D0398049

NIGHT SPEED

CHRIS HOWARD

KATHERINE TEGEN BOOKS
An Imprint of HarperCollins Publishers

Katherine Tegen Books is an imprint of HarperCollins Publishers.

Night Speed

Library of Congress Control Number: 2015952415
ISBN 978-0-06-241534-9

Typography by Joel Tippie
16 17 18 19 20 PC/RRDH 10 9 8 7 6 5 4 3 2 1

First Edition

For Allison

ONE

I'm a time bomb that should have blown already. My heart
thuds in my chest and my skin sweats inside combat gear,
fists clenched in Kevlar gloves. I can't be launched at my target until he's out in the open. I can't pursue until the target
tries to escape. But I didn't become a runner so I could waste
time being patient. I'm supposed to be making each second
count.

Puckering my lips like the world's worst kisser, I take slow
calming breaths as snipers smother the sidewalk and tactical vehicles block off the street. The slow-breathing thing
worked wonders back in basic training, when a tech was
monitoring my vitals and flashing me a nerdy thumbs-up.
But after two months of drills and demos, the Tetra
Response Unit armors each new runner and puts them on
the streets to hunt breaknecks, and calm is hard to come by
out here. No one's giving me the thumbs-up, either. A lot of

the old-timers on the unit won't even look at me till I strap on the helmet. It's easier for them to think of me as *Runner Five* than as a seventeen-year-old girl from Queens.

I feign interest as Tucker marks hazards on his map of Manhattan and guesses out loud at our target's next moves. It's a paper map, because Tucker prides himself on being old-school, but he's in fact not much older than me. He's too old for tetra, though. Too old to be an accelerator. That's why he now has to settle for being my handler. And I don't remind Tucker that Manhattan at rush hour is *all* hazard. I don't point out that to the breakneck we're after, every cross street presents escape routes that lead to a thousand more. The only known is this: to make his getaway, our target will dose up on tetra and enjoy a burst of enormous strength and incredible speed. He'll be dangerous. Out of control. And I'll dose up on the drug to go after him, hoping to bring him down before he hurts somebody on these crowded streets.

"Eighth Avenue's plenty hectic." Tucker taps his red pen at the squiggle he's drawn on his map. "Past Penn Station, then cutting down here by the Empire State Building. What do you think, Alana?"

"That he's a breakneck. Not a tourist."

"Did you just make a joke during the countdown?" Under different circumstances, Tucker's grin might disarm me.

"How much longer?" I nod at the entrance to the New York Central Bank, inside which our target aims his gun at innocent people.

"Try to relax. He's forcing them to open the vault." Tucker holds his map in my line of sight. "Giving me and you extra time to predict his exit strategy."

I push the map aside. "Predictions are distracting."

"Alana, it's *meant* to be distracting. You ever thought maybe I'm trying to cool your boots so you don't freak too far out?"

"You're sweet." I stamp my Kevlar-enforced boots at the asphalt—Adidas, special-issue. I've worn through four pairs this month.

Tucker's eyes head the way mine keep heading, past the snipers on the sidewalk and up the steps to the bank's entrance, which is framed with stenciled brass panels smudged with grime. From here in the road, we can't see much through the first set of glass doors—there's another set of doors beyond that, and the lobby is tucked inside the building, out of sight.

"You know I love your focus." Tucker gives up on the map, folding it away. "But a watched pot never boils."

He really says this. Just like he said *cool your boots* and just as he really says every other hokey expression someone back in Nebraska convinced Tucker it was okay to use. He grins again, trying hard to relax me, but sweat runs down his face, and it's not just New York in July making him a slippery mess this morning. He might not be a runner anymore, but Tucker Morgan is still in the hunt.

He sweeps his sandy brown hair up under his ball cap.

3

The hat, like the rest of his clothing, is charcoal gray, with our unit's initials—TRU—emblazoned across it in brilliant white. Tucker looks good in uniform. He probably looks good in everything, but I've never seen him in anything else.

Our lieutenant's voice wriggles out of my earpiece like a centipede of static. "We have eyes on the breakneck inside the building. All operatives: hold your positions."

The snipers stop squirming on the sidewalk; the last snatches of frantic chatter die down. And as Tucker tugs out a dose of tetra from a pocket on his bulletproof vest, my mouth goes dry as sandpaper.

Tetra—or TTZ, as the techs call it—comes in small steel cartridges shaped like bullets. You load one between your teeth then thumb the release by pressing the red button on the end as you inhale. And though Tucker's shaking the cartridge, arming my dose, he won't hand it over yet—we're supposed to give the breakneck a thirty-second window before I dose up and start after him. The rush lasts for only nine minutes, so the idea is I'll still be juiced up when my target begins to slow down.

The thirty-second plan is new, but runners have always had to wait for breaknecks to dose up first: tetra's deemed too dangerous for its use to be sanctioned unless as a last resort. Lawmakers hate the idea of minors being employed to use a highly addictive illegal drug—they'd much prefer some old-timer was standing here in my place. But past puberty the human body can't handle tetra. If people on the wrong side of adolescence try dosing up, their hormone levels are such that they can't synthesize the drug right, which is a nice way of saying their heart explodes as their brain melts down.

Those of us young enough to use tetra have to wait twenty-four hours between doses or risk a similar fate.

I peel back my sleeve, checking the stopwatch I set after I finished rushing last time. *Fifty-two hours and eleven minutes*. It feels like forever. And as I glance up at the towering crown of buildings overhead, I feel squeezed by Midtown's heat and shadows and by the rules I have to follow: the target inside the bank is familiar to us; I shouldn't have to allow him the first move.

"Need you to do me a favor," Tucker says, offering me a bottle of water, which I refuse. "When you catch this punk, make sure you wave into his camera for me."

The punk in question wears a GoPro camera on his helmet and records his getaway—all nine minutes of the rush—then posts the footage on YouTube for the whole world to see. The media loves it. Lieutenant Monroe can't even talk about it without a new curly white hair springing out of her glossy black mane.

A siren bleats in the distance, then fades. These cordoned-off blocks form an island of quiet as we wait for GoPro to exit, making the rest of Manhattan like a storm at sea.

A storm I'll soon enter.

Adrenaline plows through my veins as another buzz of

static comes over my earpiece, creaking beneath the weight of Monroe's voice. "Runner Five in position?"

"Ready and waiting," Tucker says, as if it's him that's about to juice up and go. He wishes it was him, of course. Tucker turned eighteen three months ago, and state legislature mandates all runners be retired from service if they make it to eighteen. Some runners don't even make it that far before their bodies betray them.

"Hope our Little Rabbit's feeling lucky." Monroe's voice is too big in my ear. I'm not as strong on tetra as many of the other runners but I'm one of the fastest, hence the stupid nickname. "Our boy's almost done in there," the lieutenant says. "So listen up, everyone. Despite the New York Central Bank boasting about increased security measures, this will be the third time this particular thorn in our side has ripped them off. It is up to us to make this the *first time* he does not get away. We'll have Runner Five on a half-minute delay, so our team in the chopper better keep a good eye on the target. Let me remind you, this is not some adrenaline junkie who got his sweaty hands on his first dose of second-rate tetra and is out for a joyride. Nor is it some wannabe who's wasting his precious TTZ on snatching a purse or smashing open an ATM. This is a big-leagues breakneck who will be doped up for a primo-grade rush and knows how to use it. The target is extremely dangerous, both to you and to this city we serve. If you get a shot . . ." There is a horrible pause, long enough for my heart to thud three times. "Aim to maim, people. But take the damn shot."

I need to catch GoPro for his own sake, before some slow sniper on my unit does the nearly impossible and shoots our target in the back of the head. But I'm not here to save GoPro. I'm here to save people *from* GoPro. In the last three months, his rush jobs have caused twenty-nine pileups and put sixteen civilians in the hospital. It's only a matter of time before he puts someone there who never walks out.

I pull a photograph from my hip pocket and unfold it, my fingers trembling as I smooth out the creases, my mind needing something to remind me of me before I'm speed-freaking and drowned in the now of the rush, the world spinning like a snow globe that just smashed on the floor.

The picture is a couple years old—my brother, Reuben, and I bundled in Rangers gear for our annual trip to a hockey game in Dad's honor. I began the tradition as soon as my little brother was old enough to care about the team our father loved. We didn't make it to a game this past season, though. Reuben was up for it. But he still seemed too fragile to me.

"Which do you think GoPro loves most?" Tucker says, studying the tetra cartridge he's holding for me. "The money? Or the rush itself?"

"I guess he can make the money last forever," I say. The rush feels like it's never-ending when you lose yourself inside it, but tetra kicks you to the curb too soon.

I slip the photograph back into my hip pocket, still feeling the image burn inside me, picturing the grin on my little brother's face.

Tetra is all about timing. And in the two months since I got out of basic training, my timing has been good, in the sense that I'm the second fastest runner on the unit and I've brought down more breaknecks than anyone. But no matter how fast I run, I am always too late to save Reuben.

Except at night.

In my dreams, I'm fast enough to turn back the clocks and change everything.

"You promise to wait, right?" Tucker says, holding out my loaded dose. I snatch the tetra cartridge from him, and my heart finds an extra gear to shift into. Soon it will hit the gas like a mean drunk.

"GoPro's bagged a half million, but he's not done." Monroe's voice provides a crackling commentary of what's happening inside the building. She's monitoring GoPro on the bank's camera feed, while she stays tucked out of sight, safe in one of our unit's tactical vehicles. Seven of them arc around the bank's entrance, and behind the TRU vehicles are regular patrol cars, regular cops, who are here to watch more than anything else.

The only way to stop a breakneck is to fight fire with fire.

"Ready?" Tucker asks.

I slick my black hair back and strap on my helmet—a TRU requirement I'm sure I'd rush better without—and I never loosen my grip on the tetra cartridge in my fist: a six-milliliter dose, the most any body can handle.

Tucker puts a hand on my shoulder. Any moment now, our target will burst through the doors, rushing toward us, undaunted by this trap we have set.

"Breathe deep." Tucker squeezes the tightness beneath my neck, tendons like barbed wire. I press back into his strong hands as I inhale. He understands what's about to happen to me, and I feel that in his touch. He doesn't have to ask why I do this. Has sensed never to pry about the photograph of my brother and me. For all his smiles, Tucker is good at keeping his distance. Perhaps that's why I let him get this close.

"Remember," he says, "no matter what, I'll be with you."

I wish this were true. I wish Tucker could be out there beside me, leaving the sad slow world behind. But even if he were still young enough, you can't rush *with* someone. Two accelerators too close to each other will quickly become out of control.

I shake the cartridge, though I don't need to at this point. It's armed, it's ready. All I have to do is put one end in my mouth, thumb the release, and then fire away.

"Target's on the move." Monroe's voice is calm, cold, but I am fire and lightning, every muscle inside me coiled like snake on bone.

"Doors in twelve seconds," Monroe continues. "Eleven . . ."

GoPro's gotten even greedier of late. Since tetra is hard to come by and each rush might be their last, breaknecks are always desperate to cash in as much as possible before

9

being forced into early retirement, but the way GoPro's amped up his bank habit over the last two weeks suggests he knows his days as an accelerator are almost done. Perhaps he started getting headaches while he's rushing, his body warning him he's getting too old. The biggest warning of all is the Needles, so called because it feels like your spine's drilling into your brain. At that point, your hormones have shifted such that the drug can drop you dead if you risk one more dose.

"Three seconds," Monroe announces. "Two . . ."

My heart thrums like the wings of a hummingbird.

"One . . ."

And there he is.

On the other side of the glass doors, GoPro moves at a normal speed, for a second longer. His cartridge will be armed, ready inside his helmet. He just has to bite down, hit the release.

He's in Carhartt overalls, patched up with hockey pads; a messenger bag's strapped to his back, stuffed full of bills; his little GoPro camera sticks off the top of his motorcycle helmet like an antenna; his visor's down, blocking the face we have never seen. He never speaks inside the bank. Always wears gloves. As he crashes through the doors, GoPro tosses the handgun he used to hold up the bank—most breaknecks ditch their firearms while they're merely human, afraid they might try to use them when they become something more.

When the tetra hits his system like a freight train, his

body trembles so much he almost staggers off-balance.

My cartridge flies to my lips out of instinct, and Tucker squeezes my shoulders, reminding me I have to give the target his head start. *Thirty more seconds.*

Monroe's voice echoes out through a loudspeaker, issuing the breakneck a warning he ignores. Then gunfire screams overhead as the snipers open fire in vain, their guns pointed directly at the top of the steps, the glass doors shattering into so many pieces it looks like rain, as if the bank's doorway contains a tiny shining storm and our target is the tornado at its center.

But our target is already gone.

TWO

GoPro's already cleared our blockade and is a block down Thirty-Fourth Street—a blur of brown overalls, weaving in and out of traffic, a smudge of speed amid the rush-hour crawl. Past our blockade, too many people and cars make it too dangerous for our snipers to do anything but watch as GoPro smashes through a hot dog stand, sending civilians reeling. Then, cutting across a crowded intersection, he causes three cars to swerve to avoid him and a dozen cars collide.

Twenty more seconds.

"We'll lose him," I tell Tucker, the tetra bullet at my lips, my thumb at its release.

"The chopper won't. And when you catch up, GoPro will run dry while you're still running hot."

"It's too big a head start."

"Not for you," he says.

"He's too fast. He'll go to ground before I'm even close."
At the end of their rush, a breakneck ditches their helmet
and blends into the crowds, disappearing like they've not
just left a trail of destruction behind them. "I can't just stand
here and watch, Tucker."

He tries to grab my arm, but I'm too quick. I bite down on
the cartridge, thumb the release, and the last thing I see in
slow motion is the envy in Tucker's blue eyes.

The taste is like a mouthful of aspirin. The smell is like
nail polish mixed with gasoline. Chemicals explode inside
me and I'm moving already. It's easier to feel the hit when in
motion. Can't think about it. Can't fight it. Just let it come
on.

My heart's no longer a hummingbird: it's a jackhammer,
and this first part of the rush is too much for most people to
handle—even if they're young enough, they'll likely pass out
from the adrenaline surge.

An *increased endocrine response*, the techs call it, which
means your nervous system becomes two nuclear warheads,
fight and *flight*, and they'll tear you apart if you don't control
the aggression that comes with the increased strength and
speed.

Tetra comes on quick, which is fitting. I'm knee-deep in
the rush after five yards of sprinting, then I'm fully inside it,
vaulting over the TRU vehicles blocking my path.

GoPro is no longer just a blur in the distance—it's not
that he's slowed his pace at all; it's tetra slowing the world

around me as it speeds me up. I'm able to process movement at a faster rate. It's as if the world is coming back into proper focus for the first time since the last time I rushed, and now, for nine minutes, I get to feel free.

Tempo. BPM. Bug Eye. People throw a lot of names at the drug, but Chili Powder's my personal favorite. As I sprint after GoPro, picking a thin straight line between the lanes of traffic, I flip down the visor on my helmet and feel made clean by the fire inside.

The helmet muffles the sound of the world whipping past, and I hate wearing it because that sound is the glorious noise of now. But orders are orders, and TRU wants my head protected from impact. Plus, the visor prevents grit and bugs from impaling my eyeballs, and it stops me from tearing up at the speed.

When you're this fast, blinking is bad for your health.

Everything starts to shimmer as I sink deeper inside the rush—nothing stays solid on tetra, every surface ripples as if the whole world's made of light. The city's no longer stone and steel, it's a kaleidoscope of marble and gold. Accelerators call this seeing the Fourth Dimension, which I used to think was goofy. But then I saw it.

It's like watching every atom spin.

The helmet forces me to hear my own breathing. My pulse throbs at the top of my head.

"Our boy's got eight minutes left." Tucker's too loud through my earpiece, his voice stretched and slow back in the default world. "You've got twenty seconds more than that. You would have had *thirty* more seconds, if you'd stuck to the plan."

Talking's not impossible when you're on TTZ, but I don't bother grinding out a reply.

Like GoPro, my helmet has a camera. Though mine's tiny and built-in, it sends the unit a high-res video feed of everything I'm seeing—minus the Fourth Dimension—so I get to feel like Tucker's eyes are in my head, as well as his voice.

GoPro's blitzed through a patch of roadworks, causing a maintenance truck to roll up onto the sidewalk, where an elderly couple stands right in its path. They seem to move like they're in quicksand, but I reach them just in time, shoving them to safety as the truck smashes into the building behind us.

The old lady loses her footing, almost falling, but I make sure she stays upright, and her panicked scream turns to a cry of gratitude. My own surge of relief is amplified by the tetra coursing through my veins. But up ahead, a semi's jackknifed across an intersection in order to avoid my target. And beyond it, my target is breaking loose.

GoPro's started leaping across the tops of moving vehicles instead of weaving through the traffic, which means he's begun to peak—the middle of your rush is a three-minute window that puts you at the top of your game—and I'm twenty seconds behind him, but I follow suit anyway, leapfrogging from a yellow cab to another cab to the roof of a limo, leaving a trail of dented footprints behind. Then I pivot off the back of a moped—crushing the stack of pizzas bungeed in place—and vault onto the top of a UPS truck. My right foot lands on the truck; my *left* foot lands on the roof of a bus two vehicles ahead.

It feels like I'm flying and I start hooting and howling. Roaring as the rush bubbles up inside me. Grinning as I imagine never having to slow down.

GoPro is good, but I'm gaining on him, and I mustn't get cocky. The city's too crowded for me to get carried away. Droning crowds fill each busy block. Drivers and cyclists. Pedestrians on the sidewalks and crosswalks.

Pedestrians like my brother and me, on Queens Boulevard last summer . . .

Can't think about that.

I have to stay present.

I jump from car to car, carefully sticking each landing, then launching off the roofs and hoods like they're trampolines. And despite the fact that I'm so much more careful than GoPro, I'm *still* gaining on him.

He spins around—midjump, pirouetting a perfect three-sixty—and when he sees me, he must know he's losing. I am fifty yards behind him, forty-five, forty. I'm not just a runner, I'm a hunter, closing in for the kill.

If I'm lucky, GoPro will keep running until he runs out of juice. Then I'll close in on him, still rushing, as was the plan. If I'm unlucky, GoPro will stop and make a stand. But since it allows a runner's support team to catch up, most breaknecks don't like to get caught in a tangle—not the smart ones, anyway. And GoPro wouldn't have gotten away as many times as he has if he wasn't one of the smartest we've seen.

Brake lights ahead.

The next traffic light's yellow-soon-to-be-red. GoPro doesn't miss a beat. He bounces off the top of a minivan, lands in the middle of the empty road, then vaults clear across to the other side before cars begin to stream through the intersection, blocking my path. I could dash between them, but that might cause an accident, and breaknecks are the ones who create carnage.

I am the damage control.

I pull up short on the hood of a Prius, while up ahead, GoPro cuts left and disappears onto Seventh Avenue. I'm losing him.

And I *can't* lose him.

So I jump.

Just like GoPro, I can't clear the intersection, but it's full of cars now. I have to touch down a foot on the roof of an SUV that's crossing my path. Too much velocity: I dent the roof and don't land right, tumbling off the back side of the car. For a second I'm on all fours on the asphalt, car horns blasting and a shiny grill bearing down . . . I move out of its way, rolling to safety. But I'm too late. The driver's swerved into the next lane to avoid me.

Vehicles crush together. Two cars. Four cars. A food

17

truck joins in. Then the traffic's stopped and a hundred horns wail. I survey the damage, the guilt enough to make me glitchy, and if you get too glitchy you start to unspool, which means you end up a quivering hot mess in the fetal position, vomiting, your body's way of ending the rush to spare your mind.

The horror of what's just happened makes me almost *want* to unspool.

Instead—and despite Tucker's protests through my earpiece—I rush to the vehicles and pry open their doors, making sure the people inside are all right. Their faces distort in the Fourth Dimension. Skin swims with blood and eyes swim with shock. But no one's unconscious. *Everyone's moving.*

"It's nothing," Tucker shouts, which isn't true, but worse could be happening as GoPro continues getting away.

So I turn down Seventh Avenue like GoPro did, but when I round the corner, he's out of sight.

"Gone," I manage to mumble into my helmet's mic.

"Macy's," Tucker shouts. "On your right. He's gunning for cover."

"How long?" I spit the words through clenched teeth.

"He's got four minutes."

I have twenty more seconds than the target. So I'm halfway through the rush, and I should be peaking, but the pileup has left me rattled, and now I have to go *inside*, which always makes the rush harder to control.

Macy's is *the world's largest store* according to the huge white letters on its giant red sign. Not a bad place to look for cover—breaknecks abuse the way tetra makes them stand out from the crowd, but in the end they all want to blend back in.

GoPro slowed down enough to enter the store without breaking windows or smashing the doors, but inside, he's left behind a clear trail to follow. I pick my way through the debris as alarms screech like abandoned babies. Somewhere a real baby screeches too. The sounds razor-blade through my jawbone and temple, as if I just bit down on broken teeth. I'm forced to go slower. There are too many colors and they all melt in an ugly Fourth Dimension swirl, the overhead lights a thousand suns drilling into me. My brain is like a full hard drive, my body a computer about to crash.

I bash into a display of jewelry and hear the ping of each piece of metal hitting the floor.

And the *smell*. Perfumes and powders. It's like I've been painted with plastic. Soon my hands are on my knees and my chest is heaving, mouth dry-coughing.

Dust motes trail dangling threads of light all around me, weaving me tighter inside as they tangle together. I'm about to unspool. I stare at the threads turning colors as the world turns glitchy, and I must focus on one thread if I'm going to claw my way out.

Find something to concentrate on. Something stable.

In their dash to escape GoPro's havoc, someone's spilled

Starbucks all over the floor, and I latch onto the aroma to ground me, even imagine I'm drinking a cup—black, six sugars, the way my dad used to drink it. But even with the coffee keeping me company, I'm still glitchy. Getting trapped inside was a very bad idea.

"He's out the far side." Tucker's voice seems louder than any sound should be. There's a volume control on my earpiece but I'd have to take off my helmet to reach it.

I stumble forward, trying to follow GoPro's tracks through the store, as if he's an animal I've cornered, but I haven't cornered him at all. GoPro's found the back door of this den and is escaping back into the concrete jungle. I'm losing him. *Failing.* Frustration howls like feedback inside me, and when I scream, the sound of my fury burns in my ears.

"Alana?" Tucker's voice lets me know I sound as bad as I feel. Not just glitchy, but hostile, the drug swapping all its velocity for violence and spite. "You have to get to the other side. The shop spills out onto Broadway. You have to *breathe.*"

It hurts to breathe.

"You're not alone," he says. *Lying.* "Slow breaths. Focus on my voice, clear your mind. Don't overthink this."

Overthinking can pop your rush.

"Come on, girl, keep moving." Tucker only calls me *girl* when he's nervous.

A rack of T-shirts snares me, logos and cartoons and

band names flashing past, tripping me as they wrap around my wrists and ankles, bringing me to my knees. Delirium digs cloudy claws in my skull, and I'm slipping off the back side of the rush like a surfer who just missed a wave.

But when I think about what happened to my brother last summer, rage reignites every drop of the tetra inside me, the embers of my rush bursting back into flames. Because I'm a time bomb and there is no time to be glitchy. For the sake of all those in danger, every breakneck must burn.

I stand and my feet are gooey and numb, but I force myself to hit my stride in an ugly sprint, my bearing picked at random, just heading toward a part of the store I don't recognize. And when I see daylight, a shimmer of glass and the river of traffic beyond, I push myself toward the street with everything I have.

GoPro must have escaped through a window—the remaining shards of broken glass are like sparkling teeth, and as I leap through, it's as if I'm escaping the jaws of this Macy's monster that tried to swallow me. Then I'm burped onto Broadway. I land in a roll and come up to my knees, where I wait, praying the world will stop spinning beyond my control.

"The alley," Tucker says through my earpiece. "Down to your left."

I'm on my feet. Staggering. At the entrance to the alley, a crowd of people are pointing up inside it. Because GoPro's not hiding. He's not going to ground and trying to blend in.

He's not even stopping to fight me.

He can't have more than two minutes left of his rush. And yet halfway down the alley, he's scaling a building, vaulting himself up the fire escape like it's a greased pole and gravity's ceased to exist.

He's daring me to follow.

I sprint inside the alley, the crowd of people parting before me. My insides are still creepy-crawly from the glitch, my mouth full of spiders. But the cobwebs are clearing inside my skull as I gather momentum, and when I leap up at the building, I clear the first two flights of the fire escape before I latch onto its side.

People cheer me on, as if I'm an Olympian nearing the finish line, but I ignore the magnificence of the feeling.

Just as I ignore whatever Tucker Morgan is yelling in my ear.

THREE

The building must be twenty stories high, and I'm more than halfway up when the blitzkrieg begins. Broken bricks clatter against the grated steel of the fire escape as they rain down, knocking me midflight back to the landing below. The rubble hurts my armored body more than my helmeted head.

GoPro's yanked a stretch of steel railing loose from the fire escape and he's spearing it at the wall as he speeds upward, plowing bricks loose behind him as if tilling the vertical earth, an attempt to slow me down that's working far too well.

Tucker screams louder through my earpiece. There are screams below me now too. Down in the alley, people are running from the tumble of bricks, though some remain, squinting upward, recording the action on their phones, and where's my support team? They should be clearing the area by now, making it safe.

"I'm coming for you!" I yell at GoPro. More words fly from my mouth, but I don't even know what I'm saying. I'm moving again, slower now that I'm being drilled with debris.

The chopper's right overhead, the gurgle of its blades smothering the squeak of my boots, burying the frantic sound of my lungs and shielding this alley from the small sliver of sky. The snipers onboard can't get off a safe shot with the alley still crowded below, even though GoPro's an easier target now that he's begun to slow down.

". . . not even. You have two minutes."

It's the first thing Tucker's said since I entered the alley. No—he's been screaming nonstop, this is just the first thing I've let myself hear. But why does he sound so panicked? I have two minutes, but GoPro has *less*. He's almost to the roof but I'm right behind him.

Until the fire escape comes loose.

GoPro's prying the top of it out of the wall, as if deboning a steel skeleton from a body made of bricks. He can't be strong enough to rip the whole thing clear. *Can he?* Regardless, the damage has been done to the top sections. I bolt upward before I lose altitude. And GoPro disappears onto the roof just as the fire escape above me peels all the way back.

I jump as the steel goes slack. The gloved fingers of my right hand claw at the side of the building, my left hand flapping in the air.

My knee cracks at a buttress, almost throwing me off the

wall completely, and I lose another five feet before I'm able to hook my fingers onto a ledge.

Not three feet away, a pigeon blinks at me twice.

My vision is returning to normal. *Not much time left.* And the roof is maybe six lengths of me away now. I am molten with sweat inside my Kevlar, my fingers slippery inside my gloves.

Maintaining my hold with one hand, I tug the glove off the other with my teeth, then I dangle there, wiping my palm dry, flexing my knuckles. I switch hands, tug off the other glove.

Down in the alley, a few idiots still gawk skyward.

Don't they realize they're in danger?

Not as much danger as me.

With time running out on my rush, I crimp my fingers inside the ledge, press at the wall with the opposite foot, and push up onto the next hold, working every angle I can. I dart from a windowsill to a drainpipe to the next window, edging into each nook and cranny. Two more crumbling holds, a tortuous zigzag, and now the roof is only one move away.

"You have sixty seconds," Tucker yells. "Go!"

I pull up on both arms with enough force to clear the top of the building, and I somersault forward, then hit the flat roof in a sprint.

GoPro has forty seconds before he's finished. His body will be slowing down. But at the far edge of the roof, he shows no sign of quitting. He leaps from the top of this building to the next one and disappears into a fog of white steam.

I reach the edge of the roof and leap to the next one, just as GoPro did it. Only I leap farther, faster.

The TRU chopper roars overhead.

"YouTube this!" Tucker shouts, and I think of all the videos GoPro's posted, the blur of his rush, the TRU runner looking like a fool behind him. But not this time. I'm taking him in and pulling that helmet off his head so he can smile for *our* cameras. He'll pay for all those he's injured.

But he can't pay. Not properly. *None of them can.*

I'm losing focus, but I still clear the gap between buildings, one after another, windmilling my arms through the air, then landing midstride.

I'm so close behind GoPro, I can read the brand name on his messenger bag, see the bills poking out of it, the frayed edges of his Carhartts, the cracks in his hockey pads.

"*Thirty seconds!*" Tucker yells.

If I have thirty seconds it's almost over: GoPro's rush is about to run dry.

As he lands on the next roof, he crumples on impact. He tries to roll through it but is all out of finesse.

I land right there behind him.

"Alana!" Tucker shouts in my ear. "You've done it!" He thinks this is a victory. But for me it isn't nearly enough. I'm ten feet from our target when I rip off my helmet, holding it under my arm so its camera still points at GoPro, but so I no longer have to hear my handler gloating.

The roof is mostly flat and empty. Just one exit point—a doorway to a maintenance stairwell. Steam plumes out of two HVAC pipes, shrouding everything, adding to the feeling we've traveled above the clouds and left the city behind us.

The last seconds of the rush quickly slip through my fingers. I'm withering and stiff, and I'm shaking, trying to slow myself down all the way, not wanting to grab hold of GoPro too hard and hurt him with the residues of my strength and anger. Except then he's on his feet, limping away from me, dragging his right leg behind him as if it's been snared in a trap.

He glances back at me as he breaks into a hobbled sprint.

"Wait," I yell, my voice almost back to normal, though my ears keep popping and my jaw throbs.

The steam blows thick and I lose sight of my target. Nor can I see the chopper that drums its blades overhead.

I start jogging through the steam, my joints crunchy. I'm no longer so nimble but can still catch up to this breakneck before I lose all my edge.

"You've run dry!" I scream, spotting him at the far side of the building. The chopper's so close it whips my hair and billows the steam. Visibility's too poor for the snipers onboard to take a clear shot, but if GoPro keeps running, it's only a matter of time before they try wounding him.

Or worse.

"You have to stop, or they'll shoot," I yell as GoPro turns

to face me. I yank my hair from my eyes, pinning it back.

Then GoPro sucks his sweaty head out of his helmet. And GoPro's not a *he* at all.

Her dirty-blond hair is piled in a bun, and the sweat and heat and the tetra have flushed her pointy face a furious red.

Of course she's not the first girl I've caught. But for some reason, GoPro has always been a *guy* in my head, showboating with the YouTube footage, manly in the Carhartts, and this revelation gives me pause.

Which gives GoPro an opportunity.

She hurls her helmet like a bowling ball and it hits me square in the chest, knocking me backward. I drop my own helmet as I fall. Then GoPro's running, rattling open the door to the maintenance stairwell and disappearing inside.

The rush is over, but I go after her. Through the door. Down the stairwell. "There's nowhere to run," I shout, wheezing as I descend the steps, my feet thudding, knees jarred.

Below me, GoPro crashes through a door, and I follow her into a barren post-construction zone: heavy workbenches waiting to be removed, empty pots of paint, stained rags, and cardboard boxes full of trash. Otherwise the floor is open and empty. No interior walls or dividers. No cubbyholes or cubicles. The fresh paint is blinding white and sunlight streams through the windows at the far end, everything aching with brightness.

GoPro's reached the wall of windows, glass floor-to-ceiling, and she has her back to me as she peers out at the city, silhouetted against the backdrop of buildings beyond.

I'm still twenty feet from her, but I stop moving when she slams her forehead at the glass with a horrible smack.

It's something a trapped animal might do. A bird caught in an invisible cage. And the residue strength of her rush is enough to spider the tempered glass into a fractured web as she cracks her head against it once more.

Her overalls are covered in dirt. Tiny pieces of debris are lodged between her pads, making her spiky and ragged as a scarecrow.

"Stop," I say, before she smacks her head at the glass again.

"I suppose you're nice and young," she says, rubbing her gloved hands over her head as she turns to face me. Blood drips from her forehead and her features are all straight lines. Sharp cheekbones and ski-jump nose; her jaws grinding as if she's chewing gum laced with poison. She presses her thumbs at the base of her skull. "You look about fifteen, *runner*."

I reach to grab the handcuffs clipped at the small of my back.

"Too young for the Needles," GoPro sneers.

"If I'd got the Needles"—I show her the handcuffs—"I wouldn't still be rushing."

"Sure you could resist?"

"Try closing your eyes," I say. "It's supposed to help with the pain."

"It doesn't." She shakes her head, then stops, quickly, as if shaking her head is the most painful thing she could do. "Nothing helps. Trust me. This is my fourth time through it."

I can't help but be impressed. Once you get the Needles,

you should never dose up again. Your body's setting off an alarm in your brain and it can be deadly to hit snooze. Some can't help pushing it one more time, though. I even heard talk of a breakneck who risked *three* more rushes.

Four times has to be a record.

GoPro turns back to the window, still rubbing at her cranium. As I take a step toward her, she taps a finger at the glass. "See the scaffold?"

Of course. It wraps the white bricks of the building across the street like a sleeve and tops out at about our level.

"Think I could make it?" GoPro's breathing is ragged. "The pigs will have this building surrounded. But not that one."

Even peaking, it would be hard to cover that distance.

"Your rush has run dry," I remind her.

"Yeah. Forever. So what, I just become like all them?" She peers down at the street below, then turns to face me again. "You ever look at them? Squirming about like they're just waiting to die. Half of them look dead already. You ever smell them rotting, *runner*? You know, right? Just because you wear that uniform, doesn't mean you don't know."

"All I know is you're under arrest."

"No. You know. *You* know. After your last rush, there's nothing. That moment when the moments have all passed you by."

She gasps, then sobs. I take another step toward her. I have to cuff her, read her rights, then I'll find my helmet and call for backup.

"*Damn it!*" GoPro screams. "Four times through. Four times!"

She squeezes her skull between her hands like she might pop it, but then stops, and with a flourish, shakes out her hands in the air. Her voice becomes a growl. "You listen to me, *runner*. You ever catch up to Mobius, tell him he was wrong about me. Dead wrong."

I've no idea who Mobius is, but I don't care—GoPro is striding toward me.

I'm ready for her. Aching and exhausted, but ready as she lurches closer. Only then she stops, pivots, and I realize she's been backing up from the window. And now, with room to run, she's running *at* the window, and then barreling *through* the window, and she is once more the tornado at the heart of a storm of glass.

"Wait. . . ." I stretch the word past breaking point.

The chopper has appeared outside, a giant steel insect hovering in place, and I wonder if the snipers onboard are watching like I'm watching as GoPro hurtles out of the window, aiming for the scaffold that cradles the building across the street, knowing her rush has forever run dry.

For a moment, she spins her limbs in spastic movements, as if she's traded her arms for broken wings. The building must be sixty feet from this one; the scaffold that wraps it is only marginally closer.

GoPro doesn't even make it halfway.

FOUR

That night, I dream myself faster.

Fast enough to slide to the broken window just in time to grab GoPro by the hand. I'm pulling her back inside the building when the dream morphs GoPro into my brother. The last traces of tetra in my veins make the dream hyper real. We're back on Queens Boulevard last summer. The late afternoon sun stretches the sky wide open, the streets wavy with heat. I can see Montasy Comics in the background, and I've dreamed this enough to know that I'm dreaming, but I still feel the panic as Reuben lags behind me, comic books stuffed under his arm, his face buried in the pages of some new story.

I take a few steps out onto the crosswalk without him, yelling for my brother to hurry up. He's grinning as he steps off the curb, moving toward me. But then he stops grinning because he's heard what I've heard and he knows something is wrong.

Reuben looks in the direction of all the noise just as the breakneck cuts a corner to cut down Queens Boulevard. At first all I see are Reuben's comic books scattering, the pages fluttering open.

My brother lands twenty feet away.

But this is the dream. So I dream myself faster. Fast enough to rewind and do things over. Fast enough to scoop Reuben into my arms and carry him to the sidewalk so he's safe as the breakneck blazes past.

The dream takes its time fading as I awake, and I let it replay over. But as morning seeps in through the curtains, I am a hundred years of slow. The day after dosing up means long hours in low places. I crawl out of bed, too sore to stand without leaning against my dresser. Holding the walls for support, I hobble through our small house.

The television snaps off as I enter the living room. The blinds are drawn, and in the gloom, Mom fidgets with the remote as she perches on the couch.

"Breakfast?" she asks, anxious as ever to have something to do, but I give my head a slight shake as I lower myself down on the love seat, squeezing in next to Echo, the black lab who brings my brother so much joy. Echo merely twitches at my presence and keeps sleeping, but Mom is overly attentive, smothering me with a blanket before I even sit down.

"I'm not cold," I tell her.

The shivering is just one of the postrush symptoms. We call the recovery period *derailing*. You have to wait a full twenty-four hours before it's safe to dose up again, but sometimes these symptoms last longer than that.

To combat my current ailments, I have a regimen of supplements I'm supposed to take, premade packets of goo to down, but I can't eat yet. Derailing often makes me feel too sick to be hungry. I'm also dehydrated, despite the drip the medics put me on as they hurried me back to headquarters. Once the techs okayed me to leave, some desk jockey took me home, so I never saw the lieutenant, or Tucker, but that's pretty normal. The priority is to get a runner rested so they can rush again as soon as possible. When I go in tomorrow, I'll be scoured for signs of weakness or post-traumatic stress. I've become good at answering the questions the right way to get back in uniform and back on the street.

This time it will be harder.

"How about some coffee?" Mom asks. I try a nod, and she gets the idea.

I can tell she spent the night on the couch again, eventually drifting off next to the piles of self-help books she keeps renewing from the library. Mom picks up accounting gigs, doing people's taxes, crunching numbers, but with school out, she's often too busy looking after Reuben to get out of the house much. She sometimes takes pills to help her sleep—they make her pass out hard and the next day she walks about like a zombie. She seems alert today, though. Just as well. I'm zombie enough for both of us.

As Mom clatters about in the kitchen, I tell myself the cup of coffee will be a reprieve: from first sip to last, I'll not think about yesterday, or anything other than right here, right now.

I find a pad and pen amid Mom's books and try drawing, just messing up the paper to clean out my mind. I used to draw all the time, doodling over anything I could get my hands on, filling up notebooks, scribbling on magazines and books and receipts. I'd draw cartoons to make Reuben laugh, and more serious stuff that I'd keep to myself. Just the way I saw the world, little snatches of things.

I've only been able to draw black swirls of nothing since Reuben got hurt.

My phone vibrates on the table. There are a half-dozen missed calls, no voice mails. Tucker, mostly, has been trying to reach out. But the lieutenant has tried, too. Even Jamie—one of the other runners, who is almost a friend—has sent me a consolatory text. Barely five foot and built like a gymnast, Jamie has the best vertical leap of anyone at TRU. And just like that, I'm thinking about GoPro. *Leaping.* Plummeting out of a nineteenth-floor window as if meaning to puncture the world below.

Mom brings me coffee the way I like it. She's even cut up a Granny Smith and put a few pieces on a plate, trying to bait me to eat.

"I suppose it's all over the news," I say, letting go of my phone so I can grasp the coffee mug with both hands.

Mom shrugs, but I know she's been glued to footage half the night. TRU does a good job of keeping the news cameras

35

away when we're rushing, but even if no one from the networks captures pictures or video, some slo-mo on the street will. And knowing the networks, the finale is all they've been showing. Perhaps a few clips of the rush in progress—maybe someone captured me with their phone as I stumbled through Macy's, maybe some fire-escape footage—but they'll be focusing on whatever nastiness was gathered of GoPro's body hitting the asphalt, as if flung without forgiveness into a grave no one dug.

I set down my coffee as a wave of nausea hits.

It's a good thing I was hidden from prying eyes when I pulled off my helmet. If someone got a clear picture of me, you could Google *TRU* or *tetra*, or *accelerator*, and my face would pop up, and I can't put what's left of my family at that sort of risk.

A local station once threw a runner's face on the evening news, and TRU had to retire him immediately. I heard they relocated him and his family to Kansas, which Tucker swears isn't so bad, and I'm sure isn't—when you're from Nebraska. But our identities as runners have to be kept strictly protected, to shield us from media attention, and breaknecks, and from the protestors who think we're too young for law enforcement and that we're somehow making things worse. The protestors are the ones making things worse, though. If it weren't for all the controversy, TRU would be allowed more than twelve runners. As it is, after eighteen months and almost a hundred arrests, the unit is still classified as *experimental*, so our numbers are capped. This results in a waiting list for new applicants.

I had to wait five months just to get tested.

It's only during puberty that the body has a chance to synthesize tetra safely, but not everyone who's the right age will reap the benefits: many just wander about in a daze or are knocked out by the adrenaline surge. The techs have all sorts of explanations for this, and maybe if I'd not had the right body chemistry, hormonal balance, or whatever, I'd have tried to understand it all more. But I passed TRU's tests with flying colors. Then I had to convince Mom to sign off on me entering the program. She relented only after I got Reuben to help persuade her.

"Did he see it?" I ask, meaning my brother. "The jump?"

"Only once." It hurts my mother to admit even this much, but she favors honesty above all else. "I'm sorry. You know how he gets."

My phone vibrates as another call comes in—it's Tucker again, but I ignore it. I'm too busy getting up now that Reuben's entering the room.

I jog over to my brother as fast as my sore feet will allow.

It hurts to smile. My jaw cracks and my teeth throb, but I beam at Reuben. "Hey, Doughnut," I say, wrapping my arms around his shoulders. With his doughy little cheeks, caramel skin, and eyes the color of bittersweet chocolate, my little brother could have been crafted at an expensive bakery. *Doughnut* doesn't really do it justice.

"Hector's bringing the ice," he says, his arms around my neck. At first the wheelchair made hugging awkward, but we've had almost a year to practice. "He said he'll be here by noon."

Hector runs the small grocery store six blocks away, and after Reuben read something about pro quarterbacks taking ice baths after games, he thought it might help with my postrush pain. I always shut myself in the bathroom and wait for the ice to melt enough that I can take a hot shower, but Reuben loves any way he can help.

"How's your derailing?" he asks me, his brow furrowed with concern.

My bruises feel like holes packed with swollen nerve endings. My bones buzz like an electric fence.

"What derailing?" I say, which makes my brother smile, and of everything sweet about him, his smile really takes the cake.

Mom's on her way to the kitchen but pauses to run her fingers through my hair. "Soon we'll be all done with mornings like this, babe."

"They still might let me be a handler," I say. "Once I turn eighteen."

"What happened to finishing high school and going to college?" Mom asks, still playing with my bangs. She hates that I cut my hair short, but I joke that her own hair is long enough for both of us. "What happened to being a normal girl again?"

Mom loves to bring up high school and the names of girls I used to goof off with, wondering out loud why I no longer spend time with my friends. But those girls are strangers now. School's a lifetime ago. Normal is a luxury I can no longer afford.

"You should like that I want to make a difference," I say.

"Who says I don't?"

I lean against her. "You'll be less worried when I'm a handler."

"Trust me, I am counting the days."

"Me too." *As of today, there are only twenty-four left.* Not even four full weeks, and then no more saving people as an accelerator. I'll be relegated to the slow lane for the rest of my life.

"You have seventeen arrests now," Reuben says, once Mom has disappeared into the kitchen to fix him a smoothie. "They'd be crazy not to let you be a handler."

"Yesterday doesn't count," I tell him, straightening his Spider-Man T-shirt.

On the wall behind Reuben is a framed picture of our father before he got ill. He still has the scruffy red hair and radiant grin that the cancer so quickly erased. Reuben and I have our mother's dark coloring, but my brother's sweet smile reminds me of Dad's, and Reuben offers it to me now in sympathy.

Six years ago, when our father died, I set up a little bed in my room so Reuben could sleep near me. He was only three, too small to understand what had happened, and I used to sob silently in the darkness so my brother wouldn't hear. It's been the three of us since then. Mom's relatives in Honduras are our only relatives, and they're all so far away. But I've always told Reuben that three was enough, that we'd look after each other, and most importantly that I'd always look after him.

He doesn't remember anything of that day last summer.

He doesn't know I left him on the curb. That I was telling him to hurry up when I should have been holding his hand.

He wheels himself toward me as I sit on the arm of the love seat. The wheelchair is too big for him. I guess it's hard to find one the right size for a nine-year-old. "There wasn't anything you could do," he says. "GoPro must have been crazy. People online are all talking about it. I mean if he jumped after his rush was over . . ."

TRU must have issued a statement that the deceased breakneck was male, in a vain hope this will provide less ammunition for the unit's detractors. And when I realize there'd be no easy way to tell what gender the body was after it smashed into the street, I'm almost sick all over my lap.

"You shouldn't be reading that stuff," I tell Reuben.

"I only read about runners," he says. But though he's old enough to hunt around on the internet, he's not old enough that he knows to clear the browser history when he's done. So I know my brother reads all about tetra, not just about the accelerators who take it.

He reads about how the drug stemmed from research intended to provide a cure for people with degenerative disorders. That the people who came up with the drug—researchers at a company called Trinity Pharmaceuticals—were trying to make people healthy, not condemn them to wheelchairs.

"At least no one else was hurt." Reuben is still trying to console me. A nine-year-old veteran of a war on drugs. "When GoPro fell. There was no . . . you know. Collateral damage."

I make a painful smile, force a nod. "Right. No one else got hurt."

"Thanks to my sister," he says.

"What do you want to do today?" I ask, really needing to change the subject.

"Can we take Echo to the park after you're done with your ice bath?"

Our black lab perks up at the sound of his name.

"Of course," I say.

"You sure you don't hurt too bad?"

"Never," I tell Reuben. "Not when it comes to you."

FIVE

There's no wind for us to fly the kite I got Reuben as a present and Echo is too lazy to fetch anything, so I end up kneeling in the grass at the base of Reuben's chair, weary as we watch Canada geese squabble at the joggers and Frisbee-throwers. A group of girls about my age huddle together at the edge of the lake, sharing a cigarette, and as I watch them, GoPro keeps pushing her way back into my mind. The desolation in her eyes. The pain on her pointy face. The thing she said about people *just waiting to die*.

In twenty-four days I'll face the same brutal truth she did. The bright inner light of the rush extinguished. Forever.

I can't talk to Reuben about it. The person who'll best understand what GoPro was going through—what *I'm* going to go through—is Tucker, but I don't want to talk to him on the phone. I need to see his reassuring Midwestern smile.

"I should head in," I say, staring toward the Manhattan

skyline in the distance, brick and steel brilliantly lit against an azure sky. "I can get a head start on tomorrow's evals."

"Is that allowed?" Reuben asks, worried. "You can hardly stand up straight."

"TRU never gets a day off," I say, hugging his legs against me. "Why should I?"

Mom insists on driving me into the city in our old Volvo station wagon—she can't take me all the way to headquarters, as even family members aren't allowed to know the location, but she can get me close. Reuben comes along and brings Echo, making my trip to work like a family outing, and we get stuck in traffic crossing the Fifty-Ninth Street Bridge.

The radio has an update about an accelerator who recently started wreaking havoc in Chicago, and Reuben shoots me a look. His dog is squeezed between us on the seats. His wheelchair is in the way back.

"They still haven't caught him?" I ask.

Reuben shakes his head, and Mom switches to a different station. I try not to talk about this stuff around her, but incidents involving tetra outside New York are rare, and I'm curious how Chicago is going to react.

"Maybe they'll need handlers out there," Reuben says. "If they start their own response team."

"I'm not going anywhere, Doughnut. Tetra's a New York problem." The farther you get from Manhattan, the harder good TTZ is to find. For those who want to abuse the drug to get rich quick, Manhattan provides not only the drug, but the ideal place to use it: a crowded concrete maze, where it's hard for the police to get a clean shot at you and easy to hide once the rush wears off.

"It started off like that here, though," Reuben says. "Just one. Ricochet. Now there are almost twenty."

That number is climbing. When someone ages out of the drug or gets arrested, there always seem to be two new breaknecks ready to replace them.

"This breakneck in Chicago is no Ricochet," I say. "And Chicago is no New York."

About three years ago, Ricochet ripped off everything from armored cars to jewelry stores while dosed up, then realized the big money was to be had at the largest banks and began using tetra strictly for getaway purposes. He never got caught. And he set the example, started the trend. Now a rookie breakneck typically tries their luck at a smaller bank outside Manhattan, maybe makes off with just ten thousand dollars. But the big-timers who hit the big banks come away with close to a million each time.

I study Manhattan's bristle of skyscrapers through the window and try to avoid Echo's slobbery breath. "I could crawl faster than this traffic," I mutter.

"Me too." Reuben stares at his legs.

I reach across Echo and take my brother's hand. Mom's watching us in the rearview mirror. I never told her how I let Reuben lag behind me that day on Queens Boulevard.

I've never told anyone the truth.

The media loves to come up with nicknames for break-necks. Some are quickly forgotten, disappearing after a rush job or two, but the ones who stick around gain notoriety. The one who crippled my brother was called Sidewinder.

He wore this full-body *dream suit*—made in Japan out of highly reflective materials designed to blend with the urban environment, they look faintly ridiculous when static, but when he was in motion, Sidewinder was near impossible to see. He seemed to ripple through the city, gliding like a snake over hot sand. And all I saw of him was a blur of speed blasting through the crosswalk.

He'd just ripped off the Ridgewood Savings Bank. He went on to rip off bigger banks, and hurt more people, but never got caught, disappearing from the streets before I even made it to basic training.

Mom turns the music up as we finally make it off the bridge. This song has come on that she loves. A late-'80s hip-hop *masterpiece* according to her.

"Come on," she says to us, a little desperate. "De La Soul. Don't leave me hanging."

She's started rocking a dance that involves a wiggle of the head and swivel of the shoulders, along with a shaking thing with the fingers. I don't know if a lot of people did this back in the day, or if Mom invented the dance on her own, but it is an awesome thing to see—Mom actually being like Mom, again.

It's even more awesome to see Reuben join in.

And though my body is sore and stiff, as I try to dance, I almost forget that I'm derailing. I certainly don't care about the stares coming from other drivers when we stop at a red light.

But it's impossible to forget about what happened yesterday. GoPro smashing through a nineteenth-floor window, no way to make it to the building beyond. She chose death because she was done rushing forever, and I guess that means she must not have had a brother, or a mom, or anyone she loved and was leaving behind.

"Echo's dancing!" Reuben announces.

I smile. "He's wagging his tail, Doughnut."

"That's how dogs dance." He tugs off the old Rangers cap of Dad's—which he's been wearing backward for the De La Soul jam. "It's your turn," he says, so I take the hat from him and put it on my own head. The hat's really too big for Reuben, but we switch out who gets to wear it.

I'm pretty sure Dad would have loved the dance party, though he was more of a hard rock sort of guy. Played guitar, actually. Badly, as I recall. My memories of him are just as broken-in as this old hat of his. They feel good, but are all worn out.

"We can go to a game next season," Reuben says, meaning a hockey game, for Dad. "We can go in October. You won't be so busy then—even if you are a handler."

"Is that what you think?" I stop dancing. "That I was too busy for you last season?"

"Only once you started basic training."

He doesn't mean it in a bad way, but it cuts to the bone. We're close to headquarters, though, so I have Mom pull over.

I hug Reuben good-bye, kissing his cheek and breathing in the sweet lemony smell of his hair. "You know why I do this," I whisper, my arms still around him. "You know why I have to be gone so much."

He nods his little head. Says nothing.

"Hey," Mom shouts, a new song coming on. "'Ladies First.' Alana, you love this one—Queen Latifah . . ."

"I know, Mom. But I gotta go," I say. "You guys keep busting a move for me."

I watch them till they're out of sight. Then I begin shuffling away like an old woman after a violent mugging. My hip sockets are raw, and my feet are bruised fruit, turning sloppier with each stuttering step. It's six more blocks to headquarters. The derailing makes it feel like sixty.

Another day and I'll bounce back, though. Come tomorrow, I need to be ready to go.

Headquarters is housed in an old dog food factory in a still-hellish patch of Hell's Kitchen. The building doesn't look like much from the outside, and the inside smells like Purina when the sun bakes the roof, but the location has served us well, central enough for dispatching runners, but remote and ugly enough to not snag unwanted attention.

Just like the runners themselves, TRU headquarters has

to maintain anonymity—mainly to avoid protests, but also because we store considerable amounts of tetra on-site. The higher-ups at TRU fear we might be breached by a break-neck eager to steal our supply. That would be madness to attempt. Even on tetra. But while Trinity Pharmaceuticals provides TRU with the drug free of charge, breaknecks are forced to rely on illegal sources, which have fortunately remained few and far between. Even a pale imitation of TTZ is super difficult to manufacture, and it's even harder to pro-duce it without slipping in a nasty new side effect or six.

I arrive at the back entrance in civvies, as is protocol, then I punch in the appropriate code at the delivery bay and wait as the graffitied garage door rattles open. The covert thing is a pain in the butt.

"Little Rabbit," says the guy waiting behind the door for me.

He is also a pain in the butt.

"Hey, Toby," I say, hobbling inside the cool building and breathing in the familiar scent of puppy chow and sweat.

Old Toby Moore is eighteen and was one of the first run-ners TRU trained, but is now a glorified doorman. "You look as bad as I feel," he says.

"I feel even worse than you look."

Every ex-accelerator has to endure life as a has-been, but some also have to endure looking like a fossil, and Toby's appearance jumped straight to middle-aged and bald-ing by the time he was through. He has flaky yellow skin, spiderwebbed with crooked lines. His teeth are black and fractured from biting the bullet too hard too often, the TTZ causing rampant decay.

"You're not supposed to be in today." He taps my ID card on the counter, waiting for it to process, then has me line up my face for the retinal scan. "I'm surprised you'd come back at all. After yesterday."

"Am I set to enter?" I ask.

"Almost." He leans across the desk toward me, removing his cap to scratch at his head. Toby's scalp is like a yard no one watered that sprouts an occasional weed. "You know you could talk to me, right? If you wanted. I get what you're going through."

"I'm just trying to go through security."

He grins with too much gum. "What's the countdown, Little Rabbit?"

I check my watch. It's been twenty-nine hours since my rush ended. "Hopefully I'll be back on the streets sometime tomorrow."

"I meant until you're retired."

I knew what he meant.

Toby's eye twitches as he holds up his left hand, showing me the gnarled fingers he can no longer move. "I should have had six more months." I've heard this story before but don't have the heart to cut him off. "Didn't tell the techs after I needled up the first time. Ended up in a coma and woke up with this." He shoves the shriveled claw in his pocket. "So

I know about the transition. I could help you get through it—as a friend."

"I have a handler to help with that."

"Tucker Morgan." Toby scowls. "The Pretty Boy."

"Come on, Toby. I've told you before you're too old for me."

"We'll be the same age when you turn eighteen."

"Good-bye, Toby."

I snatch my ID card from him, then head to the locker room. My plan's to hit the gym and stretch the sore from my muscles, which feel like hot coals shrink-wrapped in skin. I want to heal faster. Be ready to go again sooner. Plus, the gym is where I'll most likely catch Tucker, since he spends a lot of his off time staying in shape in TRU's workout facilities, trying to fill the void TTZ left behind.

I throw my locker door open with a clang and try to get dressed quickly, but derailing makes me so slow it's stupid. I watch myself in the mirror, weak and pale beneath the bright lights. When I'm feeling kind, I tell myself that my figure is athletic and I'm built right for sprinting and hand-to-hand combat. But today I just look like a boy—all edges, sinewy where other girls are soft. My haircut doesn't help: shaved short at the sides and back, black bangs hanging to my chin like a scythe. If I tuck my hair behind my right ear just so, it covers the nastiness above my right eye, a mangled bit of forehead that's a souvenir of my showdown with a breakneck called Dominos. He punched in my helmet, shattering the visor. Then I pinned him in handcuffs and waited for backup to arrive.

I inspect my scar in the mirror, then zip up my charcoal overalls as a rush of activity bursts through the doors at the other side of the locker room.

From the noise, I can tell it's Idra Hall—Runner Eight—and that she's fresh from a rush job, in which she was victorious in pursuit. Though I have made more arrests, Idra's the fastest runner on the unit. But Idra doesn't run for the same reasons I do. She told everyone back in basic training that she wanted to become a runner just so she could experience the rush. Now Idra likes to say she's addicted. She says this like it's some stupid joke.

There's only one way into and out of the locker room, and I pull the visor of my cap low, hoping I can somehow stay unnoticed and sneak out, but as soon as they round the corner—three bodies inside a bubble of energy—I'm trapped.

Idra's supported under one arm by her handler, spiky-haired Sasha, and under the other by Jamie, my tiny almost-friend. Idra's eyes widen in recognition when she sees me, though her pretty face is droopy from the postrush comedown.

"They still let you work here?" Idra slurs the words, but it fails to smudge her spite.

Blond hair spills out beneath her cap and falls down her shoulders and it somehow robs her of a little authority, making Idra look less like a runner, more like a girl dressed up as one for Halloween. "What happened yesterday?" she asks.

My body tingles, craving velocity as I glance toward the exit. But I'm derailing, sore and weak, and Sasha is blocking my path with her broad shoulders and spiky hair.

"Ignore my runner," she says, wearing an imitation of a smile. She rushed the streets when Old Toby Moore did, though her appearance fared better. "Idra's crashing hard. Doesn't know what she's saying."

"How convenient."

"We caught Dog Star," Jamie says, to change the subject. "I mean—all Idra, of course. I was just on hand for backup."

"As if I need backup." Idra's sagging features manage a sneer. Even in a stupor, she has beautiful eyes—the irises a startling blue, like the feathers of an exotic bird. "That was my fourteenth capture, West. I'm two behind your *record*. And I have five months left to beat it."

She knows I'd do anything for another five whole months.

"I'm surprised you even care about arrests," I say. "Thought you just care about tetra."

"You're still doing the self-righteous thing? After yesterday?"

"I hope you needle up early, Idra. You could be the next Toby Moore."

"*You're* the next Toby," she says. "Maybe they'll let you work the door with him after you finish scraping GoPro off Thirty-Sixth Street."

I turn to Sasha. "Can't you put a muzzle on her?"

"I'm just being honest with you, West." Idra makes a sloppy grin. "Everyone else'll keep talking behind your back, then cheer once you're gone."

I turn to Jamie, who won't meet my gaze and mumbles something about texting me when I ask what people are saying. And there was me thinking she was *almost* my friend.

"Did it feel good?" Idra says as I try to push past them. "In the moment, right when it happened? Right when you lost all control?"

"I don't even know what you're talking about."

"Yesterday." Idra's blue eyes sparkle. "When you threw GoPro out of that window."

SIX

I don't find Tucker in the gym and I don't stick around. And that night I barely sleep I'm so nervous. It's just gossip, I tell myself. No one really believes I'd throw a break-neck out of a nineteenth-floor window. I consider texting Tucker. He's been reaching out to me all day but never left a message. Now it's the middle of the night, though. I don't want to seem needy.

As soon as I arrive at TRU the next morning, I ask if Tucker's on-site yet, but the guy working security at the entrance won't tell me. He just summons some other drone to escort me straight to Monroe's office. My presence there has not been requested.

It is required.

The lieutenant tells me to take a seat and keeps her back to me as she wraps up her call. I fidget on the fake leather chair, trying to smooth out the creases on my T-shirt, and trying to make my shorts not so short. In my uniform, I can convince myself I look seventeen. In my current outfit, I feel about twelve.

I tuck my bangs behind my right ear but my hair keeps flopping in front of my face, and because the lieutenant's office sits right in the middle of the tactic room, which occupies the entire top floor of headquarters, I feel I've been put on display in front of the whole Tetra Response Unit. Especially since Monroe's office has windows for walls.

I glance out through the blinds, where everyone's busy working satellite imagery and data maps, fielding calls and monitoring chatter online. At TRU, we don't sit around and wait for a 911. There are people as likely to upload a picture of a breakneck to Twitter as they are to call the police.

If the tactic room is the brains of the unit, Monroe's office is the heart, and it's a messy, intuitive organ. Like Tucker, the lieutenant prefers paper maps, and they're everywhere, scattered across her desk and floor. There's a giant white-board filled with her chicken scratch, hard copies of photos and files. But unlike Tucker, the lieutenant is not just old-school—she's old.

Her glossy black hair is tied back, but I count the coarse white strands that curl out of her scalp. Too short to be bound by her ponytail, they bounce like dead branches on an otherwise healthy tree. She is midsentence and furious when she ends her call, drumming the phone against her hip for a few seconds before slipping it into her back pocket.

"Have kids," she says, turning to face me. "Or have an ex-husband. But whatever you do, never have both."

I try to come up with a witty response, but there's nothing humorous about being escorted to the lieutenant's office first thing in the morning. Especially not after what Idra said yesterday.

"What's wrong with you?" Monroe asks. "Why aren't you in uniform? Are you sick?"

"No. I—"

"Better not come in here spreading germs, West. You've caused enough problems already."

"I'm not sick."

"Yay for you." The phone rings in her back pocket, and Monroe silences it by sitting down forcibly in her chair.

"I'm not gonna sit here and quiz you about what happened." The lieutenant begins picking at the cans of Mountain Dew that litter her desk, shaking them to find one that's not empty. "It'll come as no surprise that a dead breakneck is not real high on my list of concerns."

I think of the eerie calm look on GoPro's pointy face, right at the end. Right before she jumped. But if Monroe sees me shudder, she chooses to ignore it. "And yet . . . I am *forced* to care," she says. "Since I am forced to operate this unit under intense scrutiny instead of being allowed to get on with the job in the ways I see fit. Trust me, if you were all the right damn age this would be a lot simpler. Perp commits armed robbery. Perp gets killed trying to get away. Boom, we saved taxpayers about a hundred grand a year by not having to provide said perp with room and board at Rikers."

I picture GoPro smashing through the glass.

"Problem is people like to think of breaknecks as *juveniles* instead of junkies." Monroe finds a can that makes a sloshy enough sound and she slugs it back. "Goddamn public relations nightmare is what it is. Always has been. Always will be. Speaking of bad publicity, you have any idea how many hits GoPro was getting on these YouTube videos she was posting?"

I shake my head. It's strange to hear Monroe refer to GoPro as a *her*, after all the months we assumed this target was a guy. It's even stranger to realize I don't know GoPro's real name yet. We shared more than a moment—we shared her *last* moment, and part of me wants to know all about her, but I am too afraid to ask.

"A *phenomenon*, they say." Monroe spits out the word like a broken tooth. "Kid had *followers*, an online sensation, you see how it goes? We're chopped liver, you and me. Sure, people know these speed freaks are a menace. But that doesn't stop them coming up with cute little nicknames for them. Still, you ask the people that junkie put in the hospital how they feel about GoPro taking a nosedive from nineteen stories up. Ask the families who lost a father or son or a sister because some breakneck had to grab another fix and didn't give a damn who got hurt just so long as they got away."

"I don't need to ask them."

This gives Monroe pause. She scoops six soda cans off her desk with one arm and huddles them into a recycling bin. Then she plants her elbows on the arms of her chair, studying me over steepled fingers. "I guess you don't, Little Rabbit. I guess that's why you're here. You might want to play it up in your eval. An eye for an eye. Not a bad angle. Pull the sympathy card."

"You think I need an excuse for what happened?"

"Um, to put it mildly, *hell yes*, West. I do."

"And I should use my brother as an excuse?"

"Honey, you're using your brother as an excuse every time you come to this shit hole. Every time you bite the bullet and get your burn on, you take that picture out of your pocket and say a little prayer. And it's not about what you did wrong or what you did right, it's about someone *dying*, and it's about some of the networks saying you killed your target, and so now it's about the goddamn protestors and people needing somewhere to put the blame."

It's hard to swallow, harder to speak. "Since when do you care what the media's saying?"

"Since the mayor of this city appointed me for this job. Soon as TRU was announced, people began calling for the unit to be disbanded. This building might stink like a dog's armpit, but I don't want it shut down, do you?"

"Of course not, but—"

"I got a daughter about your age, West. Pesters me to let

her apply to be a runner now she's old enough. And I'd never let her within a mile of a tetra bullet in a million years, so I guess I'm a hypocrite, but I believe you runners are vital and that this unit is the only viable defense against a threat that will otherwise continue to grow."

"GoPro jumped, lieutenant."

"Yeah, well, some of the media's not buying that. And it's hard to tell from our chopper's feed—all it shows is her coming out of that window, nineteen stories up, One Forty-One Thirty-Sixth Street. Timing shows she was done with her rush, so . . . why jump?"

Because she already felt dead, I want to say. But how could Monroe, who was born too soon for tetra, understand the dread of facing life like a stalled engine, swallowed in slow motion?

"She'd needled up." I can't stop my voice shaking.

"So she killed herself? No way to prove that now. If you hadn't torn your helmet off on the roof, we'd have your feed to go on, but—"

"You think I threw her out of that window. Seriously? You think I'd *kill* her? That I'd kill our target and risk the lives of all the people below?"

"You were still rushing, hon. Amped up and hostile."

"No. I'd finished. I was twenty seconds behind her. . . ."

"Yeah. Another thing you did wrong. Breaking protocol. It was supposed to be a half-minute head start. What is it with you? Listen, things went bad, real bad, and it's on your head or it's on mine, but one of us has to fall on the grenade. Understand? Take one for the team, or—*poof*—no more team."

When the alarm goes off in the command center, the glass walls of Monroe's office rattle and my heart plunges into my stomach.

"What do you mean, fall on the grenade?" I ask, following Monroe out into the tactic room, where even in uniform, I'd feel out of place. As a runner I'm supposed to be at the end of the long arm of the law, reaching out into the world, fingers straining as I grasp at the target. Instead, I'm stuck in here with a hundred desks full of flickering screens, and all the desks point inward, aimed at Monroe's office, putting us at the center of it all.

Above, the ceiling is a living map of New York, overlaid with filters and statistics, imagery flashing as connections are made between each layer of data on the colossal screen. It is the city as cells and synapses, and the desk jockeys glance back and forth, up and down, studying the monitors in front of them, while keeping an eye on the big picture coming alive overhead.

The alarm swells the room with sound.

Monroe's voice is even louder. "Someone shut that stupid thing off!"

Within seconds the sharp edges of the alarm have been dulled, but as I stare at the map overhead, I see a red target flashing in time to the pulse of sound—the screen zooms in, switching to a live satellite feed that gives us a real-time aerial view of Brooklyn Heights. The target is not far from an off-ramp to the Brooklyn Bridge, and the stats for the U.S. First Bank are as unimpressive as you'd expect from the location. Whoever this breakneck is, they're small-fry. It's probably a first-timer, who can be the most reckless—and dangerous—as they make their escape.

"Runner up?" Monroe yells, and six different numbers are rattled off: runners ready to be sent out on the hunt.

My number is not one of them. The urge to be there is an itch I can't scratch.

"Pick one," Monroe snaps at Vogler, her second-in-command, a man built like a bulldog with scoliosis, and who has a face to match. "Any one. I want them choppered out there with a support team ten minutes ago."

At first I think the alarm has been flipped back to its previous magnitude, but then I realize another alarm has kicked in.

The screen overhead zooms out, and once again shows the whole city. A new target pulses in the West Bronx and when the screen zooms in, it tells us this is a Wells Fargo, the stats showing another branch that offers a low rate of return to anyone attempting to rob it.

"Vogler!" Monroe shouts. "Chopper two runners out to the Bronx, one as a backup. Let's show this rookie they picked the wrong day to test us. And forget protocol, I've got a headache, so someone turn down that alarm some more. Both of them!"

Before the alarms drop, another has fired up to join the

chorus, and another target lights up the map, right in Midtown.

"I can take it," I say to Monroe. I'm good in Midtown. I know the streets better than that old map Tucker carries.

"What about that one?" she says as yet another alarm hits. "Queens is your own backyard, right?"

Four targets. All at once. There are whole days where we don't see that many. But if Monroe's concerned, her face doesn't show it. Right here, as the alarms seesaw like sirens and TRU's brain circuits blink, Monroe is in her element.

"Not today, Little Rabbit," she says, staring at the map overhead. "*I'm* heading to Midtown, you're getting the hell out of my command center."

"I can suit up and—"

"I was hoping to prep you some more, but we're out of time, kid. Two suits from the Department of Justice are here for you, and knowing the feds, we better not keep them waiting."

"Federal agents?" The news is a chainsaw, cutting through the bad news with worse news that has much sharper teeth.

TRU is part of the New York City Police Department, and debriefing is always done in-house, the TRU techs and shrinks poking at you with questions and checking for weakness.

"What do federal agents want with me?"

"Just remember what I told you," Monroe says, stomping away. "Someone has to fall on the grenade."

SEVEN

The interrogation room is supposed to be soundproofed, but the droning alarms leech in through the walls. It's hard not to squirm on the cold metal seat, knowing breaknecks are out there putting people in danger, while I'm trapped in one of the very rooms we question breaknecks inside.

The shrink who sits off to the side works for TRU and acts as if we're old friends, but if I ever knew his name, I've forgotten it. I suppose he's here to support me, to help represent me somehow. At least I hope that's why he's here.

Across the table from me, the two federal agents from the U.S. Department of Justice are Spaihts and Small, which sounds like two lawyers who can get you a thousand bucks for your carpal tunnel, but they don't look like lawyers. They look more like my judge and jury.

"Alana West," Spaihts says. He has a shaved head and

a goatee so short it looks like he painted it on. "Seventeen years old. Accepted for basic training at the Tetra Response Unit four months ago, been on the streets for almost two. Clocked as the second fastest runner in the unit. Has sixteen arrests to her name."

He puts down my file, which is alarmingly thick, crammed with printouts, pictures, and handwritten notes. "So. Let's talk about the day before yesterday, when you were climbing up the side of a building designed by Cass Gilbert in 1906."

"You mean the fire escape."

"I'm sorry?"

"I wasn't really climbing up the *side* of the building."

Spaihts's smile is tiny and quick. "It appears the fire escape was . . . how should I put it, dislodged?"

"I suppose." It's hard to remember right. Details get lost in the rush. "Yeah. You're right. Near the top."

"At which point you appeared to climb up the *side* of the building, according to the video feed we obtained from your unit's chopper. Fan of architecture, Alana? Because Cass Gilbert is a particular favorite of mine." Spaihts rubs his hands together, as if we're actually going to talk about architecture and he can hardly stand the excitement. "He designed several hundred buildings around this great country, more than a hundred years ago. Lots has changed since then. I doubt Gilbert imagined one day there'd be youths crawling over the outside of his building. You think he'd have ever dreamed that was possible?"

We are not going to talk about architecture.

"Maybe he'd have added more handholds."

Spaihts takes a sip of his coffee, and I wonder if they're going to offer me some. The coffee at TRU tastes like brewed brake pads, but it's better than no coffee at all.

"We'd like to be forthright, Alana." This is Small, she of the orange highlights and unibrow. She who is a goatee shy of being just as masculine as her partner, and whose nose twitches when she speaks, as if she's sniffing each word she says. "We'd like you to be forthright, too. It will go easier."

"Okay," I tell them. "I've got nothing to hide."

The shrink smiles when I say that, crinkling the tangled shrubbery of his salt-and-pepper beard. Behind him, there's a painting of a dog enjoying whatever brand of dog food this building used to churn out, the colors fading on the flaky wall.

"Listen, I feel terrible about what happened," I say, and I mean it more than these old-timers can ever understand. "You have to believe, I'd never have . . ." Saying it out loud sounds ridiculous. "*Pushed* her. Or thrown her, or whatever you think I did. I wouldn't . . . didn't . . ."

"Of course." Spaihts's face is mock-horrified. "We have no evidence that you did. No matter how much you might have wanted to."

"I didn't *want*—"

"We're looking at the whole situation, Alana." Small leans on the yellow desk between us, as if she's all about breaching gaps. Even their body language is calculated to trap me.

"That means we're looking at all of *you*," says Spaihts, and I wish for the thousandth time I was in uniform, as his eyes rake over my crumpled T-shirt. The metal seat is cold beneath my bare thighs, and I have goose bumps on my forearms. I don't know why they have the AC cranked. I thought the idea was to make the suspect sweat.

"Do you know how we classify this unit?" Spaihts asks.

"Experimental."

"Exactly. Like a diet pill not yet approved by the FDA. Yes, the pill *works*—six weeks on the stuff and I'd be shopping for extra-smalls." The man's not fat, but he's huge. A brick wall in a tan suit. "And yet no one knows all the side effects. No one fully understands all the risks."

"You're saying what we do here is effective."

"Yes . . ."

Spaihts waits for me to say *but it's also dangerous*, only I don't feel like stating the obvious.

"What you're tasked with, day in and day out, must be extremely difficult." Small's nose twitches extra fast when she's trying to sound extra kind. "Not just physically. Emotionally, too."

"If it was easy," I say, "I guess anyone could do it."

"And where would be the fun in that?" Spaihts smirks like I just walked into a trap.

"I don't think I follow."

"Really? You don't feel a teensy bit special because you

work here, like perhaps the laws that apply to other people don't apply to you?"

"No."

"Ever feel the state is subsidizing your drug habit?"

"I don't have a drug habit."

"He means tetra," says Small.

"I know what he meant."

I've raised my voice, and Spaihts's smirk blooms as Small's nose freezes midtwitch.

A fifth alarm begins to reverberate through the walls.

"Your file doesn't mention anything about a problem with authority, West." Spaihts pretends as if he's actually checking my file again, leafing through the pages.

"I don't have a problem with authority."

"Just with us asking you these questions."

"You do seem a little on edge, Alana," the shrink says as he scribbles something on his notepad.

"You seem to have a problem getting along with some of your peers, too." Spaihts is still glancing through my file, though I know he's already gleaned everything from it that he wants to know. He thumbs the corner of a page, adjusts a paper clip. "Idra Hall and you almost beat each other to death in combat training, correct?"

"That's an exaggeration."

"Really?" Spaihts holds up a photograph of Idra's face. Her black eyes look like used tea bags, her lips are two smashed slugs.

"Is there a photo of the dislocated shoulder she gave me?"

"She claims that was an accident, but that you then beat in her face with one fist." Spaihts frowns, as if he's struggling to understand my point.

"We were both on tetra. And we *both* got put on probation."

"Right. Accidents happen, I suppose. Martial arts seems to be something you excel at, though. Everybody was kung fu fighting, right?" He sings it. Like the song. "You must be like Bruce Lee when you bite the bullet. No—you're *better* than Bruce Lee. And I bet that makes you feel pretty good, doesn't it? Does the aggression make you feel good too?"

A sixth alarm kicks in. Each electronic bawl is separated from the others by a half second; they wash over one another as they rise and fall.

Six simultaneous targets is unprecedented.

And there are only ever seven runners on duty.

Spaihts snaps his fingers at me, calling me back to the here and now of this too-cold room with its too-thick walls. I glance up at the camera in the corner, then at the one-way mirror on the wall, and I wonder who's watching these bullies. I wonder if Monroe will at some moment yank me from this eval and have me suit up for action.

Or perhaps Tucker's in the next room. The thought of him rubbing the stress from my shoulders makes me tense and teary-eyed because Tucker's not here and I am totally alone. Trying not to show weakness, I glance down at my hands. I used to be a girl who painted her nails. Now I have busted knuckles.

"They sent two runners to the second target," I say. "That means I'm the only one left."

"You're not a *runner*," Spaihts says, and his shaved head gleams in the harsh light. "You're a liability."

"In your case," Small adds, "we think you pose as great a threat to the public as the criminals you pursue."

"You can't say that." I'm stunned. "GoPro put people in the hospital. Breaknecks put people in the *morgue*. How many have I hurt? Does it say that in my file? Is there a page with a big fat zero?"

"Alana." My best friend the shrink makes this face like I'm on thin ice and he's so worried, it's made him constipated.

"Just because no one's been seriously hurt by your habit, doesn't mean lives aren't put at risk every time you gas up," Small says. "Your job is not just to *catch the target*, but to protect the innocent."

"I do protect them. That's the whole reason I do this!"

"We think you've been lucky."

"I'm careful."

"Were you careful when you were following your target through a red light two days ago? Were you careful when you caused a five-car pileup?"

It's hazy, but I recall the intersection and my tumble. I remember checking the vehicles after the collision, making sure people were all right.

"How about when you dosed up ten seconds before mandated?" Spaihts asks. "Or when you took off your helmet while still in active pursuit?"

This was another trap, and I walked right into it, but no one smirks this time.

"You're self-destructive," Small continues. She's all over me, when I thought it was Spaihts I had to watch out for most. "Reckless. TRU should never have trained you. You're clearly too angry about what happened to your brother."

"You don't know anything about that. Or me. You don't know what it's like out there on the streets."

"I'm not sure you know. I doubt you remember much of those nine minutes once the drug wears off."

"You are impressive," Spaihts says. "Very impressive. But I believe Agent Small is right—you're a loose cannon."

He pulls out his phone and presses play on an audio file, rocking back in his seat as the recording comes alive with distortion. A voice rises out of the noise, cresting the static. "This is your handler," Spaihts says. "Tucker Morgan. And this was captured from your inline comm, right after you entered the alley off Broadway."

"Fall back!" Tucker shouts. And he keeps shouting it. "*Alana?* You hear me? Do not engage. Do you copy? Cut the pursuit!"

"You remember this part?" Spaihts asks, placing the phone on the desk between us. "Did you hear him? Because we could show you the video, the footage from the chopper or from your own helmet, or you can just believe me when I say you began climbing up the fire escape so fast we had to slow down the clips to actually see what you were doing."

"It's too risky!" Tucker's saying. "Do not climb after the target. There are too many civilians below."

"Which part of *fall back* did you not understand, West?" Spaihts pauses the audio. "Because you know what I hear on this recording, beneath the static and hiss and the sound of your handler giving you a *direct order*—you hear it, buried in there? That is the sound of your silence. That is the sound of you being unreachable and totally out of control."

"We can't have that," Small says. "Or this . . ."

Now we can't hear Tucker on the audio because I'm screaming inside my helmet, swearing all the things I'll do when I catch up to GoPro. Terrible things I have no memory of saying. And somewhere in there, mangled amid the rush of my voice, I stop threatening GoPro. Instead I'm threatening the breakneck who crippled my brother. I'm shrieking his name.

Sidewinder.

"I didn't mean that," I say, horrified as Spaihts clicks off the audio. My whole body is shaking. "I didn't mean any of it."

"Yeah you did. And good for you. This is war, kid." Spaihts shakes his head as if he doubts I fully understand. "Soldiers need a killer instinct, which you might well have in spades, but soldiers also have to obey orders. Especially in combat."

I think of the grenade Monroe mentioned, how I'm

71

supposed to fall on it. I don't want to fall on it, but it seems I have no other choice. The heat and shrapnel is already piercing my skin, and my hands are drumming the tops of my thighs under the table, because why *didn't* I hear the order to fall back?

Spaihts leans his elbows on the table, cracks his knuckles. "You're lucky no one was killed when your target started smashing holes in the wall to slow you down. Let alone when your target smashed into Thirty-Sixth Street."

When another alarm kicks in, smoothing the rise and fall into one continuous screech, I scrape my seat back across the floor to stand.

"Sit down." Small's nose twitches furiously.

"There are seven targets out there."

"I'm aware of that. Your lieutenant will have to manage this without you."

"I can still run on probation."

"You're not *on* probation," Small snaps. "Now take your seat."

"I don't understand." I don't sit down.

"Think of it as a leave of absence." Spaihts picks his phone off the table and flicks at the screen, as if he's already moving on to what's next on his busy agenda. "My advice, enjoy the time off. It's summer, right? Spend some time with your friends."

"I don't have any friends."

"You can hang out with that little brother of yours." The

shrink beams through his beard at me. "Go watch a movie. Get out of the heat."

"But I can't stop now," I tell them. "I only have a few weeks left till I turn eighteen."

I picture GoPro, smacking her head at the glass, staring down at the city, the pounding sting of her spine jabbing the base of her skull, like a nail being driven into a coffin.

Spaihts looks at his phone. "Then I guess you're all done running."

"I didn't do it. You have to believe me. I was careful! I would have stopped her—I *tried* to stop her. She thought she could reach the scaffold . . . the building across the street."

"How could she think that?" Small says. "Even on tetra it'd have been pushing it. This breakneck was experienced—"

"But she'd needled up. She was finished. She didn't *care* if she made it. It's like . . . she had lived too much already. The drug—it . . . it shows you this truth."

"What truth?" the shrink asks, frantically scribbling notes.

"I can't explain it . . . but it holds you inside the moment, like you're gonna live there forever, being the very best you can be. And then to never get that back . . ."

"What does that even mean?" Small says.

"It means GoPro smashed through the glass and smashed onto the asphalt and smashed herself into a million pieces because she burned too bright for too long so she'd rather just be ashes."

73

The three faces staring at me are old, old, and *old*, and even if they tried, they could never understand. "We're suspending you," Small says. "Indefinitely. Dr. Fenkman here will talk to you about potential withdrawal symptoms."

"What will change your mind?" My throat feels like a fist squeezing shut, barricading my heart in an airless cage.

"Nothing," Spaihts says.

"You're firing me."

Small furrows her unibrow at the suggestion. "We think that would look bad—if word got out, the way the media might spin it. A leave of absence sounds better, less of an admission of guilt on behalf of your unit."

"You need to speak to the lieutenant."

Spaihts is sliding his chair back to leave. "She has no authority in this matter."

"She *runs* the unit."

"Not for much longer. The Department of Justice is intervening."

"You have your whole life ahead of you, Alana." Small gathers up my file as she stands. I'm surprised by how short the woman is now that she's on her feet. "We're doing you a favor—sooner or later, a runner is going to wind up dead."

"You say that because you've never done it."

Her smile is smug and ugly. "Even if it feels like it, tetra doesn't make you immortal."

"I meant about my whole life being ahead of me."

Now Small just looks sorry for me. "As I said, the doctor

will go over withdrawal symptoms."

So he does.

As the chorus of alarms howls in the distance, the two agents leave and the shrink goes over paperwork, talking about what he calls the *readjustment phase* when you give up the drug. I tremble so much I can't sign the forms properly; Fenkman has to help me hold the pen steady. As he prepares me for the shock of life in slow motion, he never explains how to deal with being meaningless and weak. He never says anything about how I'm supposed to look at my baby brother and not think about Sidewinder. And he pretends not to notice the tears that stream down my face.

EIGHT

My feet crunch gravel as I follow the trail through the woods, mocked by the faint applause of raindrops smacking leaves. Every time I shift gears into a sprint, Echo can barely keep up, straining the leash between us as he lags behind.

"You call this fast?" I yell back at him.

Soon we'll be back in the park, looping around the basketball courts, running past the lake. Then we'll be entering these woods again. Two more times around and I'll have gone ten miserable miles while going nowhere, just running in circles because Dr. Fenkman said I need to be careful about managing my endorphins, and I tried not managing them—schlepping about the house, eating cereal on the couch, watching TV, and drawing swirls of black nothing in old notebooks. I even dyed a hot-pink streak in my bangs, an attempt at embracing a life of no dress code. But by the end of the third day of not-managing-my-endorphins, I got the shakes so bad I couldn't leave my room for fear of scaring Reuben.

I check the watch on my left wrist. I never reset the stopwatch since the end of my last rush. The silent digital seconds have monitored every wasted moment since. *Ten days, four hours, thirty-six minutes, and fifty-two seconds.*

Fifty-*three* seconds.

Fifty-*four* seconds.

It's been eight days since I was thrown off the unit. Despite Dr. Fenkman's assurances, I don't miss being a runner on the streets any less than the day I got discharged.

I only miss it more.

I let Echo off his leash and he bounds into the woods while I drop to the ground and knock out fifty push-ups, hold side planks for a hundred Mississippis, then go into cartwheels—the gravel biting my hands. The cartwheels are a dizzying approximation of coming up on tetra, making me feel strong, agile, and briefly unstoppable. Making me feel as if I'm about to be tossed off into space. But then I botch coming back into a straight-ahead run and my left foot splays out, losing traction. I'm a jumble of limbs, crooked as I flail off the trail: I nearly break my jaw against the trunk of a monstrous elm, then end up with a face full of ferns, my forearms and knees skinned and bleeding.

My left ankle is horribly sprained.

I crawl to the nearest branch to pull myself up, peering

through the drizzle and trees.

"Echo!" I shout. Reuben came up with the name, thinking it'd be funny if we kept yelling *Echo* over and over when we took the dog to the park.

It has never been less funny than now.

Returning to the trail with a branch as my crutch, I have to drag my left foot behind me, traveling in the wrong direction up the path to retrieve Echo's leash from where I dropped it.

"Echo!" Leaning on my makeshift crutch, soggy from the rain, I struggle back into the trees, where I keep up a search for more than an hour, but eventually I have little choice but to admit defeat and start shuffling home for reinforcements, knowing that if I've lost my brother's dog I will have broken my brother's heart.

At the edge of the trees, the rain has mostly cleared out the park; the Manhattan skyline looms in the distance, bulbous stumps and skinny spires shrouded in clouds. It's almost rush hour, but the city looks peaceful from here. Meanwhile, my left ankle is a squeal of hot pain, and I'm groaning along, as noisy as I am slow, and I'm trying to remember if Fenkman said paranoia was one of the symptoms of withdrawal, because as I follow the path around the lake, I imagine this old blue truck is keeping pace with me on the road about thirty yards to my right.

I'm not imagining it though—when I finally get sick of denying myself the paranoid pleasure of turning to catch a look at the driver, Tucker Morgan stares back at me from behind the wheel.

He's squinting, as if I am too-small words on a page. Then he pulls the truck over to the side of the road and comes jogging across the grass toward me.

My clothes are drenched with sweat and rain. My hair's greasy. My skin's either dirty, scratched, or both. I try to stand up straighter with the help of my crutch, equally excited to see Tucker and mortified at my appearance.

"What the hell, Alana?" He looks mortified, too, and picks up his pace. "Are you okay?"

"Just busted my ankle." I shrug, like me bleeding and limping with a branch as my crutch is no big deal. "I fell. . . ."

"Looks like you had a fight with a tree."

I don't return Tucker's smile. I haven't returned his calls either.

"You just happened to be passing?" I ask.

"Not exactly." He examines the sole of his old leather work boot as he steps off the grass. "What do they call this place, anyway? Goose Shit Park?"

"It's not so bad if you stay on the path," I say, feeling defensive of the only training ground I have left.

He nods at my shoulder, where Echo's leash is looped. "Didn't know you had a dog."

"It's my brother's." Tucker glances about expectantly. "He ran off."

"Just now? Hell, we should go look for him."

"You want to tell me what you're doing here?"

"I'm checking on you. Hasn't been so easy to reach you."

"Nothing's been easy," I say. "You remember what this was like? The *readjustment phase*?"

"Cold turkey. Yeah, of course I remember. I still get the shakes sometimes, but only at night now. You been able to sleep?"

"Hardly." I've not even had the dream where I'm fast enough to save Reuben. My nights are as painfully slow as my days.

"You gotta try constellations," Tucker says. "Imagine one and count the stars inside it. Idea is you drift off before you get done."

"I don't know any constellations," I tell him, which is true. New York's big on shadows and short on sky.

"Maybe I could give you a lesson." Tucker glances up at the clouds as if at any minute now we might be able to begin stargazing together. His red plaid shirt brings the Nebraska out in his features, teasing sunsets and cornfields from his sandy brown hair. His faded jeans are the same shade of blue as his truck. "The problem then is the dreams," he says. "Once you actually manage to sleep. You almost feel like you're back inside the Fourth Dimension."

"Doesn't sound so bad." It in fact sounds amazing.

"I thought the same thing," Tucker says. "At first. But it's this cruel reminder of something you can't get back. Now I dread the night, asleep or awake. But at least we're still here.

At least we made it through in one piece."

"Not like GoPro." I force myself to hold Tucker's gaze. "Are you gonna ask if I killed her?"

"Don't need to. Come on. I know you better than that."

"You just know Runner Five."

"Then it's nice to meet you, Alana West."

I stare at him, on the verge of tears.

"You should loosen those shoelaces," Tucker says, glancing at my feet. "They're cutting off circulation."

He's right. My left ankle is now the size of two grapefruits.

"Come on," he tells me. "I'll help you to the truck and we'll go look for this dog of yours."

I shake my head. "I can just get my mom to drive around with me. My house isn't far."

"I know where your house is. That's where I just came from. Your little bro said you like to run around here, said it's helping with your PTSD." Tucker makes quotation marks with his fingers. "He seems to think you're on some sort of break."

"I couldn't tell him and my mom I got kicked off the unit. I keep up the lie for fifteen more days and I'll be eighteen, anyway."

"Seems fair enough."

"None of it's *fair*. Did you tell him who you are?"

"Just said a friend."

"Good. He needs to take a break from TRU and everything that goes with it."

"What about you? You need a break from me?"

I glance at the truck—an old Ford with a smoky chrome bumper, rust patches like nicotine stains—and I picture falling into the passenger seat, Tucker tugging my sneaker off my swollen left foot. I'm still picturing it as I turn around and start shuffling away. "I'm a liability, Tucker. Too dangerous to be around, in case you hadn't heard."

"You bring a flashlight?" he calls after me. "The sun will be down before you make it halfway home."

"Never knew you Midwestern boys were afraid of the dark."

"I never knew New York girls were so stubborn."

"Then you must not get out much."

He jogs up the path, catching up to me easily, and takes away my crutch as he gives me his arm.

"That's my walking stick," I say.

"It's a branch."

"It's a branch that's my walking stick."

I lean against him, his arm around me. His plaid shirt is soft, his body hard beneath it. "The truck," he says. "Now. I'm carrying you."

"Try it and I'll break your arm."

"Swallow your pride for ten seconds."

"It's all very well you showing up now, but you ditched me, Tucker."

"How do you figure?"

"You let them think I killed her." I can't look at him. "You were my handler. You should have had my back."

"Is that why you've been ignoring my calls? It didn't make a damn bit of difference what I told them. The Department of Justice is on a warpath, and you were just the first step of their march."

I push myself away from him, just enough that I can look up at his face. He looks different outside of work—younger, out of uniform, but also older, this close. Burst blood vessels cloud the whites of his eyes, a leftover from his days as an accelerator, and the image is at odds with his fair complexion and tousled sandy hair, which both scream a life lived well, rather than a life lived already.

"Even Monroe's on probation," he says. "Which basically means the whole unit is. Spaihts has taken over her office. Guy's trying to run the show while he gathers enough evidence to shut the place down. Damn feds are everywhere. Special agent this, special agent that."

"You say it as if I should care."

"You will." He glances at the path behind us, then across the grass, at the lake, the road, as if he's watching for something. And then, apparently satisfied it's just us and a couple hundred Canada geese, Tucker looks me in the eyes and lowers his voice. "I'm here to offer you a job."

I let him carry me to the truck.

NINE

Tucker helps me get my left foot propped on the dashboard and pads a blanket under my thigh, and it all involves lots of his hands and my bare legs getting to know each other.

"Sorry," he says, his fair skin blushing, his fingers fumbling to undo my shoelace. Rock steady in the face of armed robbery, but alone with me makes Tucker nervous.

As he tries to close the door, a lone goose waddles close enough I'm worried the bird's going to get inside the truck. Tucker tries to shoo it away, but it waggles its head at him with a mighty squawk.

"Back home, I'd shoot the thing." Tucker nudges it aside with the toe of his boot.

"You eat them raw in Kansas or bake them in pies?"

"Nebraska."

"That isn't *in* Kansas?"

He smiles. "It's the truck, right? You think I'm a hick now."

"You think I needed confirmation?"

"Yeah, well, you're a real city slicker based on your current appearance." He nods at the dyed streak in my sweaty hair. "Nice pink, by the way."

I glance down at my tiny running shorts, my tank top covered in dirt, the split-open skin on my knees. "Pretty sure only a hick says *city slicker.*"

When he starts up the truck, the radio plays loud music too quietly. He turns it off before I can tell what it is, but from the guitars I'm guessing more classic rock than country bumpkin. Definitely old-school, though. That's Tucker's thing. The truck probably dates back to the Dust Bowl.

"We'll drive while we talk," he says. "Look for your dog."

Right. *Echo.* I should definitely be thinking more about Echo. But all I can think about is what Tucker has come here to say. "Behind those trees." I point back at the woods. "Follow this road around, there's a neighborhood on the far side. It must have gotten lost somewhere over there."

"*It?*"

"*He.* Echo. It's my brother's. A black lab. A *huge* black lab. You say *Echo* over and over and it sounds like—"

"An echo. Cute. You checked the woods?"

"Every inch. Slowly. And it's not cute, it's annoying."

He checks the rearview, shifting the truck into gear. "So I'm guessing you're not much of a dog person."

"They're fine, when they don't run away."

"I always wanted one. Never enough space."

"Didn't you grow up milking cows on a farm or something?"

"My *uncle* has a farm. And no cows. Just a ton of corn in every direction. Gets real pretty out his way. At night the fields kinda look like the sea. But me and Dad lived in town—he worked at the Dollar General and we rented the place above it. No pets allowed."

"What about your cousin's place?" I ask, because I know that's where Tucker lives now, in Jersey. "No room for a dog?"

"My cousin's allergic."

"You should get your own place."

"I thought about it. But I might be heading back home soon."

"Really?" The idea of him leaving puts a lump in my throat. It's like everything is ending. First tetra, and now Tucker. "Why would you go home?" I ask, putting on a brave face. An edge in my voice. "The Dollar General's hiring?"

"They might be," he says, with a sad smile. "My dad passed on."

"Oh . . . Tucker. I'm so sorry."

"Almost six months ago now. He got diagnosed about a year before that. Lung cancer. Dad never smoked a cigarette in his life."

"My dad died of liver cancer. Six years ago."

"Something else we got in common."

"Else?"

"Tetra." Tucker shrugs.

"Right. A couple of has-beens." I catch the look on his face. "Sorry. I guess that's a crappy thing to say."

"Only because it's true," Tucker says. "But you could still rush."

"Theoretically."

"I started getting the headaches near the end. Almost eighteen, anyway. All out of time. But you could dose up right now."

"Not a helpful reminder."

"So you would?"

"Of course I would. Why?"

We're following the road around, leaving the park, but then hit a light. "I'm sorry about your dad." Tucker drums a thumb on the steering wheel. "Never knew that."

"I know. Six years, and I still miss him so bad. I miss the way my mom used to be, too. She's still like her old self sometimes. . . ." But less and less since Reuben got hurt. "Six months, though? Tucker, that's so brutal. It's like it just happened, and you were out here. You must have been so lonely."

"Yeah. My dad was with my uncle toward the end, though. Dad liked it better that I was out here trying to do some good."

"I bet he was so proud." I reach across and give Tucker's forearm a squeeze.

"They all were, back home." The light goes green and I take my hand off Tucker's arm as he pops the truck into gear. "But they didn't know how much I enjoyed it. I mean, there's not words you can put together that come close to describing it right, but I felt, I don't know, *endless* on tetra. Like the moment was endless and I was the moment."

"You were never this poetic at TRU."

He looks sheepish. "I in fact wrote down once that the feeling was like a flash of lightning filling up the night sky, illuminating everything, all at once. . . ."

"Go on."

"Electric and alive. But then gone way too soon."

I crave the feeling he's described so much I can't speak for a moment.

"Don't laugh," Tucker says, slumping his shoulders.

"Why would I laugh?"

"Because I'm a has-been who has no way with words."

"I don't think of you as a has-been. And I think what you said was beautiful. Just so sad."

"Tell me about it. I got hooked before I even came to New York." Tucker hangs a right, taking the road that curls around the back of the woods. "Played tight end in high school and an assistant coach hit me up with some cheap TTZ knockoff at the state championship. Four minutes left, down by five. I carried so many defenders into the end zone, the crowd went *silent*."

"You were state champions?"

"You ever watch football, Alana?"

"Not if I can help it."

"I scored too soon. The other team marched down the

field and kicked a field goal to win. But I was already busy bugging the coach about how I needed more of what he'd given me. He said he'd only had three doses and he'd wasted the other two on our fullback and a wideout, both of whom passed out."

"You dosed up in Nebraska. That's pretty wild, Tucker."

"I know. Low-grade bootlegged stuff. I'm lucky the crap didn't kill me. But I'd heard about the TRU program, so I was all over it. I guess I feel bad that it was the feeling I loved, though. Even my dad . . . I never told him the truth. Right before he died, I tried." Tucker shakes his head. "Guess I wanted him to think I was better than I was."

"That's not the only reason you joined TRU." I think of Idra Hall, who thinks it's hilarious to brag about her addiction to tetra. "You didn't become a runner just for the rush."

"Sometimes I wonder." The road straightens, and Tucker steps on the gas.

"But you're still here. Still helping. Still doing the right thing."

"Guess I got hooked on that feeling, too." He pulls the truck over and peers out through my window, into the woods. "What does your dog look like?"

"Black as a ninja and running wild off its leash. Now tell me why you're here."

"I'm here because Monroe thinks there's a way to stop it." He cuts the engine as he meets my gaze. "No more break-necks."

My brain spins in stunned silence. My heart skips beats.

Then my voice slips out. "How?"

"Idra caught Dog Star," Tucker says. "And the skinny little punk wanted to trade information for a lesser sentence. Didn't have a whole lot, but he backed up a story Monroe's heard before. Said he always got his tetra from the same dealer. . . ." Tucker glances in the rearview, then out at the street. "This is all supposed to be off the record."

"I am so far off the record."

"Yeah. That's what the lieutenant said. Anyway, according to Dog Star, every breakneck meets with this dealer, direct. It's the only way they can get their hands on a dose of the good stuff. And he gave us a name. I mean, it's a fake, obviously, but apparently the name keeps coming up—Mobius."

"Wait. I heard that before. GoPro said it. About how Mobius was right about something. No—she said Mobius was *wrong*. Said it just before she jumped."

"I know. The lieutenant saw the name in your report. And she thinks this Mobius is the guy—all the tetra on the streets comes through him. I mean any tetra that's worth taking, that gives the full-on for the full nine minutes. Mobius either figured out how to brew TTZ properly or he's working with someone who did. According to Trinity Pharmaceuticals it'd take a genius with a whole lot of dollars to spend on research to crack their formula, but if we can catch this guy, then we could eliminate the breaknecks' source. Hey, you keeping your eye out for your brother's pup?"

"Of course."

"He's good about avoiding traffic?"

"He's a dog. He specializes in sucking at avoiding traffic. But how come Monroe told you all this, if it's so hush-hush? You get a promotion or something?"

"She told me so I could tell you. Didn't want to come meet with you herself—said it might raise a red flag." Tucker avoids all eye contact as he says, "She apparently thought me and you were dating."

"Isn't that against protocol?"

"Since when did you care about protocol?"

Now it's my turn to avoid eye contact. "I wouldn't. I mean, I did. But not now I'm off the unit." I make things more awkward by making this super loud noise when I swallow.

"To be honest I wish I came here to ask you out, Alana."

I sneak a peek at Tucker, who has both hands on the wheel and both eyes on the road, despite the fact that we're not moving.

"But you didn't."

"We're not gonna be able to see each other much," he says. "You know. Red flags."

"No. I don't know. *Red flags?* I appreciate the inside knowledge and all, but what does any of this have to do with me?"

"Like I said, Spaihts is running the show now. Not Monroe. And Spaihts has got no time for Dog Star's story or Monroe's theory. And if things keep going Spaihts's way, there's not even gonna *be* a Tetra Response Unit in another few weeks. There's more pressure to get rid of us than ever—the White

House hounding the mayor's office. I guess everyone's all ready to decide runners are not worth the risks. But Monroe says you present the perfect opportunity. You have the training, the skills. And you're someone she trusts."

"To do what?"

Tucker stares at me, his bloodshot eyes red, white, and blue.

"She wants you to track down Mobius from the flip side."

"You mean go undercover."

He nods. "Run for the other team. Though she didn't know you were gonna tear up your ankle."

"I'm a fast healer."

"I know." Tucker releases his grip on the steering wheel as he turns to me. He takes a big breath, makes a little smile. Then he reaches across the cab and brushes the sweaty bangs from my face. I hold perfectly still as he traces the scar above my right eye, his thumb hovering over the crinkled skin, barely touching me. "I remember when you got this," he says, and he no longer seems nervous to be alone with me. Just concerned about what he came here to say. "I watched them sew it up after you brought in Dominos. Remember? You didn't even flinch."

"They let you be there, though it was against regulations. Said you could hold my hand."

"I should have. Held it, I mean."

I bite my lip. Never mind that I'm sweaty and dirty and bloodied. Never mind that my ankle feels sawed in half. I pull my foot off the dashboard, so my leg's not in the way of us being closer.

"Always thought it would be too dangerous," Tucker says. "If we were to . . . you know. Like it might be a distraction."

I put my hand on his arm, in case he was thinking about stopping the way he's touching me. He strokes the scar again. Then runs his fingers through the mess of my hair.

"You're blushing," I say.

"Because I'm angry. The danger you'll face if you do this. The risk. I wish it was me."

"But you'll help me, Tucker."

"You won't even be able to tell your family. No one can know."

"*You'll* know."

"Yeah. And Monroe will know, but that's it. This is all going so far against the rulebook. Spaihts would never approve it, and Monroe doesn't want to risk anyone else's career, so the whole unit's in the dark. Unless you get caught." He stops dead still, his hand on the back of my neck. I lean toward him, but he pulls back. "Or killed. You'll be dodging bullets on both sides. To get to their dealer, you have to become one of *them*. According to Dog Star, you don't find this Mobius guy—he finds you, and the way you attract his attention is by making a splash and making some headlines using any low-quality tetra you can scrape up. You won't have to risk the low-grade crap, of course. I can help you out there. But making headlines means committing armed robbery, and I don't want you to do this alone, but . . ."

"Breaknecks don't have handlers."

He still has his hand on the back of my neck. He's still close. But there's a new void between us. "I'll have to keep my distance," he says. "Monroe wants you to be convincing."

"She wants me to start robbing banks," I whisper, and my hair falls back in front of my face. I wait for Tucker to move it away, but he's letting go of me. And I am so swallowed by the enormity of the task ahead, I almost don't hear him yelling that he's just found my dog.

TEN

T he HSBC squats in a pollution-stained Astoria strip mall, and if you were just passing by, you might miss the bank's white sign with black writing, its small tinted windows, the ATM to the right side of the front door. But if you weren't passing by and in fact planned to rob the place, you'd likely determine this HSBC lands on the safe-but-low end of the risk/reward spectrum. A bank is a bank, though. Armed robbery is armed robbery. So no matter how much I slow my breathing in an attempt to stay calm, my body has entered the full panic zone.

To make matters much worse, I'm still suffering from withdrawal. And because I've spent most of the past week on the couch, resting my ankle, any hope of me managing my endorphins has gone down the drain.

It's been more than two weeks since my last rush. *Less than ten days till I turn eighteen.* But now I'm operating undercover, I'm off the record and out of sight and TRU protocol no longer concerns me. The only thing that will stop me rushing is when my body can no longer handle the drug. So I'm still running out of time, but at least it's on my own schedule.

On the other hand, the HSBC closing in twenty-two minutes is totally beyond my control.

I huddle in the thin shade of a maple outside the Walgreens across the street from the bank. Shoving my hand into the front pocket of the giant sweatshirt I'm wearing over my hockey pads, my fingers find the tetra bullet Tucker gave me and I grip the small steel cartridge in the vise of my fist.

He gave me three doses of tetra to get started, along with the handgun I'm carrying—a Beretta that can't be traced to anyone since the serial number's been filed off. No bullets, though. The Beretta's only here to keep up appearances.

I suppose that should make me feel better about the fact I'm going to be pointing the gun in people's faces. But I've yet to discover a way to feel better about any of this.

It's necessary, though. When they first announced TRU, the mayor defended the controversial new program by saying some problems require *problematic solutions.*

I should tattoo those two words on my forehead.

Zipping open my duffel bag, I take out the Beretta and shove it in the waistband of my sweatpants, then check over my Rangers goalie helmet. The helmet has a grille to hide my face, but no visor, so I'll be protecting my vision during the rush with a pair of flight goggles—the sort people wear skydiving. My shoes are the chunkiest New Balances I could find at Foot Locker, and though they're not reinforced with Kevlar or anything, they should hold up to the rush okay. They're heavy and slow as I jog on the spot, testing my left ankle. I've taped it, and it's no longer so swollen, but it's still only been six days since I sprained it. Six days since Tucker came to make me an offer I'd never refuse.

End their supply of tetra and we rid the streets of every breakneck. But to end their supply, I have to attract the attention of their dealer, and I'm not going to do that unless I cross the street and enter that bank.

I don't want to have to come back tomorrow. Especially since I arrived in plenty of time to hit the *morning* rush hour today.

I was standing right here, right at nine, when the HSBC opened its doors, and I watched one of the tellers come out to pop into the Burger King next door. She had a puffy hairdo like something out of a dog show, and when she reemerged from Burger King, sucking on a soda, I was still trying to imagine waving a gun in the poor woman's face. Then here came the HSBC's first customer of the day, who was swallowed-a-beach-ball pregnant. So of course I waited for *her* to leave. A half hour after that, the bank was packed with people and the roads had thinned out.

Ended up riding a bus and sitting in a Starbucks. Then

ended up being sick in the Starbucks bathroom, because my tetra withdrawal and armed robbery anxiety did not mix well with a Strawberries & Crème Frappuccino.

Next time I'll stick to black coffee, six sugars.

I check the gun's secure in my waistband, pull on a thick pair of gloves. Then I hide my face with a pair of sunglasses and my dad's old Rangers cap tugged low—this bank probably has cameras outside as well as inside, and putting the goalie helmet on too soon would give away my intentions as I make my approach. Instead I look like the Michelin Man going incognito, thanks to my bulky hockey pads and ridiculous baggy clothes.

Just a quick in and out, I tell myself, jogging to the crosswalk and hustling across the street. I'll have them empty the cash drawers. *I'll be careful on the getaway.* People are going to be scared of me inside the bank but my gun's not loaded. *No one's going to get hurt.* It's all a show. Just the first step of the plan Tucker and I made to break me into the world of breaknecks.

A world I plan to burn to the ground.

"Coming in?" An old woman holds the door to the bank ajar for me on her way out, and as I approach her, I do the cold turkey shakedown.

My eyes twitch and my feet tap, my head pecking around like a chicken with Tourette's.

Before I enter the bank, I need to get on my goalie helmet and flight goggles. Which is going to be harder than I thought, seeing as I already have on the ball cap and sunglasses.

I stare past the woman at the ATM in the wall. "I'll use the m-m-m-m . . . mmmm-m-m . . ."

"The machine? Use the one inside, dear." She pushes the door a little wider, smiling. Lipstick on her teeth. "Nice and cool in there."

I come forward to grab the door, feel a blast of air-conditioning and am hoping the woman will leave me alone, but we get tangled together, and the Beretta slips down the inside of my sweats, then lands with a clatter on the sidewalk.

Squatting to grab it, my hands won't stop shaking as I stuff the gun in the pocket of my sweatshirt, trying to conceal it from the old woman's view. I'm sure she's about to start screaming. But instead she lets the door slam and scurries off down the sidewalk, oblivious.

Through the glass, the poodle-haired teller chats with a security guard, keys in her hand, coming to lock up for the night. I freeze, still squatting on the sidewalk. But thinking about having to come back and do this all again tomorrow makes me *un*freeze.

I rip off my hat and sunglasses and pull the goalie helmet down over my head, tugging on the flight goggles as I stand. Then I cock back the safety on the Beretta and charge into the bank.

The first thing that hits me is the screaming. So many

voices all shrieking so piercingly loud. I'm shuffling sideways across the lobby, hopping along like a tap-dancing crab, and my flight goggles are steaming up, so I end up slamming into the counter as people dive to the floor.

Then silence. Except for some guy whimpering. And the sound of my New Balance shoes drumming like a one-man-marching band.

"F-f-fi-fi-fill it!" I scream, tossing the duffel at Poodle, who's cowering over by the door. The hairdo makes her an easy target, but I should have chosen one of the tellers already *behind* the counter, because Poodle is taking a long time to get back there.

I convulse and hiccup, my withdrawal partying with busloads of adrenaline. It's like mixing Mentos and Diet Coke.

I used to spend hours every week studying security footage from breakneck bank jobs. So I tell myself I'm prepared for this, and that I know what I'm doing, and I take slow straw-sucking breaths to stay calm. But then I burp Strawberries & Crème Frappuccino and I might be sick again *because I have a gun in my hand* and it is *pointed at people.*

The gun's empty. *Just for show.* And my goggles keep fogging up, clouding my vision, so I tell myself that this hand is someone else's hand. The gun is not mine. And this actually works enough to settle my stomach, though not my nerves.

I locate the security guard and keep a jittery eye on him. Everyone's facedown on the floor, as far as I can see, but seeing is getting increasingly difficult thanks to the steam inside these stupid goggles, so I tug them up on top of my helmet.

"Poodle!" I shout, which really only makes sense in my head. "H-h-ho-how we doing?"

"One more," she says, meaning one more cash drawer to empty.

"Just h-h-hand it here."

She can't get the bag over the counter. It's too heavy. So I have her stagger around on her poky high heels to bring it to me. Her glossy bottom lip is quivering and she's older than I thought. Might be someone's grandmother. Probably has nine kids with six kids each and no one in her family will ever forgive me if this woman has a heart attack right now.

Nor will I ever forgive myself.

"It'll b-b-b-be okay," I say, hiccupping and mangling my words.

I want to tell her the gun's not loaded. Reassure her that I'd never hurt anyone.

Probably best I just leave.

I have the duffel and I sweep the gun about to make my exit, checking that no one's moving as I jitterbug back across the lobby. I'm moving enough for everyone. Stamping my feet and grinding my teeth. Just need the tetra to smooth my rough edges. Right now I'm a shipwreck, but the drug's beautiful winds will soon fill my sails.

I jog over to the security guard and pluck the gun from his holster while he teeters on his potbelly. Leaving him armed while I make my exit would be a real rookie mistake. But now his gun's in my duffel, which is heavy and bulky, and the money's sloshing around loose inside it, and I'm thinking I should have brought something smaller, when I hear the first siren outside.

My heart dubsteps into my throat, making it hard to swallow, while the butterflies in my stomach become caterpillars, wriggly in my gut.

Regular cops, I tell myself. TRU headquarters is too far—even if they choppered in a runner, I've been too quick. I picture the call coming in, though. The alarm going off in the tactic room; the map on the ceiling zooming in on this HSBC. I wonder which runner would be sent here to chase me.

Focus, Alana.

Shouldering the duffel, I throw in a final quick sweep of the bank with my empty gun and I bounce toward the door, reaching in my pocket for the tetra bullet and shaking it to arm the dose. But when I raise the cartridge to my mouth, I keep hitting the stupid grill on my hockey helmet, my hands shaking too bad to get the drug to my mouth. I need to use both hands, while holding the gun, and the tetra, and it's beyond awkward. I get the bullet to my teeth and bite down just as I get tackled from behind.

My head snaps back as my body slams forward, my arms pinned at my sides. I crash into the floor, and the air gets knocked out of me. But I still have the tetra bullet clamped in my teeth.

I arc my head around enough to see the fat security guard who's crushing me, his knees digging into the backs of my thighs as he yanks my arms behind my back. He pries the unloaded gun from my fingers, then snaps handcuffs onto my wrists. *I should have taken those off him too.*

Gripping the tetra bullet between my teeth, I strike it at the floor like I'm hammering a nail—*whack, whack*. The third hit triggers the release, and as the tetra puffs loose inside me, it's like a drop of water falling on parched desert soil.

"Wait!" The guard rolls me over, his eyes wide as I spit out the empty metal shell through the grille of the helmet.

"Sorry," I say. No stutter. No hiccup. "You did your job. But you better back off."

He's on his feet now, recoiling as I hop up, my hands cuffed behind me.

"We can take her," someone yells from the floor. "All of us. Together."

"It's too late." The guard stares at me. His skin is badly shaved, pocked with angry ingrown hairs. "She's dosed up."

My jaw tightens, the drug swelling inside me. "He's right." I manage to grind out the words. "Please. No one try."

The tetra removes all distortion and weakness, and as the power seeps into my fingers, I strain my wrists at the handcuffs, the steel biting my skin and making me bleed . . . but then the steel breaks.

This silences any talk of the group tackle. I peel the last pieces of handcuffs from my wrists, and then, cinching the duffel against me, it's one step, two steps, and I'm out through the doors.

Patrol cars are lined up to stop me. *Regular cops.* My left ankle's a bigger concern, but it's holding up so far. I tug down the flight goggles, accelerating, then leaping, and I'm already on the street, weaving through traffic, moving like a cork out of a champagne bottle. As the world flickers in the Fourth Dimension, it's as if I've been blind for the last two weeks, but now, at last I can see.

ELEVEN

I go to ground in Jackson Heights, ducking behind a Dunkin' Donuts, where I huddle by the dumpster and peel off my sweats and hockey pads. I shake my hair dry, stuff my breakneck clothes inside the duffel with the stolen cash, and then—losing energy by the second—I limp to a bus stop, clad only in the tank top and cutoffs I left the house in this morning.

When I get home, Mom and Reuben want to know all about my first day back at TRU, but I blow them off, saying the lieutenant had me rush already to prove I'd not gotten rusty, so I need to crash early. I ignore Mom telling me I should eat something. Don't answer when she asks what I have in my bag. My left ankle is getting stiffer by the second. My whole body's sore, wretched and slow. Doesn't bother me, though. I'd take a hundred days of derailing over another minute of withdrawal.

"Which part of town?" Reuben asks, wheeling after me as

I head to my room. "Who were you chasing?"

"That's classified, Doughnut."

"Since when don't you tell me?"

I have more work to do tonight. Lots more. But I wrap my brother in a hug, leaning my head against the top of his and inhaling the sweet citrus smell of his hair. "What if I told you I was going after *all* the breaknecks?" I ask him. "What if today I started chasing every single one?"

He wriggles free of my embrace and stares up at me.

"Top secret." I wink at him and he beams. "But I think you'd better call Hector. We're gonna need a lot of ice delivered these next few weeks."

As soon as I've stumbled into my room, I collapse on my bed and use my phone to log onto one of the blogs that covers all things breakneck. There was controversy when this one's forum was being used for gambling: people placing bets on which breaknecks could evade arrest longest. I also know it's one of the sites Reuben gets sucked into, trawling for the latest news. But according to the lieutenant's information, this guy *Mobius* also trawls the site, looking for leads on new blood. Likes what he sees, Mobius then recruits the new blood so he can deal his high-quality tetra to them in exchange for a cut of their earnings.

He's like a drug dealer and arms dealer rolled into one.

With a fake email, I've already created an account to use the site's forum, a message board that mostly allows slo-mo spectators to post footage and theories, eyewitness accounts and updates.

I check the selfie I snapped of me rushing—the street's all a blur, but my Rangers hockey helmet is close to in focus, and for my first ever breakneck action shot, it's not bad. I lean over and open the duffel on the floor, snap a few pictures of the stacks of cash inside, then stuff the bag under my bed. Once my account is live, I upload the pictures to the blog's forum, creating a new discussion thread.

I'm not sure ripping off the HSBC in Astoria will prove I've got the goods to some dealer looking for new talent to exploit, but I have two more tetra bullets stashed in my underwear drawer, which means I have more opportunities to grab Mobius's attention. As soon as I recover from derailing, I can hit a bank in Midtown. A bigger bank. Where I'll make a bigger splash.

I use cellular data, since a Wi-Fi connection would reveal my IP address and make me easier to track. TRU monitors these blogs, so right now some desk jockey on the top floor of headquarters is checking out my pictures and trying to hack into my user account. But if they succeed they'll just find a fake email address that leads nowhere.

After an hour of waiting, I get direct-messaged, but it's someone asking to buy tetra from *me*.

Then I get my first piece of hate mail. It comes from someone who got tangled up in a breakneck-caused car wreck four weeks ago and lost an arm.

I get five similar messages from five different survivors, and I read them all. *This is why I must succeed.* Cutting off the breaknecks' supply of tetra is more than just damage control: it would prevent the damage entirely.

I have this Bart Simpson lamp on the dresser beside my bed. The lamp was my dad's, and I don't get his obsession with the Simpsons, but I like imagining him up late reading the sports section by its yellow light. The lampshade's in the shape of Bart's spiky head and casts a giant shadow on the ceiling, which can make you feel like you're inside Bart's brain if you spend too long staring at it.

I spend too long staring at it.

Eventually I shove my phone under my pillow and switch Bart off for the night. I'm still in my cutoffs and tank top but am too weak to get up and change. Too weak, and too wired. I think of Tucker's trick of counting stars until he slips into the sleepy space between them. I picture him in Nebraska, sitting in his truck with the chrome fenders and patches of rust, the peeling paint the same color as his faded blue jeans. I picture endless cornfields in every direction, rising and falling like an ocean in the warm summer night.

Then I dream of the crosswalk on Queens Boulevard. I dream of Sidewinder. And Reuben. And I dream myself faster. I dream it over and over, so that it never is over.

When my phone rings, my body spasms. The sleigh-bells ringtone has never packed such a punch. "Tell me you're not home," Tucker says as soon as I answer. "Can you hear me? *Alana?*"

"Yeah." My mouth's full of sleep.

"Prove it's you," Tucker says.

"Um, you like to shoot Canada geese?" I keep my voice

down, not wanting to wake Reuben in the room next door.

"Where are you?"

"Brace yourself—at home, in bed," I say, groggy and smiling, happy he's called.

"Get out. Now. They're on their way."

"Who?"

For a second, I think he means Mobius and I feel a brief surge of excitement.

But he doesn't mean Mobius.

"Spaihts," he says. "Now start moving."

"I *can't*. I'm derailing. I rushed—"

"I know. I know everything. You left a ball cap behind at the HSBC, right outside the entrance. Your fingerprints are all over it—fingerprints which are on file here."

"No." *Dad's old hat.* The twinge of sadness at having lost the thing is swallowed by fear.

"Spaihts is personally reviewing every incoming case," Tucker says. "So, *go*. I shouldn't even be talking to you. I'm hiding in the freaking bathroom."

"Monroe . . ."

"She'll take the fall if you get caught. But then this whole thing is finished. Wait—what was that?"

"That was me moving." I sound like a cow giving birth.

I try to get to my feet, but end up on my knees, one hand clawing the bedsheets to hold myself upright. "Good-bye, Tucker."

He starts to say something, but I end the call and make another.

"Hello?" Reuben says, his sleepy voice little-boy squeaky.

"It's me," I whisper.

"Alana?" I can hear him through the wall as well as the phone.

"I need you to come here."

"Bad derailing?" He immediately sounds awake, alarmed, and much older.

"Sort of."

"I'll get Mom."

"*No*. Keep quiet and come here."

I end the call so he won't keep talking. When he tries to call back I power off my phone.

I flip on Bart Simpson and tug on a pair of Converse, then start the agonizing task of retrieving the duffel from under my bed. In the state I'm in, the bag feels as heavy as eight dead bodies tied together. I don't stop to listen for the rumble of car engines on the street outside or Reuben getting himself into his wheelchair next door. I have minutes to do what needs hours. And by the time my bedroom door pops open, I only have the duffel halfway out from under the bed.

"What are you doing?" Reuben grins. He thinks this is funny.

"I have to get out of the house. And you have to help me."

"Are you insane? You ran today. Even TRU wouldn't call you in."

"I didn't *run*. Now keep your voice down and come here."

He wheels over and when I hand him one of the duffel's

straps, we're able to pull the bag all the way out. "I don't have time to explain," I say, showing my brother the stolen money. "You just need to trust me. The police are coming. . . ."

"Alana. Why do you have a gun?"

The gun I grabbed from the security guard is stuffed amid the scuffed cash. I scoop out the Rangers helmet to show Reuben that too. "I stole this money, you understand? I stole it from a bank. Today."

"That was you? In Astoria?" He's read all about it, of course. Maybe he even saw my post on the forum. I want to tell him I'm working undercover. I want to stem the confusion pouring out of his eyes. But if I make it out of here, Reuben will be questioned—probably by Spaihts. And that means I have to stick to the story.

Unable to look him in the eyes, I fix my gaze right between Reuben's eyebrows, just above his nose. "I know you saw it reported. Maybe you even saw the selfie I took mid-getaway; if not I can show it to you, because it's still on my phone. And later on you'll understand why I did it, but for now you just have to do what I say. Which means you have to go into the top drawer of my dresser . . . over there."

He screws his face into an angry question mark. But he rolls over to my dresser and pulls open the top drawer.

"This is your *underwear*, Alana."

"Stop making so much noise, you'll wake Mom. Just reach in the back and grab me the two cartridges. They feel like bullets. Like little steel bullets . . ."

"Tetra?" He fumbles around in the drawer until he finds what I need.

"That's it. Put them in the duffel for me, then zip it up."

Reuben stares at the two black bullets. "I want one," he says.

"No, you don't."

"Why wouldn't I?"

"You're too young. It won't work on you."

"So I'll save it," he insists.

"For what?"

"You think people in wheelchairs haven't tried it? I read about this one kid—"

"It's not safe, Reuben."

"You do it all the time."

"For my *job*."

He stares at the gaping duffel and the money inside. "You're going to take this tetra so you can rob more banks?"

"No, I'm . . ." *No one can know*, Tucker said. And he's right. The truth is too dangerous.

"Fine," I tell Reuben. "Just keep one. But put the other one in my duffel and give me your chair."

"My *chair*?" He looks horrified as I crawl across the floor, reaching for him.

"I'm going to get arrested unless I can get out of this house."

Reuben wheels right past me, heading for the door, and I'm too slow to stop him. "If you robbed a bank, then you're . . ." He's sniffling, making a mess of his words, and I want to cry with him but am afraid how much frustration would come gushing out.

"You're one of *them*." Reuben spits this out so forcefully I'm shocked, and seeing the surprise on my face makes him even angrier. "You think I'm weak," he says, with enough spite I have to scrape myself back together. "You act like this is something that happened to *you*." He drums his little fists against his tiny thighs. "You think you can't have a normal life because of me." Spit and tears froth on his lips and he's swallowing words now, his mouth clamped tight enough to snap off his tongue.

"No, Reuben," I beg. "Please. Don't do this. I know how strong you are."

"Liar!"

"I'll explain, I promise. I just can't right now. But everything I'm doing is to fix this."

"Fix what? *Me?*"

I try to look right into his eyes. He won't let me.

"Because you can't," he says. "No one can."

"Give me a chance to not get arrested. Just give me a chance to prove I'm trying to do the right thing."

"If you're lying," he says, "then don't ever come home."

He wheels himself next to my bed and spills himself out of his wheelchair, his legs twisting beneath him as he rolls over to face me, his precious features all puckered by pain.

He's suffered so much—every single day. And if I only

save one more person from this sort of suffering, it's worth any sacrifice I make.

I haul myself from the floor up to the bed and for a moment I'm lying beside my brother, so close I can smell the toothpaste on his breath. He blinks at me. The big sister he no longer knows.

"I'm so sorry," I whisper, kissing his cheek. Then my sore feet balance on the floor for a painful split second before I topple down into the wheelchair.

I wrench the duffel from the floor to my lap, sweating and straining, then I wheel myself across the room. "I love you," I say, not whispering now because what if Reuben doesn't hear and it doesn't count? When I reach the door, I wait, needing Reuben to say the words back to me. His face is hidden, his body crooked, and if I'm trying to make things right, why does leaving him feel so wrong?

"You know what tomorrow is?" Reuben's buried his face in the sheets.

"Yes," I say, though it's snuck up on me.

My brother got broke by a breakneck one year ago today.

I almost give Reuben his chair back and wait in my room. I could play it safe—tell Spaihts the truth, let Monroe take the fall. Perhaps in time, I could forget all about TRU, and tetra. And Sidewinder.

"I'm not one of them," I tell Reuben.

Then I tug open my bedroom door and wheel myself out.

TWELVE

As I roll through the living room, I crash the wheelchair against the back of the love seat, setting off a chain reaction that involves the coffee table and Mom's tower of self-help books, which topple noisily to the floor.

The mound of blankets on the couch twitches and I freeze, holding my breath. Mom's crashed out here again, and I don't want to have to explain things to her. I don't want to have to lie and *not* explain things to her either. But her sleeping pill must be working its magic, so off I go, less swift but more stealthy, and I'm almost to the front door when I hear cars pulling up outside.

They're here.

I try to spin the wheelchair around as quickly as I've seen Reuben do it, but I make a mess of the maneuver and end up smashing into the wall. I knock loose the framed picture of Dad. Can't catch it. And as it detonates on the floor, I crunch over broken glass, wheeling back through the living room, Echo barking at the front door and Mom thrashing around on the couch, sloughing off blankets.

I pick up speed. Zipping back past my bedroom, then Reuben's room, the bathroom, Mom's room. Then I'm all the way at the back of the house and stalling at the top of a small set of stairs.

At the foot of the steps: the back door. Beyond that: our tiny backyard.

I once found enough space to teach my brother to ride a bike out there, but now it's just the place we store trash cans and we've never put in a ramp for Reuben to use. There is no slow way to do this—as someone starts pounding a fist at the front door, I launch the wheelchair down the steps and end up all mashed up against the back door, which opens *inward*, so I have to scoot free of the duffel and shove back the wheelchair, unlatching locks and undoing the deadbolt, then squeezing the door open.

I land outside on my hands and knees.

And then . . . silence. Apart from a dog howling down the block. Echo has gone quiet inside the house, and there's no more pounding at the front door. Mom must have opened up. *Is she demanding to see a warrant?* Perhaps Spaihts is playing it cool—just saying he's here to ask me a few questions. Perhaps he's waiting at the front door while Mom goes to wake me up.

When I yank the wheelchair out into the night, it comes

within an inch of slamming into the trash cans. But I keep things quiet as I crawl back onto my ride and strain at the duffel bag, clawing at the straps until it's back on my lap. I'm so tired. *So weak.* Adrenaline courses through my veins but has nowhere to go. It's as if my muscles are dried-out sponges. My bones are stale bread.

Good thing I have a chair with wheels.

I roll to the edge of the house and peer around the wall. A narrow path separates our house from the next, and at the end, the path hooks up with our driveway, which is occupied only by our old Volvo. No one's blocking in our station wagon. But there'll be TRU vehicles just out of sight. I heard them pulling up. Perhaps there'll even be a runner. Spaihts knows I rushed earlier but he might be prepared for me to risk rushing again.

I check my watch: fifteen more hours until I can safely dose up. Hitting the release too soon is too risky. *It could kill me.* Still, it's tempting. One hit of tetra and I'd be able to move this wheelchair a whole lot faster. Maybe I'd even be able to run.

I test my left ankle and the joint feels feeble and furious, so I go back to wheeling the chair forward, which sucks up every last drop of strength, the wheels grating the palms of my hands, the duffel crushing my hips. I'm rolling down the path toward the driveway *too slow* and I can't stand it, so I start fumbling around at the duffel, unzipping it and plunging my hands inside to probe for the tetra bullet among the banknotes, a needle in a haystack of cash.

The trash cans smash like cymbals behind me, meaning someone's just exited the back door in a hurry, and my fingers close around the security guard's gun as I spin myself around.

I pull the gun out of the duffel, not really thinking. I'm halfway to the driveway and I should keep moving, but I point the gun back at the corner of the house. Just to scare someone off. Just a warning shot.

Monroe rounds the corner and I barely hear the gun fire. I just see the small circle of blood welling up on the lieutenant's forehead as her eyes roll back.

She staggers a half step, crumpling against the wall, and I glance down at the gun in my hand. *I pulled the trigger.*

But the safety is on.

The wheelchair catches at the wall as I turn, and I lose my grip on the gun as I face the real shooter: Spaihts is at the far end of the house, his face just a silhouette, the top of his shaved head gleaming in the orange light of the street lamps beyond. He holsters his gun inside his jacket, hustling toward me.

I back up but there's someone grabbing my chair and shoving it forward, launching me out of the seat. The duffel hits the ground first, spilling cash over the concrete, but the mound of money doesn't do much to cushion my fall.

I end up facedown in the darkness, arms torqued out of their sockets, wrists bound in handcuffs. The pain makes it hard to breathe, hard to focus. It's a blinding white light searing my senses, and yet I can make out Idra Hall's voice just fine.

"This is for the lieutenant," she screams, kicking me in the ribs, then she's reading me my rights, her voice ragged, and through a fog of confusion and fear I wonder if this means she is breaking my arrest record.

"I didn't shoot her." I whimper. "Please . . ."

"I saw the gun in your hand." Idra hauls me up by the handcuffs, her mouth at my ear. "Still want to pretend you're better than me?"

THIRTEEN

It's a different interrogation room than last time, but all these rooms look the same. Cheap metal chairs and a yellow plastic table. A painting of a dog and its dinner, like prehistoric art on the wall. There's the one-way mirror, and the camera in one corner of the ceiling. The AC blows too cold. The overhead light burns too bright. Just like last time, two agents from the U.S. Department of Justice sit across from me—Small, with her bad dye job and twitchy nose, and Spaihts, wearing the same tan suit, the same groomed goatee, the same smug look.

Everything else has changed.

"Where did you get this?" Spaihts asks, spinning the TRU-issued tetra bullet on the table between us. I'm handcuffed to my chair, arms locked behind me, and every time I tremble, the cuffs chink like ice cubes in an empty glass.

"Alana." Small leans across the table toward me. "Please. You have to speak to us. Try to talk us through what's happened."

I didn't see Small before I got to headquarters, but that doesn't mean she wasn't at the scene of the crime. Perhaps she was hidden inside one of the other vehicles, watching as Idra Hall bundled me into the back of Spaihts's low black sedan. Or perhaps Small was in my house, calmly explaining to my brother and mom that I had just shot a law enforcement agent while evading arrest.

Doesn't matter if Small was there or not, really. Her partner murdered Lieutenant Monroe in cold blood and is now framing me for it.

There's no way I can trust either of them.

And there is no way out of this room.

"Tell us how you think we should spin this?" Spaihts asks, still spinning the tetra bullet on the table. "You get asked to take a leave of absence and a couple weeks later, you show up, ripping off a bank in Astoria. Then, after you're ID'd, the Tetra Response Unit—*your* old unit—dispatches a team to bring you in for questioning, a team led by myself and Lieutenant Monroe—*your* old commanding officer—who you then shot in the head."

"With a stolen gun," Small adds.

The ballistics won't match. Forensics would show I never fired the security guard's gun, and instead would match the bullet to Spaihts's weapon. But something tells me that when you're being framed by the Department of Justice, details like that are easily fixed.

Spaihts snares my gaze, holding it while he squeezes the tetra bullet between his finger and thumb as if he means to snap the thing open. "Tell us where you got this."

"You're psychotic," I manage. My handcuffs rattle as I shake in my seat. I stare down at my lap, blinking back tears.

"*I'm* psychotic? That's your defense? Okay. Tell me this— are we all nuts, Alana? Is that what's going on? Everyone's crazy but you? Was your lieutenant also psychotic? Is that why you shot her? Or did your addiction to TTZ and your subsequent withdrawal turn you completely delusional? Because if you want to convince me you're a schizoid or paranoid or some other *oid* I don't know about, I could very easily be convinced. Agent Small?"

"It's possible Alana's experienced some sort of episode related to her withdrawal."

"I'll talk to Dr. Fenkman," I say, because he works for TRU, not the USJD, which means perhaps I can trust him. And he's a shrink, which means he might see that Spaihts is not only insane but insanely good at pretending he isn't.

"Fenkman?" Spaihts drums the tetra bullet on the table. "He's been transferred to a different division. But based on that quack's profile of you, I'd say his *expert opinion* is of little value."

"But I do get a phone call."

"You want to waste it on Fenkman?"

I stare at Spaihts's face for as long as I can stand. His gleaming scalp and slick goatee give him an oddly shiny appearance. His beady eyes ooze confidence. "I can call whoever I want," I say, terrified that nothing I know is true anymore.

"Of course you can." Spaihts snorts, as if my request is so ludicrous it's funny. "And a phone call you'll have. Even cop killers have rights. We'll let you make the call, Alana. As soon as you tell us where you got the TTZ."

He points at the fine print on the side of the tetra bullet. Little white letters. I can't read them from here but I know what they say.

"This tetra's from TRU," Spaihts says. "A six-milliliter dose. Premium grade. Manufactured by Trinity Pharmaceuticals. I want to know how you got it."

I close my eyes, shivering in my cutoffs and tank top on this cold metal seat. My body's so far beyond tired, it's almost past hurting, but I still feel the pain of derailing buried beneath the surface, like boiling water trapped under my skin. Maybe I should embrace it. Lose myself in the postrush agony and let it eat away the confusion.

Spaihts bangs a fist on the table. "Are we keeping you up, West?"

"You killed her," I say, as if saying it can make the world he's building around me crumble and reveal the real world underneath. "I saw you."

"Who did we kill?" Small asks.

"Not you. Him."

"Agent Spaihts?"

"Maybe you were there, too. Maybe you weren't. I don't know who is in on this or what it's about, but I'm innocent and I want my phone call."

"Alana . . ." Small says, her voice soft, like she's so concerned about me because I sound so crazy. Then her voice trails off into the oblivion of this interrogation room and there is only the echo of her partner's lies.

And it's all so much worse, because he is a liar, but he *isn't* insane. If this man across the table from me were just some nutjob, he'd not pose so much of a threat.

I try to slow down my thinking. *Spaihts is framing me because he needed a scapegoat.* Because for some reason he wanted Lieutenant Monroe dead and he seized the opportunity to kill her. *But why?*

"This is being recorded," I say. "It must be—unless you've broken that rule too. Maybe people are watching through that mirror. Or they'll watch the feed from the camera up there. And if anyone's watching or listening, I want it on record: I am stating my innocence. I saw this man shoot the lieutenant, and I—"

Spaihts smashes the table with his fist. "*You want your phone call.* Yeah, we know. But here's the thing—no one *is* watching, or listening, and no one's coming to your rescue. So don't—"

"Spaihts." Small doesn't raise her voice to match his,

rather burrows her calm beneath his lack of control.

I stare at her, wondering if she's an accomplice to murder, or if she truly has no idea what her partner has done. It could be they're playing good cop/bad cop, and if they're playing me, I am too dulled by shock and fatigue to understand the rules of the game. I'm cornered. Chained. No one to turn to.

Except Tucker.

He's the only one who knows what the lieutenant asked me to do. But I can't involve him. Spaihts killed my lieutenant. I won't let him hurt my handler too.

"I'll talk to you if he leaves," I say to Small, because I need to know if I can trust her and I need to get this monster away from me. "You have to help me."

"Honey, I can't help you."

"I'll tell you what happened. But only if he leaves."

Spaihts makes a big deal of not making a big deal out of it, shrugging as he slides his chair back with a screech. "Coffee?" he asks his partner, but Small shakes her head, which is a disappointment. Even *smelling* coffee right now sounds good to me.

Spaihts straightens his tie as he waits for the door to click open, and once he's through, it buzzes locked behind him again.

"What will happen to TRU?" I ask Small. Spaihts will be able to hear me. He's doubtless watching through the one-way mirror now. But at least he can't interrupt.

"You have bigger worries. Believe me."

"But what will happen to the unit?"

"TRU's almost finished. Any thread still holding the unit together has been unraveled by Monroe's death, and by your . . . actions. A couple more weeks and it will be official. This whole place will be shut down."

"So who'll go after the breaknecks?"

"We're not here to talk about that."

"Isn't that the only thing that matters?"

"Alana, we have footage of you robbing a bank yesterday."

"I robbed the bank because I was undercover."

"*What?* Why?"

I hesitate. But I have no choice but to see where the truth gets me. "Monroe believed I could find out who's making the breaknecks' tetra. She wanted me to find the dealer Dog Star mentioned. The dealer Spaihts refuses to believe exists."

"So you were asked to go undercover."

"By the lieutenant."

"Convenient. The person you shot is the person who can verify your story."

"It's not just a story. And I didn't shoot . . ." I picture Monroe crumpling against the wall, shock etched on her features, blood swelling in a bubble on her forehead.

"Who else knew about this? There'd have to be someone." Small's voice comes from some place faraway, calling me back to the present. "Bearing in mind, even if someone can corroborate this order you were issued, that doesn't do anything to clear up the murder charges you face."

"It's not . . ." I forget what I wanted to say. In my mind, Monroe is still sliding down the side of my family's house in Queens, staining the whole place with blood.

"Alana, I might appear more patient than my partner. But he *saw you*. So did this runner, Idra Hall."

"Spaihts did it. Run ballistics on his gun, his clothes—"

"You're saying a special agent of the Department of Justice committed murder and is now framing you. You really want to pursue that as your line of defense?"

"I never fired the gun," I say, my eyes pleading with hers. "Have my hands tested for residue. Have my clothes tested. Spaihts was behind me—"

"Stop. Listen to yourself for a moment. And then take another moment to remember that this is my partner you're talking about. The man I have worked with for the past eleven years."

"I'm telling you the truth."

"You haven't told me anything that makes even the slightest bit of sense. But I'll give you your phone call. In private." She stands, smoothing the creases out of her pants. "My advice? Get yourself a good attorney. Anyone should be better than the one the state drudges up. I can get your mom in here to help you select one. As your guardian, she—"

"No." I need to keep the people I care about far away from Spaihts. "Don't bring her here. Please."

"We'll need to question her."

"And my brother?"

"He'll also be brought in."

"But they won't be safe here."

"This is one of the safest places in the city." Small's nose twitches as she smiles. "Your old headquarters is the Fort Knox of dog food factories."

Right. And a monster is loose inside.

As Small leaves, I slump in my chair, my body wretched with derailing. I'd slide to the floor but for the handcuffs pinning me in place. I don't even sit up straight when Old Toby Moore enters the room, though it's jarring to see his familiar fossilized face.

Toby ignores me as he hooks a phone into the wall, connecting it to a landline. I know the call will be listened in on, that a trace will be put on whoever I call, but I need Tucker. He's the only one who knows the truth.

Everyone else here thinks I'm guilty. All the old-timers and the runners, the desk jockeys in the tactic room, the snipers and drivers and chopper pilots. Monroe's second-in-command, Vogler. My almost-friend, Jamie. Idra saw me with a gun in my hand, a gun that had been pointed at the lieutenant. And everyone will buy into Spaihts's story because why would Spaihts lie? He's an agent for the Department of Justice. And I'm not even a runner anymore.

Tucker had me memorize a number to call *in case of emergencies.* I don't want to put him at risk but, what other choice do I have?

"Hey, Little Rabbit," Old Toby Moore says, dropping the

phone on the yellow table.

"I didn't do it," I say as he comes behind me to unlock the handcuffs. "I didn't—"

"Don't talk," Toby whispers, and he pushes something into the palm of my hand. "Just run."

FOURTEEN

I clench the tetra bullet like I mean to pierce it through my skin and swallow it in my veins. And as my handcuffs fall free, I shake the cartridge, arming it instinctively. Too shocked to speak. Can barely swallow. I dare not look at Toby as he taps at the phone on the desk, drumming up a dial tone. He's handed me a key that can break down every door. Even here, in the bowels of this building.

Tucker must be somewhere inside headquarters. The tetra must be from him. I picture him sketching an exit strategy, red ink scribbled on blueprints. *He's telling me I can do this.* Believes I can break free.

I check my watch as I bring my arms in front of me, the tetra bullet concealed in my fist. *Eleven more hours* until it's safe to dose up again. I'm only about halfway through derailing. And I could barely handle being inside Macy's on the drug, let alone this place. I'd get glitchy, all cooped up and locked up, and what if the tetra's not from Tucker at all? Spaihts might be trying to trick me. Perhaps he wants to make me look even guiltier. Nothing makes you look guilty like running away.

But the only way to clear my name is to prove that Spaihts shot Monroe.

I'm not going to do that locked up in here.

"Be careful," Toby whispers. He has his back to me, waiting for the door to click open. As soon as he's gone, I snatch the phone from the table, cradling it with both hands, using it to shield my mouth from the one-way mirror and the camera and all the eyes watching me as I shove the cartridge between my teeth, bite down. A last hesitation.

Then I hit the release.

Instead of red-hot, my insides turn cold. My brain full of ice water, my heart swollen and slushy. Breathe in and my lungs rattle, a chill crawling all over me until everything is frostbitten and stiff.

I probe my rib cage with numb fingers, panicked as I try to stand. My hands flail at the table, then the chair, then I'm down on the floor, legs like shards of melting snow. I'm sinking inside myself, drowning in the double dose. Instead of scaling the drug's peak, I'm caught in an avalanche, tumbling down inside an endless crevasse. *I need to start moving.* They'll be coming for me—*Spaihts* will be coming.

I need to be ready to fight.

Here comes the drum of footsteps, followed by a blur of

faces peering down at me on the floor. As I try to swat them away, my limbs move at a glacial pace. My mind reaches for something pre–Ice Age, and I yearn for Tucker's warm voice in my ear. I need him to handle me. *Help* me. Tell me I can control this and show me what to do.

In my altered state, I feel his fingers caressing the scar on my forehead, his touch sizzling on my snowdrift skin. And as I abandon myself to the vision, Tucker's no longer caressing the scar on my forehead, he's peeling it open and reaching inside me, his fingers like matches made of bone and teeth.

He strikes the toothy part of the match against the inside of my skull, scraping it into a blood-red flame, and the flame trembles like a teardrop, then falls, splashing inside my cold gray depths, reigniting my engines. As the rush blooms through my veins, my heart booms like a tribal drum as every part of me prepares to explode.

It is terrifying.

And glorious.

My skin sobs sweat. And when I open my eyes I am spun gold and hellfire. My stomach wants to erupt but my throat won't let it—can't unspool before the mother of all rushes kicks in.

". . . still alive." It's Small's voice. Her fingers are at my neck, feeling my thunderous pulse, but I'm *more* than alive. Much more. Just like this is more tetra than I've ever felt and more power than I have ever imagined.

Strength surges into my muscles until I throb with it.

My heart races until I am slippery with speed.

They're backing away from me—Agent Small and Old Toby Moore. Two other sleepwalking drones who work security.

Spaihts is backing up, too.

My brain basks in reborn lucidity, bolting ahead and craving conclusions. But I need to focus on getting out of here before I try to solve the puzzle of Spaihts. And how long has it already been since the tetra hit my system?

Doesn't matter. Don't overthink, Alana. Just get off the floor.

Spaihts is reaching for his gun, but he should have shot me back at my house when I was slumped in my brother's wheelchair. He should have gunned me down like he gunned down the lieutenant. Because his gun's not even halfway out of its holster before I leap from the floor to the tabletop, and he's still staring at the floor, his eyes glued to the spot where I used to be, as if I'm still lying there and not kicking him in the head.

Everything shimmers, the Fourth Dimension a corona of luminous light. I see clearer now than I ever have. And I don't just see better, I hear better too—globs of Spaihts's blood splatter the air and his head makes crunchy sounds as it collides with the wall.

I'm still spinning, my right leg straight out at ninety degrees, mowing down Small and the two guards I don't know. I round off my roundhouse just before my foot reaches Old Toby Moore.

He dives backward, knocking the cap off his head as he bounces at the wall. Clutching his ugly yellow scalp, Toby winces in pain.

I have to rein myself in.

My crumpled victims scatter like broken branches in the corners of the room. *I don't want to hurt these people.* Not even Spaihts. Not in here. Now more than ever I must stay in control.

Toby stares up at me from the floor, his face a cartoon of slow motion, the words stretched out as he says, "Let me help you."

I don't bother telling him he no longer can.

More bodies are piling in through the door now. Gray TRU uniforms and combat gear, riot sticks at the ready. In 4D they're a spiky tongue probing the cavity of the room. I see them move almost before they do move. And when *I* move, I'm so fast, the walls seem to melt.

I lose myself to the swirl, not so much stemming the tide of bodies gushing in here as puncturing a hole *through* them. Then I'm in the corridor. Moving like a bullet through the barrel of a gun. If I blink I won't make the corner up ahead—I'll just slam into the wall. So I don't blink, I *run*, and guns fire at places I used to be.

More bodies ahead. Men and women with twitchy trigger fingers. I weave through their bullets, then stampede through the shooters themselves.

I round a corner. Another. I'm in the stairwell. Ascending. Leaving the interrogation rooms behind. Then I'm in a new corridor, racing through the building like the drug's racing through my veins, my brain keeping one step ahead so my feet can find the way out.

TRU headquarters is a code I crack from memory, a maze my mind long ago mapped. Top floor is the tactic room, but I don't need to make it all the way up there. Ground level will work fine. I cut past the locker rooms and the training rooms, everything rippling around me. Again I think of Tucker's squiggly red lines marking exit routes. And where *is* Tucker? Is he waiting for me? Ready to help me? He could be around the next corner. . . .

As a reward for losing concentration, I lose my footing. I slide, then tumble, bouncing at the walls like a gutter ball, and somewhere inside the glow of the overdose, my left ankle raises an alarm.

I slam into a closed door at the end of the corridor. Leaping up, I test my ankle—not as stable as I want it, but the pain's hard to feel through the rush.

A bigger problem is this door being locked.

Feet rumble in the corridors behind me, above me and below, the sound distorting all through the building, a song made of echoes, as molten as the chipped walls that pour like waterfalls, the painted dogs barking at me and wagging their tails. I've never seen so much in the Fourth Dimension.

It's as if the building's alive and the bricks are breathing.

I clutch at my chest, trying to inhale and exhale and not get glitchy. I mustn't unspool, despite the intensity of the trip.

As shooters round the bend, cornering me against the locked door, I feel like I'm about to peak, and I have never come close to peaking this hard.

I'm fast enough to dodge the first wave of bullets. The second and the third. But pinned against this locked door, I can't out-move all of them. A bullet slices my left thigh. Another clips my right shoulder. I have so much speed, just not enough space.

My stomach churns and my head spins as I grip the door's handle. I need strength now, not speed. I need to channel the momentum through my fingers, and it'll help if I let the aggression rise up inside like a flood. So I picture Spaihts gunning down my lieutenant. I picture Idra Hall strapping me in handcuffs.

I slam a fist at the steel door, but can't punch through it. The gunners are closing in on me, and they've stopped shooting. They think I'm cornered. They think this is over. But it's *never* over.

Not till I put right everything that is wrong.

I think of Reuben, coming toward me on that crosswalk. Sidewinder speeding toward us. Barely visible as he blind-sided my brother. And me too slow to do anything but watch.

One year ago today.

As I peel the door from its hinges, the metal rips like old cardboard. And it's as if I've never known tetra until this moment—the anger consuming me, all past and future destroyed. There's only now. Just me and these walls that cannot hold me, because nothing can hold me. I *am* the rush. I howl as the nine-minute-me melds with forever, screaming the sound of all of me all at once being unleashed.

The door's broken. Gone. And I'm running again, if you can call it running. *Flying* doesn't do justice to the way I now move.

I drag the steel door behind me, using it as a shield against the bullets. Running up on the walls and the ceiling. Still screaming. Still peaking. Still ripping through the seamless rags of time. I see colors no one's named and smell my shoes burning.

When I reach the exit, the final locked door, I take my steel shield and hurl it before me, spinning it like a boomerang I don't expect back. It punctures a hole through the last door but not big enough for me to squeeze through.

I have to slam on the brakes and grind to a stop, easing off my left ankle so I won't tear it apart. "Open the door!" I scream, my voice bubbling with rage.

Some security drone's cowering behind his desk with his gun drawn.

"Let me out!" I crush my elbow into the door. The *last* door. A door I cannot rip through. It's too huge and too heavy and I am no longer peaking.

"I didn't kill Monroe," I say, my voice strangled by the vise of my jaw. I leap onto the desk, and the guy behind it peers up at me, then tosses away his gun.

At first I think he's opening the door because he believes I am innocent.

The real reason? He's terrified.

I burst out of the building, rounding the corner to the street, then vaulting over the barricade of tactical vehicles they've already set up.

I can't have long left now, but I'm loose down the street and still so high. No helmet hemming me in. Squinting, no goggles. I breathe deep. Savoring this feeling where I'm nothing and everything. I am the sky and the concrete, the dirt on the asphalt. I slip between sunbeams and cast no shadow. And as the blocks fly by, I touch no one and see no one, and I am no one. For just a little while longer. Like a half-remembered dream, I will forget almost all of this, but not *this*.

This will come back to me, and haunt me, a ghostly angel with wings of speed. And I will know then, as I know now, that all my best is behind me. Because nothing will ever come close to this feeling again.

FIFTEEN

I hobble out of the gas station restroom, my pink-and-black bangs slicked back with water, my clothes stained with sweat and blood. It hurts to lean down to the water fountain, but my mouth feels full of sawdust. My veins feel full of sour milk and it's curdled my bones.

I cradle the water fountain with both arms and drink until the attendant behind the counter turns his TV down to yell, "Hey! You gonna buy something?"

I push myself upright, spine stiff as a rusted bike chain. I scraped sixty-two cents off the sidewalk—looking for loose change gave me something to do after the rush wore off. I've probably walked a mile since the comedown. Feels like it took hours to make it that far, but I'm not sure. My watch got smashed in my escape from headquarters, so I slung it in a trash can.

"How much is a cup of coffee?" I ask.

The guy looks like a body-mod Jesus, all tattoos and piercings, scraggly beard and scrawny shoulders. He's straight out of forty days in the wilds of Brooklyn. But what do *I* look like? My old Converse are in tatters. My tank top and cutoffs reveal the wounds on my shoulder and thigh, which I've wrapped with toilet paper. I move across the crowded convenience store like I need an IV drip more than a shot of caffeine.

"Seventy-five cents." Behind the counter, Jesus scratches an inky forearm. "Plus tax."

I count my change, as if I don't already know exactly how much I have. "How about I get a half cup?"

"We don't sell *half cups.* You hit the machine and it squirts the brown out. What you gonna do, pour half on the floor? Second thought, don't answer that. Third thought, get the hell out."

"I have sixty-two cents."

"I'll take that for the twenty-six minutes you just spent in the bathroom doing God knows what. Who do you think has to mop the floor in there, anyway?" With his fists on the counter, he props himself up taller so he can stare down at my feet. "What happened to your shoes?"

"It's a new look. Listen, how about I mop the floor in the women's bathroom for you and you let me use your phone for a minute?"

"What about the *guys'* toilet? That one's got things growing inside it." When Jesus grins, he displays a very un-Christlike piece of grimy gold bling on a snaggled front tooth. "I'm just messing with you. Go on and get out. There's a pay phone outside."

"It's broken."

"So?"

"What if I told you I got attacked and that's why I look like this?"

"You want me to call the police?"

"No police. I just need your help."

"Get some coffee," he says, turning back to his TV behind the counter. "Then get out."

I line up a cup beneath the crusted dispenser, and the coffee steams out like bubbling tar. Smells so sour, my eyes water, but my mouth waters too. I pour in six packets of sugar, then take my coffee to the counter and put down my dirty loose change. Jesus douses his hands with Purell after he's stuffed the coins in the register.

Perhaps he's worried I'm contagious.

"And?" he asks. "You want a *receipt*?"

"If I could just use your phone. My mom needs to come get me or I'm stranded," I lie. "Please, man. I'm not some homeless junkie. I'm just a kid who needs to get back to Queens."

"You washed your hands in there?" He nods toward the bathroom and the hoops in his ears rattle like tiny tambourines.

"You're out of soap, but I did my best."

He nudges the hand sanitizer toward me and I scrub my

hands with it while he gets out his phone and taps in his password. "I'm a good Samaritan for life after this. What's your momma's digits?"

I tell him the number Tucker had me memorize.

"It's ringing," the guy says, holding up the phone so I can hear for myself. Then he points at the little TV mounted behind the register. "You seen this?"

I'm focused on the phone, panicked because all it seems to do is ring and ring and then ring some more, but Jesus keeps nodding at the TV screen.

The footage he's watching is of *me*.

Someone must have captured my escape with their phone, and now whatever channel this is has the clip on repeat—you can make out the blur of me as I soar down the street, headquarters behind me. I'm followed at first by most of my old unit, but if I'm a solar flare, they're slow as sunstroke, and by the end of the block most of them must have lost sight of me, because they rumble to a confused halt.

The footage zooms in on a few of the uniforms, then points up at the sky, where—too late—a chopper has appeared to track me.

"You ever seen someone on tempo?" Jesus is still holding his phone up but it's no longer ringing. "No answer, by the way."

"Can you try again?"

"They look even faster in real life." He stares at the looped footage of me in action. "So that breaker was *moving*, know what I'm saying? They think that was like the TRU home base or something. Some breakneck escaping. Total first."

"Try the number again. Please."

"It's a big deal." He points at the TV, which I am trying very hard not to look at.

"I bet."

On our second attempt, Tucker answers immediately, shouting, "Where are you?" with such urgency I'm surprised Jesus can hold on to his phone.

"Where are we?" I ask, grabbing the phone, then I repeat the Tribeca address to Tucker. "Come quickly."

"What phone is this?"

"I'm at a gas station."

"Don't stay there."

"Then how will you find me?"

"Take West Broadway to Worth Street," Tucker says. "If you don't see me, head east to Chatham Square, then get to Sixteen Elizabeth Street. Got it? It's a hair place. *Lien Hair Salon.* Get your head buzzed or hair extensions. Anything to change up how you look."

That will put me right in the middle of Chinatown. Good place to go to ground. But so far from here. "I won't make it," I say.

"Yes you will."

"Tucker." I turn and lower my voice. "It was Spaihts . . . Spaihts killed Monroe."

"I'm coming for you. Hang tight. We'll get through this."

"But why would Spaihts kill her?"

"All I know is you should be moving already."

When I go to hand the phone back, the guy behind the counter has both tattooed hands stuffed up in his greasy brown hair. "You are shitting me," he keeps saying, shaking his head. "You have got to be shitting me."

He reaches to the TV to turn up the volume, and the escape footage has ended.

Instead, my face stares out of the screen.

It's the picture I always carried in my uniform, the one of me and Reuben at the hockey game, but my brother's cropped out of the shot—the image is zoomed in on my smiling face, and Gas Station Jesus knows who that girl is.

Of course they didn't use a shot of me in uniform, like the one TRU took at my graduation from basic training. As the footage of me speedfreaking down the street starts over, I'm only described by the news anchor as a breakneck. A wanted criminal. No mention that I was a runner. That would be a harder story for the Department of Justice to *spin*, I suppose.

"You still want to clean those bathrooms?" Jesus looks more bemused than shocked as I start backing up to the door. "I could put a sign on the wall—fastest breakneck in history once scrubbed these johns clean. Hey! Don't want your coffee?" He grins. "Come on, don't leave yet. At least sign something for me first. What d'you think I'm gonna do, call the pigs?"

"Why wouldn't you?"

"Why *would* I? What'd you do, rob a bank? No biggie to me. Banks have been robbing people way longer than tempo's been on the streets. Come on and sign something. Payment for the phone call."

"What do you want me to sign?"

He looks not at his counter for a piece of paper but at his forearms, for a blank piece of skin. "Here," he says, pointing at a still tattoo-free patch near the inside of his left elbow. He holds up a pen. "Might just make this permanent, if you turn out to be as big a deal as I think."

"You want me to write my name on your arm?"

"Yeah. Your breaker name. Which one are you, anyway?"

"No one." At the counter, I take the pen from him. "I'm . . . new. I guess."

"Then pick a name, sister."

I pluck the cap off the pen and scrawl on his forearm. I do a nice job of it too, giving him a little drawing instead of writing something.

"What's this?" he asks, trying to make out my doodle upside down.

"It's a time bomb," I tell him.

He hands me a ragged denim jacket that reeks of old smoke and older sweat. "You better take this. Can't head out on the street like that."

I pull the jacket on, and it's way too big, but that means it covers the wound on my thigh as well as the one on my shoulder. "Thanks," I tell the guy. Then I get the hell out.

The cabs steer clear of me. I don't blame them, but getting a ride to Elizabeth Street would be infinitely preferable to the painful slog of walking. The subway's another option, but even though it's cheaper than a taxi, it would still cost more than I've got. I had a duffel stuffed with thousands of dollars beneath my bed last night, now I have less than nothing. So I keep on toward Chinatown, holding out hope that Tucker finds me on West Broadway, before I reach Worth Street.

Then I reach Worth Street.

Next stop is Chatham Square, where there is still no sign of Tucker or his blue-jeans truck. And double the dose means double the derailing, so I'm really dragging, hoping Tucker will spot me, *rescue* me, but this is a mistake. I can't dawdle out here in public. My face has been plastered all over the TV, so it's on the internet, too. The story will be on people's phones and on people's minds and I'm not going to be outrunning anyone anytime soon. The further I get from the rush, the more haggard I feel. If tetra smoothed out my rough edges, they're now rougher than ever. My left ankle once again held up when I needed it, but it's starting to feel like a land mine I have to keep stepping on.

Reminds me of Monroe telling me how I needed to fall on the grenade to protect TRU, to protect her, to make sure others could keep fighting the good fight. But now the lieutenant is dead and TRU is in the hands of Spaihts, who's going to use my own unit to catch me, then shut the unit down.

Unless I can find out why he's doing all this and prove what he's done.

My limp is drawing attention, and more and more faces turn to stare at the skinny girl in the oversize denim jacket, shoes barely on her feet.

In dire need of a break, I lean against a graffitied wall for a second. I'm on the edge of Chinatown now. Elizabeth Street's not much farther, and these bricks are so toasty from the heat and I'm so drowsy from derailing, but a guy runs out of the bodega on the other side of my beautiful wall, yelling at me and shooing me away.

I pass restaurants, meat shops, and pharmacies, signs for foot rubs and eyebrow threading and legal advice. Windows full of koi. Flimsy carts full of fruit. The air is swampy, pungent with exhaust and onions, every smell sautéed by summer. Dizzy bright colors sprout off every inch of each battered block.

I shove my hands in the pockets of my jacket, dirty bangs falling across my eyes. The toilet paper bandaging the wounds on my thigh and shoulder starts peeling off as it wilts in the heat. And I've just turned onto Elizabeth Street when a car horn blasts behind me.

"Yo!" The girl's driving a cream sports car and shouting through its open window. "Hey! Gimpy!"

I glance about, hoping the girl's spotted a friend or something, but she's definitely talking to me. Others on the sidewalk are turning to see what's going on—correction, *everyone* on the sidewalk is turning to see what's going on. As I start shouldering my way through the onlookers, the sports car holds up the traffic behind it, driving slow to keep pace with me. It's one of those expensive electric things. A Tesla. Silent as a knife. Probably costs close to a hundred grand, and the girl driving it is about my age.

"Come on," she shouts. "Let me get a good look at you!"

She blasts her horn again. The girl has skin almost as dark as my hair. Her own head's shaved smooth, and from her left ear dangles a feather earring.

"Knew it!" she exclaims, bringing the car to a halt at the curb beside me. Someone honks in the crowded road behind her, but the girl doesn't seem to care. "I knew from those feet, kid."

She points a phone out through the open window—its case like a playing card, the Queen of Hearts—and compares me to something on her screen. "Better get in, love." Her accent makes her stick out even more than she already did in her expensive electric car. "Before someone less friendly finds you."

"You must be confused."

"Nah, love. Not confused at all. You're *her.* And it's lucky I found you, innit. Been looking for you *all* over. Go on and get in. We'll talk."

"I'm meeting someone."

"Yeah? I'll give you a lift, then. Better than walking after a skin full of tempo."

148

A couple of blocks away, a siren shrieks, sending a shock wave down my spine.

"No time to argue," the girl shouts.

Where's Tucker? And where the hell is 16 Elizabeth Street? It should be close, but there are only nail salons and a dentist's office. No hair salon.

I glance about for somewhere to hide as the siren wails louder, *nearer.* There's a tiny shop full of teapots to my right—too small to go to ground in there. Same with the place selling Malaysian beef jerky. The Amour Nightclub up ahead appears to be some sort of sweaty French-Chinese fusion, but it's an over-twenty-one joint, and is, regardless, *closed.*

The crowd on the sidewalk is setting like concrete around me, fingers pointing to lock me in place. The chatter's full of words I do not understand, Mandarin or Cantonese, and curling between the words is the sound of that siren.

I push through to the edge of the sidewalk, throwing a desperate last look at the street for Tucker's truck.

Then I yank open the door to the Tesla and plunge inside.

SIXTEEN

We glide off Elizabeth Street as a cop car turns onto it a block behind us, its howling siren spinning blues and reds. I twist around in my seat, holding my breath till the squad car blasts past the turn we just made—they're continuing on Elizabeth. But if someone alerted the cops to my presence in Chinatown, they'll likely soon have a description of this car.

Two more turns and we're down an alley, then popping out into uncharted waters: some narrow tributary of Chinatown I've not seen before. The shabby signs are less burdened with broken English, the awnings more droopy, the windows more clogged. The road's soupy with cyclists, which makes driving a stuttering frustration.

"I could walk faster than this."

"You sure?" the girl at the wheel says. "No offense, but you look like complete shit. Now make yourself useful and tell me you know how to get to Baxter Street from here."

She is long-necked and wiry, and her head and shoulders bob in a constant state of motion. Not jerky and twitchy, but fluid, rhythmic, as if she's undulating to music only she can hear. She taps a beat at the steering wheel, her fingernails the color of seashells.

"*Baxter Street?*" she says, catching me staring at her. "I know you're derailing, love, but do you know where it is?"

"I'm not going to Baxter Street."

She glances at her phone in its Queen of Hearts case. "Baxter, where are you, you bugger? We find it, we'll take that toward Bleecker, yeah?"

An old man sails toward us on a bike, boxes balanced on his handlebars. He jostles his front wheel left and right as if he can't decide if he should play chicken with the Tesla or get out of our way.

"*Crazy* man!" the girl yells, her accent chewy it's so thick. She slams on the brakes, hits the horn, and the cyclist scowls at us as he swerves to avoid the front end of the car. "Go on. Get out of it!"

"I need to go back to Elizabeth Street," I tell her. "I'm meeting someone."

"You no hear that *whoop-whoop* behind us? Only thing you're meeting down there is the police. Now come on and help us get unlost. I ain't native's the problem."

"No kidding."

"Sri Lanka, love." She grins like she's used to making

people smile. Not smug about it. More like she's just excited to be passing on the good news. "By way of South London. Hear my accent, yeah? Makes the boys *crazy*. Problem is, this city's a lot of streets for a new kid. And half the signs down here don't make any sense."

Lost or not, she starts working the Tesla forward through a gridlock of bikes, pedestrians, and delivery trucks. She checks her rearview, and snatches up her phone again. "JB'll know," she says, pulsing her shoulders a little harder, as if the music in her head has picked up intensity. "The boy's got a mind like a GPS."

As she starts to make a call, I hear the sirens behind us.

"Take the next right," I say. "You can't go north on Baxter. We'll take Mulberry to Bleecker."

The girl drops her phone, beaming at me as she navigates through the murky crowd, and I imagine more than the accent, this girl's *smile* drives boys crazy.

I'm bedraggled and tattered beside her. The runaway hitching a ride with the rich kid.

"What am I calling you then?" she asks.

"You don't have to call me anything." I make sure my door is unlocked, planning to bail out a safe distance from Chinatown. I'll find a way to call Tucker again and regroup.

"Bit prickly, aren't you? Come on. You can call me Rapunzel, on account of the long, flowing locks." She rubs a hand over her smooth head, giving her shoulders an extra groove and flashing another incandescent grin.

I remember what Tucker said about shaving my head, or getting extensions, or anything that would change how I look. Something tells me I wouldn't rock a shaved head quite like this girl. Something tells me I wouldn't rock *anything* quite like she does.

She's a breakneck. Has to be. The expensive car. The talk of *tempo.* She knows I'm wanted by the police and has tracked me down.

"Just call me Lana," I tell her.

"There you go. You even *look* like a Lana."

I smile. Only Dad ever called me Lana, and it's nice hearing someone say it again.

"*See.*" The girl takes my smile and grows it bigger, then throws it back. "You'll warm up to Rapunzel. Everyone does. And JB's gonna be tickled pink as Santa's knickers at Christmas when he finds out I'm bringing Public Enemy Numero Uno back to the pad."

"You're a breakneck," I say. Not a question. I wonder which one she is. Did I chase her when I was a runner, both our heads hidden inside helmets?

I'd best make a run for it at the next red light.

But then what? I've been framed for murder by an agent of the Department of Justice, and even Tucker can't keep me safe from Spaihts. Perhaps I'll be safer with breaknecks, until I can find some way to clear my name. I need to find out why this has happened and what Spaihts is up to. I still need to find Mobius, too. *Keep on down the rabbit hole,*

Little Rabbit. I can hear just how Monroe would have said it. *Keep on with the mission and stick to the plan.*

Besides, breaknecks have the thing I'll need most if I want to remain one step ahead.

Tetra.

"Here's Mulberry," I say, and after she turns onto it, Rapunzel hits the accelerator, making us shoot forward, the electric car whispering speed and putting plenty of distance between us and Chinatown. Taking me farther from Tucker. I feel the ache of missing him, just when I was so close to seeing him again, feeling his hand on the back of my neck. Seeing his warm, reassuring smile. Maybe we'd have leaned against each other in a restaurant booth as he outlined a plan on a paper napkin and we downed buckets of cheap chow mein.

The thought makes my stomach growl.

"Jaffa Cake?" Rapunzel asks, reaching to the backseat and bringing forth a box of cookies. "I hated these when I lived in London; now I can't get enough of them. They're well tasty, though not exactly filling. You must be starving after the rush you had."

They're not bad—cheap chocolate with fake orange spongey bits. There are eight in the box, and I eat seven before I offer her one.

Rapunzel laughs, shaking her head. "You enjoy it, mate."

So I eat that one too, and start to feel sleepy. The double dose and double derail are catching up to me. And I couldn't sleep the night before I ripped off the HSBC. Couldn't the night after, which was *last night*, when I was still at home, telling Reuben I'd fix things.

But how can I? And what must Reuben think of his big sister now?

"You all right?" Rapunzel asks, and I blink hard to hold back the tears.

"Fine." I lean against the door, peering out through the window at the tiered blocks and narrow shaded streets. Above old St. Patrick's, curling wisps of clouds turn the sky a smoky blue, and I try to recall the way the world looked when I broke out of headquarters, every building blooming toward the sun as the rush sonic-boomed through my heart. *Like a flash of lightning, filling up the night sky* was how Tucker described the feeling. But all that's burned out, and something thin and cold is left in its place.

The Jaffa Cakes aren't sitting well in my stomach, and the closest I can get to recapturing the rush is the chewed-up taste of aspirin in my mouth.

"Sleep if you need," Rapunzel says. "I got the directions no problem from here, believe. And you have had one hell of a day."

"Hell of a year," I murmur, not meaning to be funny, but she laughs as I start to nod off. It's a kind laugh. The sort that makes you want to join in, to taste the same joy.

She's a breakneck, I remind myself.

She is the enemy.

SEVENTEEN

I dream I'm sprawled in the back of Tucker's truck, sunset staining the skies, the cornfields like oceans of gold in the thickening dusk. The truck is still but I crave motion. I need to be fast and I want to run, but Tucker's holding my hands in his, slowing me down beside him, promising that when the stars appear he'll show me the constellations.

"Try not to move," he says. He presses something cool to my forehead, and I realize I'm no longer dreaming.

And that Tucker Morgan's not here.

"Easy," the boy says as I jolt up. He's pulling plush sheets over my bare shoulders, careful to look away, and I realize I'm nearly naked as I recoil from him, squirming back in the bed and pressing myself into the pillows.

"Where's Rapunzel?" I ask, my voice less awake than the rest of me.

"She flaked out." The boy meets my eyes for the first time.

"Nurse duties fell to me."

"What do I need a nurse for?"

"Bullet wounds," he says, and I find gauze pads taped to the wound on my shoulder. Then, reaching down, I find he's patched up my thigh, too. "You were lucky."

"Not lucky," I say. "Fast."

"Right." He pitches the damp cloth he's holding into a bowl full of ice. "I've seen the footage. You rush well. But you derail harder than anyone I've ever seen. Been almost two days since Rapunzel brought you home."

Two days gone. It's hard to take in. I look for my watch, then remember I broke it in my escape from headquarters. "What did you do with my clothes?" I ask, since I'm in nothing but my underwear.

"Rapunzel said they weren't worth keeping. I'll grab you something to wear, now you've stopped sweating it out." He puts the back of his hand against my forehead. "I thought you might have a fever but it seems like your body just needed to detox. What kind of tempo were you rushing?"

I shrug. "Scored some on the street."

"Yeah? Well, you rushed legit." His tangled mop of curly hair is almost as dark as mine, his complexion a shade darker. He's lean, but broad-shouldered. Long legs. *Fast.* Could be any one of the breaknecks currently posing a serious threat.

He arches his back to crack it. Looks exhausted.

"You seriously nursed me back to health for two days?" I ask.

"Oh yes." He furrows his brow to match mine. "Very seriously."

He bundles up some books and magazines off the floor, stacking them on the table beside my bed. "Something to pass the time. Till you feel up to moving about."

"Which one are you?" I ask, again trying to make his body into a breakneck I recognize.

"Why?" He smiles. "Have you met a lot of us?"

"So you are one." I'm disappointed. Somehow he doesn't look like a breakneck. Something about his brown eyes. Soft and sweet, and a little sad. His cheekbones are sharp, his skin smooth. A sculpture of a boy carved from expensive wood and polished to perfection. I'm more like a soggy blown fuse. Grubby and ugly beneath these sheets, my skin bruised and bandaged. My face feels swollen, eyes gummy with sleep.

A plastic tube plugs into the vein on my right arm, IV tubing hooking me up to a clear bag of fluid, which hangs upon a little metal tripod. The tripod would make a flimsy sort of spear, and a blunt one, and one that really looks more like a hat stand than anything else, but it's still a potential weapon.

"Are you planning to keep me here?" My voice is hoarse.

"You want to hobble on home, that can be arranged." The boy cocks his head to one side, studying me with his bottomless brown eyes. "But I've a feeling you'll want to stay once you talk to JB."

"Another breakneck?"

"Not exactly. He's my brother."

"And you are?"

"Ethan." He offers me a hand but I don't take it. I'd have to extend my arm out from beneath the sheets and I already feel too exposed. He seems to realize this, and mumbles, "Sorry," as he withdraws. But this boy patched up my shoulder and thigh, so he's already seen me in my underwear. So I take his hand.

"You need another pillow?" he asks.

"I'm ready to stand," I say, but as I prop myself up on my elbows, too much blood rushes in every wrong direction, making my head swim.

"Easy." Ethan's stuffing more pillows behind me, holding the back of my head up.

His breath is sweet black coffee beneath minty gum. His overalls are splattered with paint, all different colors, a Jackson Pollack with a boy inside. The traces of paint fumes make me even more light-headed, but his breath makes my mouth water.

"Don't let me sleep," I say, desperate not to lose more time. As I reach for his shoulder to pull myself up, the sheet falls away and he averts his eyes from my body.

"Ethan?" calls a voice from across the room. Someone stands in the doorway. "How we looking, bro?"

"She's not ready." Ethan straightens up. "Still recovering."

"It's been two days." A young man's voice. Impatient. "This ain't a bed and breakfast."

"Give her time."

"No," I whisper, and I pull Ethan toward me as I try to sit up again. The room turns fuzzy; his handsome face fades in and out. "I'm ready."

He helps wrap me in a sheet as I climb out of bed, holding my arm to steady me. "You are a wild one," he says, our faces close. Then he turns to the door. "Says she's ready."

"My office," comes the reply. "In five."

Ethan brings me two mugs of coffee, each with six sugars, just as I ask. I gulp down the first, then have him carry the other for me as I struggle out of the room, wrapped in the sheet, carrying my IV tubing and bag of fluids. My left ankle has the stability of a spaghetti noodle and the pain is shark-bite bad, but I don't let Ethan carry me down the hardwood stairs. If this house is full of breaknecks, now is no time to show weakness.

At the bottom of the stairs, Ethan holds open a door for me, and inside the room, a spidery fossil sits behind a desk, his phone sandwiched between the rotten slices of bread that are his scrawny shoulder and flaky ear.

He taps his call dead as I enter.

"Better sit down," he says, gesturing with his phone to a seat across from him. "Before you collapse on my floor."

A broken nose that never healed right is his finest feature. His lips appear to have been nibbled away by his horrific yellow teeth. Perhaps an accident disfigured him, but more likely it was too much knockoff tetra and too little regard for proper dosing and purity. He looks like Old Toby Moore plus a hundred years of no sleep.

"Christ, Ethan," he says. "Can't you get the girl some clothes? And what's with the IV?"

"She was in a rush to meet you." Ethan hands me my coffee as I sit down. "I'll grab her something from Aces or Rapunzel."

"And leave me alone with her?" The fossil across the desk grins at me, the smile splitting his face open like an earthquake in the worst part of town. "Not gonna bite me, are you?"

I'm more likely to bite a sewer rat.

Ethan leaves, and I fiddle with the tube in my arm. The sheet I'm wearing is soft as silk and I've twisted it around my torso like a towel. I have to pin it against me as I lean forward to set down my coffee.

The fossil leans back in his leather chair and stretches his legs out across the desk. The room's otherwise sparse, yet feels decadent. Chocolaty hardwood floors. Creamy walls like slabs of cheesecake. Heavy curtains drape the window, snuffing out the sunlight, and fluffy pockets of grime web the corners, as if someone moved out a decade ago and took the maid with them.

"Rapunzel wants to take all the credit for finding you," the fossil says, waggling his spotless skate shoes on the desk like two puppets. "But homie at the gas station gave us a heads-up. Said he overheard something about Elizabeth Street."

Body-Mod Jesus. "That guy called you?"

"He called someone who called me. Chinatown was good thinking—best place to go to ground in the whole city. Who were you planning to meet on Elizabeth? You already working with someone?"

"A friend."

"Another breaker?"

"I thought breaknecks work alone."

Lone wolves, Monroe always called them.

"Not anymore." The fossil scratches his flaky bald scalp. "Not here."

A pack of wolves, then.

"So which one were you?" I ask, and it is hard to know how old he really is, but it is also hard not to imagine this ex-breakneck as the breakneck who crushed Reuben's spine.

I feel the IV pinch in my vein as my whole body tenses.

"No one you've heard of," he says, waving away the question. "And now I'm just plain old JB. I was never much good, to be honest. Not as good as my brother. And definitely nowhere near as good as you." He swings his legs off the desk and plants his elbows on it instead. His face is closer now, and it is the sort of face you prefer far away. His eyes are so bloodshot, there's hardly any white left at all. "*Timebomb.* That's what the media's running with. New York One ran an interview with our gas station friend while he was at the tattoo parlor, inking up your design. I like it. *Timebomb.* Catchy, and to the point. And speaking of time, how long would you say you have left?"

"Rushing?" I shrug.

"Sure. No one knows *exactly*. But how old are you?"

"Sixteen," I lie.

"When'd you start getting your period?"

"When did you?" I snap.

JB smiles again. Another earthquake of ugly teeth. "I know. Bit personal. But it's the best indicator of how much longer you get to keep hitting the tempo. Later a girl starts her period, longer she can rush."

I shake my head. You have no real idea how much time you have left until you needle up. You might get the warning headaches, but that's the only heads-up there is. "That theory's out of date."

"According to who?"

According to the techs at the Tetra Response Unit.

"I read it online," I say. "But I was a late bloomer, if that's what you want to know."

"No headaches?"

"Not when I'm rushing. My skull feels split in two right now."

Ethan returns, dropping a hoodie and a pair of jeans in my lap. And wanting to appear bold, I dress as if I'm at the beach and wrapped in a towel, pulling the jeans on beneath the sheet, then pulling the hoodie down over the top.

"She tell you how she did it?" Ethan asks his brother.

The IV tubing's out of sight but still hooked in, my body

slowly sucking the bag of fluids dry. "Did what?" I take a sip of my coffee.

"Escaped from TRU," JB says. "That was their home base, right? The protestors are having a field day about it. Got the place surrounded with their dopey signs." He wags a bony finger at me. "So we want details—no one's ever escaped once they've been caught by a runner. And yet you somehow got up-tempo and broke out."

"Start at the beginning." Ethan sits on the side of the desk. "How'd you get caught?"

"It was my first bank job. I was sloppy."

"No, no. Skip to the good part." JB leans forward. "How'd you get *out*?"

I remember Spaihts in the interrogation room, tapping the tetra bullet on the table.

"They found a dose on me when they brought me in and this guy kept waving it around in front of me, asking where I got it. Waved it close enough me for me to snatch it right out of his hands."

I think my lie's pretty smart. For about two seconds.

"And where *did* you get it?" JB asks.

"You want me to reveal my dealer?"

"There's only one dealer who deals that sort of rush."

"Mobius," I say.

JB claps his hands. "You have done your homework. But you didn't get your tempo from Mobius. He never deals to rookies. You have to earn his respect by surviving the cheap stuff first. So, what happened? A breaker needle up and have tempo left over so they resold you a Mobius dose?"

"Maybe."

"Give me a name to go with the breaker."

"Never knew it."

"You get it from this friend you were gonna meet in Chinatown?"

"What does it matter?"

"Mobius is the only source of the good stuff. Always has been. Far as I know, anyway." JB taps his fingers on the desk. "And I pride myself on knowing everything there is to know about tempo. And breakers. And if enough of Mobius's primo tempo slipped through the cracks, I'd like to know which crack we could find it in. Meaning if your buddy has a store of the good stuff, I'd be interested. Competition brings the price down. Good economics."

"I don't think my guy had any more tetra for sale," I say, hoping I sound convincing enough we can drop the subject.

"*Tetra.*" JB exchanges a look with his brother.

"Chili Powder," I say. "Bug Eye. Or whatever."

JB grins. "The rookie knows all the names."

"She's real eager." Ethan helps himself to a swig of my coffee.

"You connect me with Mobius," I tell JB. "Maybe I could check with the guy I got my doses from. See if he has more."

"All in good time, *Timebomb.* Let's skip to what happened after you took your hit," JB says, changing tack.

"You used to rush." I retrieve my coffee. It's grown cold and the sugar sits like syrup at the bottom. "Don't you remember how it works?"

"I never broke out of a massively guarded building."

"It's all a blur once I got started," I say, which is true. More than ever, the rush is like a continent I can barely recall visiting: every bruise on my body is a postcard the other me sent home.

"Yeah." JB runs his finger along a groove on the desk. "Tempo can be cruel that way."

"I thought you said I'd not want to leave after I spoke to your brother," I say to Ethan. He might be too chivalrous to sneak peeks at me in my underwear, but now that I'm fully clothed he looks at me as if we're the only two people in the room. His brown eyes are less sweet and soft, now that we're talking business.

"Better impress her quick," Ethan tells JB. "She seems in a hurry."

"What's your rush, Timebomb?" JB asks. "This is the safest place in the city."

"So that's what this is? A safe house?"

"You know, there was a time that was the extent of my vision. Ethan and me had all sorts of breakers staying over in those days. Some for a few weeks, some for even longer. Some just for a night or two. But there got to be too many. I couldn't trust everyone in the end. Got let down majorly, in fact. So now I have a new house, and a new vision."

"A team," Ethan says.

"An *exclusive* team," JB clarifies. "Breakers with the right pedigree. You're new. A talent, but a rookie. You scrounged up a dose of the good stuff, and your body synthesized it just right, so your brain started cranking at the idea of never having to worry about money ever again."

"Sound familiar?" Ethan asks, and I nod.

"They all start off like you," JB pushes on. "Armed robbery, but probably some dump of a jewelry store or a Wells Fargo the size of a toilet. Small-time. Rookies don't know what they're doing. Some have too much fear, others don't have enough. But if they get lucky, they come away with a decent haul and end up connecting with Mobius, and that vampire sets them up with a consistent supply, for his fee, so our rookie starts to set their sights bigger. Bolder moves. Targeting the big-time banks. Like Ricochet did."

"More risk," Ethan says, "especially with new security measures popping up, but a lot more potential to earn. If all goes well, a breaker can bring in a lot of cash."

"It's a numbers game," JB adds. "But soon you're forgetting the whole thing wasn't just about the money. It was supposed to be about so much more."

Ethan nods. "The money's for the future. The rush should be all about now."

JB spends a long time scratching under his chin, his eyes distant, like his mind is stuck on the memory of his days as an accelerator. "You know Kerouac?" he asks me.

"A breakneck?"

"A writer. *The beauty of things must be that they end.* You get me?"

I wonder if JB has the dreams Tucker mentioned. The dreams that do not let him forget.

"When did you last dose up?" I ask. "I bet you know right down to the day."

"What I know is you should be enjoying it while you can. And you should be out there showing the world everything you can be. Don't think about the end of the line till you've crossed it. I can help you with that. I worry about the future for you, and you get to enjoy the here and now."

The two brothers mostly look nothing alike, but the high cheekbones give it away, elevating JB's fossilized face from merely ghastly to *haunted* and ghastly, while making Ethan look much more distinguished than any breakneck has the right to appear.

I wonder how many innocent people he's put in the hospital.

Or the morgue.

"Good girl like you wants to take care of her family," says JB. "Am I right? Thing is, it doesn't matter how much you steal, you gotta make the money legal. You need a way to make your money die so it can get resurrected, see what I mean? Else how do you explain all your income to the IRS? Yeah, yeah, you're not thinking about paying taxes, since you're still thinking you'll be young forever. But you will have to think about it. You'll need a way to make the money come clean."

"You'll launder my money for me? That's your big sales pitch?"

"And what will you do with it?" Ethan asks. "I don't suggest you open a checking account any time soon."

"Seeing as I'm wanted by TRU, seeing as they *know who I am*, laundering money is not my biggest concern."

"I can help with that, too." JB points at his phone. "I got connections. People who can make you someone else entirely. Someone legit. Set you and your family up someplace. I'll take care of all of it."

"In return for what?"

JB sits back in his chair.

"I keep twenty percent of what you steal. You get your here and now and I take care of your future. Plus, I keep you safe here. You never have to leave this house if you don't want to risk it, except when you leave to rush. I also keep you supplied with premium tempo. You're good enough for my team, you're good enough for Mobius. Kinda sweetens the pot, right?"

He's right. Mobius definitely sweetens the pot. *I have to track him down.* And now maybe he'll come to me.

"We share our know-how," Ethan says. "Beta on any place worth robbing. And we'll be coordinating the team's movements, staging rush jobs at the same time to pose problems for TRU."

JB winks at me. "Not that they seem to pose much of a problem for you."

I recall my last real day at TRU headquarters, when I'd been summoned to Monroe's office, then sent to face Spaihts and Small in an interrogation room. So many alarms had bounced off the walls at the same time. Unprecedented. *Coordinated movements.*

"Breakers hitting different banks all at once," I say.

"That was my idea." JB bares his yellow teeth in a proud grin. "Too dangerous for you all to rush in close proximity, but this way we spread out TRU's resources. This way we work *together*. All earnings go into the pot, after my twenty percent. It's win-win."

"Sure." I think about my brother in his wheelchair and want to reach across the desk to smash the grin off this fossil's face. "Sounds like a pretty good deal."

"We held tryouts a couple weeks ago," he says. "Gave seven breakers a shot. I wanted to see who could make the grade, and whittled things down to four. I'd like to keep it small. An elite group. Only the best breakers. A team of people I'll know I can trust. I thought the team was set, but I'd make an exception . . . for someone exceptional."

"He means you have to prove yourself." Ethan takes the last sip of my coffee, wincing at all the sugar congealed at the bottom. "If you want to be one of us."

EIGHTEEN

E than is as gentle as he promised he would be, sitting beside me on the bed as he removes the IV. The tubing pops free and a single drop of my blood splashes onto his thigh, joining the myriad mottled patches of dried paint. His overalls are like color-blind camo, too bright to blend in anywhere. But just thinking about *breaknecks* and *blending in* makes me think about the reflective suit that Sidewinder wore.

"Your pulse is fast," Ethan says, taping a Band-Aid over the small hole the IV left behind.

"How long have you rushed?" I ask, rolling down my sleeve and scooting my thigh away from his.

"Almost a year."

Sidewinder disappeared from the streets before I could even start basic training, and I feel a flood of relief that the timing is off. But it should be the other way around—I should wish this was him. Just because I never had a shot at Sidewinder as a runner doesn't mean I can't still track him down. *He probably left the city.* Got far away from the scenes of his crimes. But maybe JB helped him set up a new life. Maybe these people know where he is. And if I can track Sidewinder down, maybe I can make him pay for what he did to my brother. And for what he did to me.

"You paint pictures?" I ask, just to keep Ethan talking so I can mine for more information. "Or are you renovating your big brother's mansion?"

"*Older* brother." Ethan tilts his head to one side, brown eyes fixed on mine as he smiles. "I took up painting when I started rushing. Seemed I had all this extra space inside me I needed to fill."

"Really? I used to draw a ton. Pencil-on-paper stuff. Just doodling. But after I rush I feel like my brain is wet wool."

"Give it time. You only just started."

"Right." I nod. *Because I'm a rookie.* "I imagine I'll be a little too busy for drawing, though. If I make the team, you'll be putting me to work."

"Maybe you can make that a work of art, too."

"Armed robbery?"

Some tide turns in his brown eyes, revealing a sadness in their depths that's so raw, I instinctively turn away. "You can make anything a work of art," Ethan says, his voice remaining steady as he gets up off the bed. "Especially the rush itself."

"I'd love to see what you're working on."

"Maybe when it's finished," he says. "If you stick around that long. Speaking of which, this'll be your room for as long you're here. House rules include no outsiders, so no guests. Ever. No one outside these walls even knows the address. *You* won't even know it—unless you get cleared as part of the team. That happens, you get a key to the front door, can come and go as you please. In the meantime, lay low and finish getting healthy." He points to the magazines and books he stacked by the bed earlier. "JB has plenty more books, if you dig reading. Feel free to roam about the house, but don't try leaving. If you no longer want to stay, we'll escort you someplace else in a way that keeps our location under wraps. Cool?"

"I have no plans to leave."

"Then you won't want to miss dinner." Ethan flashes a brief smile. "Not even Rapunzel breaks that rule."

"The breaknecks that eat together, stick together?"

"Something like that."

"You have a phone I can use?" I ask. "I really need to make a call."

"Earn the right to stay and you'll have a phone you can use as much as you like."

"But not before? Even TRU let me have a phone call."

"We're not TRU."

"Then when do I get to prove myself as part of this team?"

"Focus on the now." Ethan gathers up the IV tubing.

"You're spending too much energy on things that aren't right in front of you."

"Maybe you're confused—I'll need something stronger than coffee to get my rush on."

"See, that's your problem. You're just killing time between rushes." Ethan heads for the door. "There's a bathroom down the end of the hall. This is the girls' floor, so there should be all the girl stuff you need."

I don't want him to leave yet. I've not learned anything about Mobius, or Sidewinder, or anything else. And I'm already so lonely, I can't stand the thought of actually being alone.

"Thanks for nursing me back to health," I say, but instead of resuscitating our conversation, this kills it dead.

"Just one breakneck looking out for another," Ethan says, making me feel not in the least bit special. Then he closes the door behind him, leaving me in a house full of break-necks, unable to leave or make a phone call. No way to reach Tucker, though I need him more than ever to steer me in the right direction and whisper encouragement in my ear.

I think of his bloodshot blue eyes and sandy brown hair, his strong hands on the steering wheel of his blue-jeans truck. So solid, in a world that's too slippery. He is the only person who knows I am innocent. The one person who knows who I really am.

I fidget with the window, but can't get it open. I press my face against the glass, but can see only the bricks of the house next door. The third floor is the top floor of this old mansion: just an attic and a roof above me, then all the freedom of the open sky.

Muffled music bounces around distant parts of the house. There are occasional footsteps, broken snatches of laughter. Eventually I venture onto the landing, checking the doors down one end of it, and when I at last find an unlocked door, I enter a bathroom bigger than my bedroom at home.

There's a huge claw-foot tub and a brass-framed mirror. The wood toilet seat was probably carved from some rare Amazonian tree. The marble shelves are cluttered with soaps, lotions, and bubble bath. Two sinks perch on white pillars; plush towels hang on gold hooks.

Dirty money made clean, I suppose. But I don't care. I feel like something rescued from a dumpster and peel off my clothes in a frenzy, desperate to scrub off the last few days.

Though the mirror's the fanciest I've ever looked into, it can't do much to spruce up my reflection. My skin looks paper-thin, and the pink streak I put in my hair is the only thing about me that doesn't look faded. In fact, the pink is somehow *brighter*. A cartoonish slice of color grafted onto monochrome me.

My bruises are mossy smudges, stretching all down my right side, and I finger the bandages on my thigh and shoulder, vaguely remembering being grazed by bullets at TRU headquarters. My body remembers it better.

Peeling back the bandages, I conclude that the wounds

can get wet. And though the shower is hot and powerful, it doesn't feel as cleansing as I crave, so I run hot water into the tub. Getting in makes me instantly drowsy, and the derailing lingers, even after two days of sleep. The double dose really knocked me out. But it was worth it. *I escaped.* And not just from headquarters. I broke free of the twenty-four-hour rule. I even rushed with no helmet. And the double dose broke me so open and so loose. As I soak in this breakneck bathtub, the rush is a too-distant thrill.

The water's cold by the time I get out, and as I'm toweling off, I hear a voice—Ethan's, I think—yelling from somewhere downstairs, announcing it's time to eat. I pull the sweatshirt and jeans back on, and when I run a comb through my hair, I end up looking too clean-cut, so I mess with my bangs, spiking them to highlight the pink bits and show off the scar above my right eye.

I take long deep breaths, the slow, straw-sucking kind they taught us in basic training, as I leave the bathroom, following the sounds of feet echoing on the wood floors below me, *the wolves gathering to feed.*

I prepare myself to be one of them.

NINETEEN

T he chatter turns silent as I enter the kitchen, turning my
insides hollow and amplifying the boom of my heart.

"Here she is," JB announces. "Straight out of TRU headquarters!"

He claps, which makes things even more awkward;
Rapunzel is the only one who joins in. Ethan's busy at the
stove, his back to us, and the other two—a guy and a girl—
seem to be taking part in a contest to see who can ignore me
the most.

"You already know Panzer." JB's sitting on the counter,
and as he talks, his skate shoes waggle like puppets, his bony
legs like strings inside his voluminous jeans.

"Panzer's the name of a *tank*," Rapunzel says, chewing the
words through her South London accent. "Do I look like a
tank to you, boss? Strong as one, maybe, but that's it."

"You don't look like a tank." JB inflicts upon her one of

his gruesome smiles. "But Rapunzel's a mouthful. I'm going for brevity."

"That'd be a first," his brother mutters. JB waves off the remark, but Rapunzel slaps the back of Ethan's head as she laughs.

The blond girl sitting cross-legged on the counter is apparently too busy being pretty to pay me any attention. And her being so effortlessly cool makes me feel even more of a hot mess.

"And we're supposed to call you what?" says a kid with jagged shoulder-length hair that falls across his face like curtains. His sleeveless hoodie shows off his sleeve tattoo.

"Name's Lana," I say. "Didn't catch yours."

"Miles Davis." He flicks his hair back to reveal his fake smile.

"Nice pseudonym."

"Nice thesaurus you swallowed." He'll be handsome when his skin clears up, and if he ever stops scowling. For now his face is a battlefield wrecked by explosions of acne, his eyes two snipers taking aim at me. "What are you, some sort of brainiac?"

"Just making conversation."

"Don't."

"You really needn't work so hard at being an asshole, Davis." When JB slides off the kitchen counter, it's the first time I've seen him standing, and despite his haggard appearance, I'm unprepared for the severity of his stoop. He's bent over, not just forward, but sideways. "It comes natural to you, breh."

Miles Davis uses his scowl like an instrument, bending it through each note on the major scale of majorly ticked off. "Thought we were ready to eat," he says, peeling his gaze off me and throwing it at the back of Ethan's head instead. "You call us down here to watch you cook, boy?"

"Called you so you'd actually be here on time," Ethan says, not turning around. "Chill out, man. You can't rush greatness."

"Give me some tempo," mutters Davis, "I'll rush greatness for you."

JB laughs, waggling his fingers and snapping his knuckles with such ferocity, I'm worried his hand might fall off. "See, Davis, you can be funny when you're not being a complete dick."

No one else is laughing. Not even Rapunzel, and least of all Davis. And when JB's laugh sputters out, the kitchen goes as silent as it did when I entered.

I steal another glance at the girl sitting cross-legged on the glossy granite countertop. She's still not acknowledged me, and I'm wondering if that should fuel my paranoia, like maybe somehow she knows who I really am. But that's impossible. And why would she stay quiet if she knew me? She's just not interested in the new kid, that's all. I try to follow her lead in looking relaxed, but when I attempt to slouch my shoulders, they're stiff as rebar, and then, when the girl meets my gaze at last, her eyebrows arch as if she's amazed by how awkward I look. Her complexion is nature's answer to whoever invented airbrushing. Her lips pout without trying, and sun-kissed locks tumble down past her shoulders.

I fiddle with my spiked bangs and ill-fitting clothes, and a tiny smirk appears on the girl's mouth.

She probably bathes in stolen money, exfoliating with crisp hundred-dollar bills while she dreams of her next dose. And speaking of next doses, I could use a tetra bullet between my teeth right now. I'd not be awkward at all if I was thumbing the release.

"Who's ready to eat?" Ethan says, and the breakneck girl on the counter breaks her gaze from mine, her eyes cold and regal.

Ethan's fixed tacos, serve-yourself style, and we serve ourselves using paper plates and mismatched cutlery. Though there's a dining table in the next room, it's covered in cardboard boxes and books and we all eat in the kitchen, sitting on the floor, which is checkered with black and white tiles, like a giant chessboard that needs a good cleaning.

The food would be excellent even if I wasn't totally starving, but it's hard for me to eat surrounded by breaknecks, wondering which one of them I should be afraid of most.

"Any good at cooking?" JB points a greasy fork in my direction. "I order in takeout on Fridays and Saturdays, but you could take the Sunday spot."

"In JB's mind you made the team as soon as he saw the footage of you in action," Ethan says. He's sitting across from

me, his back against the dishwasher, his paint-stained overalls rolled down to his waist to reveal a tight white T-shirt
and muscular arms.

I turn my attention back to my food.

"Come on." JB's hunched on the floor beside his brother.
"You saw the footage, too. She broke out of TRU headquarters, leaving a whole army of pigs in her dust."

"We all get to decide," Davis says around a crunchy
mouthful of taco.

JB wipes at his mouth with the back of his hand. "Relax.
We'll all vote. But she's lightning, I'm telling you. Can barely
see her blur in that footage. Reminded me of Sidewinder in
that suit thing he used to wear."

"You OK, love?" Rapunzel asks, because I'm choking on a
bite of red pepper and beans.

I nod and manage to swallow my food as I set my plate
aside.

Miles Davis looks disappointed I'm still breathing.

"Speed's not everything," he says, turning back to his
food. "How many times you hit and run, Lana?"

"Hit and run?" I picture Reuben stepping onto the crosswalk, comics in hand. *I am too slow. And too far away . . .*

"A&R jobs," Davis snaps. "You know, *armed robbery*. How
many times?"

"I held up a bank in Astoria."

"Astoria?" He sneers. "Small-time shit. What else?"

"That's all," I say. "So far."

"Seriously?" He aims his scowl at JB. "One bank and she wound up in custody."

"She's raw. So were you once."

"I never got *caught*." Davis scowls at Ethan instead. "You buying this?"

"I say we give her a shot," Ethan says. "You can't teach someone to rush the way she did."

Davis rolls his eyes. "One day you might wake up and do us all a favor by thinking for yourself, boy."

"JB's in charge." Ethan shrugs. "His house, his rules."

"Supposed to be a team."

"Every team needs a leader."

"Ethan's right, Davis." Rapunzel plays with the feather earring that dangles from her ear. "Give Lana a chance."

"Girl, you kiss JB's ass so much I'm surprised you never give him a piece of yours."

Rapunzel throws the last of her food at Davis. She misses, and bits of taco scatter on the black and white tiles as Davis snorts with laughter. "I understood why JB was so desperate to recruit Aces." He nods at the pretty girl, who still keeps silent. "At least she's a looker. But this girl . . ."

"You're an asshole, Davis." Ethan glares at him from across the kitchen. "On so many levels."

"What? Aces can't even understand me—unless . . . I talk . . . really . . . slow. . . ."

"Talk slow to this." JB gives Davis the scrawniest middle finger in history. "Or, better yet, shut the hell up. I said you'll all get a vote, so relax."

"Ought to vote Davis off the island." When Rapunzel laughs, it's hard not to join in, and Davis catches the smile on my face.

"Bet you'd like that, *newbie*." He snarls. "We already held tryouts, but here you come trying to steal someone's place."

"There's room for one more." JB points around at the kitchen. "Big house, breh."

"You said four breaknecks was solid, after the tryouts. You said four was easy to trust. Now you're getting greedy."

"Greedy?" JB grabs at the kitchen counter and hauls himself as upright as his stoop will allow, then he shuffles across the kitchen until he's peering down at Davis with bitter bloodshot eyes. "How long have I let you live here?"

"I don't know. . . ."

"Six months, two weeks, and four days. Promised I'd keep you safe as long as you're under my roof. Have I done that?"

"Sure." Davis studies the scraps on his plate. "For a fee."

"And when I assembled this team for the coordinated attacks, I gave you a shot. Let you prove yourself. Makes it a little easier to get away when TRU gets spread thin, right? And yet you sit in my kitchen and question me. *Insult* me. And you insult these girls." JB stomps a foot onto Davis's plate. His voice gets soft, but more sinister than any scream. "Look at me, breh."

"I'm looking." Davis glares up through his long greasy hair.

"It's not about being greedy." JB's hands are shaking and he shoves them in his pockets. He breathes as if trying to cool himself off but his face burns red. "It's about what's best for the team. We're supposed to be a unit. It's the only way this will work. . . ."

"Your house," Davis mutters. "Your rules."

During the long silence that follows, JB shuffles back across the kitchen. And as he retakes his seat on the floor, he makes eye contact with his brother, relaxing visibly as Ethan reassures him with the sort of wordless support only siblings can share.

"Tomorrow night's Italian." Rapunzel almost succeeds in changing the whole mood of the room with her smile. "Aces is from Rome. Doesn't speak any English, but she don't cook English, neither. Best night of the week."

Aces can sense enough that Rapunzel's paying her a compliment, and she rolls her eyes, flashing a tiny yet dazzling smile. I try to catch her eye again, so we can exchange a grin, or a look, anything that might mean she could become an ally. But she is too cool to notice, or too cold to care.

Eventually Davis stands and stuffs his smashed paper plate in a garbage bag in the corner. He scowls at me as he rips off a nasty burp, then strides out of the room.

"Don't mind him, love," Rapunzel tells me. "Has a hard time trusting people. Just wants to keep the team as it is. Speaking of which, when do we put Lana through the wringer?"

"She's not ready." Ethan gazes at me with his brown eyes but speaks about me like I'm not even there. It bothers me that this bothers me. He cocks his head to one side, all thoughtful, and I wonder if he thinks this head-tilting thing makes him look cute, because he does it all the time. But then I suppose it wouldn't look cute if that was the intended effect. "She was passed out detoxing for two days. Should keep resting."

"We'll give you a day or two," JB agrees. "Let you get your strength back."

"When's the next job?"

"Tomorrow morning. But we got this one covered. You'll be safe here, Lana. Everyone inside these walls is my responsibility, and I might not have been the world's greatest breaker—"

"He was a terrible breaker." Ethan throws a handsome grin at his brother, who throws an ugly one back.

"True. I was shit. But I take care of my people. Am I right, Panzer?"

She grins, too, kicking his foot with hers. "I told you, it's *Rapunzel*."

The tension's leaching out of the room now Davis has gone, and I try not to feel envious of the ease with which these breaknecks lounge on the kitchen floor, comfortable despite the hard tile, confident in the company of friends.

"Let me rush tomorrow," I say, my impatient heart quickening at the thought.

"Save your strength," Ethan says. "Just a couple more days."

"I could rush right now."

"Sure. So could I, up *here*"—JB taps at his skull—"but my body has different ideas. Best to wait till you're in top shape if you want a part of this action."

"She wants to rush, let her rush," Rapunzel says. "Give her Davis's spot in the morning."

"Davis's spot?" JB grins and we bear it. "Yeah, that'd teach him for being such a dick. I guess if you're sure you're up to a little trial by fire, Lana."

"Just light me up," I tell them. "Then watch me burn."

TWENTY

Instead of Dad's Bart Simpson lamp keeping me company, I have a high-wattage chandelier that sparkles like a small sun upon the ceiling. A dimmer switch would be nice. I can do total darkness, or blazing yellow light. I've tried both, but no part of me feels like sleeping.

I keep telling myself that if I help stop the breaknecks' supply of tetra, it'll prove I've been undercover the whole time. Tucker has to find someone we can trust. Someone we can go to with whatever I find out about Mobius. Someone who believes I'd have never killed Lieutenant Monroe.

But as I lie on my plush bed, staring at the ceiling, I don't want to think about Monroe. Or Mobius. I don't even want to think about Tucker. I just want to imagine the rush I'll feel tomorrow. Amid the messy tangle of unknowns, tetra is such an easy thing to focus on: those next nine minutes when I get to leave all this behind.

Can't wait to bid the last vestiges of this cruddy derailing good riddance. The tacos I ate earlier sit rock-hard in my stomach. My brain is all hot static, as if it's been tumble-dried.

I kick the sheets off and sit up, deciding to take a walk about the place and dig for information. Maybe find some-one to talk to. I'll go crazy cooped up in this room.

I creep down the landing of the third floor, listening at each door, but all I hear is night sounds from the outside world—the hum of wheels, a bleating car alarm. I've no doubt this is a city mansion; I've just no idea where in the city we are.

On the second floor, I catch the sound of a jazz band, a little late-night listening party. Miles Davis's room, I guess. Rest of the floor is quiet, though.

Downstairs, everything's quiet, too.

I poke at cardboard boxes on the dining room table—empty, except for foam packing peanuts—and glance through the stacks of books, mostly novels, but also every-thing from plays and poetry collections to some of the graphic novels I've told Reuben he's too young to read. I find that issue of *Rolling Stone* with a single bullet of tetra on the cover, the headline *Live Fast, Die Young*. Someone's scrib-bled on it so it reads *Live Slow, Die Anyway*. As I trace the tetra bullet with my finger, I lick my front teeth.

Another room is home to two giant leather couches and the largest flat-screen TV I've ever seen. Speakers that look loud enough for Madison Square Garden loom in the corner;

Xbox controllers litter the floor. I step in someone's old microwave dinner and gross cold noodles squish between my toes, and I'm just wiping my foot on a rug and thinking I'll head back to my room, when the music starts. Electronic and wordless, the sound throbs up through the floorboards, a siren song calling me underground.

Doesn't take long to find the basement. At the bottom of the stairs is a dank passage, so poorly lit I have to feel my way along the crumbly walls. I focus on the music, ahead of me now, much louder. Squelchy beats and belchy screeches form a muddled ambient noise that escalates into swells of storming sound, then detonates in furious breaks. It's unlike anything I've heard but is somehow the sound of everything I love turned up super loud.

The passage ends at a door that's not all the way shut, and the light that seeps out is like synthetic sky—an electronic approximation of the outside world, just like the music, cranked up with voltage until it becomes better than real. I'm mesmerized by the melodies, as if caught in the song's spell. The music seems to have twisted its way inside me, wiring my heart to the rhythm of its beats. It feels like the first flutter of a rush, after you've bit the bullet, your brain basking in the glow as your blood starts to blaze.

Then the music becomes silence and I drop out of the feeling. I am once more barefoot in a basement, surrounded by breaknecks and wanted for murder. A runner who bolted down a rabbit hole.

"Lana?"

Ethan's silhouetted in the doorway, light pouring out around him, but the silhouette of his head is bulged and distorted, and his breaths crackle and hiss.

He takes a step toward me. "What are you doing down here?"

"I heard music. I'm sorry . . . just couldn't sleep."

He's wearing goggles, and some sort of respirator, hence him sounding like Darth Vader after a grueling sprint. "You okay?" he asks, pulling his goggles onto his forehead, yanking the respirator down to hang from his neck.

I've stumbled to the wall and am about to slide down it, but he comes forward and grabs me, holding me up by my elbows. He stinks of chemicals. *Paint.* And I'm all up against him, my face smushed into the mask he was wearing.

"I knew you were pushing it," he says. "No way you should rush tomorrow."

"It's nothing," I mumble, feeling loose and woozy in his arms. It's like the music untied me, but I need to pull it together. "Don't tell the others. Please. I'm tired and couldn't sleep. I'll be all right once I'm dosed back up."

"I don't know, Lana. I didn't play nurse for two days so you could collapse on the streets."

I try to straighten up against him.

"You sure you've not had any headaches?" he asks, brushing my bangs back and peering into my eyes. "The Needles can come early, maybe as early as sixteen. It's dangerous to push it if you're close to the end."

"My head is fine. *I'm* fine. Really."

"Let's see how you feel after a coffee," he says, still holding me. "Want some?"

"I always want coffee."

He grins. It's a good grin. He should use it more often. "I know the feeling. Can you walk? Or do you want me to carry you to the kitchen?"

Ethan's arms are strong and I need something strong right now, someone to lean on. But I've already shown too much weakness for one night.

"I can walk," I tell him.

In the kitchen, he scoops coffee beans into a grinder, and when he powers it on the thing is Weedwacker loud.

"You'll wake the others," I say, filling a kettle with water.

"Ah, who sleeps before dosing up? And JB hardly ever really sleeps. Says the dreams torment him—like he feels fast but not fast enough. Comes with the territory, I guess."

"Small price to pay."

"Hard to know till you've paid it." His eyes dig deep into mine. "You know, you don't seem like a rookie."

"How so?"

"I don't know exactly. I guess you could take it as a compliment. I've seen a ton of breakers come and go."

"At the safe house JB ran before this one?" I'm eager to steer the conversation to safer ground, which is basically anything that has nothing to do with me.

"Those were wild days." Ethan flashes a guilty grin. "Lot

of kids coming through. I mean, pretty much everyone did back then."

"Whiplash?" I ask, referencing a well-known breakneck who never got caught.

"God, yeah. We were all scared shitless of her. Heard she's in Mexico now."

"Yeah? So, who else? What about, I don't know . . . Sidewinder?"

"Yeah." Ethan stops smiling. "Him too."

Him. I've been right about Sidewinder being a guy. *But it's too little information to do me much good.*

"That house got too nuts," Ethan says. "Too many people knew the address, and some people couldn't be trusted. JB was right to move here, downsize in a new spot." Ethan stares at the kettle, and I think of Tucker's hokey expression, about how the watched pot never boils. "You like my brother?"

"Define *like*?"

"Enough to trust him? Because you should. He wants things to be different this time. Wants the team to be like a family. He tries too hard, but he's coming from a good place."

"Which is what?"

"A place with no family." Ethan keeps staring at the kettle. "Mom wasn't around much, and Dad wasn't around at all. And then one morning our mom never came back, so we had to fend for ourselves."

I don't know what to say, so I don't say anything.

"It was almost better at first—Mom's losers were out

of our life. But JB got in trouble and ended up in juvie, at Tryon, so I wound up in this foster-home thing in Jersey where it got rough. Guy running the place had a freaking *cane*. Said he would beat the scum out of me. And when JB got out and heard what had been going on, he dosed up on tempo and nearly tore that guy in two." Ethan glances at me. "Didn't kill him, but close. I was screaming for him to stop. My brother had no control on the drug. That's why he never made much of a breaker—stone-cold sober, he's smart as hell and twice as shrewd, but on Chili Powder the aggression made him stupid. You can still see it in him, sometimes."

"Didn't stop you wanting to try it."

"Tempo? Sure. We needed the money."

"How much?"

"What?"

"How much do you *need*?"

"Enough so we don't end up back on the streets. Ever." Ethan cocks his head, studying me. "What you into it for? The money? Or the rush?"

"Both," I say, because that seems like a breakneck sort of answer, and I can't even come close to telling Ethan the truth about why I am here. The truth about what happened to Reuben. The truth about how I left him behind on that crosswalk and can never be fast enough to save him now. The truth that I'm here to stop breaknecks by cutting off their supply of tetra. But maybe there are other truths now, too.

193

Like how I have nowhere else I can go.

And how maybe tetra has changed me.

The kettle rumbles to a boil and I dump the ground beans into a French press. "So what's your expert opinion—you think I'll impress the team tomorrow?"

"You got the hunger. I can see it all over you. But can you use it to focus only on the now?"

"You don't think I focused on the now when I escaped TRU headquarters?"

"I think your body processes tempo to the max. Congrats. But what about your mind? Lose control and you'll end up glitchy. The rush is no place to get sidetracked."

"Thanks for the vote of confidence."

"You wanted my expert opinion."

"What about your personal preference?"

"Trying to remain neutral."

"Come on." I punch his arm playfully. "You want me to make the team and prove your brother right, don't you? Besides, who else is gonna listen to your life story in the middle of the night?"

"Life story? I didn't even get to the good stuff." He turns to grab the kettle so I can't see his face, but I sense his mood shift.

"Wanna try me with a little good stuff?"

He pours hot water in the French press. Shrugs as he snaps its lid in place. "Just memories."

"You should let it breathe," I say. "The coffee should bloom first. Makes the taste smoother."

"This from the girl who drinks her coffee with six sugars." He unplugs the lid anyway. "So how long am I meant to let it breathe, barista?"

I pop myself up onto the counter, sitting beside the open French press, peering down into the hot black liquid. "Okay, give it a stir. Now put the lid on and hit a timer—four minutes."

"You're the boss." He sets a timer on the stove, and I keep staring at the French press so I'm not staring at Ethan. I should steer the conversation back to tetra, try to talk about Mobius. Or Sidewinder. But I'm more curious about the stories behind this breakneck's sad brown eyes.

"This is one of the good things about not sleeping," he says. "Feeling like you're the last people awake in the entire world."

"Sounds like being on tetra."

"Why d'you always call it that?"

"Tempo, whatever."

"Tetra's what the media calls it. Them and everyone too old or too scared to try life in 4D. The *blogs*." He rolls his eyes. "People rambling on about something they can't understand."

The timer goes off. And when I look up, Ethan's studying me, like I'm a book and he's making up his mind if he wants to turn the next page. And there's a tingle, a fleeting hot rush inside me. A desire for him to turn all my pages. To be the book he cannot put down.

"You sure you want to do this?" he asks.

"The six sugars?" I smile, coy about it, and I don't lean toward him, just let him know it's okay to lean toward me.

"I mean tomorrow," he says, and I feel it like a slap in the face, but why do I want him to want me? This boy is a breakneck. It doesn't matter that he nursed me to health. It doesn't matter that he has exquisite cheekbones and deep brown eyes I could seek shelter inside if he let me. It doesn't matter that I'm totally alone.

"I don't just mean the bank job," he adds, "I mean all of it. You've rushed, what, twice?"

"Feels like more times than that."

He's close enough I can see speckles of red paint like fine dust on his cheeks.

I reach to plunge down the French press, but he reaches for it at the same time and our hands touch, our eyes locked together.

"You wanna grab some cups?" I ask, still waiting to push down.

"You're trembling." Ethan tilts his head to the side, but his eyes don't waver. He seems to stare inside me. One blink and he'll make it no deeper.

I don't blink.

"What do you like best about it?" he asks. "When you rush."

"The peak," I say, without hesitation. "The way I feel right at the topside. The way it feels like flying—no, more than that. Like I'm soaring and the world's not so cold and lonely because everything's all ablaze."

"As if you set fire to it."

"Yes. Like I'm a spark." I remember how Tucker put it. "Like I'm a flash of lightning filling up the night sky."

"Not bad." Ethan smiles, and I feel I've betrayed Tucker by using his line. But I'm sick of Tucker's distance. Sick of isolation.

Tucker doesn't deserve that, though. He's out there worrying about me, and he knows me, and he's proof of life after tetra, proof that you can give up the drug but still help keep people safe.

On the other hand, Ethan's going to waltz into a bank tomorrow, waving a gun in people's faces.

And so am I.

"What's wrong?" Ethan asks, our eyes still locked together.

"You ever think about the people who might get hurt? Killed?"

"When?"

"How can you ask that? You commit armed robbery, Ethan."

"No breaker's ever shot anyone." He frowns, like he's confused.

"But the threat's there. It only works if you mean it."

"Only works if they *think* you mean it. And people can't risk not thinking you do."

"What about in the city, then? On the streets. You don't think there's a—"

"I think you think too much. Might someone out there get hurt because they're too slow to get out of my way? Is that what you mean?"

I busy myself with plunging the French press because I'm afraid I might slap him. The coffee's sat too long anyway. It'll be bitter now.

"You think that's cruel?" he asks. "I'm careful out there. More careful than most. I never let myself lose control all the way. But you can't rush if you're too afraid of the consequences. You know what tempo's taught me? That the thing creating limits is *this*." He shakes back his hair and taps at his forehead. "In here. All the fear. All the lies we tell ourselves, the stories we spin. Guilt and blame. It's a life sentence. It's the way we keep people at a distance and lock ourselves away."

"We have to take responsibility, though. That's not just a story." I think about Reuben. Left behind. Just for a moment. Because he was too slow, but also because I was too fast.

"Sucks having a conscience, doesn't it?" Ethan tugs at the sleeve of his overalls, and his fingers come away smudged with wet paint. "You gonna pour that coffee or wait till it's cold?"

"So you're a breakneck with a conscience."

"Maybe. Maybe not. Maybe I haven't figured it out yet."

"At least you're thinking about it."

"You say that like it's a good thing. But what do you know about breaking, about rushing? You don't know anything yet. How could you? There are breakers who *never* care about the consequences. They accept all of it, the beauty and the pain."

"You wish that was you?"

"I'm not sure. Someone so on their own trip . . . I hate it, judge it, but a part of me wants to be that way too. To experience everything and not give a damn. Just live without fear. Each moment, totally free."

His eyes are the same shade of brown as his tangled hair, as dark as the coffee still waiting to be poured, as dark as the bark of old trees and rich dirt, and it is the saddest color of all as he stares at me. He hangs his head and his hair falls in front of his eyes.

"What is it?" I ask, and I almost reach for him. I almost reach out and touch his face.

"I should get back to work." He shoves a hand at his curls, sweeping his hair back.

"At least let me see this picture you're working on. . . ." His overalls smeared my own borrowed clothes with paint as he held me downstairs, and I show him the rainbow of colors he left on my jeans. "Only seems fair, since I'm part of the project."

"I gotta finish it before I show it to anyone." His stare is icy enough that my smile freezes, then fades.

On his way out, Ethan stops in the doorway. "It's not

too late to turn around, you know. You could leave all this behind pretty easy. The longer you rush, the harder it'll be to quit."

"I can't quit. I'm doing this for my family."

"Sure you are," he says, slipping away. "Unless you're just doing it for you."

TWENTY-ONE

A s soon as Miles Davis pulls off my blindfold and lets me up off the floor, I crawl onto the seat and try to get my bearings. The bright sky and busy world stream in through the windows.

Rush hour approaches.

The other three breaknecks left the house on foot at first light, shouldering bags stuffed full of gear, heading for the subway to get in position.

"Sorry about the theatrics," JB says, watching me in the rearview mirror as we wait out a red light.

"That's one way of putting it." I blink till I'm used to the dazzle of morning. We're on the Upper East Side, heading down Fifth Avenue, parallel to the billowing green of Central Park.

"We don't want you knowing where we live till you're officially on the team. Can't be too careful."

I'm on the middle row of seats, with Davis behind me. He twirls the red bandanna he blindfolded me with around his wrist. "Nervous?"

"Not yet."

"I can smell the crap in your pants, newbie."

"Ignore Davis," JB says. "He's just pissed you stole his spot this morning."

"May as well get it over with," Davis mutters. "Throw her in the deep end and watch her drown. You'll find Midtown a little different from Astoria."

As a runner, I was always good in Midtown. I know the streets well, which will help when I'm rushing.

I struggle to come up with anything that's going to help with the armed robbery part.

"How come we're not in the Tesla?" This old minivan has stained gray seats and a peeling ceiling.

"Prefer not to draw attention when we're working." JB hits the gas as the light turns green, the motion making me nauseous. "Besides, Ishmael here has more seats for picking you all up when you're done."

"Ishmael?"

"Thing drives like a boat and looks like a whale." JB slouches behind the wheel, one hand fiddling with his flat-brimmed Jets cap. "It's a *Moby-Dick* reference. Herman Melville."

"How very literary of you."

"Oh, I'm a big reader. Started in juvie. Now I got me a

library at the house twice the size they had. Anyone can borrow a book." He glances at me in the rearview again. "Can help you through a sleepless night."

Davis groans. "One of JB's books doesn't put you to sleep, nothing will."

We cross Fifty-Ninth Street. It's still early; traffic's steady.

"How long till rush hour?" I ask.

"Don't worry about it. I got shit calibrated. Here." JB tosses me a chunky watch, and I strap it on. "Four alarms are programed. First one's Aces, then Panzer, then Ethan. Fourth one goes off—four chimes—means it's your turn. You enter the bank, do the deed, then dose up on the way out. Your bank's a New York National."

"In Midtown? I know it."

"Good. Take any route you want once the tempo hits, but hightail it toward Park. I need you to go to ground somewhere near there and wait for your pickup. You know Saint Bart's Church?"

"Sure."

"Makes life easier." JB nods. "Panzer gets lost half the time. I have to strap a beacon to her so I can track her down."

"Knowing the city won't help you," Davis says. "You gotta know how to control yourself. How to pace the rush and use your peak. Takes practice."

"Give it a rest." JB's shaking his head, but he's enjoying this. Even Davis can't dull the thrill of the countdown. "I'm starting to think I should have left your ass at home, breh.

Now, Lana, there's a backup meeting point if you can't make it to Saint Bart's—"

"She won't." Davis leans forward so he's hanging on the back of my seat.

"—or if you wait a half hour and we're a no-show for some reason. Then make your way to Riverside and West Eighty-Second. There's a laundromat with laser tag in the back, Suds'n'Glow, you wait there till rush hour this evening. I haven't shown up, the *third* meeting point is the Mark Hotel." He tosses a roll of bills back at me. "You shouldn't need this, of course. But if you have to ditch your winnings to play it safe, then do so. If no one's there to meet you at the hotel, shit's gone bad for someone so we're all laying low. I'll have a room rented for you, under the name Lana Kishiro—a fake ID with that name on it is in your pack."

"With what picture?"

"That one the media keeps showing except I morphed it into something more Japanese. Along with the name, it will throw people off. Just keep your hair over your face as much as you can. And put this on." He tosses me a retro Knicks beanie with a bobble on top. "You end up staying at the Mark, enjoy. Place is upscale. Stay in your room. Order room service. Sit tight until I can come pick you up."

"Sounds like you've thought of everything."

"Not our first rodeo. There's a change of clothes at the Mark. Kinda one-size-fits-all stuff, shoved in an orange Nike day pack in the lost-and-found. Don't spend any longer on the street than you have to, and don't get in a taxi. Subway's all right. But keep your head down."

"How do I communicate with you?"

"You don't. We don't do phones out here. If someone gets caught, calls can be traced. Opens up a whole can of worms. Till we pick you up, you're on your own."

Right. No support team. No overhead chopper.

No Tucker.

But a Midtown bank this size, I'll be drawing a runner, for sure. Even if I am the fourth breakneck to strike this morning, the New York National is too big a target for TRU not to send out a team to catch me.

"Nervous now, ain't you." Davis sniffs at me. "You're sweating."

"Sorry." JB fiddles at the air vents up front. "This gas-guzzling piece of shit doesn't really do AC anymore."

It's not the lack of AC. Davis is right. Lose any of my edge today and I'll end up back in custody.

Or dead.

Aim to maim, Monroe used to tell the snipers. But now Spaihts is in charge, and he seems to be a big fan of *shoot to kill.*

I count the money JB's given me, just so I have something to do as we drive. Two hundred bucks. Enough for a Greyhound somewhere far from here. Or maybe I should just show up at Saint Bart's later and say I ripped off the New York National but had to drop the cash in my getaway.

Probably won't make the team if I do that, though. And hopping a bus out of the city gets me no closer to Mobius, or to clearing my name. Plus, the Fourth Dimension awaits me. The tetra bullet is practically between my teeth, its sweet relief only minutes away.

Keep on down the rabbit hole, Little Rabbit.

"What do I wear?" I ask.

"Hook her up," JB says, and Davis dumps a green backpack on my lap. "I'm a good judge of size, but I bought some extras just in case."

I pull out flight goggles, then black pads and spandex. Streamlined stuff. Nothing too bulky, except the silver helmet, which looks like something a dirt biker might wear.

"What's with the spandex?" I ask JB.

"Figured you'd want to be fast, so I went with lightweight gear."

Davis snickers. "You should see the getup he's got Aces rocking."

"Shut up, Davis. Aces digs maximum speed, minimum bulk."

"And you dig seeing her dressed like she's about to do yoga."

"She can wear what she wants, breh."

"Which one is she?" I ask.

"Aces?" JB hangs a left on Forty-Seventh. We're getting close now. "Media calls her Vespa."

"Why you telling her that?" Davis says. "She's not on the team."

"She already knows you all are breakers."

And I know Vespa. I never ran after her, but she's been rushing the streets for almost a year. She wears the slick motorcycle helmet with the Italian flag. Davis is right, the rest of her outfit *is* a little on the tight side.

"I found her on the streets in Spanish Harlem," JB says. "More than a year back. Used an app on my phone to translate the deal I was offering her."

"You just found her on the streets and offered to make her a breakneck?"

"I offered her a chance at a better life. Got a good eye for accelerators."

Davis laughs like a mean dog barks. "JB, you are the ugliest player in the city and the smartest pimp of them all."

"I'm no pimp, breh."

"Hook people on tetra, then take twenty percent of their earnings. Sounds like a pimp to me."

"Yeah, well, if I'm a pimp, Davis, then what does that make you?"

"Screw you, man. And screw you for giving up Aces's breaker ID to this girl. You've no idea if we can trust her. It's just like when you ran your first safe house into the ground. You're too cocky, JB."

"*The best way to find out if you can trust somebody is to trust them,*" JB says. "Hemingway said that, breh."

"Some old dead guy, I suppose. Means it must be true." Davis leans forward across the seat so he's right beside me.

His greasy hair smells like old french fries, which does nothing to help the icky feeling in my gut. "I'll be rooting for you to crash and burn."

"Thanks for the extra motivation. Now if you wouldn't mind blindfolding yourself with that bandanna, I need to get suited up."

TWENTY-TWO

Rush hour means the square is crowded with coffee jugglers in sweaty suits, headphone heads, and bagel munchers. People thumb texts and scroll screens, too late and too bored and too busy to look at the girl by the fountain rummaging in the top of her forest-green backpack, checking on her drugs and her gun.

No one sees the time bomb in their midst.

No one hears the tick-tick of my heart.

The fountain glitters right in the center of the square. Beyond it, the New York National Bank's walls are polished steel, and the sun makes the building come alive, turning it silver and gold. As the fountain's mist clouds my vision, it's almost as if I'm on tetra already, seeing the surging splendor of the Fourth Dimension.

I can't wait for the rush to come.

JB dropped me off two blocks away. The minivan—

209

Ishmael—is a Chevy the color of chickpeas, and it's off to pick up Aces, seeing as she's the first one to rush so she'll be the first one going to ground and reaching her meeting point.

Staring at the doors of the bank, my heart thumping the countdown, I'm reminded of how Tucker and I would wait in position together, our watched pots never boiling, and I imagine him here, rubbing my shoulders, telling me I'm not alone.

Imagining it makes me even lonelier, though. And my shoulders grow even tenser.

An alarm beeps once on the watch JB gave me—it's time for the first breakneck to enter her bank, which means somewhere across the city, Aces is striding through a set of glass doors, her snazzy helmet strapped on, the tinted visor flipped down. *Vespa* is about to order people to the floor with a wave of her gun or perhaps a shot at the ceiling. She's ready to disarm security guards; scan for hazards and potential heroes. Ready to grab her cash and bite the bullet.

When I imagine the flavor of tetra on my tongue, my mouth waters. My blood sings.

The second alarm chimes twice on my watch—Rapunzel's turn, whoever she is once she suits up and hits the release. I wonder if she moves like she's dancing when her rush comes on, her heart a bass drum kicking at a thousand beats per minute.

The third alarm hits. Ethan's turn. But I don't try to

imagine who he is when he's breaking, nor how careful he will or won't be when he makes his escape. I must focus on here. Now. *It is almost time.*

I flex my shoulders, stretch out my hamstrings. Left ankle feels pretty good, wrapped up in an Ace bandage, and these sturdy Nike high-tops offer decent support. I reach into the top pouch of my backpack to pull out my dose, and I can't help smiling, a tremulous thrill in my belly.

This bullet's a dark red color and the casing is different from the ones I'm used to. Feels lighter. The release at the one end is white, a red *T* the only lettering on the whole thing.

Breakneck tetra. *Tempo.* From Mobius.

The fourth alarm chimes and I cross the square with my silver helmet gripped in my fist, bouncing it against my thigh as I walk. The New York National's heavy glass doors have been smudged by countless fingers and I add my own sticky smear as I shove inside.

The lobby is huge. A high, bright ceiling and glossy marble floor. Eagles are engraved on the walls, overseeing the drone of people who wait to see tellers or perch on tiny couches, hoping a banker will call out their name.

I count the security guards as I pull Kevlar gloves from the top pouch of my backpack and slip them on. I don't care about leaving fingerprints: just want to be ready for the rush.

My hands don't shake like they did at the HSBC, but they still tremble. I aim a Glock 9mm overhead, pointing high at the ceiling, and fire two shots, which grabs everyone's attention much better than shouting. There is no voice as loud as my gun.

I drop my helmet; letting it thunk on the marble tiles, then pull flight goggles out of my pocket, tugging those on for protection instead. The world already knows my face so there's no need to hide it, and the helmet has always made me feel claustrophobic. No stuffy rules now. No TRU mandates.

I can rush however I want.

I have the five security guards hunker down together where I can keep an eye on them, then I pluck their guns from their holsters and toss them into my pack. Over near the ATMs, a little kid's crying, and her dad's trying to shush her quiet, but at least the wailing is honest. When it stops, the terrified silence is so much worse.

The cash drawers are too sparse for my liking, and I suspect the tellers are holding back. *They're playing games and playing with fire.* But I need a haul that is going to impress.

"Take this to the vault," I say to the teller who seems the least panicked thus far. He has a feathery moustache but a steely gaze and I shove the backpack at him. "Be quick. But make sure this gets full."

I wish I didn't have to wave the Glock in his face to hurry him along. I wish this gun wasn't loaded. But off he goes and now I have to force myself to be patient.

When the guy comes back with my withdrawal ready, the

backpack's stuffed so full of money I can barely lift it onto my shoulder.

It won't feel heavy much longer.

My insides are fluttery and tight as I shake the tetra bullet to arm the dose inside, then I clamp it between my teeth. This feeling alone is electric. I'm giddy as I head for the doors. Stepping over the bodies that face-plant the floor, arms cactused out at their sides. No one tackles me this time because I know to keep turning, keeping my gun trained on everyone, even when I'm at the glass doors and stalling because a TRU squad is swarming the square outside.

Snipers slither on their bellies, surrounding the fountain. Tactical vehicles line up behind them to block off the streets.

I adjust my flight goggles and clamp my jaw tight, trying to stop my teeth rattling on the tetra bullet. My spandex is slippery with sweat.

The people in the bank are still facedown on the floor behind me, but I fire another warning shot at the ceiling to make sure they all stay there as I peer out through the glass doors, plotting my best route across the square. That's when I spot a runner halfway between me and the fountain. With the helmet on, visor down, I can't tell who it is until I see the spiky hair and broad shoulders of the handler beside them.

Sasha.

So I'm up against Runner Eight, and I wish she could lose the helmet: I want to see the look on Idra Hall's face when she realizes her target is me.

I hit the release, then shove through the doors, dropping

my gun as I bolt straight at Idra and Sasha and the snipers that pool at their feet. I leap as the bullets begin, the tetra surging through my veins, my body floating skyward like it's been injected with helium and I'm never going to touch down.

I do touch down though, right inside the fountain, in the very center of the square. The snipers are all aimed at one another, so they can't open fire as I dart and splash, and then I'm out of the fountain and don't even feel wet. Must have danced through the jeweled beads of water like I bet Rapunzel's dancing through the city right now.

I bound over the tactical vehicles and out of the square, tetra smoothing life into something simple. All that matters is the next step, which is this step because every moment is now. I let it feel just as good as it deserves and open wide to let out a glorious scream, my insides moaning, my tongue reaching out and up like I'm licking the blue sky between the tips of the buildings and tasting the tang of the popcorn clouds.

The Fourth Dimension rains down in light all around me. Every atom unmuzzled, all the colors unleashed. The buildings become battleships, thorny with turrets. Then they're crowded tombstones of some extinct giant race.

And up there's a steel bug, a TRU chopper, pointing its camera and guns at where I ought to be but struggling to keep up. My mind goes where it wants, twisting things as it paints 4D pictures, so the chopper becomes less steel bug and more tin dragon. *Don't get too close, or I'll slay you.* I will drink your gasoline and bite your bullets for breakfast.

I'm on Madison Avenue. Crossing Forty-Ninth Street.

They can't catch me at Fifty-First Street.

Can't catch me at Fifty-Fifth.

I'm threading through traffic, letting it dictate my movements—a light turns red, so I cut a new way. I leap across cars only when I need to. I steer clear of pedestrians clogging the sidewalks. Don't even dream about going inside a building. I can do anything I want because I'm not following, I am way out in front.

And I'm careful.

So I don't take out this cyclist ahead—I vault right over him. That crowd of people on the crosswalk? I grab a street lamp and spin around it, then launch into the air and land on the far side of the crowd. No danger. And I never had to slow down.

I'm going to start peaking. The soupy city streets jumble up out of order, kaleidoscopes melting inside the melting pot. I'll rearrange them in new blocks, new neighborhoods with new names. *And why shouldn't I love this?* This is the best I can be and the world can't stop me.

But I'm crying. It was those people on that crosswalk. I avoided them. But I can't avoid the memory of that day on Queens Boulevard last summer. The day my brother and I got broken.

The drug speeds up the tears, making it hard to breathe.

It's slowing me down, slicing off my peak like a hot spoon through ice cream.

I spin a three-sixty to see how far Idra is behind me. She's not a full block back, and closing in. *Runner Eight.* She doesn't know I'm undercover. *She's a fool.* But she's a fast fool, *the fastest*, and I'm not fast enough anymore. I shouldn't have started crying: I lost the peak, lost the moment. And now the feeling I'm feeling doesn't feel like enough.

I got spoiled by the double dose. And I'm used to what Trinity Pharmaceuticals brews for the runners. This is counterfeit crap, from Mobius. He's ruining everything. But I don't care about Mobius. All that matters is Idra Hall's gaining on me and *I should be better than this.*

I start sliding to a stop, my Nikes shrieking as they burn on the asphalt, rubber soles dying a painful death. I'm dimly aware of cars. Brakes slamming. The traffic crunching to a standstill. People scatter in slow motion on the sidewalks to escape me.

I barely notice.

I come to a grinding halt. Then turn to face Idra.

TWENTY-THREE

dra hesitates. Running after a breakneck is one thing. Facing one who has stopped to make a stand is a whole different beast.

I cinch my backpack tighter. Pull my goggles down so they hang from my neck. I have to make this quick. Too long and her assist team will catch up. I have to remember the chopper. The tactical vehicles. *Snipers*. My old unit has no idea what I'm really doing out here: they're just puppets dancing on the end of Spaihts's strings.

"Why don't you take off that helmet?" I force the words out, my tongue thick, jaw locked. "Take a break from the rules."

"That what you're doing?" Her voice comes out as warped as mine.

"I'm changing everything. You're just getting in my way."

"This about your brother, West?" She leaves the helmet

on, but flips the visor up. There are those pretty eyes, the blue of an exotic bird. A thick strand of blond hair sticks to her cheek, all of her glimmering in the Fourth Dimension. "Spaihts told us about your personal vendetta and how it's made you unhinged."

I want to throttle her skinny neck till her eyes bulge out.

"Hard to understand," I spit out. "For someone only in it for the rush."

"At least my rush is legal."

The anger shakes up the tetra inside me, making me fizz. Aggression growing over my rush like mold. But I lost the peak. I need more tetra. *Maybe when I make Idra bleed, I can drink the drug from her veins.*

She leaps first.

She's five feet off the ground and hurtling toward me. In training they taught us to sidestep this sort of maneuver, let the attacker wear herself out.

But we're not in combat training now.

I launch off my right leg, left fist out in front, and my knuckles sink into Idra's chest as we collide in midair like two heat-seeking missiles. But we don't explode into pieces: we meld into one.

My momentum cancels out hers and we drop to the asphalt, wrestling, but wrestling is not what we want, so we let go of each other, spinning back onto our feet to set up the way TRU taught us. I remember Spaihts singing a snippet of song in the interrogation room—*everybody was kung fu fighting*—and thinking about Spaihts reminds me it's because of him this is happening, not Idra.

Run, Little Rabbit. Don't do this . . . come on, Alana. *Run!*

"Back down!" I scream, wrenching the words from inside me. But as Idra slips closer to engage, I don't want her to back down. I want to feel this adrenaline and feed off its power.

This is wrong, a voice inside reminds me. Until Idra's fist connects with my gut and sends me flying twenty feet through the air. I land on my back, my head smacking the asphalt, tetra dulling the agony as my brain spins around. That little voice inside?

Totally gone.

People have fled the scene—the cars around us abandoned, doors left open, the sidewalks home to nothing but whispery pieces of trash. *Evacuated.* Good little snails. They've given us a safe zone so they won't get stepped on.

If there was still anyone here to watch us, all they'd see is two bodies blurring together. Our limbs move faster than the wings on a hornet, and each hit kicks like a thousand mules.

When I wrap my arm around Idra's neck and yank off her helmet, her blond hair spills out of its ponytail and sprays like a fan. She has blood on her lip. So very *red*, and her skin so pale, and those eyes are even bluer now that she's angry.

She feels it. Like I feel it. A bonfire of ego. The rage flaming on. I can tell she likes it, and her smile distracts me.

Idra rips loose of my grip. Spins free. She sets up to launch at me again, but I'm ready for her. I leap before she does and when we collide, I overpower her. We hurtle together, tangled like two hands making a fist; swimming inside shadows as we bounce off the street.

Disengaging, I roll to a standing position, my eyes getting used to the darkness. We're inside a parking garage, empty cars all around us. The chopper can't sink down to join us in here. But TRU can surround the building.

How much rush do I have left? I need Tucker. I need him screaming into my ear.

What if I only have seconds?

I need so much more.

We bounce against parked cars, setting off every alarm, cars honking and headlights flashing. We're like two balls in a pinball machine.

Idra slams me down on the concrete, but I punch out her elbows, roll free, and she's slow to recover. I catch her by the ankle, spinning her around me, then smashing her against the side of an SUV. She manages to get to her feet again. But after a swift kick to her kneecaps and a chop to her sternum, Idra turns limp. Staggers. I let her fall.

She flops on broken glass, skull thumping the concrete. Her eyes are shut and blood seeps out of the back of her head. It's dribbling out of her mouth, too.

"Idra," I moan, kneeling beside her. There's too much static. The headlights flash as the car alarms bleat and all of it *hurts*. I can't have much time left. *I barely peaked* but I am coming down hard.

I check the pulse on Idra's neck, but my hands are too shaky. Her eyelids flutter, which means she's alive, but realizing I've almost killed her makes me glitchy. The Fourth Dimension whirls around me, everything picking up speed. Too much color and too much motion.

I'm going to unspool. Then it'll all be over. They'll throw me in prison for killing GoPro and Monroe and for poor Idra Hall, who ended her life as a hero. My little brother will see me locked up; he'll see the real me, the rotten me. The me I tried to pretend that I wasn't. I just couldn't run fast enough to get away from myself.

"Idra." I say her name over and over. I want her to come to and hit me. Snap handcuffs on me and read me my rights.

"Please!" I scream. "Wake up."

"What are you doing?"

A voice. Behind me.

"Tucker?" I shout, spinning around and wanting him, *needing* him.

"Who the hell is Tucker?" Ethan pulls off his helmet.

"How are you here?" I mumble, focusing on him with everything I have so I can crawl out of this glitchy hole.

"On my way to my meeting point when I saw people running off Eighth like a bomb had gone off. Lucky for you I decided to check it out. Come on." He checks his watch. "I have two and a half minutes left, you should have more, but we gotta move."

He talks so easily on tetra. *Two and half minutes.* He's still got almost a third of his rush left.

"She's hurt," I say, turning to Idra. Her eyelids still flutter like she's trapped in a nightmare. Unconscious but still rushing—that's a nightmare all right.

"She's a runner," Ethan says. "Getting hurt's an occupational hazard."

"But what if she doesn't pull through?"

"There'll be a whole medic team on its way here. Her support team, her TRU buddies." Ethan rubs his quads. "This standing around is making me cramp. Where's your helmet?"

"I lost it."

"Man, you are a wild one. How did you like the New York National?"

"Like it?"

"Easy, right? They got a big take-no-chances policy when it comes to us. And all those columns. Makes you feel like you're in ancient Greece."

"I liked the fountain," I mumble, unsure how I'm having this conversation. I keep staring at Idra. She keeps not waking up.

"Well, I'm out." Ethan sounds bemused more than anything. He tugs his helmet back on, straps it in place. "Thought a fellow breaker might need a hand, but it looks like you want to stick around here."

Sirens wail out on the street. The thrum of the chopper's blades loom close.

And there's a scratchy sound. A grinding. I glance down at Ethan's feet—he's rolling a skateboard back and forth, crunching broken glass beneath its wheels.

"You're Half-Pipe," I say. I never chased him.

Idra did.

"That's what the drones call me." Ethan kicks at the deck so it snaps into the air, where he catches it. Then he tosses the board ten feet ahead and it rolls on without him, but he leaps for it, effortless, *weightless*, then sticks the landing and starts gliding away.

"Wait," I yell, sprinting after him, pulling my flight goggles back down.

But there's a girl's voice, behind me, calling my name. I turn back, thinking it's Idra. *She's calling for me. She's awake.* But it's not Idra—it's tiny Jamie. She must have been on standby as backup.

"I have a message for you," she says, sprinting closer, flipping up the visor on her helmet. "From Tucker."

Jamie grinds to a halt at Idra's body, then drops to her knees.

"You did this?" She stares up at me, looking horrified, and glitchy.

Ethan's gone—and my body yearns to catch up to him.

"What's the message?" I snap. "Quick."

"Tucker says Vogler can help." The rush distorts Jamie's words. "He wants to talk."

Vogler. Monroe's second-in-command. What can Vogler do against Spaihts?

The sirens howl outside. The chopper's blades rumble. Idra bleeds.

"Don't come after me," I tell Jamie, and I run.

TWENTY-FOUR

B reakneck or runner, you rush alone. Always. You isolate yourself because you're too volatile, too powerful and too fast to be close to someone burning as bright as you. But when I catch up to Ethan, it doesn't feel dangerous that we're both dosed up.

It feels incredible.

I forget about Idra. Vogler. Spaihts. Tucker. It's too much fun watching Ethan move. He pops off his board and snaps the deck into his hands so he can run with me, weaving through the traffic—he's right behind me, then in front of me, like he's playing a game. When we jump, he's fond of somersaults. And after a block of leaping car rooftops, Ethan signals for us to take the next right, leading me down a side street, where he hops back onto his board without slowing down, kicks a foot at the asphalt, then *flies*.

It's like he's surfing through the city. Though I've seen footage of Half-Pipe before, up close and on tetra, his moves aren't just impressive, they're beautiful. He's not banking off concrete walls and shredding the blacktop—he's riding swells of light through the Fourth Dimension.

The tetra swells stronger in my veins, making the 4D world glow more brilliantly, and it's so dazzling it glows *inside* me too, a warmth spreading out from my chest. My skin prickles with heat, and I wish cool fingers were touching me. *Ethan's fingers.* Because I'm not just surging through the city, I'm surging *with* someone. *Not alone.* I feel his rush magnify mine.

Two bodies, no shackles.

We burst through sunbeams on the shimmering streets of my city, and as I run, I barely remember the first parts of my rush or what I was feeling guilty about before. I use Ethan as a pacer, pushing myself to keep up with him as we start to wind down. And when we go to ground on the far side of Midtown, both of us are far from our meeting points.

"You ever done that?" I ask, staggering after Ethan into an alley off Forty-First Street. "Rushed with someone? So close like that?"

"First time for me, too. How did you like it?"

"Loved it."

"Yeah." His grin is huge as he tugs off his helmet. "I know what you mean. But we got work left to do. Better keep focused."

"I was supposed to go to Saint Bart's," I say. "Then some laundromat."

"Suds'n'Glow?" He doesn't even seem out of breath. "Let's both head there and wait for JB."

Ethan shakes out his mop of tangled hair. He's dressed in a beat-up black leather jacket and skinny gray jeans, chunky pads covering his clothes at the elbows and knees. He's unpeeling his gloves, unclipping his pads, fast about it. All of a sudden his board and everything else is stuffed in his pack.

"You getting changed?" he asks, seeing me still leaning at the wall.

"I don't have anything to change into." I peel off my goggles. "Left my other clothes in the van."

"Well, at least get out of the pads. You'll blend better. You should have been wearing a helmet. What were you thinking?"

"They already know what I look like. TRU caught me before, remember?"

"Yeah, well, a helmet would still protect your head." Ethan's studying his torn-up skate shoes. They're simple Vans, and there's not much left of them, despite all the duct tape he's bandaged them with.

"Should try sturdier shoes," I suggest.

"Nah. I'd lose my feel for the road."

I still haven't moved from the wall. "You don't even seem like you're derailing."

"Had a lot of practice."

"So have I."

He glances at me, eyes narrowed, and he looks more suspicious than confused. "How so?"

"I mean I derail hard. You took care of me last time, remember?"

Ethan reapplies a scrap of duct tape to his shoe, seeming satisfied with my explanation. "You'll get better at the comedown," he tells me. "The trick is to still feel the rush as much as you can."

"My nine minutes is long gone."

"But the drug's still in your veins, right? Dig deep for the afterglow. Breathe into it. Not the same, of course. You can't move like you just did. But it feels *awesome*."

"For how long?"

"Thinking about that's a surefire way to make it end sooner."

I breathe deep as I start pulling the pads off my arms and legs. Still feel the opposite of awesome. My body is brutally sore.

"Can't believe you faced off with a runner," Ethan says, cinching the straps on his backpack to make it shrink smaller. "Second bank job, and you made a stand."

"She was gaining on me . . . I think. She might have caught up to me if I didn't . . ."

"Beat the crap out of her?"

"It's a blur."

"Yeah. Again, you need practice." Ethan taps at his forehead. "I remember most of it. Sometimes all of it. Trying to take it with me. You know, while I still can."

"How bad did I hurt her?"

"You sure you wanna know?"

I hesitate, then nod.

"Let's just hope the medics scrape her up carefully," Ethan says, grimacing. "Else they might leave bits of her behind."

I lean back at the wall, feeling sick. "Have you ever done something like that?"

"Faced off with a runner? Nah. Not my style. I learned from JB's bad example to steer clear of violence."

"You just held up a bank at gunpoint."

Ethan shoulders his pack. "I told you last night—you just have to convince people you mean it. The gun's only for show. I've no intention of firing it anywhere but at the ceiling to grab their attention. They always submit. It's what people do."

"What if a security guard called your bluff?"

"Then I'd run. I guess. Hasn't happened so far, and I doubt it will. No one cares enough about someone else's money to risk their life for it—except for the runners. But they're even crazier than you."

"Runners are trying to protect *people*, not the bank's money. They protect the innocent who get hurt in your getaways."

"Big fan, huh? Seems to me they're just making it worse. They speed us up. Harder to be careful when a runner's on your tail."

"Right. Because safety's such a priority to you."

"What's your problem?" Ethan unzips his leather jacket.

His shirt's all sweaty beneath it.

"You being a hypocrite."

"*I'm* the hypocrite? I've rushed dozens of times and never hurt anyone. You just put someone in the hospital. And who the hell's Tucker, anyway?"

"What?"

"When I showed up you thought I was *Tucker.* Like you were expecting someone to be there. . . ."

"I said something?" I turn from Ethan, stuffing my pads into my pack so he can't see my face. "Just a name?"

Please let it have been just a name.

"You really don't remember any of it? Come on, who is he?"

"I don't know. *No one.* I was high, wasn't I?"

"You were high, all right. JB's gonna be stoked on your performance. Little out of control for my tastes, but he doesn't mind that sort of thing."

"What thing?"

"Rage." Ethan steps closer, wipes the sweaty bangs from my face and lifts up my chin. His gaze is calm but intense as he cleans blood from my forehead with the sleeve of his jacket. Apparently, I have a cut just above my left eye, and I tell myself whatever happened with Idra, she must have started it. She's had it in for me since basic training, after all. "Maybe that's why Davis doesn't like you," Ethan says. "He's super pissed at the world, too. People are like magnets: they repel those too similar."

"So I don't repel you?"

"Not so far."

We cross Broadway toward Bryant Park, then drop into the subway, Ethan carrying my bag as well as his, since I can barely walk.

I end up leaning against him on the platform, mostly because I'm exhausted, but also because I'm afraid someone might recognize me—despite the Knicks beanie JB gave me, which I wear tugged down low, my bangs tucked up inside it. I use Ethan's body as a shield, pushing my face into his jacket, breathing in its leathery stink and the salty fresh smell of his sweat, which is a much better combo than the hot-tar-and-ashtray stench of subway. We must look like a couple. Destitute kids, maybe, all we own in the packs at our feet.

"I'll find you a seat," Ethan says, smuggling me and the bags onto an uptown train.

"No, this is good," I say, leaning against him as people bustle around us.

He puts his arm around me, hand at the small of my back, pressing me against his hip. "This okay?"

"It's fine."

"I don't wanna be sleazy."

"You're just holding me up."

The subway rocks and rattles, tunneling deep beneath the city, and our train thins out a little more at each stop. Eventually there's room to move but I don't move away. Ethan holds on to the bar overhead, one arm still wrapped around my waist, and we rock back and forth with the pulse of the train.

"Derailing hits you quick," he says, voice low, his mouth close to my ear so only I can hear him.

"And hard. Always so hard."

"You're not all the way done unless you think you are. Trust me. It's in there, still burning."

I reach up and put my arms around his shoulders so I can hang off him. I'm like deadweight but he doesn't seem to mind standing for both of us, and it feels good to stretch out. I crack my neck and breathe in slow, feeling Ethan's rib cage expand and letting him pace me.

When I tip my head back to stare at him, his eyes are closed. My forehead's the same height as his chin. Tiny drops of green paint smudge his curly dark hair.

"When are you going to show me what you're painting?" I ask.

"You gotta stay present."

"I am present."

"Don't you want to still feel it?"

"Of course," I whisper. "I don't think I ever felt it enough though. Even at my peak, it seemed a little flat. I don't know. Maybe I'm used to something stronger."

"There's nothing stronger," he whispers back. "The tempo we get is the best there is."

"Right. From Mobius. But where does *he* get it from?

Who's making it—*him?*"

"Why? You want to put in a special order?" Ethan laughs, but keeps his voice down. "Remind me not to be there when you tell Mobius you want to score higher-grade BPM just for you."

"I get to meet him?"

"He meets with every breaker worth a dose of the good stuff. Mobius sells direct. And delivers regular."

"Delivers? He'll come to the house?"

"You'll see. If you make the team."

"Just admit it." I smile. "I'm in."

"Depends what the team wants."

"*You* want me, though. Right?"

He opens his eyes, and I have to tilt my head back a little more so my gaze can meet his.

"You are way too aggressive," he says, smiling back at me. "Not to mention unorthodox."

"You like unorthodox. No rules. No limits. Like the breakers you mentioned last night. The ones who don't fear consequences."

Ethan's smile disappears. "Stop, Lana."

"What?"

"You gotta stay present if you want the afterglow. And you need to quit standing on my feet."

"Thought you were a big tough skater boy."

"Not as tough as you, *Timebomb*. Perfect name. Hang around you long enough, I'm bound to get hurt."

"Don't say that." I picture Reuben slumped in his too-big wheelchair. Crippled for life because Sidewinder was too fast and I was too slow.

"How did you know her name?" Ethan asks.

"What?"

"That runner," he whispers. "The one you beat all to hell."

The memory's so hazy. My brain feels like it's been chewed. I didn't *beat* Idra, though. We fought, and I did what I had to do to make sure I got away. Ethan makes it sound worse than it was.

"You were crying it out when I found you with her. *Idra*, you were saying."

"Maybe I was just moaning or something."

"No. You knew her name."

I break away from Ethan's gaze, burying my face in his chest, my eyes bugging out of my head as I search for a lie I can use.

"She's who arrested me," I say. "Before. After my first bank job."

"And she told you her name?"

"That's what the rest of them called her. Kind of unusual . . ."

"Yeah. Unusual."

"The name, I mean. *Idra*. It's unusual."

His silence scares me.

"I just don't really remember much of the rush. . . ."

"So you said."

"But I feel awful about hurting her," I say, to remind Ethan I faced off against a runner this morning so he should trust I'm as breakneck as they come. "I want you to show me how to still feel it," I say, my face still pressed at his chest as I change subjects. "Like you are."

"The afterglow? All right. Are your eyes closed?"

"They are now."

"Then hold on."

"To what?" My arms are still wrapped around his shoulders.

"Everything," he says, and I tense every bit of me. "Now let go. It's all right, I've got you."

The train rumbles along, drilling through the earth and rubbing me against him. We're like two pieces of wood trying to strike up a spark. "Almost . . ." I say. "There's something there. I know what you mean, I'm just not sure how to reach it."

"Stop trying so hard. It's inside you. Relax."

I let go of him just as the train makes a violent shake and I lose my balance, but Ethan presses me against him, keeping me from falling, keeping me safe.

Starting with my shoulders, I let the tension out of my body, working down to my hips, making things feel bigger inside me, reaching for a place where the tetra's still burning, the embers not quite gone out.

"Don't fight it," Ethan whispers as I arc back, my face turned up to his. I feel his warm breath on my lips and my

235

mouth hungers for more of him. I keep my eyes closed but stand on tiptoe, moving toward where his mouth must be. It's as if our lips are kindred spirits that need to find each other and as I breathe in this boy's chemical heat, it mingles with the tetra inside me, which makes my tongue so happy it starts wriggling around in my mouth.

The heavy backpacks at our feet are almost knocking me over but Ethan has his arms around my waist so I don't need to worry, and as he holds me, and we breathe, it's as if I'm breathing back in the tetra already inside me, slowly at first, but then there's plenty. *So much.* It's rushing through me and lighting me up and as I press closer to Ethan, we create enough voltage to power the city. Just one flip of a switch and the whole world would turn on.

"You feel it?" he asks.

"Yes," I tell him, and it is the best word my mouth has ever tasted. So I keep whispering it, over and over again.

TWENTY-FIVE

T urns out a laundromat is the perfect place to hide. Ethan and I are two more strangers with giant bags at our feet, biding our time as the washers cycle and the dryers drone. No one knows our bags are full of dirty money instead of dirty clothes.

"Only bad thing about this place is the seats." Ethan slumps down into the hard plastic chair beside me.

"Tell me about it." I put my head on his shoulder, which ups my comfort factor considerably. "How long do we have to wait?"

"Mostly depends on how lost Rapunzel gets and how long it takes for JB to track her down." Ethan stuffed our gloves and his sweaty T-shirt in a washer so we'd blend in as legitimate customers, and when I angle my head just right on his shoulder I can glimpse down inside his half-unzipped jacket. I feel a little guilty about stealing a look at the tops of his abs, but then I remember he practically saw me naked when he was nursing me back to health.

"You're not gonna fall asleep on me, are you?" he asks, shifting an arm free so he can put it around me. I snuggle closer to him, sore and exhausted, but sleep is the last thing on my mind.

"I swear I'll stay awake if you promise not to move."

"How can we play laser tag if you're not willing to move?"

Suds'n'Glow is, as JB promised, laundromat in the front and laser tag in the back.

"If you want to carry me in the back and shoot me with some toy gun while I curl up on the floor then you can go right ahead."

"Man, you are no fun at all on the comedown."

"I'm more a go-big-then-go-home kinda girl."

"Or in this case, go do laundry."

"Sit still and watch a washing machine? This much I can manage. Run around in the dark shooting at plastic targets? Not happening."

"Good thing you're here with me, not my brother."

"Agreed. His shoulders are way too bony to make a decent pillow."

"Glad I could help. But JB would have you up and playing at least one round. Dude loves laser tag. Is convinced it's retro and hip and that Suds'n'Glow's popularity is on the verge of a massive comeback."

"Seems pretty busy to me," I say, glancing about the place.

"The laundromat is. But check out that woman in the leopard-print scarf, or her, with shoes like ballet slippers. Also that kid with a jacket like bubble wrap. See what they all have in common?"

"They wouldn't be caught dead playing laser tag?"

Ethan laughs. "Exactly. But JB doesn't get out much. He likes to play stealth—the lights on the targets switched off—and insists on sudden death, so if you take a shot to your target, you're all done."

"High stakes."

"You should see him. He gets really into it. We all played a few times to humor him."

"It's kind of sad," I say, though I'm laughing, too. "Humoring the old fossil."

"Hey, we'll all be has-beens one day. Reminiscing about the good old times."

"That's depressing."

"Can be. Got to find another way to think about it. Got a lot of life left after this."

"It's hard to imagine Miles Davis playing laser tag to humor your brother," I say, because I'd prefer we don't get into life-after-tetra. Especially not while I'm derailing this hard. The afterglow Ethan taught me to feel has all fizzled out.

"In typical Davis fashion, he insisted on doing everyone's laundry instead of playing the damn game. Said laser tag is for kids and managed to shrink a bunch of Aces's clothes while he sulked out here."

"They're not the kind of clothes that leave much room for shrinking."

"Nor do they leave much to the imagination."

"Perv."

"Hey, I'm just stating a fact," Ethan says. "Your own getup is pretty skintight, too."

"JB's idea."

"Of course. My brother. New York's classiest appreciator of the feminine form."

"So who does he have a bigger crush on, Rapunzel or Aces?"

"I'd say JB is able to crush on both with equal magnitude. Guy's got a big heart."

"And you?" I risk going there. "Which one of those two lovely ladies has stolen your heart?"

"Who says I have a heart to be stolen?"

"Right. You probably just paint pictures of girls but never pine over them."

"The best part of the game," Ethan says, seeming keen to change the subject, "was how we'd all wait it out for someone else to make a move, seeing as it was stealth, and sudden death, but each time, Rapunzel would lose patience first. She'd end up yelling some sort of Sri-Lankan-South-London war cry, charging about the place, and would always be the first to get eliminated."

"Are you sure your brother's the big laser tag fan? You sound awfully fond of the whole experience."

"You're right. I'm like a has-been, reminiscing already."
Ethan reaches into the top pouch of his backpack and pulls
out a thin notepad and a pen. "Best way to avoid looking
back is to make something new. Want to draw something
for me?"

"You carry a notepad when you're rushing?"

"Not like the extra weight is gonna slow me down. I bring
these too." He shows me some cans of spray paint stashed in
his pack. "Just in case I can go to ground early."

"Graffiti?"

"I prefer to call it street art." He holds the notebook toward
me. "Creating stuff on tempo is amazing. You should try."

"I don't feel much like drawing."

"Come on. I want to see your style."

"You're the one with the big painting project you won't let
me see."

"It's a work in progress, but I'll sketch you something now
if you want."

"All right." We're shielded by the shake and hum of the
machines, but I whisper when I say, "Draw one of the people
in here. Like leopard-print lady. Or bubble-wrap guy."

"Not usually much for realism, I warn you. But I'll give it
a shot. Can you close your eyes while I draw it but not fall
asleep?"

"My eyes have been mostly closed for the past five minutes."

I don't peek until he says it's ready, and when I open my

eyes, the fluorescent lights sting.

"I thought you were gonna draw someone in here," I say.

"I did. It's you."

"I know, but it's me rushing. It's me in 4D." I suppose I should be glad he didn't draw me derailing. I look like a sloth with the flu.

"Don't you like it? Kind of impressionistic—"

"I love it. So much movement."

"Not too swirly?"

"How could it be?" His drawing is like a labyrinth, tiny pathways spiraling to white space at the center where my heart would be. "Why's it so blank in the middle? This part."

"I guess that's the part I don't know."

"You make me sound so mysterious." I try to keep my voice light.

"No. That's how *you* make you sound."

"What do you want to know about me?"

"Why you beat the crap out of that runner, then started sobbing about it, all glitchy with guilt."

"It wasn't like that," I say, but how would I know? The rush is choppy water I can't see down into, like a nasty dream I can't quite recall. But when I picture Idra's blue eyes, the guilt is a crackling jolt of clarity, painful as touching a Taser to my tooth.

She hurt me too, though. I'm all bruised and battered, my beanie pulled down over the new cut on my forehead. Feels like a crash test dummy somewhere must want its body back. But I want my *memories* back. Those nine minutes are so dead to me now. And what if that blank space at the center is something dead inside me? A part the rest of me pretends doesn't even exist.

"You're tickling me," Ethan says, and I realize the bobble on this stupid hat I'm wearing is bristling under his chin. I pry my head from Ethan's shoulder and hang forward, elbows on knees.

"Big Knicks fan?" he asks, meaning the hat.

"It's your brother's."

"I know. Just joking around."

"I like the Rangers," I say, thinking of Reuben. And Dad. "Hockey."

"I guess basketball's not violent enough for you. . . ."

"Can we drop it?" I snap.

"Wasn't expecting *both* of you to be here," JB says, and I sit upright as he and Rapunzel appear.

"Crossed paths with Timebomb." Ethan flips his notebook shut.

"Sounds dangerous." JB grins. "I already have Aces, so let's split. Unless you all want an impromptu game of laser tag. How about it, Panzer?" He cracks his knuckles. "Care to take on the master himself?"

"I'm knackered, boss." She falls into a seat across from me. "Else you know I would."

"Too bad." JB turns to me. "I am the LeBron James of laser tag."

"So I heard."

"Looks like you had some success." He picks up my backpack. "Allow me to help you with this."

"I had them go to the vault," I say.

He struggles beneath the weight of my pack. "Feels like it."

"My shirt's almost done." Ethan nods at the washing machine.

"We can buy you a new one, bro. Can buy you a dozen."

"Seems wasteful."

"You ain't poor no more." JB kicks his brother's foot. "Besides, I think the girls like you shirtless."

"Yeah, stud!" Rapunzel's whole body shakes as she laughs.

"Come on." JB's heading for the door, and Rapunzel grabs my hand to drag me to my feet. We're almost out of the place when I realize Ethan's not coming.

"I'll catch you back at the house," he says as I glance back at him. He's pulled his notebook back out.

"He does this." Rapunzel's holding the door open for me. "Best to leave him be, love."

Ethan's sketching in his notebook again, his long legs stretched out and his curly hair shoved back, his hands swift upon the page. As I follow Rapunzel out onto the sidewalk, I can't help but think of the blank space he drew inside me.

A mystery. Or a void.

TWENTY-SIX

T he first thing I do with my freedom is borrow a scooter from Aces's fleet and head out of Manhattan across the Triborough Bridge. I reach Queens by early afternoon and wait in the park near my house, hot and itchy as the sun beats down.

Overdressed for the heat, I'm forced to cling to the shade of a tree as I wait for Reuben, hoping he and Mom might come to the park with Echo. I watch the skies for the kite I got my brother, but there's not much wind, and this whole thing is a long shot. I didn't dare reach out with a text or email, since I'm sure Spaihts has my family under careful surveillance. I can't go any closer to our house for the same reason.

I check the snazzy new phone JB gave me—no missed calls, and no texts since the one I got back from Tucker. I'd wanted to hear his voice but he wouldn't pick up, and the number he had me memorize didn't even go through to voice mail. He just texted back where to meet him. Tonight.

I robbed the New York National three days ago, and that evening everyone but Davis voted me onto the team. So I got a key to the front door—the house is on a beautiful treelined street in Sugar Hill, not far from the Harlem School of the Arts. I also got a few thousand dollars in spending money. I'm free to come and go as I please.

I don't feel free, though. Even out here, under the bright summer sky, I am trapped by the dark knowledge of how bad I hurt Idra. According to the media, she's still in critical condition, and I can only guess at how out of control I became. It's like tetra forged a counterfeit me, a substitute. Yet my hunger to return to the rush is the realest thing I know.

I want to crawl back into that dark space and not care for nine minutes. As I stand in this park, hoping to glimpse my family in the distance, tetra feels like a shortcut to a different sort of home.

My bangs are all sweaty, but I have to keep my beanie snugged down like it's winter. Along with my sunglasses, the hat's to keep me from being recognized. The beanie is black, the sunglasses red. Rapunzel gave me both—a stylish upgrade from the baggy clothes and borrowed Knicks hat I was planning on leaving the house in. Along with the paisley leggings and leather jacket she gave me, I look like the funkiest member of some indie rock band. Mom and

Reuben probably wouldn't even recognize me if I walked right past them. But I keep my distance when they show.

No kite. It's just the two of them, and Echo. About a hundred yards away from me, my brother's dog fetches the ball Reuben throws. I want to call out. I want to run to them. I want to be squished between my mom and brother in a suffocating hug. I'd even be happy for Echo to slobber all over me and whack at me with his wagging tail.

But I can only watch, and from all the way over here in the shade of this tree, the two people I love in this world are so, so far away. I can't even see their faces, which means they can't see mine. Which means they can't see the tears rolling down my cheeks.

They leave before the sun sets. But I wait till it's dark. Alone, except for the mosquitos that begin to hug the warm air around me as night falls.

Then I mount my borrowed Vespa and head back into the city, and my sadness lifts a little as I cross back over the Triborough Bridge. With the East River below me and Manhattan glittering up ahead, I feel I'm at least heading in the right direction. I've done what Monroe wanted, after all. I'm on the right side of the law to meet Mobius. If I can find a way to end the breaknecks' supply of tempo, there'll be no more breaknecks at all.

The theater's off MacDougal Street, right in the heart of the Village, and it shows foreign films and festival winners, the sort of highbrow titles hardly anyone actually wants to see. Instead of popcorn, there are vegan goods for sale from the bakery next door, and I get a chocolate doughnut and a coffee, telling the dreadlocked girl behind the counter to keep the change.

Tucker texted that I should meet him at this theater, this time, and this movie, which is something French, I think. I'm unsure how to pronounce the title. But I enter Screen Two and plop down in a velvety red seat in the back row, tucked off to the side, giving me a good vantage point and putting me far from the entrance but close to the emergency exit.

There are three other people here for the 9:10 showing.

None of them are Tucker.

Rusty violins punctuate the fragmented mumbling of the film, and despite getting sucked into reading the subtitles, I'm having a hard time following along. More than half an hour goes by, and I've finished my coffee—which was pretty good—and I'm just checking my phone to see if I've heard from Tucker when he slumps down into the seat in front of me.

"What are you doing?" I hiss, my whisper barely audible above the discordant noise of the film's soundtrack.

"Tucker," I say, a little louder now, but he raises a hand up to silence me. His head swivels about as he surveys the theater. Mapping out exit routes, I'm sure.

"Hold this," I say, basically putting my coffee cup and doughnut in his lap. Then I crawl over the velvety seats, climbing into Tucker's row to take the seat next to his.

He stares straight ahead, bloodshot blue eyes glaring at the screen, and judging by his white-knuckled grip on the arms of his seat, he is terrified, or furious, or both.

"You want me to get you caught up on the movie?" I ask. "The old guy is kind of a douche, and the chauffeur is secretly a woman. She might be the old guy's daughter, but I'm not totally sure."

"If it was a good idea to sit next to each other," he hisses, "don't you think I would have sat next to you?"

"How are we supposed to talk if I'm back here and you're up there?"

"Someone's tailing me."

"But you lost them. Right?" I glance at the entrance. "Tell me you lost them."

"Of course I lost them. Had to make it look like I wasn't *trying* to lose them, but I made the world's weirdest subway connections to get here."

"Then it's okay. You wouldn't be here if you were still being followed. Come on." I put my hand on his arm. I need him to be kinder than this, more calm. I need him to be in control. "Tell me it's okay."

For the first time he looks at me. His eyes study mine in the dim light, and a thin trickle of sweat runs down his cheek. "It's not okay."

"Try to relax," I say.

He lifts up his Yankees cap, wiping his sweaty hair from

his forehead. He has on a plain gray T-shirt, and black shorts with too many pockets. I miss the plaid shirt. He looks so much less Nebraska.

"We're blending in," I tell him. "Breathe slow." I try to pry his fingers from the arm of his chair. "Take my hand."

He recoils as if my fingers burn.

"I'll be right back," Tucker says, shoving the coffee cup and doughnut back at me as he bolts out of his chair, making so much noise, the person sitting four rows in front turns around to flash an irritated frown.

So much for not drawing attention.

When he gets back, Tucker looks a little better. He even sits next to me right away. "No sign of anyone out front," he says. "I guess they'd be here already, right?"

"Who?"

"Spaihts and his people. The feds. I don't know. But *some-one's* following me. And don't keep calling—if I don't answer, it's because I *can't* answer."

"You said to call that number in an emergency. I'm pretty sure this counts."

"I can't talk to you when I'm at TRU. . . ."

"So turn the ringer on the phone off. Here, you want this?" I hand him the doughnut and he eats the whole thing in two bites.

"Tastes like sawdust and sugar," he says.

"It's vegan."

"In that case it's not bad."

I wipe some crumbs off his nose. "Are you gonna tell me what's going on?"

"I'm losing it, Alana."

"Yeah, apart from that."

"I almost *want* them to shut the unit down—it's insane. Spaihts is watching everyone, all the time. He wants to know everything we know about breaknecks, tetra. Anything."

I take a break from staring at Tucker. I used to like staring at him. Now I'd rather watch a subtitled movie about a cross-dressing chauffeur.

"Spaihts has me working with him," he continues. "Acts like I'm his number one guy in the unit, but I know it's just because he suspects I can lead him to you. Toby Moore took the fall for smuggling you the tetra at headquarters. Kept my name out of it. Said he acted alone, blamed it on prolonged symptoms of tetra withdrawal and the crush he had on you. Ended up thrown off the unit with a suspended sentence. The crush part was true, by the way. It's how I convinced him to help."

"Poor Old Toby Moore."

"Yeah."

"And poor little Tucker. What about *me*?" I say this as loud as a whisper will let me. "I robbed a bank. Make that *two*. The police think I murdered our lieutenant—no, *everyone* thinks I murdered the lieutenant, my own family, most likely, even my little brother. And if getting arrested wasn't enough to worry about, what happens if the breaknecks I now *live with* find out I used to be a runner?"

"You're right. It's bad."

"However bad I'm making it sound, it's worse."

"So is being trapped with Spaihts," Tucker says. "You said the bastard shot the lieutenant—why'd he think twice about killing me?"

"He wouldn't. You're right. But you're still my handler."

"So?"

"So *handle* it."

"I'm trying."

"What about Vogler?" I recall a vague memory from my rush—Jamie giving me Tucker's message. "Can we really trust him?"

"I think so. He buys what I told him. But he seems as scared of Spaihts as I am. Vogler says we need proof—concrete proof—about Mobius and whoever he might be working with. We do that, Vogler will take what we find to the mayor and the chief of police, keep it out of the hands of the feds. Said that could go a long way to making you look innocent."

"It's a start. But why do we have to worry about the feds? Aren't we supposed to be on the same side?"

"The feds all back up Spaihts. He's running the show."

"So do you have any on you?" It's a miracle I waited this long to ask.

"Tetra? Are you crazy? I told you how I'm being watched."

"You have to get me more. What if I need to get away from the breakers? What if I'm caught by the police? I need to have some on me. Permanently."

"You want tetra, go find some," Tucker says. "You're the breakneck. Find Mobius."

"I am not a breakneck. And besides, I'm not sure theirs is as strong. I hardly even peaked on what they gave me."

"Sure didn't seem to slow you down."

"Yeah, but now that I've double-dosed, it's hard to feel like one hit is enough. . . ." The guy four rows in front tells us he can't hear the film over all the noise I'm making.

"So read the subtitles," I yell.

Tucker grabs my arm, like he's scared a fight's going to break out, and apologizes to the guy like the good Midwestern boy that he is. Then he leans into me, still holding my arm, his voice lower. "What do you have for me, Alana?"

"What do *I* have for *you*?"

"We need information. About Mobius."

"I don't have any. He hasn't shown up at the place I'm staying yet. But you were right. Or Monroe was right. Dog Star. Whoever said it—the only way to get decent tempo is through Mobius. Some might trickle down once it's street level, but it all starts with him."

"*Tempo?*"

"That's what they call it."

"I know what breaknecks call it. Seems like you're playing the part pretty well."

"You said I had to be convincing. Wasn't I supposed to convince even my mom? Even . . ." My voice catches, but I make myself say it. "Even my brother. I'm sure he thinks I'm a murderous breakneck. I'm sure he's reading all about me online."

I picture Reuben and Mom at the park earlier. Throwing a ball for Echo to catch. *Did they talk about me?* Reuben's head must spin with questions about me that Mom can't possibly know how to answer. Maybe he doesn't even know how to ask.

"I saw them." Tucker lets go of my arm. Sits back. "I went around to your house to check on your bro and stuff. Said I was a friend. Figured you'd want me to."

I want to hug him.

"And? How were they?"

He glances back at the entrance as the door comes open, but it's just someone coming back from a bathroom break. "Not so good. Your mom acted like she was keeping it together, but . . . you know. And I didn't see your brother much. He stayed in his room. Your mom said he's having a really hard time."

"Upset."

"Right."

"Because of me." I'm worried my increased decibels are going to earn us another warning from the guy four rows in front, but the rusty violins on the soundtrack have swelled enough to smother my voice. "Tucker, you have to stop him checking things online. You have to go back and make sure he's not reading things about me. He goes on all the blogs and he gets lost on there and I can't have him reading that stuff. Not about me."

"How am I supposed to stop him?"

"Whatever it takes."

"Maybe if you'd worn a *helmet* your brother wouldn't know what you did three days ago."

"The world already knew my face. I was trying to impress breaknecks."

"And I'm sure you did. Idra just got out of the ICU—not that you asked. She *walked* out. But she'll never run on tetra again."

Relief floods through me, but I can't soak it in. I'm still reeling from this news about Reuben.

"Idra shouldn't have got in my way," I snap.

Tucker looks at me as if he doesn't know me at all. "Four broken ribs, a punctured lung, and a concussion. Remind me never to get in your way."

"I couldn't risk getting caught. She was gaining on me. She's too fast."

"Not anymore. You could've killed her."

"Oh, come on. I wasn't that out of control."

"You sure?"

I flex the swollen knuckles on my right hand. An atlas of bruises covers my abdomen, and the new cut above my left eye balances out the old mangled scar above my right. "She held her own," I say. "It's like back in training, when I busted her face and everyone forgot she'd dislocated my shoulder first."

I try to remember the rush, the *fight*. All I see is Idra's blue eyes.

"So you're actually happy there's a precedent for you doing this."

"She's gonna be okay. That's the important thing. You said she's gonna be okay."

"I said she walked out of the hospital." Tucker wipes another trickle of sweat from his face. "But she'll never rush again—she'll be too old by the time she's fully recovered."

Idra was supposed to have more than four months left.

"Hard to know what happened after you pulled her helmet off, but from her feed it looked like you were waiting for her." Tucker stares at the screen, too angry to look at me. "I suggest next time, no matter what, you keep running. Understood?"

"The next time is tomorrow. First thing." I can taste my desire for the next rush as I say the words, my pulse quickening. I'm afraid, too. Afraid of what I'm capable of doing and won't remember once the rush is over. Afraid of that dead space that lets me lose control. But it's like tetra's tunneled holes inside me that only it can fill. "How long do I have to keep doing this?"

"Till we get the proof. Until we get Mobius."

"But what if I hurt someone like I hurt Idra?"

"That's why you have to be more careful. Remember your training. Just a little longer now. Try to imagine I'm with you, helping you."

"Right. While you keep your distance. Something you seem to excel at, by the way."

"That's not fair. We're in this together, no matter how alone you feel."

I lean against him, staring at the movie screen without watching it, just resting my head on Tucker's shoulder and reminding myself that he alone knows me. And I tell myself he's right—he's there for me, even when he feels far away. But it isn't enough anymore. And when he asks, "Who do you have? In this house. This team," I even feel like I'm being used.

"They're not important. We need the source of the drug, not the breaknecks who use it."

"I'd say we need both."

"I guess. I mean, yeah, of course."

"So? Who are they?"

"You already know—the breakers who rushed the day I did."

"Half-Pipe, Vespa, and Uncle Sam."

Rapunzel hates the name the media's given her but it seems to have stuck. She had Ethan paint the stars and stripes of the American flag on her helmet—it's supposed to be ironic, she says, has something to do with the movie *Easy Rider*—but she's mad that *Uncle Sam* makes her sound like a guy.

"The media calls you the Never Never Gang," Tucker says. "Never get caught. Never grow up."

"Guess the media will never get sick of cute nicknames."

"Give me the real names. Maybe I can find out something we can use."

"I don't know their real names. Maybe one of them, just the first name, but . . . I don't know, it's probably a fake, too."

"So what is it?"

Ethan. It's *Ethan.*

"Miles," I say.

"Which one is he?"

"The other one. The one who didn't rush three days ago. He wears that gross wolf mask instead of a helmet."

"The Beast of Brooklyn. *Miles*, huh? Not much to go on."

On the screen, the chauffeur has just revealed she is in fact a woman, and—*bingo*—the daughter of the old guy she's been driving around.

"So what's my plan when Mobius shows up?" I ask. "Assuming I make it that long, what do I do, hope he's in the mood to get chatty?"

"You think you can have your phone with you when you meet him?"

"I guess."

"Have your phone stashed in a pocket. Call me, I can listen in. Just get him talking as much as you can. Act like maybe you want to stay in the game after you needle up, like maybe you're thinking he could hook you up with a job dealing or something. Anything to get him to spill the beans."

"*Spill the beans.* Who says that? Are the beans in your watched pot that never boils?"

This makes Tucker smile, and it's nice, sharing a smile with this boy, despite the distance between us. The distance that sitting side by side in this theater cannot erase. Tetra is Tucker's past. It's my present. And perhaps that's too big a chasm to cross.

"Okay," I say. "But what if I can't have my phone with me?"

"Then you wear this." He reaches into one of his many pockets and pulls out a wire coiled up like a lock of hair. "This end like a Q-tip's the mic, so make sure it's clipped on you somewhere it can pick up what's being said, but keep it out of sight." From a different pocket, he pulls out a black plastic box about the size of a C battery. "You have to put the recorder within a fifty-yard radius of the mic. You have somewhere you could stash it?"

"Sure. In my room upstairs. That should be close enough—if I meet Mobius at the house. And then I just ask him stuff? That's the plan?"

"You have a better idea?"

"Me not having a better plan doesn't make yours suck any less."

"I'd trade places with you, if I could. You know that."

"Yeah. For one more hit of tetra, I bet you would."

"I'd do it for you, Alana." He leans closer. "I'd shoulder the weight of all this."

He pushes my beanie back from my forehead, wincing

when he sees the new cut I've earned. "You gotta know how much I care about you." Tucker studies my face. His breath so close I can feel it on my lips. "I wish I could smuggle you back to Jersey with me."

"Not Nebraska?"

"You'd hate it." Tucker beams and I love his smile, but there's no spark when he goes to kiss me. Tucker is safe and strong and the opposite of electric.

"We can't." I turn my cheek, tugging my beanie back down over my forehead.

"I'm sorry." His voice is small as he sinks back in his chair. "I always thought I was crazy not to do that."

"It's not that I never wanted to."

"Just not now." He sounds hurt, but also hopeful, like I might want to again in the future. And maybe I will. But I'm trying to stay in the present. Like Ethan says—focus on the now.

I put my hand on Tucker's. "Will you go to see my mom again for me? Talk to her about my brother?"

"I'll try. Of course. Alana, I . . . I know your bro got hurt by a breakneck," Tucker says, his voice tender. "Monroe told me when I was assigned as your handler. I never wanted to pry. But your mom . . . she said you were there when it happened."

I lean back in my chair, keeping my eyes on the screen. Sealing myself off.

"Why'd you never tell me, Alana?"

"I don't see how it's any of your business."

"You never wanted to talk about it? I've always been here for you. I've tried. I mean, I . . . your mom thinks you blame yourself. She said you feel like you should have been able stop it."

"I should go." I'm already out of my seat.

"Alana, please . . ."

"Just get me out of this, Tucker." I'm pushing past him, heading for the entrance. "All of this."

"You can't blame yourself. It wasn't your fault."

"How the hell would you know?"

The guy four rows up starts yelling for us to be quiet.

So I do him a favor, and leave.

TWENTY-SEVEN

I stride through the foyer, heading for the glass doors to the dark street outside, dressed in another girl's clothes, holding the keys to another girl's scooter, but I just want to be the girl I was before all this. Before Reuben was injured. Before Sidewinder struck. Before tetra.

The girl with dreadlocks leans over the counter and asks me what I thought of the stupid film. I stare at her, tears streaming down my face. Then I glance back toward the door to Screen Two, half expecting Tucker to come running out after me to make sure I'm okay.

He doesn't. And at the exit, I have my hand on the glass door, ready to shove back out into the warm night, when I stop cold.

The cars are black-hole black. Shiny in the electric night. Three sedans, two SUVs. All unmarked. Not TRU vehicles, but it's clear from their formation that they're here for me—federal agents, keeping their distance from the theater's entrance, giving themselves room in case I burst out through these doors, rushing on tetra.

But I don't have any tetra.

The scooter Aces lent me is locked up along with my helmet, just a little ways down the now-cordoned-off block. I'd never get to it before getting arrested. Or shot.

I dash back through the foyer and push through the door into Screen Two as Tucker's making his way out; we run right into each other, him holding on to me so I don't fall over.

I back up to get a good look at him, shaking myself loose of his grip. "Did you bring them here?"

"Who?"

"Whoever's in the unmarked vehicles lined up outside."

"The feds?" His eyes grow huge, his fear unmistakably real. "Why would I have brought them?"

"I don't know. Because of Idra. Because I'm out of control . . ."

"I lost my tail at Canal Street, Alana."

"Then maybe you had another tail. All I know is they're here."

"Emergency exits might set off an alarm." Tucker glances about, prospecting for a better plan. "There has to be another way out."

"Yeah—it was called you bringing me tempo."

"Will you stop calling it that?"

"Oh, quit being so delicate." I sprint back into the foyer, where the girl working the concession stand is in the middle of making a smoothie that involves a lot of spinach.

"Excuse me," I say. "This is awkward, but I'm kind of on a date here." I gesture toward Screen Two, and Tucker, who is sweating profusely in his Yankees cap. "Anyway I found out he's been seeing my best friend behind my back."

"Son of a bitch." Dreadlocks throws a fistful of spinach on the floor.

"I know. Right? So anyway—she's outside. Waiting to talk to me."

"Give her hell, sister."

"I was thinking more of taking the back way out of here and, I don't know, maybe crying in bed and listening to Coldplay for two weeks."

Dreadlocks looks disappointed. Probably *hates* Coldplay.

"So . . . *is* there a back way?" I ask.

She gestures for me to follow her, opening a door in the back of the concessions area, but Tucker's running over to join me. "What are you gonna do?" he asks.

"What I always do. Run." I keep my voice down. Dreadlocks is waiting for me, probably eavesdropping, and Tucker is supposed to be a two-timing rat, not my lifeline to the world I've left behind. "Maybe you should come with me. This must mean Spaihts is a hundred percent onto you."

"I know," he says. "But if you get away then he can't prove I came here to meet you. If I run, it's like saying I'm guilty."

"I know the feeling. But what if something happens to you? What if Spaihts goes after you like he did Monroe? I should just turn myself in."

"And then what—we both end up dead?"

Tucker's right. And if Spaihts kills us both, he wins whatever game he's playing. And Reuben gets to spend the rest of his life thinking his sister was a breakneck.

"Come with me," I tell Tucker. "Run with me."

"And leave you without an ally inside TRU?" He takes a step back, shaking his head.

"Then be careful," I tell him.

"You too."

I follow the girl's natty dreads through a storage room where obscure movie posters go to die, and I search for something I can use as a weapon or as a disguise, but it's slim pickings. The mop in the corner could double as a bad wig and a half-decent shinai, if I pulled the stringy part off the long wooden handle. But I'm desperate, not crazy. Okay, perhaps I'm crazy—I'm considering hiding inside a box full of compostable cups.

Just inside the back door, a vintage-but-sporty bike leans against a box full of T-shirts. The front tire's flat, but beggars can't be choosers. After she unlocks the back door, I grab the girl by her dreadlocks and yank her backward so I can steal the bike. She screams as I haul her past me, tripping her legs out from under her, then throwing her into a cardboard box full of fluorescent bulbs shaped like lightsabers. She's been super helpful. The least I can do is cushion her fall.

"Sorry!" I yell as she curses behind me. I swing the door all the way open, grabbing the bike. Then I hop onto the skinny saddle and rattle down a series of concrete steps.

Since the front tire is flat, the shock of concrete travels up through the handlebars and all through my body, as if the bike's an extension of my slow-motion bones. Then, when I hit the end of the steps, I make the last drop with a little too much momentum and go flying over the handlebars. My spine hits the ground with a crack.

This crap is *way* easier on TTZ.

"West?"

It's a woman's voice, yelling from one end of the alley. The shape of her is silhouetted against headlights. The other end of the alley looks clear, though, so that's the direction I point the bike as I jump onto the skinny saddle again and start pummeling the pedals. *Why is this bike seat the size of a toothpick?* It's like the bike's kicking me in the butt as I haul my butt past the trash cans and dumpsters and all the trash people have carefully not put in the trash cans and dumpsters. There's so much broken glass in this alley, I'm sure my back tire is flat by now too.

"West!" The woman shouts behind me. "Stop! Hit the ground now or I shoot!"

I duck down against the bike, pressing into the frame and handlebars, bracing for gunfire, hammering at the pedals, but my escape route up ahead is being closed off—a black

SUV's sealing that end of the alley.

I skid to a stop, then spin around and start pedaling again, pointing the other way, holding on to the fact that whoever I'm now hightailing it toward silhouetted up ahead has not taken a shot at me.

Yet.

"West!"

The voice is louder now. So loud I'm almost—boom! I slam into whoever it is.

And it's Small. *Agent* Small. Her face is about two inches from mine as we roll on the concrete. I scramble off her, reach for the bike, and find the front wheel tacoed.

"Please," she says, scrambling around on the ground for her gun. "Let me bring you in."

I throw aside the bike and start running. I'm out of the alley. Heading away from the theater on an empty street. I'm exposed. An easy target. But Bleecker Street up ahead is bustling. There, I can get lost in a crowd of people and go to ground.

My legs feel like they're sinking in quicksand. Come on, *accelerator*. Burn some adrenaline. Burn *something*.

A car's coming up behind me, gaining on me, breathing down my neck. It's like a predator, silent but hungry, and I glance back, expecting to see Agent Small behind the wheel of something ferocious, but instead there's the Tesla.

Rapunzel's car, though it's not really hers. It's *ours*, which means it's really JB's. But who cares whose name's on the title, it belongs to the breaknecks. The Never Never Gang. And I'm ready to Peter Pan my way back to Harlem.

The car slows as it pulls alongside me, and I grab for the door, cranking it open, then I'm diving inside and pulling the door shut as the Tesla squeals out, hanging a left on Bleecker.

"Keep down!" Davis yells as gunshots ring out and the rear windows shatter.

"What the hell are you doing here?"

"Following you," he says, stomping down the accelerator. "*West.*"

TWENTY-EIGHT

irens explode on the street behind us, and the street
ahead's crowded with slow-moving cars. Davis swerves
into the wrong lane, dodging oncoming traffic.

"Are you insane?" I yell.

"I'm trying to get us out of here." He spares me a quick
scowl. "Or do you want to hang out with your buddies back
there some more?"

"What are you talking about? They're after me. They had
me cornered—"

"I was parked close enough to hear that woman calling
you *West*. Shouting at you like she knew you."

"They do know me. I've been arrested, remember?"

"And then they track you down at the movies. No. *No.*
Something's not right." He takes a hand off the steering
wheel so he can point a finger in my face. It's close enough
I'm tempted to bite it off. "You've got some explaining to do."

The Tesla rides up onto the sidewalk, scattering pedestrians and clipping a stop sign.

"Keep your hands on the wheel," I scream. "You're gonna hurt someone."

"Who was that guy you met at the theater?"

"What guy?"

"The guy you were whispering to before you headed out back and I split for the car. I was in the foyer. I saw you."

"He's no one."

"First I thought he was your boyfriend. Thought I'd followed you all the way to Queens and then all the way here for nothing."

"You followed me to Queens, too?"

"Been watching you all day."

The sirens shriek louder behind us, and Davis hangs a left through a red light—causing a thousand car horns to howl in protest—but up ahead's a wall of brake lights. Davis decelerates, and all of a sudden we're not moving at all.

"Tell me you have some tempo," I say.

"There's one hit in the glove compartment. Stashed for an emergency." Davis backs up, spins the car around. Then takes off again.

"One of us should dose up," I suggest. "Draw them off."

"Yeah? Let me guess who you think that should be."

"You take it then. Something. This car's too slow."

"Not the car—the city."

"What if we split it?" I say as Davis cuts right onto

Thompson, our back end sailing up onto the curb before he gets it under control.

"Split the tempo? How? You want to bite it in half?"

Up ahead's another red light, and cross traffic's streaming through the intersection but Davis guns the Tesla toward it anyway.

"Tell me you see that city bus." I fumble for my seat belt, pulling it across my body to strap myself in.

"I see it."

The bus blasts its horn, blistering my eardrums as we shoot into the intersection, and we are six inches from being steamrolled.

Two inches.

No inches.

The bus clips the back end of the Tesla, sending us into a tailspin, and we're still spinning as we smash through a wall of glass. A mannequin crashes through our windshield, its head in my lap as we grind to a halt amid crumbling drywall and tumbling shelves.

The mannequin's eyeless face stares up at me, her curly black wig off-kilter, while Davis moans in the seat beside me and I fight to control my breathing. Can't go into shock.

This is not a safe place to hide.

Can't get my door open, though. Something's pinning it shut.

"Come on," I yell at Davis, unclipping my seat belt and shoving aside the mannequin. I start to crawl out through the broken windshield, jagged glass snagging my leggings and piercing my skin. It's as if the car's grown talons and is clawing at me, trying to hold me inside it.

Davis claws at me, too.

He's shuffled over to the passenger seat and has both hands wrapped around my right ankle, blood gushing from the top of his head. He must have been trying to stem the bleeding, because his fingers are all wet and sticky.

"Help me," he wheezes. "Please."

A woman's dress floats down and lands on my head, and I snatch it away.

The people coming after us can help Davis better than I can. They can get him the medical care he needs. Then they'll lock him up someplace, which will keep him away from me. As sick as it sounds, Davis being hurt is a neat solution to the problem of him being onto me.

But neat is not my strong suit. And I am sick of sounding sick.

I twist around and crawl back into the Tesla, recutting myself on the jagged bits of windshield. "Show me," I say, finally getting my ankle free of his grip. "Show me the places that hurt."

He does.

"You just pointed at all of you."

"My ribs," Davis whispers, then winces, and, man, I thought this kid could *scowl*. His wince makes his face look like a punctured soccer ball.

I snatch the dress off the hood and rip it in two, wrapping half of it around Davis's head like a turban to stem the bleeding.

"Are you cut anywhere else?"

"Don't know."

"Can you move?"

"Give me the tempo," he says. "In the glove compartment."

"You can't dose up. You're hurt too bad."

"Fastest way to reach a hospital. Only way to not get arrested. Come on. Don't let me go out like this."

"I don't think—"

"It's not your decision." He goes to say something else but passes out, slumping forward against the dashboard, his face pressed at the glove compartment.

"Miles!" I shout, as if he's still conscious.

Those shiny black cars could already be circling like buzzards outside.

I have to put all my weight against all of Davis to leverage him back in his seat. *Dead* weight, but he's breathing, still has a pulse, so he's not dead yet.

The glove compartment's full of the usual useless glove-compartmenty things—parking tickets and gum wrappers, a mini flashlight and broken sunglasses. I find a pack of Marlboro Reds but no bullet of tetra. I squeeze the carton of cigarettes in my fist instead of screaming. And that's when I notice something small and hard hidden inside the pack.

I find the single dose of tetra concealed between the cigarettes, and before I even think about what I'm doing, I've shaken the dose to arm it and the bullet is at my lips, then slipping between my front teeth and I'm biting down, my thumb at the release.

Instinct kicking in.

I hear the sirens now. They're out there already, and they'll be able to help Davis much better than I can. But that's not what he wants. So as I hit the release, I lean forward and grab Miles by the back of his head with my free hand. Then I have both hands on him, pulling his punctured-soccer-ball face toward me. I get my hand on his jaw, working it open, and then, like I'm doing CPR and giving him the breath of life—definitely *not* like I'm kissing him—I puff half my mouthful of tetra into his mouth. I close his jaw and he shakes as his eyes pop open.

"Can you move?" I ask, and Davis responds by moving in to kiss me. Not breath-of-life style, but not like he's trying to suck my face either. He just pecks a little kiss on my cheek.

It's sweet, which is weird.

And then Davis is crawling out of the broken car in his makeshift turban. And I am crawling after him, wading through the carnage of the store, feeling my rush come on.

TWENTY-NINE

I've always been strictly a day tripper. Running for TRU meant rushing at rush hour, which never meant when the sun was all the way hidden and the city burned lights in its place.

But now as I move, those lights move with me, as if each one's a comet, smearing the sky and showering me with their sparkling tails. It's like Manhattan was never really a city at all—it's a spaceship we've been building, one that's finally been launched into the cosmos. And tetra is at the controls.

Davis and I are on Broadway, weaving between moving cars as we pass them. Traffic is light and fast, but we're the fastest thing on the road. We've left the feds in the distance behind us, and we're safe now.

Except that Davis is injured. Bleeding out. I have to get him to a hospital or at least get him home. On half a dose each, I've no idea how long we have left.

But the lights.

Everywhere.

The buildings are volcanoes in endless eruption. Every car crawls with fireflies. And I wish Tucker could point out all the constellations to me as I spin through the ripple of headlights, marveling as the Fourth Dimension sets fire to the city, illuminating the spaces where colors get born.

If only Ethan were here to feel this with me. His skateboard straddling a supernova and swooping down wormholes. *I have to show him.* And to think I imagined Mobius's tempo to not be strong enough. *This was only half a dose.* Imagine what a whole dose would feel like. Imagine double-dosing, then feeling the magic of the glittery witching hour at a thousand BPMs.

I have to keep squinting, since the glove compartment had an emergency dose of tempo but not an extra pair of flight goggles to go with the ride. Having to squint because of the speed is frustrating. It gets in the way of seeing the lights. But I soak them up and throw away all my thinking. I wriggle through the traffic at warp speed with the world aflame.

But Davis is hurt. He could be dying.

He's fast. Even faster than I am. His turban head is glistening, blood seeping through the shiny dress I bandaged him up in. And I know this is dire, that Davis needs help, soon, but I can't help laughing when I see him in the Fourth Dimension, racing through the city with a bright green dress wrapped around his head. He looks like something out of *Aladdin*. Apart from all the blood.

It's not funny. The dress is more red than green now. But I laugh anyway. Can't help it. And I've never laughed on tetra, just like I've never rushed at night, and it suddenly occurs to me we have been doing this all wrong.

Davis glances at me, sharing the moment inside our blur of speed, and he's grinning—a new look for him. So much better than wincing or scowling. Perhaps it's because he's all glimmery, but he even looks beautiful. Just as beautiful as everything else is tonight. All these buildings. So many stories. Each monstrous block a puzzle piece melting into the next one. Davis and I feeling everything flow. And just like the stars are only constellations when you connect them together, maybe we only have meaning when our stories collide.

He tries laughing with me. He must like it as much as I do, since he keeps doing it. We are drunk on laughing and lights.

"Want to leap?" he shouts, pointing at the cars we're hurtling past.

"You shouldn't," I try to say back. Hard to speak. Laughing's better.

"I'm peaking," he shouts.

"It'll be over soon."

"Don't say that."

"It was just half a dose."

"I'm going to start leaping."

He bounds ahead of me, then he's up on the traffic, leap-frogging from car roof to truck roof to downtown bus, the vehicles like glowing lily pads fireworking beneath him, step by scintillating step.

And as I follow, my feet landing in the small dents his left behind, I'm not laughing. I'm just screaming his name. Soon I don't even notice the lights anymore. Davis needs help. But he's so fast, and so far ahead.

I don't reach him until the Williamsburg Bridge. Don't even know why he was heading this way but we're both coming down, and the less Davis is feeling the rush the more it seems like the top of his head is missing. His movements are jerky, all stiff joints and floppy limbs as he stumbles onto the deserted pedestrian walkway, clawing at the guard cage to hold himself up. He's facedown by the time I've closed the last distance between us, and when I turn him over, he is greasy with blood.

His face is pale, features sinking inward. Never mind punctured soccer ball, it's as if his brain's been sucked out and his skull has collapsed. Blood trickles from beneath his sopping makeshift turban, pooling into the craters of his eyes.

"Miles," I say. "You have to hold on."

Traffic growls past on the bridge.

"I'll get help," I say. "I can flag someone down."

"Don't leave." His voice is all shredded.

"I have to. You need an ambulance."

"Matt," he whispers.

"What?"

"Matthew Miller. My name . . ."

"Your real name."

When he nods, I tell him not to move.

"Please." His eyes droop closed, then flash back open. "I got two sisters. Make . . . make sure JB gets them their money. My share."

"Of course." I sit so I can cradle him in my lap, and a rush never came to a more screeching halt.

"JB knows where they are. I don't want them . . . going back. On the streets. My dad . . ." Davis—*Matt*—pauses to cough up blood. "He sold us. I never told anyone at the house. Was ashamed."

I don't really know what this means—his dad *sold* them, to what?

Not sure I want to know.

"Can't let them go back," he says. "The *money*."

"JB'll give it to them. I promise."

"You're with TRU."

I shake my head, but then nod. "I used to be."

"Gonna take down JB and the others."

"A breakneck crippled my brother," I say, as if I need an excuse. "That's why I went to Queens this afternoon. To that park."

"Kid in the wheelchair. I saw him. Watched you watching him."

"I should have taken better care of him. The day he got hurt. I should have . . ."

"Nothing can change it."

"I know."

"Whatever you're doing . . . make it wait till my sisters have the money. Please wait."

He can't die. I won't let him. *If he lives, he'll tell JB who I really am.* But that doesn't matter. I mean, it matters. Of course it matters. But even if they know the truth, even if I can't stop Mobius and even if everything I've done is for nothing, Davis—*Matt*—cannot die.

"Hold on," I say. "Let me flag someone down. I'll get you help."

"I'm so cold." He reaches up, feebly trying to clutch at my arm and pull it across him. "No help now. Just promise. My sisters . . . they're so . . ." He starts coughing again. It's more like choking. His lungs are probably wet with blood.

"They're so what?"

"Small," he says, and a tiny smile pries its way onto the wreck of his face.

"Yeah. My brother's like that."

"Then you know how they need you." His eyes flutter, trying to remain open. "Nice rushing with you, West." He slurs the words, but they're sweet anyway. Surprising and sweet, like when he pecked me on the cheek after I gave him his last dose of life.

"You too, Matt," I say, and as his eyes close and his head

droops, I let go of him too harshly, the horror of his dead body rekindling the rush inside me in the worst possible way. As his skull hits the concrete with a thud, I'm twitching and glitchy and seeing things that aren't there. It's like I'm flipping through TV channels—one second it's Davis dead on this bridge, but then it's GoPro, then Tucker. It's Ethan, then me. And it keeps being me as I slap my face and claw at my cheeks, trying to make the vision stop. I want to pluck my eyes from their sockets but I'm too busy grasping at the back of my neck, right where my spine meets my skull, as if my fingers might possess some hitherto untapped power to peel back my skin and pluck out pain. Because shooting up into my brain and the bone that surrounds it is a pain unlike any I've ever known before.

I know what to call it, though. Just like I know what to call Miles Davis now.

Matt Miller is the name of the dead breaker before me.

The Needles is the time bomb exploding inside.

THIRTY

The sun's about to creep into view as I creep up the steps to the front door. My key's new enough it sticks in the lock, and I work it loose with fingers covered in dried blood. Some of the blood is mine. Most of it is Matt Miller's. His death is a secret I can share with no one, and as I scuttle inside, my brain picks at the scab of that secret, while my endorphins float like dead fish in the rivers of my veins.

The Needles have subsided, in the sense that I no longer feel my spine like a javelin piercing the base of my skull. But the Needles don't end. They are the ending.

We have bank jobs scheduled for this morning's rush hour, so there's a good chance people are up already. Ethan's probably wide awake, painting down in the basement, and doubtless JB's been up all night reading some book.

No one's in the hall, though. No sounds echo out of the kitchen.

The stairs screech as I climb each painful step so slow, spiders could spin webs around me. My clothes are bloody and ripped. My bones seem to be gnawing their way out through my skin. A gash on my right thigh probably needs stitches, and my left ankle, which never fully healed, is swelling back up. But I am so much more broken on the inside, my body betraying me, aging past its point of being useful, just when I needed it most. I was a runner. An accelerator. Now I'm a slo-mo has-been and no good to anyone. Inside my room, I slide to the floor, wedging myself against the door to make it snap shut.

So much blood. These clothes. This skin. I should go scrub it off. Wish I could scrub the truth off too. Because though I gave Matt a fighting chance, I lost control to the rush. Again. I should have been steering Matt to a hospital, not staring at the pretty lights. Maybe because I only had half a dose, I remember the rush clearly—too clearly—so I remember all my wrong choices. I remember how much I liked being out of control.

Matt got what he wanted, though. Knew his time was up and he chose the same thing GoPro chose when she leaped through a nineteenth-floor window and smashed onto Thirty-Sixth Street.

"Lana?" It's Ethan's voice through the door. "You ready? JB wants everyone downstairs."

Of course he does. Rush hour is approaching.

"I'll be ready."

"You okay?"

There's a dull ache behind my left eye, as if the eyeball has swollen up and is pressing my brain. I'm as cold as the worst parts of winter. "I'm okay," I tell Ethan, sobbing in silence, leaning my head against the door and wishing I could let him in here with me. I crave his warmth. The afterglow we shared. The rush we felt together, side by side.

But who I really need is Tucker. I need him to show me how to survive a cruel cold world of slow motion from which I'll never break free. I need him to take me somewhere safe and show me the constellations. Perhaps the stars could feel like enough.

I hug my arms around my torso, trying to rub warmth into my arctic bones.

"I'll be down in a few minutes," I say, then wait till I hear the creak of Ethan's feet down the stairs.

In the shower, I make the water so hot it burns my skin but I still feel so cold inside, my body chemistry all frozen flawed formulas. I sit in the tub, letting the water gush over me, feeling like I might die from exposure as two thousand cold turkeys approach, gobbling and gloating, ready to peck me to pieces.

I want to dose up with the others. *Bring on the bank job so I can bite down on the bullet.* I'll risk it. *I will do whatever it takes to not feel like this.* Some animal lurks in the pit of my stomach, pumping my heart with noxious blood. A creature that demands I feed it. And I don't know how to cut the creature out of me. I only know how to satiate the need.

Scared I'll break down and dose up, I decide to make it so JB and the others won't let me rush, even if I beg them for tempo. They mustn't know I'm derailing, of course. Or that I've needled up. I can't tell them about Davis—*Matt.* I have to just look like I woke up sick.

Shouldn't be too hard, the state I'm in. But I can't take any chances. So after I bandage my left ankle and dress my wounds, I pull on jeans and a long-sleeved shirt, then chug as much shampoo as I can handle, thinking it will make me throw up when I get downstairs. Being sick will be my savior, keeping me from temptation. Because I can't risk never going home again. *I need Mom. I need Reuben.* And I need to tell my little brother the terrible truth about what happened on that day last summer. Perhaps I'll tell him the even worse truth about the person I have become.

The shampoo smells like orange icing and lavender. It tastes like poison. I don't bother toweling off, so I arrive in the kitchen soggy and queasy, and try to move like I woke up ill, not like I'm derailing. This means slow is acceptable, but I can't be as stop-animation stiff as my body would like.

"Jesus," JB says, upon seeing me enter the room. "You look like ass."

"I don't feel so hot."

"Yeah. Hold that thought." He turns back to the others.

Ethan and Rapunzel are ready for action—dressed in jeans and leather jackets, bags at their feet with pads and helmets stuffed inside—but Aces is perched up on the kitchen counter, looking like she just rolled out of bed and is planning on heading back there. Her flimsy pink tank top's rumpled, and her cotton booty shorts were definitely not built for breakneck speed.

JB's barking into his phone, waiting for it to translate what he's saying, then showing the screen to Aces. She responds by saying something in Italian to the phone, then bounces the conversation back into JB's court, courtesy of whatever app he's using.

My left eye throbs in its socket, a terrible reminder of the Needles. As the shampoo thunders deep in my guts, a storm brewing inside me, I have to hold on to the granite counter to hold myself up.

Even if JB's too preoccupied to be concerned by my appearance, at least Ethan and Rapunzel ought to be fussing over me by now. If only they'd look at me, they could see how sick I am. But they seem determined to *not* look at me.

"What time was this?" JB says into his phone, then he stares at it, waiting. This is followed by the handoff to Aces, who arches her eyebrows as she reads his translated words on the screen.

"Ten," she says, her accent adding a little *ah* sound to the end of the word, but her saying it in English has saved JB and his phone a step.

JB looks at me, chews his lip, then goes back to his phone. "Why?" he asks.

Aces knows this word, so she rattles off something in Italian, and the words drip with the same icy confidence she pours on everything, but she spoke too soon for JB's app to keep up, so she has to repeat it, more slowly this time, and I catch my name—Lana—in the middle of whatever she's trying to say.

The shampoo's rumble of thunder evolves into a serious low-pressure system while JB spends what seems like forever reading the translation on his phone. It's as if whatever Aces said can only be expressed in English using five times the number of words she just used in her native tongue.

Then JB turns to face me. Behind him, Aces remains cool as gelato, but JB's face is sunburn-red.

"Where did you go last night?" he asks me.

When I burp, it smells like lavender. And tetra—the tang of nail polish and gasoline.

"Is there a problem?"

JB glances at Ethan and Rapunzel, who keep staring at the floor. "Just answer the question, Lana." JB holds up his phone, as if it's Exhibit A. "Seems like you went to the Village."

"I don't remember *following me* being on the list of things you do for your twenty percent."

"I didn't follow you. Davis did."

Matt Miller, I want to say. He had a real name and real little sisters, and now he is dead and the Never Never Gang is one member short.

Never Never Gang.

I think of that Peter Pan movie, the Disney thing, the little Lost Boy saying *to die would be an awfully big adventure.* And when I think about Matt being dead in my arms, I don't think dying is a big adventure. I think it's more an awfully small reward for having lived.

"Why would Davis follow me?"

"Beats me. But he took the Tesla and followed you as you cruised about on one of Aces's scooters. They all have anti-theft trackers," JB says. "Sends a GPS signal to an app."

"Handy."

"So we know Aces's scooter is still there, parked in the Village."

My shampooed stomach issues a hurricane warning.

"I can go get it back," I say. "No problem."

"I'd rather you tell us where Davis is."

"How should I know?"

"You two don't get along, it's no secret. Davis doesn't really do *getting along*. But if you saw him . . ."

"I didn't."

JB's face turns even redder. "That's strange," he says. "Seeing as Davis pocket-dialed Aces at about ten o'clock last night. She says she answered and heard gunshots—along with your voice. Screaming."

"That's crazy."

"Pretty crazy," JB says, nodding, like he agrees with the sentiment but not with me pursuing this line of defense.

So I need a new line of defense.

"I was trying to score tempo," I say, which isn't totally untrue, and now even Ethan and Rapunzel stare at me. "I went back to my original source. What? That's not allowed?"

"You never told us who the source is," Ethan says.

"Someone who gets better tempo than any Mobius comes up with. Yours is weak."

"There's only two types of tempo worth taking," JB says. "The tempo Mobius deals, and the tempo TRU gives its runners."

"So maybe my guy got some of that—they're little black bullets. Straight from Trinity Pharmaceuticals, it says on the side. They invented the stuff, right? You ever thought theirs might be better?"

"How did your contact get his hands on that?" Ethan asks.

"Beats me. But he wanted more money than I'd brought along." I start to get on a roll, snowballing my lie till it's big enough for these breaknecks. I'm good at lying, I realize. Far too good. "He tried to rip me off. And he had a gun. Started threatening me. But then Davis appears, getting in the guy's face, telling him to back off. You know what he was like." I pause the lie long enough for me to let out a very real sob, and I put my face in my shaking hands. "I'm sorry . . . it's all my fault."

"Where's Davis?" JB takes a step toward me.

"We managed to get into the Tesla, under fire, but Davis crashed the car as we were trying to escape. Had to split up. And Davis was injured. I was hoping he'd be here and now I don't . . . I don't know."

I crumple to the floor. Remembering Matt Miller dead in my arms and the Needles detonating my brain. *And I just left Matt's body behind for someone to stumble upon.*

Now Rapunzel's beside me, holding my shoulders. "Take it easy, love. Shit got bad, but it's gonna be okay now. Right, JB? Lana just made a mistake."

"What about Davis?" he asks.

Rapunzel waves a hand in the air, dismissing the question. "He shouldn't have gone snooping around after her. He's a pain in the ass."

"That's cold," Ethan says, his brother momentarily too stunned to speak.

But then JB grows as tall as his crooked body allows. He straightens his stooped shoulders and puffs out his chest, bellowing, "That pain in the ass is one of us! He's been here for months, Rapunzel. Living here, under this roof. Under my protection!"

"Then you should bloody well go look for him," she snaps.

"I told Davis to get to a hospital," I say.

"And this was in the Village?" JB glowers at me as I nod, his fists shaking at his sides.

"Calm down," Ethan tells his brother. "It's not Lana's fault. And it's not your fault, either."

"No. It's this dealer." JB gets in my face, spitting the words. "You'll tell me who he is. You'll set up another meeting, and I'll make him pay for hurting my boy."

"Take it easy." Ethan has his hand on his brother's shoulder, pulling him away from me. "We gotta find Davis. That's all that matters. You take Ishmael, and we'll take Aces's scooters. We'll split up. Divide and—"

The phone buzzes in JB's hand.

"What?" he barks, taking the call without first looking to see who it's from. Then he doesn't say anything. Just listens.

The shampoo stomach situation has moved beyond force of nature. I'm a soapy suicide bomber and sick is about to hit the fan.

"Mobius is coming," JB says, ending the call, and he no longer looks angry. He now looks afraid.

"What?" Ethan looks pretty afraid, too. "When?"

"*Shortly* was the word he used."

"Why don't you tell him what happened?" Ethan drums his fists together. "If Davis gets caught, things could unravel. He could hand us over, cut a deal and give up this address. Him being missing undermines the whole operation. Mobius needs to know."

JB shakes his head. "Davis won't say anything. He cares too much about his sisters. Betraying us would mean they don't get his share of the money—and besides, you're getting too far ahead of things. We don't even know Davis has been caught. It's not like he's been leaving fingerprints behind at his bank jobs. Far as people know, Davis is just some greasy-haired kid. He probably got fixed up at some clinic and is about to walk back through our door."

I throw up everything inside me. The orange icing and lavender shampoo, the chewed-up aspirin taste of tetra, coffee swirls, and chunks of vegan doughnut. I'm like Ben & Jerry's on a really bad day. Rapunzel holds on to me despite the fact my sick's splashing on her legs. She holds my head up, not letting me fall.

"Smells like soap," she says, laughing. "And petrol."

"Smells like *derailing*," JB says. "And bullshit. It's a shame Davis didn't pocket-dial someone who spoke English. Timebomb's not telling us the full story."

"I had to dose up," I whisper, spitting out lumps of sick. "We split the tempo in the glove compartment so we could get away."

"That complicates things." Ethan looks to his brother. "If Davis has been snatched up by the police, they'll suspect he's derailing and test him for tempo. Any hospital or clinic would too."

"Davis is no rat," JB says. "I'm telling you. Not with his sisters in the picture."

"And what if his sisters were offered a nice little witness protection action into the bargain?" Rapunzel asks.

"Then we roll with a contingency plan. We relocate. I told you, I worry about this stuff so you all don't have to. The important thing right now is Mobius not knowing anything about this." JB looks at each of us in turn, holding my gaze the longest.

"I don't like it," Ethan says.

"I don't either," JB mutters. "But I'll put the word on the street, see what I can find out about our boy. In the meantime, we meet with Mobius and you all say nothing. Can't have him thinking we're screw-ups if you want to keep scoring tempo."

JB offers me a gnarled hand as he steps around my sick on the floor. Then he's helping me up, pulling me away from the mess I've made. He is surprisingly strong, and gentle. "That's what this all comes down to, right?" he says to me. "Scoring tempo. But going to this other dealer . . . I can't have that, Lana. And I *will* have his name from you." He leans me against the counter. "You come to me when you want anything. Don't matter what it is. We have to trust each other going forward."

"You still trust me?"

"I *understand* you. I've been there, remember? The next rush is all you want. But you came back here to face the music when you could have kept running. Means you know where you belong."

I hug my arms around the crooked stoop of his body. "I'm so sorry," I say into his bony shoulder.

"I know," he says, shushing me.

Ethan puts his leather jacket over my shoulders, since I can't stop shaking. *I'm freezing.* And Rapunzel's cleaning up the mess I made on the floor, telling me everything's going to be okay, while Aces just sits on the counter, silent and cold as she studies me. *She knows.* Perhaps they all do. They all know something is so wrong with me.

"Better get you cleaned up," JB says. "Gotta put on a good show for Mobius."

THIRTY-ONE

Mobius flicks the cherry of embers from the end of his cigarette, scattering ash on the hardwood floor. He ignores the empty mug JB nudged across the desk to serve as an ashtray, just as he ignores the chair JB's offered him. The man is deaf to attempts at small talk. When JB breaks the news that we're a breakneck short, Mobius remains expressionless, his gray eyes void of emotion as they roam around the room.

"Call Davis," Mobius says, interrupting JB's excuses. The man's voice is water dousing flames. "Get him here. Now."

"Already tried, breh." JB's working too hard to appear relaxed. "Davis isn't answering. You should have given me more warning that you were swinging by."

Mobius puts a hand on the desk, then leans across it and blows smoke in JB's face.

He waits until JB's finished spluttering.

Then he does the same thing again.

Ethan tenses beside me. We're huddled with Aces and Rapunzel in the corner, watching JB lose his cool in his big leather chair. The four of us could take Mobius down, but that's never going to happen. Mobius is the one source for the only illegal TTZ worth taking. That gives him all the power in this room.

He prowls over to us while JB pretends to call Davis.

"Still no answer," JB says, but Mobius is now busy staring at me. He is a shark dressed in scuffed Doc Martens and scruffy black clothes and I feel dead in the water as he studies me, leaning in so close I could count the hairs on his pockmarked jaw. His black hair's scraped back in a ponytail. His features are sharp enough to draw blood. He's too old to be an accelerator, but not so old he couldn't have been one. Bone-white skin and bad teeth, but no telltale signs he once was a breakneck.

I'm derailing, limp, and withered. The needling pain behind my left eye is searing my brain. But I force myself to meet the man's gaze.

"I'm new," I tell him, my voice feeble.

"You don't look new," he says. "You look all used up."

I study my bare feet on the hardwood floor, and he steps closer, his Doc Martens an inch from my bruised toes. "You're derailing," he says, sniffing at me. "I can smell you sweating it out."

"I gave her a dose last night." JB comes to my rescue.

"Lana needed a little extra practice."

"Lana's been all over the media." Mobius takes my chin, forcing me to look at him, his black leather gloves sticky on my flesh. "She doesn't need practice. She needs a leash. Do you know where Davis is, Lana?"

"No idea."

"You're lying." Mobius takes a final drag on his cigarette, then snuffs it out on the floor with the heel of his boot. "You can stop calling his phone, JB. Davis rushed last night, too."

"Copy that." JB's voice shifts several octaves higher. "Okay. We're on the same page. Great. I got the word out on the street for our boy . . . just wanted to get the full beta before I came to you—"

"I have more contacts than you." Mobius releases his grip on my chin and strolls back to JB's desk, as patient as he is powerful. "I have better contacts. So, rest assured, I know when we're on the same page."

"Hey, I'm an open book." JB attempts a smile. "You know all my pages."

"That's why I knew when you brought this wildcat home. *Timebomb*. She's a complete liability to your whole operation, which means a complete liability to me. It's also why I know one of your breakers showed up dead on the Williamsburg Bridge last night."

Everyone but Mobius stares at me.

My right eye twitches and my left eye throbs. Both eyes fill with tears.

"Dead?" JB shakes as he says the word. He takes off his Jets cap and sets it on the desk.

Ethan puts his arm around me.

"The truth," Mobius demands, lighting another cigarette. "From one of you who has the guts to speak it."

"Davis and Lana had bad blood between them," Ethan says, and JB's eyes go wide. He frantically shakes his head at his brother, but Ethan pushes on. "Was no fault of Lana's. Davis had it in for her since day one. She ran into some trouble last night and Davis was following her—he intervened, tried to help her, but he got hurt."

"Your brother should learn to talk as straight as you do," Mobius tells Ethan, and JB flushes a bitter shade of red. "Perhaps I can leave it in your hands to get rid of this wildcat?"

Ethan hugs me against him. "She's one of us, man. And she rushes as good as anyone."

"You're vouching for her?" Mobius studies the way Ethan is holding me. "Personally?"

"I trust her. So should you."

"How touching. It's on you, then. She either cleans up her act or I no longer come here, which means no more tempo— for any of you."

"Understood," Ethan says. His arm is warm around me, but I'm so cold I tremble against him. Hard to think right. My brain is like a city shut down by a blizzard.

Mobius turns to JB. "I suppose we can't expect accelerators to play it safe, can we? You at least have my money?"

"Give me a break, man. You just told me Davis is dead."

"Oh, I'm sorry. What did you want me to break?" Mobius takes a briefcase from the floor and sets it on the desk, crushing JB's Jets cap beneath it. "Your teeth?"

"Touch my brother, I'll break *you*," Ethan says, and I'm too weak to hold him back.

"You all want your tempo." Mobius sounds almost bored, but Ethan freezes beside me. "So get me my cut of the earnings."

"I gotta finish counting out all the cash," JB complains. "But I'll have it ready before you leave, I swear."

"Go on then. Get counting. I'll get started with your newest addition. Everyone not named Lana can get out."

Ethan gives my sore shoulders a final squeeze, then files out with the others, and I try to think of a way to buy some time. I need to get upstairs and set up that recorder Tucker gave me, hide the wire on my clothes.

"I have to go to the bathroom," I say.

"Perfect timing." Mobius rummages around in his briefcase and pulls out a clear plastic cup with a screw-on lid. He tosses it across the room to me. "You can piss in this."

He follows me to the bathroom, then waits outside the door. Inside, I need to drum up a few drops or risk pissing off Mobius, but why does he need a *urine sample*, anyway?

I have more pressing questions, though. *Need to focus.* I have to get information from Mobius. Uncover enough that Vogler can bypass Spaihts and go to the mayor and the chief of police. *We can make the streets clean of tetra.* But my thoughts are all scrabbled. *Too much static.* The only clear thing inside me is my hunger for the last thing I need.

I lean on the sink, splashing water on my face and rinsing my mouth out. *Just one more rush.* I could push it. Push through the Needles. I peer at my face in the mirror, then down at my body in disgust, all wiped out and whiplashed and *old.* But why does my body get to decide I can't do tetra? I'm not ready to be a has-been. If I want to rush one more time, my body can *deal.*

Mobius bangs at the bathroom door, and my adrenaline starts flowing enough to get my pee flowing too.

"Here," I say, stepping out of the bathroom and handing Mobius the still-warm plastic jar. "Knock yourself out."

He's ready with a Ziploc, so I drop the little cup inside, then follow him back to JB's office.

"Sit." Mobius points at a chair facing the desk, and I wonder if he'll take JB's spot on the other side but he doesn't. He stands above me. And his questions get straight to the point.

"Name." Mobius has pulled a clipboard out of his briefcase. He slides a printed form onto it, clicks the nib out on a pen. "Real name."

"Lana."

"Last name?"

"Why do you need a last name?"

Mobius puts the clipboard on the desk and plucks the pack of cigarettes from his chest pocket—he takes one out and lights it, then studies its burning end. "You do know who I am?"

"I just know you're the dealer."

"Right. And you're the user. And seeing as I'm the only one dealing the drug you need, it stands to reason you should make a habit of not wasting my time." He sucks up a lungful of smoke. "I'm gonna need all your pedigree info. Real name. Date of birth. Social. You got a problem with this, that's fine, just get out. Plenty other would-be accelerators out there."

I give him a bunch of fake information, and he starts asking me about allergies, my medical history. He asks me when I first took TTZ, and how many times I have rushed. I stick to the lies I told JB when he recruited me. Then Mobius asks about headaches, pains at the base of my skull.

"No," I say, my left eyeball ballooning with each boom of my heart. "Nothing like that."

Such finality to the feeling. I'm not finished with tetra but the drug is finished with me. *I could risk one more rush, though.* GoPro pushed through four times after she'd first needled up.

I remember her smashing through the window. *Nineteen stories high, 141 Thirty-Sixth Street.* Before she jumped, GoPro said something about Mobius and how Mobius had been wrong.

Dead wrong.

He finishes scribbling on the form, then rubs out his cigarette on JB's desk and tells me to roll up my sleeves. Mobius digs into his briefcase again, and produces three plastic vials and a syringe.

"You okay with needles?" he asks, popping a needle out of silver foil and attaching it to the syringe.

"Not even remotely."

"Tough shit. Make a fist. Left arm . . . there you go."

He puts my arm on the desk beside him, makes me pump up a vein inside my elbow, then plunges the needle and begins to draw blood. After he's filled three vials, he labels them and drops them in a Ziploc.

"What are you testing me for?" I ask, my skin clammy and my insides queasy.

Mobius removes the form from the clipboard and staples it to the Ziploc. Then he packages everything into his briefcase.

"Here." He hands me a Band-Aid. "Keep some pressure on it."

"I don't get it. Why take my blood?"

Mobius scratches at the back of his neck, adjusts his skinny black ponytail. "You think you're special. So you think you're owed explanations. Maybe you even think you're doing me a favor. But you're replaceable, Lana. And you're owed nothing at all."

"Meaning you won't answer my questions."

He taps out another cigarette and sits on top of the desk as he lights it.

"Where does your tempo come from?" I ask.

He blows smoke in my face. Then taps ash on my lap. Hot red embers burn black on my jeans. "Why can't you tell me?" I bolt up, brushing off my thighs.

"Why do you need to know?"

"I bet *you* don't even know. I bet you're just the dealer, working for someone with more money and smarts than you. I bet it eats you up that you're stuck watching us from the sidelines."

"You'll end up on the sidelines, too." He holds his cigarette between us. "Burning all the way to nothing. And when you're gone, I will still be here, lighting them up and smoking them down."

"I hope you choke."

A faint smile flickers on his face. "I can see why they like you. Enjoy it while it lasts."

He kicks me toward the door. When I find Aces waiting outside, I don't need to say it's her turn. She just pushes past me into the room.

I climb the stairs as fast as my body allows. I have to get to my room and get my phone and get through to Tucker so I can tell him his plan worked even worse than I predicted. I need him to get me out of here. *Now.*

I've told too many lies. JB and the others are going to want to know more about this fictional dealer of mine. And as soon as Mobius looks up my pedigree information, he'll find out none of it's real.

So in my room, I grab my phone and call Tucker, but he

doesn't answer, no matter how hard I squeeze the stupid phone in my fist.

I try letting it ring once, then end the call, counting to five and calling back again, as if this is some signal we rehearsed or talked about and not something I just made up.

Still no answer.

I text him: *I need you. Here. Now.* I text him the address. I make sure the messages have sent. Then I text him the same thing again anyway.

My left eye feels twice its normal size and I squeeze it shut as I stuff a couple hundred dollars in my back pocket, along with my phone and the key to the scooter I left in the Village. I grab the black beanie. Pull on my Nikes. Must get ready to run. But I end up sitting on the edge of my bed, trembling, derailing, needled and panicked. I start thinking about Matt's two little sisters, and how, if I run now, I can't keep my promise to make sure they get his share of the money.

But there are other reasons I don't want to leave.

And tetra is the greatest reason of all.

My pack full of pads and spandex is open next to the bed and I rummage through it, thinking maybe JB stashed an emergency bullet in my pack like he stashed one in the Tesla's glove compartment. That would have been smart, and JB's a real thinker. So I start checking the little compartments and around at the seams because maybe the bullet's sewn in some special secret spot nobody knows about. I squeeze every inch of the backpack like I'm trying to get blood from a stone, and I'm sweating now, though still so cold, and this pack is totally devoid of the drug I need. But there are all sorts of nooks and crannies throughout the house, places where a dose of tempo might be stashed. Maybe I should hurry back downstairs for the fresh batch Mobius must have in that briefcase.

He'll answer my questions once I hit the release and start surging.

I get as far as imagining a bullet between my teeth, the taste of tetra on my tongue, then I'm bent over on the bed, clutching a pillow to my face as I scream.

If only I could scream this craving out of me. But all I can do is slam my fist at the mattress, then my thigh, and when I smack myself in the face, I'm afraid my left eyeball might pop because I'm hurting myself and I'm out of control and I am not even high.

So I go back to screaming into the pillow. And I bite my fist till it bleeds.

I have to be worth more than this. For Reuben. And for Mom. And for me. Otherwise what am I? Just a vessel for desire? Just a user that uses a drug that uses you back? It's like a snake eating its tail. And Sidewinder is the snake that did this to me, but I'll never find Sidewinder. I just have to go home, and give up. I have to crawl out of this rabbit hole, no matter how much I want to run.

THIRTY-TWO

I'm trying to get the window open when Ethan finds me. My plan's to find a fire escape or a solid stretch of drainpipe, slither down to street level and hail a cab.

"Need some fresh air?" Ethan cocks his head as he stares at me.

"Thought I might be sick again," I lie.

"Yeah, Mobius can have that effect on people. Want me to get you a bucket?"

"I'd rather you get this window open."

"Pretty sure it's painted shut. But Mobius split, if that makes you feel any better."

It doesn't. But I give up on the window. Just lean back against the wall.

"That bucket . . ." Ethan suggests.

"No. I'll be all right."

He shuts the door. "Just me and you," he says. "Want to tell me what's wrong?"

"Everything. Davis. Mobius. All of it."

He nods. Keeps his distance.

"So why'd Mobius take my blood?" I ask.

"Always been part of the deal." Ethan slips off his leather jacket, shows me his own arm—a Band-Aid inside his elbow. "JB says it's something about running tests to help fine-tune the tempo. Makes sure the formula's dialed in right. Mobius takes samples every time he meets with a breakneck to deal them their next doses. You get used to him."

"He threatened JB."

"I know he did." I've struck a nerve. "But what can we do? Mobius holds the drug over our heads."

"And you don't ever wonder how he's making it—or who's making it for him?"

"I didn't come up here to talk about Mobius. I came to talk about Davis."

I'm shaking. My whole body trembling like it did from withdrawal, as if those symptoms just can't wait to kick back in.

"You want this?" Ethan asks, offering me his jacket.

"Only with you in it."

He wraps his arms around me and I shudder against him. And he tells me Davis's death isn't my fault as I press my face into his chest.

"JB's gonna want vengeance," he says. "You'll have to give him the name of this dealer, and I won't be able to stop my brother from striking back. But we don't blame you, Lana.

We want you to come downstairs and join us."

"I need to stop," I say, my arms around his waist. "I need to leave."

"Where would you go?"

"Somewhere I can stop hurting people."

"I'd miss you," he says, so quiet I almost miss him saying it.

I pull back from his chest to stare up at him. "You don't even know me. I'm a blank space inside, remember?"

"Then let me in." He brushes my bangs from my face, tucking them behind my ear.

"What if you don't like what you see?"

His eyes study mine. "Try me."

I shake my head.

"Some other time, then." He runs his fingers through my hair. "I'll tell JB and the others you need a little space right now. They'll understand. Today's a hard one for all of us."

He kisses my forehead, and it feels so much better than anything I deserve, but it's over too soon. He's letting go of me. "I'll be downstairs if you need me."

"I need you."

I hold him against me. And he kisses me again. He kisses the scar above my eyebrow, his lips slightly open. He kisses my eyelids, my cheek, he's nearing my mouth.

He's a breakneck. I should not want to want him. But it's like trying not to want tetra. His fingers are on my neck, tracing patterns, touching my jaw. I open my mouth to kiss him, waiting for him to move his mouth close to mine, but he's taking too long to get there, so I take his face in my hands, taking control. When my lips touch his it's like I just hit the release, our tongues colliding, his mouth is so warm and so soft I could crawl up inside it. But then Ethan's pulling away from me, shaking his head.

"I can't," he says. "Not today."

"Because of Davis?"

"No, it's . . . listen, I know right now should be all that matters. Experiencing everything, no fear of the consequences. And I want to. I want *you*. It's just . . . come downstairs, okay? You'll understand."

"Kiss me again."

"I finished the painting, Lana. In the basement. I finished it last night and I'm gonna show it to everyone. We're doing this thing, like a send-off. I mean, JB's calling it a *memorial service*, but you know what he's like."

"It sounds sweet."

"I want you to see the painting. It's the right time and I want you to see it more than anyone."

"So show me," I say. "After you finish kissing me."

"You'll come down." Ethan grins. "If I kiss you?"

"Don't make it sound like a chore." I tug at his hair, pulling him toward me.

"Oh, it's not," he whispers, picking me up, and I wrap my legs around his waist, feeling myself come alive as I kiss this boy who is a breakneck, and I don't even know what I am anymore. I just know I'll go downstairs to see Ethan's painting. I'll join them for the send-off as a way to say good-bye. Then maybe I'll kiss Ethan again and feel the rush of his tongue touching mine, before I disappear from him forever.

THIRTY-THREE

I t looks more like a séance than a send-off. This room in the basement is where I found Ethan the sleepless night I crept around this house alone, and with the lights off, it's impossible to tell how big the room is, but a circle of candles flickers on the floor—a ring of fire that illuminates the three bodies sitting inside it.

"You're not worried about an open flame with all these paint fumes?" I murmur to Ethan.

"So safety-conscious." I hear the smile on his lips. And I still feel the warmth of his lips on mine.

"Mission accomplished," he says to the others, leading me over to them. "Told you she'd come down."

I sit beside Rapunzel and she squeezes my knee, leaning her shoulder against mine. "Glad you're here, love. Rotten business. But Davis got to live the good life, and he took care of his family. Must be worth celebrating, yeah?"

"They'll be taken care of?" I ask. "His sisters?"

"Of course." JB sits across from me. Aces is next to him, and I'm grateful for the gloom, because now that I'm here, I feel too exposed and this feels like a mistake. I should have run while I had the chance. I could have slipped out the front door while they were all down here in the darkness. But when Ethan sits down on the other side of me, I can't wrap my head around the idea of leaving. This room smells like him: fresh paint and smoking heat.

"When do we get to hear the music?" Rapunzel asks, breaking an awkward silence.

"Lana might want to add something first," Ethan suggests. "About Davis."

"No." I respond much too quickly. "I don't want to interrupt."

"Davis deserves a few words," JB insists. "From all of us."

"No pressure," Ethan says, though clearly there is. "But you were with him. You know. Near the end."

"Yeah." JB sniffs, and I realize he's been crying. "The end."

"Davis and I split up," I lie, and I shiver as I remember cradling his head as he died. His face becoming GoPro's face as I got glitchy. Ethan's face. And mine. "But we tried to get away together at first."

I feel them all lean toward me, hanging on my every word, but how much weight can my lies hold? "We just had that one hit of tempo in the Tesla, and Davis was already injured, but he wanted to rush to have a chance. Just a half dose after we split it, but it didn't feel like less. I can remember so much of it. And I should have tried to get Davis to a hospital sooner, but it was so beautiful. The lights. The city. Everything so alive. I wish you all could have seen it."

The words don't do it justice. I would do anything to show them. To glimpse the Fourth Dimension with them and feel its flow one more time.

"Then what happened?" JB's ragged voice snaps me back to the reality of now. I want to tell them Davis died in my arms and how he told me his real name. They should know that all he cared about at the end was the two sisters he was leaving behind.

"We got separated," I say, because I have to make this lie fit the others. "I was telling him we had to get him help, but he started leaping and . . . then I lost him in the night."

"Sounds like Davis went out on a high," Rapunzel says.

"He's dead." JB noisily wipes his face with his sleeve. "Like every other accelerator, his time came to an end too soon. So now we honor his memory—all their memories and the thing they all stood for, before they got arrested, or too old, or wound up dead on the streets."

"What did they stand for?" I ask. "Speed and greed?"

"The world gives us nothing," JB says. "So we learn to take it. But I ain't talking about the money. I'm talking big picture. I'm talking about the thing that you stand for, too. The time bomb ticking down. The alarm bells ringing. Reminding people they'll be ravaged by time, so they better ravage it back. We should be scaling the stars and diving down deep, embracing the pain and breaking the rules and piercing through numbness to peer into the blinding blackest wildest light. And I ain't even quoting this. This ain't stuff I read, it's stuff I know and keep forgetting and relearning the hard way."

"Damn, boss," Rapunzel whispers.

"Yeah, well. That, and it pays good, too." He tries to laugh, but gives up and clears his throat instead. "Ethan—hit the music, bro. Let's hear a song recorded by one of our fallen brethren, and send them all on their way to their next point in time."

Rapunzel bounces next to me in anticipation.

"When do I get to see the painting?" I ask Ethan, my voice quiet, my mind warped by the fossil across from me. Because no matter how true JB's words sound, what about the people who get hurt when the rules get broken? What do *they* stand for? And who celebrates them?

"Don't worry." Ethan fiddles with a remote and somewhere in the darkness, speakers hum to life as he switches them on. "You didn't miss it."

The song is a tsunami.

I'm surprised the sheer force of it doesn't blow out the candles and drown us in darkness. It floods around me. It throbs and pulls. Monstrous beats jackhammering inside a primordial swirl. The same song I heard that night I found Ethan working down here, but now I'm inside the music, and it is as loud as the sun, its heat searing me apart and boiling my bones. The sound of the *rush*. The noise you feel when you are nothing but speed.

By the time the music begins fading out, the five of us are on our feet. Not much room inside this circle of candles, but we huddle together, our arms around one another, and it feels right to be all linked up.

"You lot should try this," Rapunzel shouts as she dances between JB and me. "Start moving, yeah?"

"Wait." Ethan's arm is gone from my shoulders—he's fidgeting with the remote again, and the music's like a wave that keeps on receding but as the music becomes silence, Ethan flips on the lights.

The effect is beyond blinding. Blue-white bulbs flood the space like dawn just broke a dozen times over.

Ethan's painting is everywhere.

We're at the very center of it, since we're in the middle of the room and the room is the painting. It's on the walls and the ceiling, even the floor.

Our circle breaks down so we can all stand alone, rotating to gaze at the streams of endless color. You could spend a lifetime staring at it but never take it all in. The room must be fifty feet by twenty, but Ethan's made it infinite. If the song was the rush preserved in music, then Ethan has painted it inside out, showing that the rush was never about being fast or strong. It wasn't about the roar of the Fourth Dimension or the way it turns the world to light. It was about the truth of this feeling he's captured, where each now is endless if you live in the now and every moment matters when you're truly alive.

"You see?" JB cries, spinning his crooked body around to stare. "The wildest light! You did it, bro. I tried to describe it, but you made it speak for itself."

"I love that it's you who made this." I lean into Ethan. "That this is what's inside you."

"It's what's inside you, too."

"Not a blank space?"

"Hey, what's life without mystery?" He grins. "Look at the painting. The blank spaces let the rest of it breathe."

"So you like that I'm mysterious?" I want to believe him. And I want to grin with him. But all I feel now is the void, because thinking about tetra and this truth it has shown me makes me hunger for tetra till I'm hollow inside.

"I want to see some of your work," Ethan says.

"I could never do something like this."

"No." He takes my hand. "You'll do something different."

My left eyeball throbs in its socket as I stare at the light and the darkness and all the colors between. And when Rapunzel, laughing, shouts, "We should hit tempo, *then* stare at it," that seems to me like it'd be cheating. Because if tetra can show us how to unlock this feeling, why do we still need the drug to feel that way?

And why do I still want to cheat?

"We should hit tempo, check out the painting, *and* listen

315

to the song," Rapunzel says.

"You're just being greedy." Ethan grins. "What about JB? We can't abandon him to slow motion all on his own."

"You kids go ahead." He makes that smile of his I used to think was ugly but I now find endearing. "This old fossil's happy to sit back and watch you enjoy."

Rapunzel's hopping up and down, and she rubs JB's scrappy bald scalp. "For real, boss? We can spare the doses?"

If they offer it to me, I won't be able to say no. Timebomb never plays it safe. *Just one more time.* One more risk. One more taste.

I squeeze Ethan's hand. My palms sweating. My scalp prickles with heat.

JB scratches his chin, and it's driving Rapunzel crazy. Even ice-cold Aces has a glint in her eye. "I think"—JB pauses for maximum effect—"that seeing as this is a special occasion, and that I'm sure it's what our fallen brethren would have wanted, then hell yes, we can bend the rules a little."

A cheer goes up. My own voice joining in.

To rush now would be a double dose, since the drug is still in my system, and I can't pass up the double dose. I'm not ready to give up this dream I keep dreaming, the lie I keep lying.

"Lana can't," Ethan says. "She rushed last night."

"Ah, bugger." Rapunzel stops moving and smiling. It's like she just got unplugged. "He's right. Can't double-dose."

I resent Ethan for making the call. But I'm also grateful to him, since he might have just saved my life.

"We wait," Ethan says. "Do it when Lana can. It'd be claustrophobic in here, anyway."

"Nah," Rapunzel says. "Not with all these colors to look at."

"I've been looking at them for weeks. Besides, I want to do what Lana and Davis did—at night, with the lights all around us. No one chasing us. Just for kicks. Just for the rush."

It's decided, and the new plan buys me plenty of time to get out of here. If I can work up the courage to leave.

"So what do we do now?" Rapunzel asks. "Wait for the candles to burn down and sing 'Kumbaya'?"

"I got an idea," JB says.

"Oh no." Ethan puts his head in his hands. "You finally did it, didn't you?"

"What?" Rapunzel demands, laughing. "What did he do?"

"He's gonna make us turn the lights off." Ethan's mock-horrified. "Tell us straight, JB. You bought all the gear, right? You're gonna make us play laser tag, you son of a bitch."

Rapunzel's in stitches, and for a moment I think Ethan's actually right.

"That is a genius idea," JB says. "Can't believe I didn't think of it myself. It'll happen. Soon as I can get us equipment. State of the art, you'll see. But, no, no, this is something serious." He glances at the ceiling, the walls. "Point it at the right spot and it just might work."

"What the hell are you talking about?" Ethan follows his brother's gaze.

"Remember way back at the old safe house, when we used to watch movies? We fired the projector up. Movie night. We still got that thing?"

"The projector?" Ethan frowns. "Yeah. It's down here in the basement somewhere. I could dig it out."

"Good. Set it up."

Rapunzel curls her lip. "Tell me you did not make a slide show."

"This is way better than that." JB steps out of the circle, careful not to knock over the candles, and Ethan goes with him, the two of them dashing out of the room. When the brothers come back, joining us once more inside the painting, Ethan has a digital projector and an orange extension cord, which he plugs into a paint-splattered outlet.

JB carries a black laptop.

"We'll point it there." He gestures to a spot on the ceiling that's covered in lighter-colored paint than the rest—a burst of yellow-almost-white. "With the lights off we can lie down and watch it right overhead."

"You're thinking like a greatest hits?" Ethan hooks the projector into the laptop.

"Not exactly," JB says.

Rapunzel lies down on the painted floor, getting ready. "This what I think it is?"

"Best way to honor her." JB grins. "The painting Ethan made for her. The song she made for us. And now we watch one of her films."

My body goes taut as a piano string, my voice a quivery high note. "Who?"

"Someone you should have had the chance to meet," Ethan says. "You would have liked her." He's working on the angle of the projector, avoiding my gaze. "Though you might have hated her, too. Emma was even wilder than you are."

"Emma." I can't swallow for the lump of terror in my throat.

"She's who made the music." Rapunzel grins. "She made these mad blurry movies when she was rushing. Used to set them to her tunes. You ever see them online?"

"GoPro," I say, the name like a knife in my gut. I remember her smashing through that nineteenth-floor window. Leaping to her death because she didn't want to spend the rest of her life waiting to die.

"Emma lived it like she loved it," Ethan says, still too busy with the projector to look at me, and I should be glad for that small mercy, but I'm not. I want to see his face. I want to know how well he knew the girl he made this painting for.

"She lived without fear?" I ask, the swollen ache behind my left eye stretching all the way down the side of my face.

"Tried to." Ethan glances around at the room he's brought to glorious life because of a girl who is dead. "I started painting this because I wanted to remember her, but she wouldn't have wanted me to remember her at all. Emma always wanted everyone to be in the moment. But if you don't remember someone, it's like they never . . ."

"Of course you want to remember her," JB says, seeing his brother is unable to go on. Then JB turns to me and my brain pounds like a hammer at the nail of his words. "Our friend got thrown out of a window. By a *runner*. Nothing I could do. No way to strike back. The system don't care when one of its own breaks the rules. But forget the system. We're here to celebrate Emma, now Ethan's finished her painting. We're celebrating Davis and every other breaker who ran the razor's edge. Ceremony's important—"

"Here comes the quote." Rapunzel rolls her eyes.

"*A ritual is the enactment of a myth.*" JB grins. "Joseph Campbell said that."

I cover my left eye, unable to stem the pain leeching out of it into every part of my body.

"GoPro was a good name, eh?" Rapunzel says to me. "Better than *Uncle Sam* by a hundred miles."

"We all were close," JB adds, concerned as he glances at his brother. "Real close. And we're about to see the last film she ever made. The live stream. Remember, bro? Me and her were testing it out."

"You were *recording*?" Ethan looks how I feel—only I feel more shock and anger inside than any one face could convey. "That day?"

"Straight from her camera to my laptop. I was in Ishmael.

320

She wanted to make sure it all worked right so we could do the live broadcast next time how she wanted. Show everyone her rush in real time. Man, she was ballsy."

"I don't know, man." Ethan flips off the projector. "Bit morbid, isn't it?"

"It's her last rush, man. Her last minutes. You don't want to see it? You don't want to feel like you were there?"

"She *died*. You want to see that part, too?" Ethan says. "You want to see her hurtling toward Thirty-Sixth Street, because I sure as hell don't want to see that."

"She didn't have the helmet on. She took it off before she got . . . you know."

"You were watching?" Ethan asks, aghast. "You watched it happen? Live? Through her video feed?"

JB shakes his head. "I was too busy heading to the place I was supposed to pick her up. Thought about watching it a hundred times since, but never could bring myself to do it. Almost deleted it. But the reports said she didn't have a helmet on, and the camera was on her helmet, so that part, the ending, it won't be . . . I just thought . . ."

Some small part of my brain is still functioning enough to realize that JB is right—GoPro took her helmet off before she jumped. I know because I saw her do it.

But I took my helmet off before she took off hers.

"Maybe you're right," JB says, apparently losing faith in his idea. "I thought it'd be a good final send-off. A way to say good-bye. But let's forget it."

There needs to be something I can say to agree with him. To make everyone see how this would be a very bad idea.

"No," Ethan says. "Let's do it."

"You sure?" JB asks.

"I'm sure." Ethan fires up the projector again. "We'll see the last things she saw, minus the Fourth Dimension. Her last rush. You knew Emma. She'd have loved the idea."

"I'll be right back," I say, trying not to sprint as I head for the door. "Gotta pee. I'll be quick. I promise. Wait for me— don't start it yet. Please don't start it."

"It's just nine minutes," JB says, but Rapunzel comes to my rescue.

"You're not a girl, boss. Unless you been keeping something secret." She starts laughing. "And you would be one ugly girl, bruv. Thought you was ugly enough as a bloke."

"I'm beautiful on the *inside*, Panzer," JB says, cracking up a little, too.

I'm halfway to the door now. Surrounded by the spiral of Ethan's infinite painting that doesn't end or begin and has no edges, and it makes me feel even more trapped, caught in a vortex. This rabbit hole is an eternal loop.

"Trust me, I was gorgeous before I started hitting the tempo." JB's on a roll now. "Should have seen me. I was like a model. Me and Ethan were all Abercrombie & Fitch."

"No way," Ethan says, almost laughing as well, but reluctant. Still somber. "If anything you got better with age."

Their voices are faint now. Just a few more feet and I'll be in the corridor. I should be running faster. They wouldn't think that was strange, would they? They'd think I was hurrying to the bathroom so I can hurry right back.

"What the hell?" It's Ethan's voice, louder than it was, and no laughter's left in it. Then JB's saying, "No, no. Start it over. Wait. Switch it off. This must be the ending."

"Don't switch it off." Ethan sounds about fifty years older, his voice draining every ounce of color out of this room.

I'm at the door now. And I don't want to turn back.

But I do.

THIRTY-FOUR

The projector casts a big enough picture on the ceiling to show all of me. The old me. The TRU overalls and Kevlar body armor, the special-issue Adidas worn-out from the chase. My helmet is clutched at my side. The letters on my chest say RUNNER FIVE. My sweaty black bangs whip about as the chopper churns the air above.

And there's my face—huge on the ceiling. My cheeks are flushed, mouth gasping for air, eyes bulging, pupils massively dilated. My body trembling. Jaw clenched shut. I look so angry. *Ferocious.* I'm a devil inside Ethan's Sistine Chapel. And it is impossible for me to turn away.

Though I'm a giant on the ceiling, my voice is small out of the laptop speakers. "You have to stop or they'll shoot," I'm yelling as I pull my bangs from out of my eyes.

Then the image twists as GoPro yanks her helmet from her head, her camera pointing at sky, steam, a muffle of brown, and everything's spinning, because GoPro's tossed the helmet at me. There's a thud as it connects with my stomach. A crack and blur as it hits the concrete.

Then there's just the scuffling sound of feet.

The then-me is running.

The now-me needs to run, too.

If I'm fast, perhaps I can make it through the dingy passage, up the stairs, and out the front door before they catch me. I'll get out of Harlem and go to ground.

"I didn't kill her," I say, not moving.

They're all still staring at the ceiling, as if they're watching the credits roll and have forgotten I'm here. Or perhaps they refuse to believe I have wormed my way inside their wolf pack.

JB's holding the laptop, and as he folds it shut, the projection shuts off. The silence that follows is the sound of my time bomb exploding.

"What are you waiting for?" At first I think JB means why aren't I running. "Why are they not already here?"

"You don't understand," I say. "I don't work for TRU anymore."

"Really?" His voice is brutally calm. "Who do you work for now?"

"No one. I swear to you. I used to be a runner but I got thrown off the unit. I didn't kill her. You have to believe me. *Ethan*. I promise I didn't hurt her. She jumped out of that building. She said something about Mobius being wrong . . . then she jumped."

"Why should we believe you?" Rapunzel says without looking at me. Ethan's staring not at me, but at JB, as if his big brother is somehow going to make all this make sense. "And Davis?" Rapunzel asks. Her body has shriveled inward. Her frown puckers her mouth all wrong.

"I didn't kill him, either. I swear it's the truth."

"The truth." Every bone in Ethan's body looks ready to snap. Then he snaps.

"How can you even talk about the truth?" He screams the words as he kicks the projector into pieces, shards of plastic and glass splintering through the air and scattering the candles. Their wicks snuff out on the floor. Ethan still will not look at me. "I played you her music. I showed you her painting! The painting I made for *her*. You made me betray her . . . for you. A *runner*."

Aces is the first to sprint toward me, and I am too shocked to try to run so I'm just standing there as she slams a shoulder into my chest and knocks me backward. She pauses only to spit in my face and say two words in Italian, then she bolts out of the room.

"We need to stick together," JB screams after her. "Aces! Come back!"

"Forget her," Rapunzel shouts, and she's above me now. I think she's going to spit on me like Aces did, but she spits words instead. "I'm gonna mess you up, girl. I'm gonna *ruin* you."

"Panzer, no . . . please!"

"The name's *Rapunzel*."

She kicks me in the gut, then the ribs. She only stops because JB's pulling her off me. "What?" she screams at him. "You don't think she deserves it? She killed Emma. And Davis. She's here to send us to prison."

"We'll make her pay, but not yet. We have to stay calm now. Gotta focus. Or we're screwed." JB's kneeling beside me, shaking me, his face burning red. "When are they coming? Tell me what they're waiting for."

"They don't want you," I say, between gasps for breath. "They want Mobius. They want the drug. They want tetra off the streets. . . ."

"So you do still work for them," he says. "You weren't *thrown off the unit*. You're, like, undercover."

"She's lying, boss." Ethan's blocking Rapunzel from me, but her voice is vicious enough to make me flinch. "Everything she says is a lie."

"Ethan!" JB yells. "Get the keys and pull Ishmael up out front."

"TRU could have people watching the house," Ethan says, frantic.

"You're right." JB smashes his fist at the floor. Then his hands are all over my body, squeezing each part of me. "She could be bugged. Wired. *Shit*. They could know she's in trouble and be about to beat down the front door."

JB finds my phone. The key to the scooter. He holds

them both in my face and makes me keep my eyes open by screaming what he'll do if I don't.

"Are they watching the house?" he yells.

I just whimper. Shake my head. *I'm going to die.* I'm going to die as a thief and a murderer.

"Please don't kill me," I beg.

"Kill you?" JB's red face is all veiny. "You being alive is the only thing keeping us safe." He shoves my phone and the scooter key in his pocket. "Ethan—get the van ready. Rapunzel, you take a Vespa. We split up. If we're being watched, it'll make us harder to follow."

"And then what?" Ethan asks. "What do we do with *her*?"

"One step at a time, bro. I'll call Mobius. Tell him things got compromised. I'll take responsibility. . . ."

"She killed Emma." Ethan's voice bleeds like an open wound.

"We'll deal with it," JB says. "Just go get Ishmael and meet us out front. I'll grab some supplies."

"Get some tempo," Rapunzel tells him.

"Yeah. So you can leave my ass in the slow lane."

"Get it," Ethan says. "Get all of it."

"I'll get it. Now *get out of here.*" JB's hands are on me again, pulling me up by my shoulders. "Upstairs, runner! Do what I say or I'll set Panzer on you now instead of later." He gives me a shove and I stumble toward the door. "Must say, TRU staging you breaking out of their headquarters was a stroke of genius."

328

Ethan sprints ahead of us, disappearing through the door, and as we follow him into the passage, I am so sore from the beating Rapunzel already delivered and so weak from derailing, I let Rapunzel push me and pull me and bounce me along.

Upstairs, she presses me against a wall while JB crashes around, trying to decide what to take. He ends up with two duffel bags and an armload of books, and he keeps calling for Aces, but his voice echoes unanswered—she's already gone.

"So much for family," he mutters, glaring at me.

"I'll stick with you, boss," Rapunzel says. "Me and Ethan and you. We'll get through this."

"Aces'll be in touch, you'll see," he says. "Wanting her money."

"I thought you said breaknecks are about more than just the money," I say.

"And I thought runners are the ones trying to keep people safe." JB kneels down to zip his bundle of books inside one of the duffels. The bag's half full of money, loose bills and thick rolls. "Listen up, Panzer. If her people are watching the house, they can't know she's in trouble or they'd already be in here. So you go out first, and you just smile and shit and look like all's right as rain." JB nods at me. "Then she follows. I pull up the rear. She tries running, I shoot her."

He pulls out a handgun.

Rapunzel stares at me. Then back at JB. "For real?" she says.

"Start moving," he tells her.

"Like, in the leg or something?" Rapunzel steps between JB and me. I want to hug her for it.

"Let me go," I plead. "I'll never tell anyone anything. Not about you, or Mobius, or any of this. I'll just go home. Just let me go home to my family."

"This." JB points his gun around at the house. "This was *my* home. My family. Rapunzel, you first. Out the door, come on."

She stands her ground between us.

"Move!" JB screams at her.

"You can't kill her. Say you won't, boss."

"Why do you care?"

"Because we ain't murderers."

"Not even after what she did to Emma? She killed Davis too, no doubt. This is all our lives at stake now, Panzer. I ain't gonna rot in some cage and neither are you."

"You go first," she says. "Then her. *I* pull up the rear. She starts running, I'll grab her."

JB stares down at the gun in his hand.

"It's like you said," Rapunzel tells him. "She's worth more to us alive than dead."

"Yeah. For now." JB tucks the gun in his waistband, concealing it with his shirt, then hustles toward the front door and cracks it open to stick his head out. "Ethan's got the van pulled up. Looks clear."

"Of course it bloody *looks* clear."

"I'm going for it." He throws the door open and jogs awkwardly down the steps, lugging the big bags on his shoulders.

"Thanks," I say to Rapunzel.

"Shut up." She drags me toward the door and when we reach it, she pins me against the wall while she peers outside. Her elbow digs in my ribs. Her hand claws at my throat.

"I just wanted to get to Mobius," I rasp. "I didn't kill Emma. Or Davis. You have to—"

Rapunzel thumps me in the gut, knocking the wind out of me. "I thought we'd be friends, me and you." She studies me as I choke. "Figured we'd both done the same things to survive." She peers outside again, then peels me off the wall. "Try to run, I catch you, *runner*. Shoe's on the other foot now."

The daylight hurts as I step outside. The minivan's idling in the street, where there are plenty of parked cars, but no moving vehicles.

A safe street for rushing on.

JB's getting in the passenger seat of the van. The driver's side faces the house, and Ethan's at the wheel, his window down, his handsome features etched with suspicion and disgust as he watches me.

"Move." Rapunzel shoves me forward.

My left eye pounds in its socket. My ribs are so sore, it hurts just to breathe. It's fifteen yards to the van, and halfway there, I have my best shot at running. I'm an equal distance between Rapunzel and the van, and Ethan's distracted by something in the road ahead—someone's pulled onto the street and is heading toward us.

The pickup truck is the color of old blue jeans.

THIRTY-FIVE

T ucker doesn't look right with a gun in his hand. Maybe he would if he had a rifle and was dressed in his plaid shirt and old jeans, about to hunt wild turkeys, or Canada geese. But he's dressed in the same Yankees cap and cargo shorts he had on at the movie theater. And he's carrying a handgun, not a hunting rifle. It's pointed at the minivan's windshield as he marches down the middle of the street.

Behind him, his pickup truck blocks both lanes; the door he hopped out of hangs open. "Get in the truck, Alana," he calls, not taking his eyes off the minivan, or, rather, not taking his eyes off the two brothers sitting in its front seats.

I don't move. My feet have grown roots and tunneled down through the sidewalk.

"Tucker . . ." I cry, trying to warn him, but it's too late. JB's pulled out his gun and is pressing its muzzle at the windshield.

"You better get the hell out of our way!" he calls from the passenger seat, his window down.

"I'm leaving with her." Tucker's six feet from the front of the van when he stops. "And no one gets hurt."

"We don't have time for you acting the hero," JB shouts. "Some other day, maybe."

Tucker grips his gun with both hands. I'd much rather he had his old paper map and was showing me an escape route.

"He'll shoot," I say.

"You warning him or me?" JB yells.

Tucker glances at Ethan, who sits rigid behind the wheel of the van, engine running. "Let her go, man."

"Talk to my brother."

"Lana!" JB yells. "Get in the van now or I blow this dude's head off!"

"You shoot, I shoot." Tucker's arms tremble as he squeezes the gun.

"JB, don't do this," I plead. "Just let me go. You're not a killer."

"You think you know me?" JB's voice bursts and breaks. "Then go right ahead and start running for that truck. We'll see how fast you are when you're not high on tempo."

"Put the gun away," Ethan yells at him. "You're not gonna shoot her. That's not you anymore."

JB howls, jamming the muzzle of the gun harder at the windshield.

"Both of you stop!" I scream. "Put the guns down.

Tucker—I'll go with them. I'm getting in the van. Just walk away."

"Good choice," Ethan says, glancing at me. "You got enough blood on your hands."

As I start toward the van again, Rapunzel calls out from the house, where she's still hiding. "I come now?"

"Take a scooter," JB yells back.

"Bugger that. I'm getting in the van."

"Take a scooter!" he shouts. "We'll meet up later."

"I'll get my brains blown out on a bloody moped!"

"Head for my truck, Alana," Tucker says. "We're getting out of here."

"It's too late," I tell him, and as I reach the van and slide open the rear passenger door, Rapunzel sprints from the house. She piles with me into the backseats.

"Don't shoot," I yell as I peer between Ethan and JB, staring out through the windshield. "Tucker. I'll be all right."

"I'll follow you," he shouts back. "I'm not letting you go."

Ethan turns to his brother in the passenger seat. "Justin talks big."

"Yeah." JB nods. "Always did."

"You don't know him," I snap. "You don't even know his name."

"Stop talking, lads." Rapunzel squats low on the floor beside me. "Start driving."

"She's right. Start backing up," JB says. "Let's get out of here, bro."

Ethan shifts the van into reverse, takes his foot off the brake, and we start to drift backward. Tucker's just standing there. Still pointing the gun. Still unable to shoot.

"You got a good look at his face, Lana?" Ethan asks.

"I don't need to. I know him."

"Yeah. You know him like I knew you."

"Give it some gas," JB tells his brother, and we start picking up speed.

"*Justin Tuck*," Ethan says. "That's what he called himself back then."

"Yeah." JB's still pressing his gun at the windshield, his eyes on Tucker. "He was the reason we had to shut down the first safe house. Bastard switched teams on me."

"Fitting name for a snake in the grass," Ethan says, and just as he says "Sidewinder," Tucker opens fire on the van.

THIRTY-SIX

T he windshield splinters and there's glass in my hair and blood on my face, and I scream so loud but JB screams louder, and then the engine starts screaming and drowns us out. And all I'm thinking is *Sidewinder* and Tucker and it's a lie, it has to be a lie, but it's a lie sharp enough to burst things inside me, popping my heart like a balloon, because maybe I've been sidled up next to Sidewinder, letting him rub my shoulders as he whispered in my ear.

I'm tossed forward as the van hurtles backward and my face slams into the back of Ethan's seat. The tires shriek on the asphalt, then our rear end thuds into something, and I'm thrown back, sideways, and down.

I don't know whose blood is on me. I'm tangled up with Rapunzel, and JB's shooting—at least I think it's JB, but then why is JB flopping into the rear of the van, all covered in blood?

337

He's been shot.

Now he's bouncing around, splayed out, upside down, head jiggling, and Ethan is gunning us forward in an angry burst of speed.

The engine's trapped in too low a gear and it roars in protest. It's Ethan who's firing the gun—aiming it through the broken windshield, shooting wild as Tucker sprints out of our path.

I drop to the floor. Cover my head in my arms, bracing for impact as we smash into the side of Tucker's truck like a cannonball into the side of a tank.

The tank wins.

Ishmael's last breath comes out in a hiss of steam and creaking steel and Rapunzel wails but beneath all that noise, I hear Ethan cursing in this weird whispery voice. He's rattling at the gearstick but the van's never going back into gear. Smoke gushes in through the broken windshield and oozes from the dashboard.

I crawl over JB and peer out through the remains of the windshield and smoke. Our whole front end looks like something big took a bite out of it, but the truck just has a missing door and a crumpled side.

Still has an engine, at least. Might still move.

I should get to the truck and start driving, put distance between me and all this. But what if Tucker has the keys, and what if Tucker is Sidewinder?

Just run, I tell myself. Get out on the street and run.

338

Ethan keeps shouting his brother's name. He's still behind the wheel but reaching back between the front seats to where his brother's flopped and bleeding. Rapunzel keeps whimpering. She's been hurt in the crash and they all need help and I don't want to leave them.

"Alana?" It's Tucker. He's close. *So close.* He's right outside but can't see me through the steam and smoke gushing out of Ishmael's engine. "Can you hear me? Tell me where you are, I'll help get you out."

I reach over Ethan to flip the locks shut.

Please don't let it be true. Please make Ethan be as big a liar as I am.

"Ethan," I whisper. He's slumped back in his seat now. He's hurt too—his head lolls. It's bleeding. His face busted, his eyes closed. "You're all right. Come on. You have to be okay."

"JB," he mumbles. "Shot."

"The police will be on their way. They'll take care of him."

"My brother . . ."

"Where's the gun, Ethan? What did you do with the gun?"

I grope around on his lap and at his feet, then I reach into the back where JB is all sticky with blood. I want him to start screaming again so we'll know he's still breathing.

"Rapunzel," I say, and she moans in response, possibly concussed. "You have to get out of here."

"Alana?" Tucker calls, trying to get the door open, still blocked from view by the steam and smoke. "Where are you?"

I find the gun where it's fallen under Ethan's seat. And while I'm bent down at the floor of the backseats, I inspect JB's stomach, where all the blood is pooling. I trace the wound back to his right shoulder, just above his armpit. I find a thready pulse on his neck.

Then I reach into his back pocket and grab back my phone and the key to the scooter I left parked in the Village.

"Ethan!" I hiss. "Start moving. Rapunzel, come on. Get up and get out. You have to leave JB here. There'll be paramedics. You understand? You have to leave JB behind."

"Where are you going?" Ethan wobbles his head toward me, his eyes back open.

"I didn't kill Emma. I swear to you. I never killed anyone."

Till now.

I shove JB's gun into the back of my jeans, crawling over Rapunzel to the rear door Tucker's trying to open. When I release the lock, Tucker yells as the door comes free.

He hops back, training his gun on me—but seeing it's me, he drops the gun to his side, clutching his hair with his free hand like he means to pull it all out. "Scared me. Oh God." He stares up at the sky. Barks out a laugh. His eyes are wet when he looks back at me. "Did I hurt someone? I shot . . . oh, shit. Alana, what do we do?"

"We start running."

"I wanted to save you."

"The police will be coming. We have to go."

He does what I say and starts sprinting. Away from the

van. Away from his truck. And I follow. Though my ribs sting and my legs feel crooked, I'm a few feet behind him . . . until my ankle blows out. The left ankle, the one I wrecked and never let really heal. Tendons rupture. My whole leg feels like glass shattering. And the ground smacks me in the jaw as I fall, sprawling on the asphalt, screaming in pain.

Tucker's ten feet ahead when he stops and spins around, exasperated, as if he can't believe I'm slowing him down. But then he sees the gun in my hands. The gun I'm pointing at him.

"Is it true?" I say, because I have to hear it from him. "It was you . . . Sidewinder. He was you?"

My finger doesn't want to wait for his answer. It's squeezing the trigger. Tucker looks as terrified as he should be. And him being terrified makes me feel good in a really bad way.

"What are you going to do?" he asks.

"Put your gun down."

He doesn't. "You hear that?" He means the sirens wailing in the distance. "They're going to arrest you, Alana."

"And you."

"Listen to me. I *stopped*. I quit. I don't know what they told you, but—"

"You lied to me! Everything. All a lie."

"I joined TRU to make up for it."

"Stop!"

"It's the truth."

"Why did you send me undercover?"

"That was Monroe. It was *real*. It's real, oh God, you have to believe me."

"How can I believe you? I let you . . . I thought . . ." I scream loud enough to tear out my tongue. "And all along, you're the one who made me this way. I am *this* because you are *you*."

"But we can end it. All of it. Cut off the breaknecks' supply. Don't you see? I *hurt* people. And I want it all to stop as bad as you do. I want to make up for everything I did."

"I don't know you."

"Yes, you do. Please . . ."

"Why make me pretend to be a breakneck?" My voice bends the words in painful pitches. "You already were one. You were the worst of all."

"I used to stay at JB's safe house. And I got my drugs from Mobius, but that's all."

"That's not all. There is no *that's all*."

"I mean I never knew how Mobius was doing it—how he has the drug. I told JB I was quitting to go straight. I tried to get him to come clean too. But they moved the safe house. Disappeared . . ."

I come to my knees, still training the gun on the boy I once imagined kept me safe from a distance. He's just ten feet from me. *I don't even need to have good aim.*

"My brother can't walk because of you."

Tucker goes to say something, but then lets his mouth hang open and swallows the words.

342

"Yeah. It was you!" My voice is a blender on high with a human heart trapped inside. "You crippled him. Blasted through him on Queens Boulevard last summer and you never even slowed down. *Did you even notice?* Did you feel it when you collided with his little body? Did you see me watching the whole horrible thing?"

"Alana . . ."

"I *relied* on you. I even . . ." I want to throw up. "But you're him. You've always been him."

"That wasn't me."

"Then deny it! Say it isn't true, Tucker."

He hangs his head. "I was out of control."

"Tell me all of it. The dream suit. The snaking around the city. What did you do with your money? What do you tell yourself so you can sleep at night? You just *count the stars*, I guess. You count your stupid lucky stars."

"I try not to sleep, Alana. If I do, I dream of all the things I did wrong. But I gave the money away. Wanted it for my dad, after JB laundered it. Thought enough money might make it so he could get better. But then I was worried he'd leave it to me, so I donated it all . . ."

"To what?"

"The Tetra Response Unit."

"Oh, I have hated you!" I have my gun pointed right at his chest.

"But you know what it's like. The rush. Come on. It could have been you. Could have been any of us."

Now I point the gun between Tucker's eyes and squeeze the trigger and only at the last moment do I think of Reuben's beautiful face. As Tucker throws himself to the ground, I swing the gun up to aim at the heavens or whatever else might be up there that makes down here hell. I fire off every shot into the sky so I will not shoot Sidewinder. So I will not be a murderer. So that I might be able to go home and be there for my brother again.

"I should have been holding his hand." My voice is quiet in the aftermath of the gunshots. "That day. On the cross-walk..."

"Tell me what to do," Tucker pleads. "Please. I'll make it better. I'll do anything."

"You can't make it better." I throw my gun at the ground and collapse onto my back, the pain in my ankle flooding through me to collide with the pain oozing out of my eyeball. "I already tried." I roll my head to the side so I can look at Tucker. "I tried so hard and just made everything worse."

He stands and throws his own gun down. "Alana..." His mouth trembles. Then his face scrunches up all ugly and his bloodshot blue eyes bleed tears. "I had no idea your brother—"

The sirens wail louder. The storm at sea closing in.

"I think about killing myself." Tucker keeps sobbing. Staring at the gun he's dropped at his feet. "I lie awake at night and know I deserve to die. But then how can I fix things?"

The truth blisters my brain.

"You can't. No one can."

"So what do we do?" Tucker risks a glance at me, wiping the tears from his face.

"I don't know." I struggle to my knees. "But I have to go after Mobius if I'm to end this."

"Let me help you."

"Help the others out of the van, then see if your truck will still start. Then get lost, Tucker."

"I'm coming with you." He jogs toward me. Slows down as he gets close, but I tell him, "Don't you dare stop," and he runs right past.

I limp down the street and retrieve his gun from where he ditched it. Mine's out of bullets.

But his is still loaded.

THIRTY-SEVEN

A t 16 Elizabeth Street, Lien Hair Salon smells of old ladies and new hairdos, and only the blow-dried models in the pictures on the wall are smiling.

The rest of us are screaming.

Ethan grabs Tucker by the neck and shoves his head into a sink, scattering bottles and combs and scissors, flipping on the water and plunging Tucker's head directly beneath the tap.

Tucker's not even putting up a fight. He just hangs his head. Water filling the sink. Water filling up his nose and into his mouth. Rapunzel and I try to drag Ethan away, pleading with him, but Ethan's too strong. "He shot JB!" he keeps shouting. "Killed him."

"JB's not dead," I say. "He was still alive when we left him."

Ethan keeps Tucker's head underwater as he turns his face to mine, all his features stretched into someone new.

"You mean when *you* left him. You and your boy, here, you backstabbing liars. You're as bad as him."

Ethan turns back to Tucker and punches him in the throat, forcing Tucker to choke on the water that's filled up the sink now and splashes onto the floor. It steams. Scalding hot.

"You're killing him," I shout. "Ethan, stop!"

Ethan was unconscious by the time we got him out of Ishmael. Rapunzel was in shock. Tucker and I smuggled them both here in the truck, paid off the owners to clear out the salon, handing them fistfuls of the money JB had stashed in the duffel.

"Rapunzel," I cry, both of us hanging off Ethan's broad shoulders. "Tell him. Tell him JB's alive."

"He was, bruv. I saw him. He'll pull through. I know he will."

"Yeah? You know that, do you? And will he pull through in a prison cell?" Ethan shouts. "Get nice and healthy behind bars, will he? You all left him to die or get arrested!"

"There's still a way," I say. "Still a way to save him."

Ethan snaps free of us, releasing Tucker and spinning around.

"Talk." He glares down at me. Towering above me while Tucker's head slips out of the sink and he slides into a puddle on the floor.

"Turn the tap off," I tell Ethan, refusing to back down. "Get Tucker into a chair and promise you won't try to kill him again."

"Don't push your luck."

"We can keep your brother out of prison. You and Rapunzel, too."

Ethan snorts a bitter laugh. "Have a magic wand, do you? Gonna wave all this away?"

"Rapunzel." I point at Tucker. "Get him up off the floor and make sure he's all right."

"I don't take orders from you, runner."

"We have to work together now. All four of us. I know how you feel about me, and you know what, Rapunzel? You have some nerve. You too, Ethan. You both might think you're something special, but you're *criminals*. You hide behind masks and lie to the world as you rob it blind and you put people in danger and I will not apologize for not being one of you."

"Oh, you're one of us," Ethan says, sneering. "You're the one who thinks she's special but you're the one who hurts people, Lana. You killed Emma!"

"Ethan, she jumped—"

"I saw what you did to that runner on the streets, beating her to a pulp. You're out of control on tempo."

"She's not." It's Tucker who defends me. He's propped himself up in a plastic salon chair, hair a slick mess.

"Stay out of this," I tell him. "Besides, Ethan's right. I have been out of control. I think I even like being that way."

"At least you have a good excuse," Tucker says.

"Everyone has a good excuse, you bastard." Ethan punches

348

a fist at the ceiling as he rounds on him.

"I don't," Tucker says.

"What the hell does that mean?"

"I crippled Alana's brother. I hurt other people too. You know what I was like. Reckless. Greedy."

"*Sidewinder.*" Ethan spits the word. Then he turns to me. "This is true? About your brother?"

"It's true," Tucker says for me, my own voice vanishing as I stare at him. "I didn't even know. Never wanted to know who I'd hurt or what I'd done. Pretended like when I rushed it wasn't really me. But if anyone here deserves to kill me, it's not you. It's Alana."

"Lana. *Alana.*" Ethan stares at me. "You almost gave us your real name."

"Is *Ethan* yours?"

"You know, you two deserve each other," he says. "Come on, Rapunzel."

"We're leaving?" she asks, eyes wide as she glances toward the street.

"Yeah. Before I kill the pair of them."

"That's not you," I tell Ethan. "You're the one who keeps focused, and who steers clear of violence."

"And you're the one with the dead hole inside."

I step closer to him, hesitate, then reach for his face to pull him close. He resists, stiff as a board.

"Get off me." He tries to push me away, but I won't let him. He trembles. And then a tear runs down his face and he allows me to hold him. I breathe against his neck, his pulse thundering against my cheek. Over Ethan's shoulder, Tucker is slumped in the salon chair, watching us.

I want to hurt him.

"Come here," I whisper to Ethan as he begins to cry harder. I kiss his face. I press my lips to his, hushing him.

"Jesus," Rapunzel mutters as Ethan and I kiss. When I pull away from Ethan, Tucker is staring at the floor, his face redder even than the scalding water made it. With the toe of his sneaker, he nudges at a clump of hair on the floor, staring at the clippings as if he's reading them like tea leaves.

The future's easy to imagine. Hard to predict.

"Don't do that again," Ethan whispers, shoving past me. He heads to the door but stops at the window, his back muscles barbed with tension as he surveys Elizabeth Street.

I follow Ethan's gaze outside, where dusk softens Chinatown. My whole face aches with sleeplessness, and my still-throbbing left eye has now turned mostly numb. I fill my lungs, breathing deep and slow, trying to calm myself, but my ribs are bruised and my throat still stings from the shampoo I drank earlier. As I inhale the stench of the hair salon, my stomach churns.

"You're right about JB being in serious trouble," I tell Ethan. After all the screaming, I sound like I swallowed a cactus. "There's plenty in the house to make it clear he's not the innocent victim of some drive-by. And Rapunzel left the door wide open when she came running outside.

There'll have been eyewitnesses, too. Once the police search the place and find all our breaking gear, they'll start tying things together. They'll find JB's fingerprints on everything, find he has a criminal record."

"Is this supposed to be making me feel better?" Ethan says.

"I don't believe he was fatally wounded. That's the important thing."

"I'm still waiting for the part where you convince me to stay."

"We give them Mobius," I say. "We go to the police. TRU. We hand them who it is they really want, then we can get a deal that will clear JB, and you two."

Rapunzel slumps down into the chair next to Tucker's and starts spinning, as if on a demented ride at a bad theme park.

"You're gonna make yourself throw up," I tell her, trying to catch her eye as she whizzes past, needing her on my side.

"You're the puker."

"Okay. Then you're gonna make *me* throw up."

She kicks at the floor to go faster.

"A deal. You're sure about that?" Ethan asks, and of course I'm not sure about it. I glance at Tucker to see if he might back me up, but I can't look at him without wanting to throttle him. *Perhaps I should have let Ethan drown him in that sink.*

"What are you," Ethan says, "the DA as well as the runner who killed Emma?"

"She didn't kill anyone," Tucker says.

"No? You were there, were you?" Ethan turns to face us. "I've seen her speedfreaking on tempo and losing her shit. Put one of her own in the hospital, but I'm supposed to believe she didn't throw our girl out of that window?"

"I tried to stop her from jumping," I say. "Yes, I chased her. Yes, I wanted to arrest her. But I didn't kill her. And you wouldn't be here if you really thought that I did."

"I *have* to be here." Ishmael's steering wheel punched Ethan in the face and his nose is like a piece of rotten fruit. His right eye's swollen shut at the bottom of a fleshy black crater. I pulled glass from his bleeding forehead with scissors meant for hairdressing, not first aid. Despite his savaged appearance, I want to hold him again. Kiss him again. And not just to torment Tucker. In a world full of lies, the way I feel about Ethan is real enough to cling to.

"GoPro put sixteen people in the hospital while she was making her getaways," I say. "And even more could have been hurt when she jumped through that window."

"You're saying Emma deserved it?" Ethan challenges me with his gaze.

"No. But my brother didn't deserve to spend the rest of his life in a wheelchair. . . ." When I glance at Tucker, I want to make him just as ugly as he has made me feel. "I always thought if I found Sidewinder, I'd make him pay for all the pain he caused."

"Yet here you are, side-by-side with him." Ethan sounds

smug, and I am so over the way he is talking to me.

"You want to make it simple," I tell him. "I get it. I want it to be simple, too. But it's not. You could have crippled someone, Ethan. I don't care how careful you think you are. You could have killed someone. *I* could have. And I can't forgive Sidewinder for what happened, but right now I'm just telling myself that Sidewinder doesn't exist anymore. *Tetra* does. Tetra's the thing that's screwing everything up."

"You want to get rid of Mobius. Our source." Rapunzel drags her foot at the floor and stops spinning. "You expect me to just give up the tempo?"

"I counted twelve cartridges of TTZ in that duffel we pulled out of the van. You and Ethan can split them, along with the rest of the money."

"Six more rushes?" Rapunzel's eyes grow huge. "That's it?"

"Wasn't gonna last forever, Panzer," I say.

"Don't call me . . . ah, forget it." She looks at Ethan. "I'm ready to bounce when you are, bruv."

"My brother's more important than how many times we get to dose up again."

"*Course* he is." Rapunzel stands, crosses the salon to Ethan, and takes his hands. "The boss is like my brother, too. But no more BPM? Ever? And how can we even trust this girl?"

"We have to."

"Why? Because she kissed you? Because you're gonna go all puppy dog after her like you did Emma?"

Ethan lets go of her hands and turns back to stare out the

window at the darkening street. "Stay or go, Rapunzel. But don't talk that way to me."

"I loved Emma too, bruv. But she played you. Sucked you in, then turned you away when she realized how you felt about her. All she really cared about was the tempo. And all this girl cares about is *getting rid* of tempo."

"You're missing the point," he says, watching the dying light. "Nothing lasts. Not Emma. Not me. Not you. Lana's right—the drug comes to an end too soon, for all of us. So I'll hand over Mobius, even if there's only a chance it'll save my brother. That's what he'd do for me. And he'd do it for you, too."

"All right," Rapunzel says, and Ethan turns back to face her. "Like family."

"Like people who know people matter more than a feeling," I say.

Ethan glances at me. No part of him softens. "So what's the play?"

"You're in?"

"I'm listening."

"Tucker!" I yell to get his attention, because he keeps staring at the floor. "You hearing this? We're gonna need you too."

"You're sure?" He looks up at me.

"I'm sure that I'm here and you're here and we have a chance to end this. I'm sure that when this is over, I never have to see you again."

He nods slowly. I guess it pains him to look at me. *Good.* He should suffer. Maybe when this is over I'll make him suffer even more.

"I wish *I* could never see me again." Tucker's bloodshot blue eyes are brittle things. They tremble with the truth. And the truth is a punishment he deserves. All the things he's done are still part of him, walling him in a prison, because you never get to escape the past.

Unless you only live in the moment.

Tetra has taught me that. Maybe Ethan's taught me it, too. And I long for the drug and for him, but I'll have to let both go.

Tucker stands and reaches into his back pocket for his old paper map of the city. The jumbled mess of streets and creases has been marked up and taped back together, and he carefully spreads the map flat against a mirror, using hair clips to fix it in place. "It's not gonna be enough just to grab Mobius and say he's the dealer," Tucker says.

"So what do we do?" Rapunzel asks, joining Tucker and me as we stare at the map. I glance at her and she snarls back at me. "What? I'm not leaving Ethan alone with the likes of you."

"We need to *prove* Mobius is the dealer." Tucker taps at the map. "We need to set up a meeting someplace. Somewhere in the city where he'll feel like it's safe, but a place he can't easily escape from. He trusts you, so he shouldn't be expecting a trap."

Rapunzel scowls. "And then what? We ask if he'll do us a solid—turn himself in and fess up? Not much of a plan, *Justin*. Or Tucker. Or whatever the hell I'm supposed to be calling you."

"You two know each other?" I ask, wondering if their paths crossed at JB's first safe house.

"Not yet," Tucker says.

"Not never, boy." Rapunzel scowls at him.

"I got through to Vogler," Tucker says, turning to me. "We can have him stake out the place, then he'll catch Mobius in the act of dealing. But before he's arrested, we need Mobius to reveal as much as possible to incriminate himself and anyone he works with."

"You're sure we can trust Vogler?" I ask.

"What other choice do we have?"

"I say we go bigger." I study the map. "We need more options than one guy. What if Vogler's in on whatever Spaihts is in on?"

Rapunzel interrupts us. "You wanna break this down for those of us who don't speak Tetra Response Unit?"

"The guy running the unit can't be trusted, and we don't know who he controls, so I say we set up the meeting, but we stake it out ourselves. Set up the surveillance *our* way, then invite people to watch it happening." I turn to Ethan, who's still over by the window but listening in. "We broadcast the whole thing. Like Emma's idea. The live stream she was planning. We put it right on YouTube. Once it's happening, once Mobius is on-site, we send the link to the police, to Vogler, but also to the media. Get it to the networks, the press. Announce it on Twitter, the breaker blogs. All of it. Make sure everyone knows it's happening and where it's going down."

"Aren't we gonna be a bit busy for broadcasting once Mobius shows?" Ethan's broken face makes him look like a boxer in the corner of a ring, preparing for the final round of a fight.

"He's right." Rapunzel allows herself a brief grin. "We can't be like, oh, sorry, Mobius, hang on mate, just *tweeting*."

"I could do it," Tucker offers. "I shouldn't be in the room, anyway. Mobius can't know I'm there. He probably remembers me. Probably knows I . . ."

"Became a runner," I finish, and Tucker looks relieved, like maybe this means I understand him now. "So you could try to run away from your guilt." I somehow manage not to choke on the nasty truth. "But you're right—he can't see you. And you're gonna be busy making sure Mobius doesn't get away once he's inside this trap we set."

"Seems like between getting Mobius on-site and keeping him there, we're *all* gonna be busy," Ethan says, joining us to stare at the map.

"You get Mobius to show up and start talking," I tell him. "Don't worry about the broadcast. I have someone who can help."

THIRTY-EIGHT

I park the Vespa six blocks from home, right across from Hector's store. I retrieved the scooter from where I'd left it in the Village, and now I limp through my neighborhood in Queens, my left ankle taped up and torn up, the streets swallowed in darkness.

Spaihts will still have people monitoring my house. They'll be monitoring Reuben's phone and reading his email. I need to see my brother face-to-face, in order to ask for his help. And for his forgiveness.

I check my phone to make sure there are no updates from the hair salon on Elizabeth Street. Our meeting with Mobius is set for tomorrow morning, so the others are trying to get some rest.

Two blocks from home, I abandon the street in favor of an alley, and halfway up it, I pull the hood up on my sweatshirt, then climb awkwardly over a low brick wall. I keep putting too much weight on my left foot, but at least my left eyeball has calmed down to a dull ache.

Slowly, I make my way through two backyards, then climb up and over a garage, keeping an eye and both ears out for dogs. When I hear one in the next yard over, I double back and find the alley again, then figure out a new route. It takes forever. But after more than an hour—and after a dozen splinters from climbing an old wooden fence—I scale some chain link and arrive in the scrub and dirt of our scrappy backyard.

I cower beside the trash cans in the darkness, listening. I'm worried Echo might make a racket when I try to get in the house, and it's hard to think about Echo without thinking about Tucker finding him that day when he found me at the park. But to think about Tucker is to dive too deep into fathomless water. I feel the pressure build inside as I sink in silence, Tucker's truth suffocating me, when once he was my lifeline. My handler, keeping me safe but keeping his distance. And all that time he was a snake. Small mercy I never kissed his venomous mouth.

Creeping to the side of the house, I peer around the corner to the spot where Lieutenant Monroe was killed. Down at the end of the driveway, street lamps glow, and probably some perfectly normal-looking car or van is set up nearby, filled with surveillance equipment and federal agents, well-stocked with doughnuts and gallons of coffee.

My mouth waters. I could use about six shots of espresso,

seeing as this is the second night in a row with no sleep. I imagine waking Mom and her brewing coffee and hugging me, and me telling her the truth as I tell it to Reuben. But I can't trust Mom to be involved yet. She might try to talk me out of the plan to trap Mobius, and she will almost certainly make too much noise. The whole house could be bugged. Which means Reuben and I better not make too much noise, either.

I keep low and press to the wall, locate Reuben's window, then tap at it, cringing at the sound. In my back pocket I feel the tetra bullet the others insisted I bring, saying I'd be crazy to head here without a means of escape.

I'd be crazy to dose up, though.

And not just because of the Needles. I can't trust myself on tetra. Not after what I did to Idra. Not after what I let happen to Davis. And while I'm lost in one last high or lost in the comedown, I might make the same choice GoPro made: to die instead of face the cruel slow world as just plain old me.

So why have I pulled the tetra bullet out of my back pocket to marvel at its smooth curves? I bite down on it. Just for the feeling of it in my mouth. Then I put it back in my pocket, and, leaving my low crouch, I press up at the glass and find Reuben's window unlocked.

He's not in his room, though. His bed on the far wall is empty. His wheelchair's missing, as is his laptop. I glance around at his posters—bulky New York Rangers and comic-book heroes, their color in stark contrast to the newspaper clippings about runners that Reuben's pinned to his wall. I check the dates on the clippings: nothing since Monroe's death.

I find Reuben in my room. He's asleep on the floor, curled up in a nest of sheets and blankets, the same spot where he used to sleep after Dad died. The nights I had to sob silently, afraid my baby brother would hear.

He's much heavier than he was back then, of course. In my weakened state I can barely lift him. He doesn't stir as I carry him to the bed and tuck him between the sheets. Nor as I pull over his wheelchair and sit beside him. For a while I run my hand carefully through his soft hair.

Then I switch on my Bart Simpson lamp and Reuben wakes up.

His eyes grow wide, and he locks onto the silent shushing signal I'm making, my finger to my lips. "We can whisper," I say, leaning my face close to his as he pulls himself up on his elbow.

Then he wraps his doughy arms around my neck and pulls me close.

I fight back tears. His hair against my cheek. His arms squeezing me tight. "Hey, Doughnut," I whisper. I peel him off me so I can look into his eyes. "I can't stay long. It's not safe. And I think our house might be bugged, so if you say something, *whisper*, no louder than this. Understand?"

He doesn't say anything, just nods.

"I'm so sorry," I say. "I don't even know what you must be thinking . . . but I've been working undercover. For TRU." I watch Reuben's face, waiting for it to flood with surprise and relief.

"Mom and me heard the gunshot outside," he whispers. "The night you left. And people online are saying Runner Eight almost died."

"Listen, it . . . it's all part of the act."

"The undercover act."

He knows there's more. But I don't have time to get into all of it.

"I should have told you. But I had to protect you. Mom, too." I make sure I'm still looking into his eyes. I have to do this properly. "There's something else I need to tell you, though. About the day you got hurt."

He nods.

"You were reading one of your comics while you were walking. One of the comics we'd got you at the store. You don't remember any of this?"

He shakes his head. And I need to tell him what I've never told anyone.

"The truth is . . . you were going slow, but I was rushing. Just in this stupid hurry to get home because I was supposed to meet up with some friends. We were gonna go to the beach. Just for nothing. Just to hang out. And that's why I started walking ahead. I was kidding with you, telling you to keep up, but I was annoyed and you were ignoring me. So

I . . . I wasn't holding your hand as I started onto the cross-walk. I was in too big a hurry. I left you behind."

A tear rolls down Reuben's cheek, but I must not look away.

"It makes you sad," I whisper. Just stating the stupidly obvious, filling the silence because I don't want to break down and start sobbing, too. This moment is meant to be about him crying, not me.

"Because it makes you sad," he says.

"That's not important. I mean—it does. But I am so sorry, Reuben . . . I should've protected you. I should have been there. Really *there*."

"That's dumb."

"No. *What?* No, it's not."

"I'm glad you weren't right beside me. You could have been hurt too."

"I could have pulled you out of the way." My voice has crept up in volume, and I struggle to rein it back in. "If I'd just been closer . . ."

"You don't know that. It could have been worse . . . we could have both got hurt, Alana. You could have been killed."

"But it's like I lied to you by never telling you. I was in this big rush to get home, for some stupid reason."

"It's not stupid."

"I'm supposed to protect you."

"Because we don't have a dad?"

"Because I love you."

"But you did your best to stop it happening. I know you did. Mom always says it's a miracle I'm still alive. Why can't you see it that way?"

"A miracle."

"I know." His mouth crumples in a frown. "Hard to believe."

"No, it is a miracle. Of course it is. I just . . . and whispering this is really hard, but how can you forgive me if you're not mad first?"

"I get mad when you think I always need saving. I get mad when you think I can't have a normal life and that you can't either. I get mad when you act like everything's broken and can never be good enough anymore."

He's right. I can't stand the way things are. I can't stand feeling broken. "I don't want to be like that," I tell Reuben, and that tetra bullet in my back pocket pops into my mind. I imagine thumbing its sweet ugly release. "I think I'm the one who needs saving."

"Then let me help you."

"That's why I'm here. You can help make it stop. All of it." I tell him what he has to do. Do my best to explain everything that's at stake. Reuben agrees without hesitation.

"I'm gonna call Hector for ice." He smiles. "First thing in the morning."

"You don't need to. I'm not rushing anymore. I'm never rushing again."

"Mom will like that."

"And you?" I think of all those clippings on his wall.

"I'll like it if you do," he whispers. "Will not rushing help you be happy?"

"I think being happy will help me not rush." I run my fingers through his hair. "I have to get going. You won't sleep in? You'll be ready?"

"I'll be ready." He's still propped up on his elbow and as I lean in for one more hug, he whispers, "Happy birthday," into my ear. "It's today. If it's morning."

"It's morning," I whisper. Then I start sobbing, and Reuben joins in. Our arms wrapped around each other.

"I've missed you," he says, and I don't care that my voice is too loud as I tell my brother how much I've missed him, too.

THIRTY-NINE

T ucker said the nineteenth floor of 141 Thirty-Sixth Street was cordoned off as a crime scene for two weeks after GoPro's death. Now the yellow police tape is gone. The floor is still vacant, though. The whole building has been undergoing renovations for months. I stare through the glass of the repaired window, peering down to the dark street below. When Tucker first suggested this as the place to meet Mobius, I hated the idea. But this is where tetra tricked GoPro into thinking she had nothing left to live for, so it feels like a good place for us to try to get the drug off the streets.

And Tucker was right—the nineteenth floor of this building works well for the trap we've set. The space is well lit, and the open floor plan makes things easy for our surveillance cameras. Rapunzel bought GoPros, which is fitting, and the way we have them set up means there's little room to hide. Plus, the nineteenth floor is hard to reach, and easy to seal off.

It's an island in the sky, far above the storm at sea.

Tucker paid off the head of the building's renovation project: a half-up-front, half-later deal, in return for the various construction crews all taking a day off. Tucker paid the guy to put the elevators offline too. It's costing most of the cash JB hauled out of the house in Harlem. Lien Hair Salon was cheap by comparison. But if Mobius had made a run for it in Chinatown, we might have lost him in the crowds. If he tries making a run for it here, he'll have Tucker waiting for him on the floor below while Rapunzel comes down from the roof to lock our target in place.

Rapunzel's armed with tetra. Tucker just has a gun.

But with any luck, Mobius won't realize he's been trapped. Ethan assured him the location is secure, said something about JB owning the place as an investment property. Once Mobius is here, our whole conversation will be recorded by the cameras we've stashed amid the junk the construction workers left behind. That footage will be broadcast live on YouTube, with the help of my little brother, who'll be sharing the link as soon as Mobius shows here at eight.

Forty minutes from now.

We've connected Reuben to the live feed already, so he's already watching across a four-camera split view. But over here at the window, I am out of frame, because I don't want my brother to see me sweaty and tense as my heart hammers out the countdown to rush hour, one last time.

"Coffee?" Ethan asks, joining me. He hands me one of two giant to-go cups. The bruises on his face have turned black as ink. His eye has swollen almost all the way shut. "Black, six sugars."

"You remembered how I like it."

"Don't get excited. Just figured you could use the caffeine."

"Yeah." I burn my tongue tasting the coffee. "Good sleeping weather." I nod out the window, where swollen clouds smother the sunrise. The city streets below are gloomy gray.

"Really? We're gonna talk about the weather?"

"You want to go over the plan again?"

"Why? So you can keep skimming over how we're supposed to get Mobius to reveal his secrets when he gets here?" Ethan glances about at the heavy workbenches and empty pots of paint. On the bright white walls, unfinished outlets sprout wires like weeds. "Speaking of secrets, where's Justin? I mean *Tucker*."

"Already in position."

"Packing heat?"

I nod. Since I wasted all the bullets in JB's gun, Tucker's is the only weapon we have left. Apart from tetra. Ethan and Rapunzel might need to use the dose they each carry, if things go south. But though I still have that tetra bullet in the back pocket of my jeans, I'm not going to let myself use it. No matter what.

"So we're really gonna do this." Ethan shakes his head.

"Getting Mobius arrested is the only way our testimonies mean anything."

"Just wish my brother was here to tell me this is a giant mistake." He grimaces as he tastes his coffee. "I tracked down his hospital. Used some of our connections."

"And?"

Ethan puts his hand on the window, like he's testing the glass. "He's out of ICU. Stable."

"Oh, thank God."

"I can't even risk going to see him. He's surrounded by cops. *Your* people."

"But he's okay. He's gonna be all right."

"Like you give a damn."

"Maybe I shouldn't," I snap back at him. "Seeing as JB was threatening to kill me yesterday."

"Exactly. You shouldn't, and you don't."

"You really think it's that simple?"

"No, I think you're complicated. Like, migraine complicated. But JB's alive. So go ahead and breathe a big sigh of relief. And remember, the fact that he's under police surveillance is the only reason I'm helping you."

I take a swig of coffee and it burns all the way down, but perhaps the caffeine will kick my brain cells into action, help me figure out the best way to get Mobius to *spill the beans*. Because Ethan's right, that part of the plan is foggy, at best. And Ethan's a distraction. His hair wild, his clothes slept-in.

His brown eyes menacing when he glances at me. Breathing in, I smell his leather jacket as well as the coffee he's brought me, even the faint smell of paint fumes that still stick to him. Blindfold me and I would find this boy across a crowded room.

He pushes at the glass again. Then he smashes his fist against it. The glass doesn't even crack.

I take another scalding sip of coffee and stare at the scaffolding that wraps the building across the street. Whatever they're working on, they're still working on it. And the scaffolding is still too far to jump to from here. Unless you were rushing, maybe. Right at your peak.

My left eye twitches.

"So where were you when it happened?" Ethan asks.

"You really want to talk about this?"

"This is the window, right? This part you're staring out of." He throws his plastic cup against the glass and the coffee explodes back over us.

It burns and I shriek, wiping my face off. Slicking the coffee back through my hair. "The cameras are on," I say. "The others can hear us."

"I want you to tell me, Lana. Show me how it went down."

"I told you—she jumped. There was nothing I could do. I was too far back to stop her."

"She jumped because you were chasing her. Because she was afraid of you."

"No . . . I was just doing my job. The rush was over for me

too. She said she could make it to that scaffold—"

"But her rush had run dry. And that scaffold's so far, even if you *were* rushing."

I think about what GoPro said as she stood at this window, rubbing her hands at the base of her skull, her face flushed red. "Maybe she was feeling the afterglow," I lie, wanting to spare him the truth. "So lost in the moment. Like how you showed me on the subway."

Reuben can hear this, I remind myself. Though here at the window, Ethan and I are not on camera, the mics are picking up every word we say. Tucker and Rapunzel will both be listening, too.

I stare up at Ethan as he stares out the window. And then, as I peer down at the street where GoPro died, rain begins falling, splashing against the glass, further distorting our coffee-stained view.

"You loved her," I say.

"I thought I did." Ethan's voice is scuffed and scratchy. "I tried to. I mean, she drove me nuts half the time, but there were so many good things about her. Emma could make you feel like you were all that mattered, like she was shining a spotlight only on you. And she was bold. So bold."

"Totally free," I say.

He cocks his head to one side, staring at the street below as the rain falls. "She'd needled up. That's the truth, isn't it? You knew, you just don't want to say."

"Ethan—"

"That's why she jumped." He pushes both hands against the glass.

"She told you? About the Needles?"

"I could tell by the way she started keeping to herself when she was derailing. Said she needed silence." Ethan turns his face so I can't see. "She *hated* silence. I didn't ask her about it, though. Emma pushed me away. But I'm right, aren't I? She couldn't handle life without tempo. So she killed herself."

"She couldn't remember everything she had to live for," I say. "Not in that moment."

"You mean there was no one she cared for enough."

"You shouldn't blame her—the drug uses us up, Ethan, no matter how much we think it gives in return. Tetra makes us think too much is all that's enough."

He wipes a splash of coffee off the window. "But it reveals so much."

"Or does it make us blind to what really matters?"

"But the moment. That feeling. The now."

"The moment doesn't belong to tetra," I say. "It belongs to us."

He turns to me, his face raw with bruises, eyes red with tears. "This whole thing was supposed to be about living. Not dying."

"Come here," I whisper, quiet enough the mics can't pick it up.

"Why? So you can kiss me again?" He's whispering, too. "Here? Where Emma died?"

"No. So you can kiss *me*. Here. Where you and I are alive in this moment. And you can kiss me because when this is over we're never gonna see each other again."

His mouth is hungry and hot as he kisses me, his hands in my coffee-soaked hair. I drop my cup on the floor so I can claw at his dirty white T-shirt. Everything warm inside me rushing to meet him. I reach beneath his shirt as his lips play mine, my fingers on his skin. I have to be careful not to hurt him, his bruised face. His heart that needs time to heal.

But we're all out of time.

My phone chimes as a text pops in, and I pull away from Ethan as I pull out my phone.

We're still staring at the message when the phone starts ringing.

"You got that?" Tucker whispers as soon as I answer. I put him on speaker. "Mobius is *early*. He's coming up the stairwell right now."

"Okay," I say. My heart thudding. "Stay out of sight, like we talked about."

"I will. I'll be on the floor right below you. Are you hanging in there? I heard—"

"We're hanging in there."

"I wish I was there beside you." There's a long pause. Long enough for me to imagine Tucker's hands rubbing my shoulders. "Like old times."

"We should get off the phone, Tucker."

"You sound nervous."

"Of course I'm nervous." My sweaty hand makes the phone slippery. I let my voice soften. "You know I always hated the waiting game."

"Right. The watched pot."

"Never boils."

I almost smile.

But then Tucker whispers, "Holy shit," and hangs up.

"What's wrong?" Ethan asks.

"I don't know."

Another text pops in.

"Hold the phone still." Ethan tries to grab it from my shaking hand. "I can't read it."

"Someone else is here," I say.

"Who?"

"You don't know him."

"But you do?"

Tucker calls again, but this time I don't answer.

I turn my phone to silent and slip it in my back pocket with the tetra bullet I cannot take, and I turn from the window, leaving the rain and the city behind me, heading to the door to the stairwell, the same door I came crashing through when I was following GoPro. The door that's the only way in or out of here since we put the elevators out of commission. The door Mobius is about to barge through.

And the door through which Spaihts will then follow.

FORTY

M obius sets his briefcase on a metal workbench in the middle of the room, then turns to face us. He must have been running up the stairs, because he's breathing hard.

He's dressed the same—scruffy clothes all black. His hair scraped in a ponytail. He tugs his cigarettes from his chest pocket. Taps one out. Then lights it as he gets his breath back.

"Any chance you were followed?" I ask, facing him, my back to the door, and when Mobius doesn't answer, I consider telling him that in fact he was *definitely* followed, but then Mobius will know we have the stairs under surveillance, and I don't want Mobius spooked. So I just stare at Mobius, and my back is still to the door, which puts me at a real disadvantage when it comes crashing open again.

Ethan and I spin around as Spaihts enters.

"Neutralize the boy," Spaihts says, and Mobius wraps

one arm around Ethan's chest, then smothers a black bandanna over Ethan's mouth and nose. Ethan's trembling more than struggling, and I try to pry him loose of Mobius's grip, wrenching at the man's arm and kicking his ankles with my good leg. But Ethan crumples to the floor at our feet.

I kneel down to him, shaking him, making sure he's still breathing.

"What did you do to him?" I scream.

"He'll be all right." Spaihts grabs me, holding me by the wrists so I can't pummel him. Then he thumps me in the stomach when I start kicking his shins.

The blow knocks me on my back and I realize the screeching sound of nails on chalkboard is in fact heavy metal workbench scraping against concrete floor—Mobius is sealing off the exit to the stairwell, trapping me in my own trap, since the door opens inward. The only way in and out has been blocked. Ethan's unconscious. But the cameras are rolling. *Reuben's watching.* My brother's sending the link out for our live broadcast, so whatever happens, I need to keep these two men in the cameras' view.

I start scooting backward, watching Spaihts as he peels off his tan jacket and uses it to mop the sweat off his shiny scalp. He dumps the jacket on the floor, loosens his tie, rolls up his sleeves. Mobius stands beside him, cigarette dangling from his mouth.

"Agent Odell," Spaihts barks. He knows his name. His real name. "Put that thing out."

"You quit smoking?" Mobius asks.

"More than a year ago. You've been in the field too long."

Mobius throws the cigarette on the floor and grinds it out with the heel of his boot. "You are right about that."

Spaihts claps him on the back, nodding at me. "But our hard work's paid off."

I scoot right into the middle of the floor, as if traveling to the center of a spider's web, and I wait for the two men to approach me, my thoughts all fractured but my plan still in place.

Come on. Just a little closer. Step into the shot.

At least then whatever they're about to do to me will be broadcast to the world. The thought is a small comfort. And it shrinks to no comfort when I remember that Reuben is watching this and I do not want Reuben watching me die.

Spaihts and Mobius walk toward me, joining me in the web.

"So what now?" I say as they get closer. "You're gonna kill me?"

"Kill you?" Spaihts flashes a smug grin. "We'd never do that. We're here to rescue you."

"From?"

"Oh, let's start with from yourself, seeing as you are the Katrina of shit storms."

"Right. You want to rescue me. That's why you shot Lieutenant Monroe, then framed me for her murder."

"I admit my hands have been dirtied." Spaihts squats

down so we're about level, his frown apparently an apology. "None of this has been easy. She was a good woman. But your lieutenant was close to uncovering things we couldn't risk being exposed."

"Like the fact you're a drug dealer? No wonder you didn't want TRU to find Mobius. What happened, Spaihts? You don't make enough money as a federal agent?"

"This has nothing to do with money. Agent Odell and I—"

"*Agent* Odell." I turn to Mobius. "How does that work? You with the Department of Justice, too?"

"Let's put it this way," Spaihts says. "Agent Odell and I both wear a lot of hats. You know what that means?"

"You like to dress up?"

"Ah." Spaihts mimes ringing my neck. "You know, when I get past the fact that you're a giant pain in the ass, I can see how you'd be quite funny."

"Wow."

"I'm sure I'll come to appreciate it as we work together. Oh, and happy birthday, by the way. I even brought you a present."

He tosses me my dad's old Rangers cap. The one I lost outside the HSBC in Astoria. It's more frayed than ever, more broken-in. I pull the hat on, confused rather than grateful. But Spaihts's love of his own voice is the best birthday present he can give me. I just hope Tucker and Rapunzel don't try to get in here yet—the workbench won't stop Rapunzel from opening the door if she's dosed up on tempo. But I don't want anything to alert Spaihts to the fact that he's not in full control.

"We've been fortunate," he says. "I expected you to wind up dead on the streets, a scapegoat for Monroe's death. But it turns out that would have been even more tragic of a sacrifice than I'd imagined."

To make sure Spaihts's face is showing up clearly on the cameras, I stand, then limp around to the other side of him, forcing him to turn as he stands, too.

I wonder who's watching the broadcast. *Vogler?* What about the slow-motion crowds on the streets outside? Are they watching us on their phones while they trudge to work?

"If it's not about money," I say, "then why poison the streets with tetra?"

"To find someone like you, West." Spaihts turns to Mobius. "Want to tell her the good news?"

"Your blood work came back positive." Mobius taps the inside of his elbow, referencing the spot where he drew my blood. "Extremely positive. We've had false alarms before, but the guys in the lab coats assure us your blood doesn't lie."

"About what?"

"About how you're responding to the TTZ."

Ignoring the pain in my ribs, I take a deep breath. Then I spit out the truth. "I needled up the night before last. I wouldn't call that a positive response."

A smile stretches across Mobius's pockmarked face. "Doesn't matter. The results show you correctly synthesized the new formula—we fully expect you'll continue to modulate the compound at safe levels, then move beyond the typical thresholds."

"Which in English means?"

"You'll outgrow the Needles."

"That's impossible."

"Not anymore. Not for you. This new formula will allow you to continue using TTZ past adolescence and into adulthood. Essentially allows you to use the drug forever."

"But I needled up. I got the pains. *Here.*" I show them, right at the base of my skull. "It's over. It has to be over."

"Those symptoms will disappear," Spaihts says. "You're building up tolerance. Push through the Needles one time, maybe twice, and the pains, the headaches, all of it will pass."

Push through the Needles.

"GoPro." I glare at Mobius. "What happened? What did you tell her?"

"She was one of our false alarms, I'm afraid."

"Because she kept needling up?"

"I warned her that if she experienced the symptoms one more time it meant things weren't working as we'd predicted," Mobius says. "It meant we were wrong about her. But you'll be different, Alana. The formula's different. . . ."

I gaze at the window GoPro smashed through. Rain blurs the glass and smudges the city behind it, a grim imitation of life in 4D. "You told her she could keep rushing forever, then she found out she couldn't. She killed herself because of your lies!"

"If that's why she jumped through that window, then you've no idea how much I regret our mistake," Mobius says. His face displays emotion now that he's dropped his tough dealer act.

I turn to Spaihts. I want to rip his head off his shoulders and stuff it in Mobius's mouth.

But I have to keep these men talking.

"Why are you doing this?"

"I told you, West," Spaihts says. "To find someone like you. The U.S. government has no need for accelerators who come with an expiration date. *Children* are of no use to us."

"Of no use." I shake my head and stare back out at the city, gazing through the rain-soaked glass. The coffee Ethan threw against the window is still dribbling onto the floor. "You've been leaking tetra to the streets. Providing it. Just to test it."

"To make it work *better*," Spaihts says. "Right now you're the only one responding correctly, but there'll be others like you. Many others, we hope. Look at what you did escaping your old headquarters—you were unstoppable. And now you can keep being unstoppable. Imagine that for a second. And then imagine if there was an army just like you."

My left eye feels like it's wriggling out of its socket as I pull my gaze from the window.

"An army. Soldiers on tetra?"

"*Adult* soldiers. U.S. troops, law enforcement agents, special operatives . . ."

"And for that you fed breaknecks the drug."

"Once we realized there were young criminals willing to take it. We merely tapped into what was already happening. TTZ was banned almost as soon as Trinity Pharmaceuticals inadvertently created it, but somehow the first breaknecks got their hands on the drug. Right here, in New York. We realized it provided an opportunity, the perfect testing ground. So we commandeered Trinity's research and began supplying breaknecks with the drug."

Mobius is rolling Ethan onto his side, checking his vitals.

"You leave him alone," I shriek.

"I'm making sure he's all right, Alana."

"So you can keep testing him? Using him? And why on the streets? Aren't you supposed to do experiments in a lab?"

"And risk it being known we're testing an illegal, highly addictive, and highly dangerous drug on minors?" Spaihts says. "No, West. Not when we had test subjects who asked no questions, who didn't even know they were part of a study, and who wouldn't even have cared, I'm sure. All they wanted was the drug. So we were able to alter the formula and monitor the way our improvements affected the users, checking their blood work for signs of a breakthrough. A breakthrough like you."

"So you tried to prove runners were a liability in order

to shut down TRU. Didn't like us getting in the way of your experiment?"

"You were catching too many breaknecks. And your lieutenant was asking them too many questions. We'd tried to prevent TRU's formation in the first place, of course, but no one at the city or state level could ever be allowed to know what we were doing. Very few at the federal level even know."

"And when Monroe got close to learning the truth, you killed her. In cold blood."

"I wish there had been another way," Spaihts says.

"Do you?"

"You think I'm a monster. I get it. But these crude assessments are a luxury you can no longer afford. It's time to grow up, Alana. We're providing you with an incredible opportunity."

"And that means what, exactly?"

"Homeland Security. The CIA. Does it matter? You'll be saving lives, kid. American lives."

"Saving people." My whole body goes wiry tight, ears pricked, like a dog that can't believe the scent it has caught but is ready to bolt toward it. *All that power. All that purpose.* All that time. "As an accelerator."

"That's right. As a goddamn hero who gets to use tetra for as long as she wants." Spaihts grins.

"That is what you want," Mobius says. "Isn't it?"

Some truths are hard to say. Others come out too easy.

"Yes," I say. "Of course that's what I want."

FORTY-ONE

W hen Mobius takes the call, he doesn't say anything, just listens, his spine going a little straighter, his eyes widening in disbelief, and then narrowing in anger.

"Spaihts," Mobius says, glancing around the room. "We've been compromised."

"Just call off whoever's outside."

"There's no one *outside*." Mobius strides to one corner and kicks over a box full of used rags—one of our GoPro cameras slides across the floor, and Mobius points two fingers at it, then waves a circle at the room. "Yet."

"Come on, West." Spaihts is already striding toward the door. "Time to go."

I kneel beside Ethan as Spaihts and Mobius drag the workbench clear of the door. The door does not come flying open—no Tucker or Rapunzel to the rescue. But I don't need rescuing anymore.

Ethan's eyes are open. "Can't move," he whispers.

"But you heard?"

"I heard."

"Then you know I have to go."

"Don't. Not with them."

"I can't turn down this chance."

"You said it's people that matter. More than a feeling. More than the drug."

"But if I go, I can *save* people. It's not about tetra and the person it's made me. It's about who I can become. I can do it right this time. I can be better. I can be in control."

"And never stop rushing."

"You'd do the same thing."

"And you'd try to talk me out of it."

I stroke back his tangled mop of curls, then turn to Mobius and Spaihts, who wait at the door for me. "I need to know Ethan will be all right."

Mobius waves away my concern. "A little groggy. But he'll be up and about again soon enough."

"He can't come with us?"

"What would we do with him?" Spaihts is pulling his jacket back on. "His blood work shows little potential for longevity. I'm sorry, Alana. But we really have to go."

"I'll find you again," I tell Ethan. His eyes are bugging out of his head, and I kiss him quickly, but he can't kiss me back so the kiss falls flat, and mostly I'm thinking about how soon I can rush again, the feeling of tetra surging through my veins, everything amped up so loud it's distorting, my body swimming in strength and speed. No wasted potential. No wasted moments. No wasted me.

I drag Ethan over to a wall and prop him up against it. His deep brown eyes bore inside me. "If I don't go," I say, "then all this suffering—my brother, everyone—it will have all been for nothing."

"Good luck with that blank space inside, Lana."

"But you've seen the real me. No more mystery."

"That's not what I meant." He closes his eyes, and I leave him there. *He's jealous.*

As he should be.

"I don't want Ethan being arrested," I tell Spaihts, following him and Mobius into the stairwell.

"Thanks to your stunt with the cameras, he will be. Unless he recovers in time to get out before the police get here." To my surprise, we're heading *up* the stairwell, not down. "I'll try to pull some strings for you. But you've complicated things, West."

"You're the one who broke all the rules."

"While your conscience is clean?"

"I was trying to stop the carnage your breaknecks created."

"And you've succeeded. We still need to find others who respond to the new formula as well as you, but after what you pulled here today, our work's at an end in New York."

So is mine. I hobble up the stairs behind Spaihts as fast as my ankle will let me. *I did it.* I finished things, and now I get to start over. So why do I feel like I'm going backward?

When we reach the door to the roof, both men pull out their guns.

"I'll secure the landing zone," Mobius says, pushing out first into the rain, his briefcase clutched in one hand, firearm in the other. Spaihts has me wait with him inside.

"You're doing the right thing," he says, watching me. "The brave thing."

When Mobius calls the all clear, Spaihts and I shove out onto the roof, and I'm drenched instantly, but Dad's old hat shields my eyes from the downpour. In the distance is the familiar thrum of a chopper's blades.

"There's our ride." Spaihts points toward the drooping clouds that weep overhead—a helicopter approaches through the mist. More federal agents, I guess.

"When do I get to see my family?" I ask.

"Soon enough." Spaihts is smiling. "We're not taking you prisoner. You work for us, now. With us."

Mobius approaches with Rapunzel before him, her hands cuffed behind her. She'd been armed with a tetra bullet, but has chosen not to take it.

"I want in," she says.

"This one's results have shown some potential," Mobius tells Spaihts. "Too soon to know for sure, but it seems a shame to leave her behind if the whole operation's been blown."

Spaihts pulls up his jacket collar, as if it might keep him dry in this downpour. He squints through the rain, studying Rapunzel. "I suppose you were watching. You heard our conversation downstairs?"

"Yeah." Rapunzel's body is still and solemn and the rain makes it look as if all of her is weeping. "You been testing us. Like bloody lab rats. Tricking us." She glares at me. "The government. The military. Just like the banks, eh? Ripping everyone off. And you thought breaknecks were the problem."

"Cut it out," Spaihts tells her. "You know the truth now, but you want to come with us."

"I'd like to tell you to stuff those bullets where the sun don't shine. But I'd get to keep rushing forever? Like Lana? Like military-grade?"

"If your body proves willing."

"Then I make the same choice she did." Rapunzel nods in my direction, shouting to be heard above the rain and the chopper. "But only if JB and Ethan stay free. How about it?" She turns to Mobius. "You'll take care of my boys?"

"Big mess to clean up," Mobius tells her. "But we'll see what we can do."

"You have to promise," I say to Spaihts. "You have to promise us you can make sure they stay free."

"You think after you crucify me—online, for the whole world to see—I still have the power to fix things?" he yells. "Do you really have that big of a problem with reality, West?"

And you know what, maybe I do.

GoPro leaped out of a nineteenth-floor window to avoid having to face the real world. And now, where she fell, am I going to fly away to avoid the same thing?

Spaihts surveys the roof, and apparently satisfied no one else is up here, he holsters his gun. The chopper's close above us now, churning the rain as Spaihts points out at the city that sprawls and towers, the streets where I ran and rushed and hid. "You got what you wanted," he shouts. "Looks peaceful, doesn't it? No more breaknecks."

I reach for the tetra bullet in my pocket, but I don't take it out. I just squeeze in my fist the drug I can safely take now. Forever.

But when has tetra ever been safe?

"It's a weapon," I say, just a whisper, drowned beneath the drumming sound of the chopper and the rain and the slow world spinning. Round and round it goes. And I've been caught in a web that never stops being spun. Unless I'm brave enough to stop spinning.

I release my grip on the bullet.

Maybe tetra's not the weapon. Maybe I am.

But it's time for this time bomb to be disarmed.

"I can't do this anymore," I shout. "I can't go with you."

"Yes, you can," Spaihts yells back. "You've got this, kid. We'll be behind you, helping you every step of the way."

"Take Rapunzel. If that's what she wants." I take two steps back toward the door to the stairwell. Small steps. Like maybe Spaihts won't notice.

"You're our breakthrough," he calls.

"Thanks. I mean it. But I have to stop now."

"You can't *stop*." The chopper touches down, whipping the puddles into spray. "This isn't about what you want. You think *I* wanted this? We're focused on the greater good here. That's what we do. To keep people safe. We endure the horrors."

"I've endured enough."

"Your country needs you, young lady."

"I have a little brother who needs me more."

"You'll be protecting him," Spaihts says. "Him and your family, this city. This entire nation."

"From who?" I ask. "From people like us?"

"Get in the chopper."

"No. I have to go home now."

Spaihts pulls his gun from its holster. "Get in the chopper, West. That's an order."

"I don't work for you." I keep facing him as I back up to the stairwell, each step shredding my left ankle a little more. "And you're not gonna shoot me. Not if you need me so bad."

"You're right." He points the gun at Rapunzel's head. "But I am willing to illustrate a point. You walk away from this, from your duty, people die as a result."

"Spaihts," Mobius says. "Come on, man. Let it go."

"I've made a lot of sacrifices for this, Odell. We both have."

"Lana." Rapunzel's eyes are as big as two planets, and I stop backing away.

"Okay," I tell Spaihts. "Put the gun down. Don't hurt her. I'll do what you want."

I'll go with him. For now. The people Spaihts works with can't all be as crazy as him.

Right?

The shot comes from behind me, and, for a split second, I'm deaf in both ears as the bullet zips past. My eyes clench shut, and when they open, I see Spaihts's belly blooming red. He's been thrown off-balance, and he loses his gun as he goes down—it slides toward the edge of the roof, then stops, ten feet from him. Twenty feet from me.

Spaihts is already crawling toward it.

"Stop!" Tucker yells behind me, bursting out through the stairwell door. "Spaihts. Give it up!"

Mobius starts dragging Rapunzel toward the chopper, and Spaihts drags himself through the puddles. He's five feet from his gun now.

I'm certain I can get to it first.

"He won't stop," I shout, dashing toward the edge of the roof, my eyes locked on the gun, my left ankle exploding in pain. "I'll get it. Tucker—don't let them take Rapunzel!"

My left eye goes all bubbly, like it's begun boiling over, the rain blurring what's left of my vision, and I'm almost to the gun but my ankle's all floppy and the roof is all slick.

Behind me, across the roof, Mobius has ducked for cover behind a concrete pipe. He's halfway to the chopper, holding Rapunzel beside him, and he starts opening fire at Tucker, who's pressed back against the door to the stairwell.

Two federal agents climb out of the chopper, their guns

pulled—we're outnumbered. And Spaihts is now upright. He clutches his bleeding guts with one hand while slowly reaching down for his gun.

I drop and slide on my right leg, kicking the gun away from him. He follows it to the edge of the building, steadying himself just before he topples over the side, and then he's picking up the gun and I do not wait to watch him point it at me.

I'm on my feet again. Or my right foot, anyway. I'm dragging the left foot behind me.

"West!" Spaihts yells with a groan. "Wait . . . please . . ."

I'm almost to Tucker. Almost at the door to the stairwell. I'm hopping and slipping as bullets echo and crack. Then Tucker's catching me. He pulls me through the door and pushes me against the wall, telling me to stay down. He leans back out. Takes two shots. And when he pulls back inside, his arm is covered in blood.

"It's nothing," he says, following my gaze. Still gripping his gun, despite there now being blood all over his hand, too. "Just a graze, Alana. Just a graze. We're getting out of this."

He cracks the door open. Takes another shot.

"But Rapunzel," I say, grabbing his leg. "She could get hurt."

"They're coming this way." Tucker pulls back inside. Checks the door. "No way to lock it. And I'm almost out of bullets."

"I have one." I pull the tetra bullet from my back pocket and hold it between us.

"You can't run on that ankle."

"I'm not planning to run. I'm gonna stand my ground and fight."

"You can't even stand."

"On tetra I can."

"You needled up," Tucker says. "I heard you. I heard it all."

"Then you heard *them*. I can still rush."

"Like GoPro could? What if they're wrong about you like they were wrong about her? You could die, Alana."

"Someone has to stop them. And Rapunzel's only up here because of me." My thumb's on the release. My hand is shaking. "I have to take that risk."

"No you don't!" Ethan yells, sprinting up the stairs toward us. He pulls out his own dose of tetra. "I'll do it. I'll get her back." He glances at Tucker. "Don't try to cover me."

Tucker blocks him from the door. "Breaknecks run from a fight like this one."

"Then I guess no one will be expecting this."

Ethan bites down on his bullet, hits the release, and barrels outside.

FORTY-TWO

The showdown rages as Tucker and I hide behind the closed door.

But the showdown is brief. And the silence means it's over.

I let my unused tetra bullet clatter down the stairs as Tucker helps me up. Then we venture back out onto the roof, me leaning against my old handler, his arm around me as I hop on my one good leg.

The rain has eased to a drizzle. The chopper's rotors slow and then stop, its engine stalled—the pilot's slumped across the controls, unconscious. The two federal agents who leaped out of the back of the chopper are now splayed out cold.

We find a handgun with a crushed barrel, the end pinched shut by the type of strength few ever experience and which I will never forget.

We find Mobius half conscious, each breath a sputtering wheeze.

Then we find Spaihts at the edge of the roof—his stomach no longer bleeding, his eyes rolled back in his head.

Still holding me, Tucker bends down to close Spaihts's eyelids.

"Guess Ethan and Rapunzel didn't think they'd get much of a deal after this," I say, scanning the nearby rooftops, as if they might still be in view.

Tucker's still bent over Spaihts, awkwardly holding me against his hip, and I realize he is too weak to stand back up straight.

"You don't have to carry me," I say, breaking free of him. "You're injured."

"So are you."

"It's just my ankle. You've been shot."

"Barely."

"Let me see."

"It's fine." He drops to his knees. "But look at your ankle. You need to loosen the shoelace. Cutting off circulation. Like that day at the park. Remember?"

"Tucker, let me see."

I kneel beside him and pull his arm from his side where he's been clutching it. As I do, he cries out in pain.

"You need to lie down," I tell him. The bullet went in under his collarbone, and it's not a graze. A graze would mean the bullet almost missed him entirely. Instead it's buried inside.

He shivers as I help him into a recovery position. "They'll be here soon," I say, my voice catching. "I bet Vogler's on his way up those stairs right now."

"Don't leave."

"Try not to speak."

"This might be the last chance I get to tell you."

"Don't say that. You're not gonna die, Tucker Morgan. Not today."

"Will you hold me?" he asks, closing his bloodshot blue eyes. "I'm so cold."

I curl next to him, facing him, trying to stem his bleeding with my bare hands, nothing else to do but wait for help to arrive. This is our now. Tucker and I, and the waiting game.

"It's not just because I'm cold," he says, trying to smile. "I've not had a hug since my old man died."

"I'll have words with your cousin." I want to make Tucker's smile bigger, but he winces instead.

"There is no cousin. I've always been on my own out here."

"Why didn't you just run away?" His blood is warm on my hands, his skin so cold. "You could have gone back to Nebraska. You could have run and never looked back."

"Like them?" Tucker briefly opens his eyes, glancing up at the sky and out across the skyline at all the somewheres where Ethan and Rapunzel are disappearing as they leave us behind. I imagine them leaping from rooftop to rooftop, shadows darting against the pale gray sky. Too fast for my slow eyes to see.

"I guess they have nothing worth sticking around for," I say, thinking of Ethan. Thinking of a life without tetra and a life without him.

"But you do," Tucker says. "You could have gone with Spaihts."

"No, I couldn't." I squeeze my left eye shut, trying to stop the throb of pain. "I have enough consequences to face as it is."

"Yeah." Tucker makes a grim smile. "Me, too."

"That's why you stayed. You tried to do the right thing."

He makes no answer, but I'm sitting up now. "I hear them coming. They're here. . . . Help!" I start screaming. "Man down! Over here. We're over here!"

I lean back down to Tucker. "Hold on," I tell him. "Just a minute longer."

"I stopped dreaming of tetra," he whispers. "Started dreaming of you. Like you were my flash of lightning, filling up the night sky. But it's getting dark, Alana. So dark now."

"Then you can see stars, right?" I say. "If the lightning's gone that means the storm has passed. You can see the constellations, Tucker. You can pick one and count the stars inside it."

"I picked one," he says.

Then he slips into the endless black.

FORTY-THREE

Washington State looks a lot like how I pictured Kansas, or Nebraska. At least this part does.

I'd hoped we'd end up closer to Seattle, which may not be much of a city by New York standards, but at least is an actual city. Out that way are endless swaths of forest, great stretches of glorious mountains, big and bald on top, capped in ice and snow. There are rough cliffs and cold ocean, and probably tons of other stuff you can't find in Kansas, or Nebraska. But that's the western part of the state. We're way east, where there's no ocean, forests, or mountains. Just lots of crops, sun, and wind.

Reuben calls it good kite-flying country, and he's proclaimed that today boasts the best conditions since we were moved out here.

He said that yesterday, too.

I struggle to get the kite launched, and Reuben laughs

as I run back and forth while he mans the controls. Then, once we achieve liftoff, he shows me how it's done, making the kite spin and soar above the park while Echo chases its shadow.

I mostly just stand around then, watching the kite and our dog and my brother. The way Reuben smiles with his eyes all squinted against the sun is pretty much why kites were invented.

It might be why the sky was invented, too.

There's a lake, and Canada geese, but no woods on the edge of this park. No Manhattan skyline in the distance.

The sunsets here last forever.

We're in no rush to get home, so I try sitting on the grass, but the grass makes me itchy, and I grow antsy. This thing happens where it feels like I have a shirt full of spiders, and I want to jog around for a bit, but Echo comes and crash-lands on my lap, pinning me down, as if he knows what I was about to do.

"Did you bring it?" I call to Reuben.

"I always bring it."

"Let me see."

From the pocket of his baggy jeans he pulls out the tetra bullet I once gave him in return for the use of his wheel-chair. He has a better wheelchair now. He has one that fits.

The sun glints on the black metal as Reuben holds up the cartridge with one hand, his other hand wielding the kite overhead.

"Today's the day," I tell him. I've said this before, but he doesn't roll his eyes. He's good like that.

"You ever wonder what would happen if we gave it to Echo?" Reuben grins.

"We are not giving it to Echo."

I get up, stride over, grab the cartridge, and walk down to the lake.

I have done this before, too.

"Alana," Reuben calls.

"Right here, Doughnut."

"Good luck."

I hold the cartridge up and study it: the black steel, the red release button. I shake the six-milliliter dose of tetra inside. As far as I know, this is the last of its kind.

"I'm going to do it," I shout, glancing back at Reuben.

He looks at the lake. Then at me. Then he stares up at his kite.

I turn to the water. Shield my eyes from the streaming glare of the sun. Out here, the fall feels like one long late summer. And I feel like a stopped clock.

I bounce the bullet in the palm of my hand. I guess it's not good form to throw stuff in the lake. I mean, what if one of the Canada geese swallows this thing? There'd be goose crap *everywhere*. But there's already goose crap everywhere. It's a defining feature of the park, just like the park back home.

I stop myself—because *this* is home, now.

I study the little steel bullet again. The metal warm in my

fingers. Dropping it in the trash won't seem like a big enough deal. This should be ceremonial. And I smile, thinking how me making this ceremonial would have made JB proud.

Maybe I should hit the release and puff the dose into the air before I toss the cartridge. But that would be weird, hitting the release without the bullet between my teeth. It also might be too tempting. And I could save this last dose—in case my body *can* keep handling this drug and I'm put in some situation where I need it again. Despite all the precautions and assurances, someone Spaihts worked with could hunt me down one day and try to recruit me. *Perhaps they won't take no for an answer.* I'll need to hit the release one more time so I can get away.

"Alana?" Reuben calls.

"Hang on."

I squeeze the bullet in my fist and wish I hadn't thought about Spaihts. *I should try again tomorrow.* Yeah. Tomorrow. I'll stride right to the edge of the lake and toss this thing in the water, no thinking.

I twitch, and it's a bad, full-body one. I almost drop the bullet in the lake on accident, which would really ruin the ceremonial aspect. The withdrawal twitches make me imagine a big cold turkey is pecking at me, and I shouldn't still think that way. But it's only been a few months, so I try not to be too hard on myself. I better stop thinking about twitching, though, because thinking about it always . . . too late! The shakes start up in my right leg, work their way to my arms and head, then settle on my nose.

I wait for it to pass, glad my back's to Reuben. My nose twitching reminds me of Agent Small, which is better than thinking about Agent Spaihts, but just like that, I'm thinking about him, too.

When Small and Vogler found me, regular cops swarmed the roof, but help had come too late for Tucker.

I sobbed as they pulled me away from him.

I screamed when they zipped him inside a body bag.

And then, once we got off that roof, Small shepherded me through the whole process. Said she'd only been trying to help me when her team had me trapped inside the movie theater in the Village. Said she'd suspected Spaihts was part of something *wrong*. I started to think I'd been underestimating Agent Small, but these days I'm not so sure. Letting me go could have been necessary for the story she had to spin. After our YouTube stunt, the pressure from the media was enough to force an investigation into all things tetra. The official word is that Spaihts had been heading up a *rogue initiative*, unsanctioned by the federal government. But seeing as the U.S. Department of Justice are the ones looking into it, I guess they would have to say that.

Thinking about it all makes me angry enough to want to gobble down every last drop of this last dose of tetra, my brain careening the wrong way down a one-way street.

So I hit the release. The TTZ puffs into the air and sparkles in the sunlight. And when I toss the bullet into the lake, it doesn't land as far away as I'd wanted. Nor does it feel as satisfying as I need. But I do feel lighter.

"Alana!" Reuben yells, and when I turn back to him, he's pointing at someone striding across the grass toward us.

"It's okay," I tell my brother, but I'm a wreck. I have a hard time with strangers.

There's a number I'm supposed to call if I need help. Not sure if stranger-in-the-park warrants me making the call, but I do call over Echo. He wags his tail, pants, then curls up at my feet.

"He looks ferocious," says a voice I know. "Should I be scared more of the dog, or of you?"

Ethan's shaved his head. And he's thinner, almost gaunt, his black clothes baggy. His skin not so polished-looking.

"You look terrible," I say, which is not entirely true. Especially not when he smiles.

"And you grew out your hair," he says. Of all the things he could mention, this is charitable. I've lost weight, too—in all the wrong places. And I'm paler than I used to be.

"I'll be right back," I tell Reuben.

"Who is he?" my brother asks.

"Just a friend," I say. "We'll be right over there, okay? Those swings. I promise. You'll keep an eye on me?"

"Of course."

I sit on a rubber tire swing, facing my brother, out of earshot but not too far away, and neither Ethan nor I talk for a bit.

"You're not gonna arrest me?" he says, finally. Trying to make a joke as he leans against the swing next to mine.

"Why?" I push at the ground with my feet. My left ankle's almost healed all the way. "Did you just rob a bank?"

"Nah." He pushes at an empty swing. "I'm out of that game."

"You mean out of tetra."

He cocks his head. Grins. But the grin fades quickly. "Yeah. You made sure of that. None to be found anywhere."

"I'm sure it's still somewhere."

"Yeah, well, not on the streets. None that's worth taking."

"So." I stare out at the lake. "How's your withdrawal going?"

"Lots of time trapped in here." He points at his forehead. "Didn't think it could get any worse after the first few weeks. . . ."

"But it did."

"Yes, it did."

"Mine's started getting a little better," I tell him. "Just this last month, really."

"Lucky you."

I shrug. "One step at a time, right?"

"That's what JB says. Moment by moment."

"How is he?"

"The same," Ethan says, but then shakes his head. "No. That's bullshit. He's not the same, but he'll be better once he gets back outside. Two more years on his sentence. Could have been worse, I suppose. And he healed all right. You know JB. Picture of health."

"He's still angry at me?"

"Not like he was. He knows you helped him get the reduced sentence. He knows nothing was what we thought."

"And Rapunzel?"

"She's going by Charlie, now."

"That's her real name?"

"For the time being. She's at this thing in Arizona. A center . . . doctors and shrinks. Hot springs and shit."

"Rehab."

"She'll get better," Ethan adds.

"It's hard not to think of her smiling."

"Or dancing. You know. That thing she used to do." He kind of bobs his shoulders, and it is a very poor approximation of that thing she used to do.

"Maybe I could visit her," I say.

"Is that allowed?"

"I don't know. I mean, I guess. You're *here*, aren't you? How did you find me, anyway?"

"The Vespa. You know—the one you stole."

"The Vespa?" I laugh. It was the one thing I kept. "I didn't *steal* it. Aces could have it back if she wanted."

"She's in Rome by now. But she hooked me up with this." Ethan pulls his phone out, shows me the tracking app.

"Oh my God."

"Yeah. I figured you forgot about that. I tracked the

scooter all the way to your house."

"So now you know where I live."

"I'm not here to bother you," he says, sensing me grow tense. "I just came to give you something. Your mom said you'd be over here somewhere."

"What's this?" I say as he hands me a flash drive smaller than my thumb.

"It's the song."

I glance over at Reuben, who's watching us more than he's watching his kite.

"Emma's song," I say, trying to hand it back. "I think it's best I move on from all that."

"Move on?" Ethan says. "From the moment? You don't ever try to get lost in the now?"

"All the time. But the song, all of it, that was then."

"I was then, too, I guess."

He watches me, his face stoic but his eyes sad, waiting for me to confirm that I've been trying to leave him behind. But the truth is I still dream I'm faster at night. Not fast enough to save Reuben. Even my dreams have accepted I'll never turn back time. Instead I dream I'm fast enough to catch up to Ethan as he disappears across the Manhattan skyline.

I dream we're rushing together again.

"Enjoy it for me," I say, handing him the flash drive. "If you listen to it."

"I listen to it all the time." He looks embarrassed, and

hurt. "There's one more thing, though," he says, staring up at the kite my brother's flying. "JB had money stashed away that no one found—money he made clean. He wants you to have your share."

"Did Davis's sisters get their cut?"

"Of course."

"Make sure JB gives my share to them, too."

"All you want's the Vespa, huh?" His mouth smiles. His eyes do not.

"Sure. I have the most stylish scooter in town."

"Guess that wouldn't be hard in a town this size."

I laugh.

"Seriously," he says. "What's there to do here?"

"You will think it horribly boring," I say, "but I'm working on my GED."

"Whoa. For, like, college?"

"That's the plan."

"And do *you* think it's horribly boring?"

"Most of the time," I say, but I laugh again. "And you? Still painting?"

"Not so much. The withdrawal makes it tough some days just to get out of bed. I took up surfing, though."

"I bet that suits you." I think of the way he used to surf through the city, cresting upon waves of speed.

"I'm down in SoCal now," Ethan says. "JB's gonna move out there when he gets out. He wants to open a bookstore. Christ. I'll probably end up working the cash register or something. Anyway, he said he hopes you get that *the beauty of things must be that they end.* It's from some book."

"Kerouac. Yeah. Tell him I looked it up."

"Then he'll be even less mad at you. And so what else? GED. Family time at the park. That's it?"

"I started drawing again. I know what you mean, it seems so pointless sometimes. But I'm getting back into it. Some nights when I can't sleep, I try to draw my way through it."

In fact I've filled notebook after notebook with doodles. Just pencil on paper. Lots of gray. But some of it looks the way I remember the Fourth Dimension in my dreams.

"That's great, Lana." Ethan smiles.

"It's *Alana*."

"Right."

"And you? You never told me your real name."

"Just Ethan." He shrugs. "I guess not everything's a lie."

"No." I study his face. The lips I kissed. And the thought of kissing them now makes me tremble, not in a bad way, but I'm worried if I keep thinking about it and trembling, the shakes will really kick back in.

"I heard about Tucker," he says.

I nod. "Another minute and I would have said I'd forgiven him. Just a few more seconds, really." I don't give in to the shaking. "It's almost the thing I regret most. How weird is that?"

"Had you, though?" Ethan asks. "You'd really forgiven him?"

"I want to talk about the future," I say quickly. "Not the past."

"Sure. Your artwork . . ."

"Yeah. I actually have some pieces being shown. Not a gallery or anything, but my mom approached a coffee shop a couple towns over and they put some of my best stuff up on the walls."

"They have good coffee?"

"Terrible."

"Well, I'd still like to check it out."

"Sure," I say. "I'll give you the address."

Ethan gazes out across the lake. And Reuben's turned the other way, watching his kite. So I stand up beside Ethan and put my hand on his chest, feeling his heart beat. Feeling his countdown. Then on tiptoes I kiss him. Just for a moment. And for that moment I am of that moment alone.

When I pull away, Ethan smiles, his eyes wet with tears.

"I was gonna ask if you might want to go," he says. "With me, I mean. To this coffee shop. While I'm in town."

I almost tell him yes, of course. But I'm trying not to make quick decisions. So instead I ask if he wants to fly a kite with my brother and me.

Ethan takes me up on the offer, sticking around and sticking close as the sun starts to drop.

I don't introduce him to Reuben, not properly, since I'm not ready to explain how Ethan and I know each other. But Reuben acts as if Ethan's presence is perfectly normal. My brother's good at acting as if things are normal. Maybe in time, I'll be as good at it as him.

The sun takes its time setting and when I peer east where the world is already dark, I imagine all the way to that far edge of the country where the Manhattan skyline is full of storms and stories and speed. But then I turn back to where the sun is still winning, and I put my arm around my brother's shoulders, staring with him up at the kite that puts such a smile on his face. It is slow, beautiful, and fragile, blowing this way then that way. And though tethered, it moves as if it were free.

ACKNOWLEDGMENTS

A huge heartfelt thank you to my agent, Laura Rennert, and to my editor, Ben Rosenthal, both of whom challenged me as a writer, cheered me on as a person, and championed this book. I'm also grateful to my publisher, Katherine Tegen, and the whole team at Katherine Tegen Books, as well as the larger HarperCollins family, who all helped create such a wonderful home for *Night Speed*. A special mention to Katie Bignell, Kathryn Silsand, and Megan Gendell, for their editorial assistance. Also to Joel Tippie, for his brilliant cover design. Three cheers to my five beta readers: Kristin, Jackie, April, Mandy, and Christina . . . and then three hundred more cheers, because you all rock! Much love to my friends and my family: your enthusiasm for my stories helps me keep writing them. I thank my lucky stars for my wife, my first reader, my biggest fan, and my best friend, Allison. And finally, I thank you for reading.